ALSO BY JANE ODIWE

Lydia Bennet's Story

Willoughby's Return

"Rollicking good fun with a surprise twist."

—Austenprose

"An absorbing read."

—Austen Blog

"Jane Odiwe has caught Lydia's gushing, breathless manner beautifully... I daresay Lydia would have written like this, all dash and full of enthusiasm. A book that gave me more food for thought than I was expecting."

—Random Jottings

"An absolute delight to read."

—Historical Novels Review

"Not only a terrific story but also a wonderful example of Jane Odiwe's talent at character development... It changes nothing of the original Austen creations, instead it digs deeper and adds personality to a secondary character."

—Book Zombie

"Austen enthusiasts will enjoy this novel, but even those readers looking for a fast-paced 'romance' will enjoy *Lydia Bennet's Story*."

—Savvy Verse & Wit

"Odiwe's writing style made me feel almost as though I were actually reading Austen."

—Diary of an Eccentric

Praise for *Willoughby's Return*

"Odiwe's elegantly stylish writing is seasoned with just the right dash of tart humor, and her latest literary endeavor is certain to delight both Austen devotees and Regency romance readers."

—*Booklist*

"Beautifully written… Jane Odiwe writes with such eloquence and style that you can't be helped for thinking that you are reading Jane Austen."

—A Bibliophile's Bookshelf

"A well-plotted and elegant romance…*Sense and Sensibility* is my favorite Austen, and it is quite a treat to have the story continued in such an accomplished and satisfying sequel."

—Jane Austen's Regency World

"Fans of happy endings will be delighted with how the author spins her story, weaving suspense and intrigue into a well-crafted tale."

—The Jane Austen Centre

"Charming… Odiwe has captured Marianne's spirit superbly. Odiwe's research and passion for the Regency era shine."

—Austenprose

"The sequel for *Sense and Sensibility* I have always wanted! I am so very delighted that Jane Odiwe has supplied us with this compelling and expressive sequel to cherish and enjoy! …Odiwe has done a magnificent job."

—Austenesque Reviews

"Superb...the best sequel to *Sense and Sensibility* that I have ever read! The characters are captured perfectly and the story is wonderful. I highly recommend it to all lovers of *Sense and Sensibility*, Austen, or just a wonderful romance."

—Laura's Reviews

"Readers who love Jane Austen sequels will find this charming book a more than satisfying read. Jane Odiwe is developing a keen style of her own."

—Jane Austen Today

Praise for *Lydia Bennet's Story*

"Odiwe pays nice homage to Austen's stylings and endears the reader to the formerly secondary character, spoiled and impulsive Lydia Bennet. Odiwe grants readers unfettered access to Lydia as she flirts with her many beaus... falls hard for George Wickham... and finds true happiness in the most unlikely of places."

—*Publishers Weekly*

"Elizabeth Bennet's naughty little sister takes center stage in a breathtaking Regency romp all her own, told with authoritative period elegance by Jane Odiwe's eloquent pen."

—Diana Birchall, author of *Mrs. Darcy's Dilemma*

"Odiwe emulates Austen's famous wit, and manages to give Lydia a happily-ever-after ending worthy of any Regency romance heroine."

—*Booklist*

Mr. Darcy's Secret

JANE ODIWE

sourcebooks
landmark

Published by Sourcebooks Landmark, an imprint of Sourcebooks, Inc.
P.O. Box 4410, Naperville, Illinois 60567-4410
(630) 961-3900
FAX: (630) 961-2168
www.sourcebooks.com

Library of Congress Cataloging-in-Publication Data

Odiwe, Jane.
  Mr. Darcy's secret / Jane Odiwe.
     p. cm.
   ISBN 978-1-4022-4527-5 (pbk. : alk. paper)   1.   Darcy, Fitzwilliam (Fictitious
character)--Fiction. 2.   Bennet, Elizabeth (Fictitious character)--Fiction. 3.   Gentry-
-England--Fiction. 4.   England--Social life and customs--19th century--Fiction.   I.
Austen, Jane, 1775-1817. II. Title.

PR6115.D55M7 2011
823'.92--dc22

                                        2010043735

       Printed and bound in the United States of America.
          VP 10 9 8 7 6 5 4 3 2 1

...To sit in the shade on a fine day, and look upon verdure, is
the most perfect refreshment.
—Jane Austen

For Jenny, Caroline, Penny, and Mavis, whose friendship and
love of gardens inspired this book.

Chapter 1

WITH LITTLE EXCEPTION, THE anticipation of a long-awaited and desirous event will always give as much, if not more pleasure, than the diversion itself. Moreover, it is a certain truth that however gratifying such an occasion may prove to be, it will not necessarily unite prospect and satisfaction in equal accord.

Mrs Bennet's musings on the affairs of the day at Longbourn church were similarly divided. The ostrich feathers on her satin wedding hat quivered tremulously as she surveyed her surroundings with a self-satisfied air. Evening sunlight streamed through the long windows of the sitting room gilding her hair and silk pelisse, simultaneously burnishing the top of Mr Bennet's polished pate with a halo of amber softness.

"Hardly has a day passed during the last twenty-three years when I have not thought about my daughters' nuptials with the certain foreknowledge that my beautiful Jane and clever Lizzy would do their duty to their parents, their sisters, and themselves," said Mrs Bennet to her husband on the day that her eldest daughters were married.

"Yes, my dear," Mr Bennet replied with a wry smile, "even when you professed your resolution that they should both die old maids not two months ago, I am sure you knew better in your heart."

"Such weddings as Longbourn and, indeed, the whole county have never seen before," exclaimed Mrs Bennet, fingering the new lace about her shoulders with an air of appreciation whilst ignoring her husband's bemused comments. "Not that there were some matters that would have pleased me better had I been allowed to have a hand in the arrangements myself. I should have liked to host a party if I had been permitted, but Elizabeth did not think it fitting. I am sure our neighbours would greatly have appreciated the celebration, but who am I to be considered? I am only the mother of the brides married to two of the richest men in the kingdom! It is not as if it was a question of money. I am sure dear Darcy would have liked it if not for Elizabeth's opposition. Still, it was something to see the condescension of our neighbours; I daresay Lady Lucas will not feel herself so superior now. But truly, nothing will vex me today; all has surpassed my greatest expectations."

"I am glad to hear it, my dear, because without a doubt, if such long anticipation had been disappointed in some way, I am not entirely sure I could have borne the next twenty-three years with the same equanimity."

"Who would have thought it, Mr Bennet," said his lady, talking over the top of him, "that I should live to see two of my daughters so exceptionally advantaged in married life?"

"Quite so, my dear," replied he, "though I must add that however well placed I believed my daughters might find themselves, I had always planned on exceeding my own five and forty years to witness their felicity. Indeed, possessing the knowledge that your own long surviving line of aged relatives are still thriving as I speak, I must confess that I am a little astonished to think you had supposed to be dead before our daughters attained the matrimonial state."

"Oh, Mr Bennet, you speak such nonsense. But you will not tease me out of my present happy disposition. And, I must say, I received some comfort from the fact that Miss Bingley and her sister Mrs Hurst were forced by a rightful sense of obligation and due civility to treat our family in the correct manner today. Oh, yes, Mr Bennet, I cannot tell you how much it gratified me to see the smug, self-satisfied expressions they generally display upon their ill-favoured countenances quite wiped away. I thought Miss Bingley looked likely to choke when I turned to see Elizabeth and Jane walking down the aisle by your side."

"I did not observe any greater condescension towards our family than that which they usually bestow, Mrs Bennet," replied her spouse, "though I must admit I did not really pay them any great attention. My own thoughts and looks were only concerned with our dear girls."

"What a double blow it must have been for Miss Bingley. I expect all the while she was hoping that Mr Darcy might break his promise to Elizabeth and leave her at the altar. And I am sure, whatever she might have said on welcoming Jane to the Bingley family, that the sincerity of her wishes was entirely false. Well, I cannot help feeling our advantage over those Bingley women. And Mr Darcy was as charming and obliging as ever. I think him quite superior to dear Mr Bingley in many ways, even if I hadn't always liked him."

"I'm sure Mr Darcy would be delighted to hear it."

"I daresay he would, for he certainly needed to earn my good opinion after the way he strutted about Hertfordshire with his proud ways. However, I'm not entirely convinced by Lizzy's partiality, whatever she might protest on his having been misunderstood and winning her round. A man ought to have a tongue in his head, indeed, especially a man of such consequence."

"I should hate to hear you on the subject of despising a man if this is your approbation, Mrs Bennet. And I loathe to be contradicting you once more, but I cannot agree with you. I believe Lizzy to be very much in love with Mr Darcy, as much in love as dear Jane is with her Mr Bingley."

"Well, I certainly think I might fancy myself in love if I knew I was married to the owner of Pemberley, with a house in town and ten thousand a year, at least!"

"I am sure such good fortune helps love along. No doubt, my own prospects animated the feelings you had whilst we were courting."

Mrs Bennet looked at her husband in exasperation. "Oh, Mr Bennet, it was nothing like the matter. There is no comparison. The wealth of Mr Darcy and Mr Bingley is a hundred times your consequence, as well you know. La! With Jane and Lizzy so well married; 'tis enough to make me distracted!"

"I am pleased to discover our poverty is in no way dispiriting to your outlook, my dear. But I cannot join you in your exertions. I find myself feeling most melancholy. I am delighted that I need not worry that our daughters will suffer any lack of wealth or hardship; but despite the satisfaction these assurances bring, I cannot help but add that I shall miss them very much."

At this point Mrs Bennet burst into tears. "With my dearest Lydia so lately married and now Jane and Lizzy having left home,

I shall have little to do, especially now Mary and Kitty will be gone to their sisters by the bye. I do not know what shall become of me; indeed, I do not. I shall be quite alone in this house with only my memories coupled with the dreadful understanding that William and Charlotte Collins are counting the days to your demise. What misfortune to have our estate entailed away for that odious pair to inherit. It is all Lady Lucas ever talks to me about these days: of her daughter's delight at the prospect of being able to return one day into Hertfordshire."

"Come, come now," insisted Mr Bennet, passing over a pocket handkerchief and rising from his seat with the intention of leaving the room. "I see no reason for tears. I am sure one or all of your daughters will accommodate you when that unhappy day befalls you and, until then, I flatter myself that you will have the comfort of knowing that you are not entirely alone. I am here, or at least I will be when I am not away."

"Away! Do you intend to leave me, sir? Where are you going, Mr Bennet?"

"To Pemberley, of course," came his emphatic reply.

"To Pemberley and you never said a word of it. But do you intend to go alone and without an invitation?"

Mr Bennet stroked his chin thoughtfully. "I suppose if you should wish to accompany me, then you may enjoy your share of the invitation."

"An invitation! Has Lizzy invited us to Pemberley so soon?" asked Mrs Bennet, scarcely able to keep the astonishment out of her voice.

"No, Mr Darcy himself, no less," came the triumphant answer, "has not only issued the invitation, but also expects us for Christmas!"

Elizabeth Darcy looked out of the carriage window, her spirits in high flutter as they crossed the ancient stone bridge on the road into Lambton village. Nestled at the foot of a hill, on the western side of the river, a number of stone cottages, a church, and a few handsome buildings formed the landscape. Her eyes were drawn to the rich and romantic scenery of the place, enhanced in beauty by the noble appearance of wood-clad hills, wreathed in mist on this damp, November morning. She could not help but remember her first journey to Lambton, accompanied by her uncle and aunt Gardiner on their northern tour. How different had her feelings been in August when the trees had been lush with greenery, the sunshine dazzling her eyes and burnishing her skin to tones of golden brown. Elizabeth recalled her feelings of dread at the thought of being in near vicinity to that of Mr Darcy and how she had feared visiting Pemberley, the house that was now to be her home. She laughed out loud.

"Are you happy, dearest Elizabeth?" Mr Darcy enquired, taking her hand between both of his and raising it to his lips to kiss her fingertips tenderly.

"I am indeed, though happiness was not the emotion at the forefront of my mind just now. I was engaged in other, quite dreadful recollections, I must admit."

Fitzwilliam Darcy's brows knitted together in consternation. He studied Elizabeth's countenance, noting her expression which had suddenly changed to display a look so serious and grave that he could hardly bear to witness it. "I shall never forgive myself for the things I said to you in the past, nor for the way in which I behaved. I only trust that in time I shall make sufficient amendment. My wish is to make you feel as I do, to have you love me as I love you. Please, Elizabeth, do not dwell on such bleak remembrances."

Mrs Darcy turned her face toward him and, being unable to look anything other than completely amused, caused her husband to look searchingly into the dark, fine eyes which he so admired. "You have clearly forgotten some of my philosophy. Think only of the past as its remembrance gives you pleasure." Elizabeth paused, her curls trembling as she suppressed the mirth bubbling inside. "I am teasing you, Fitzwilliam. I am perfectly happy to dwell on the memories of my first trip into Derbyshire, even if my initial feelings were concerned with mortification and distress. When I first set eyes on Lambton village, I could not help but think of you, and knowing that your estate was but five miles from here, with the possibility of your being in residence, was enough to overturn all my feelings."

"Am I to deduce from this statement that you felt an incli-nation toward me that was beyond your own will? You always gave the impression of total disinterest, a self-sufficiency and aloofness. This description of your feelings gives quite a different picture. I think if you really had been so indifferent to me as I believed you were then, no such agitation could have been expe-rienced. No one suffers anxiety when they are truly detached from feeling. I suspect that this distress you speak of was the deep acknowledgement that you were falling in love with me, regardless of your resolution to despise me forever."

Elizabeth laughed again, her dark ringlets trembling prettily as she shook her head. "Oh, you insufferable, darling man. I hate to admit it, but I think there may be some element of truth in what you say, although I would certainly have denied it at the time. I felt most uncomfortable at the thought of looking around Pemberley, and yet I was most curious to see the house where I could have been mistress, had I not turned down your wretched proposal."

"Oh, do not remind me of that dreaded conversation at Hunsford."

"No, I shall not be so cruel. Instead I shall remind you that your second proposal was infinitely more acceptable to me, so much so that I am sitting here next to the man who has made me the happiest woman alive."

"Have I made you happy, Elizabeth? I know we are just at the beginning of our life together, and two days spent in exclusive company is hardly enough time for you to know whether or not you were right in your decision to accept me a second time. But I hope you do not regret the outcome. I only want your happiness."

"Mrs Reynolds is a very wise woman, I have come to believe."

"Whatever do you mean?"

"Your housekeeper was the person who made me think again about my prejudice against you. Her description of you as the sweetest-tempered, most generous-hearted boy in the world could not be without foundation. She, who had known you since you were a child, had to know something of your true character. I suppose it was from that day my idea of you really changed. And what is more, I believe she was correct. I know now just how sweet-tempered you really can be."

Mr Darcy smiled and looked into her eyes at that moment with such evident longing that she felt her cheeks blush. The pressure of his fingers upon her own increased and though she reciprocated with a returning squeeze, it was too much to sustain his gaze. She must keep something in reserve, Lizzy felt, or her husband's vanity, so recently curbed and tamed, might stir again like a beast unleashed. In any case, it would be far more fun to keep him wondering quite how far her admiration for him extended. She turned once more to seek the view through the window, simultaneously extracting her hand from his firm grasp and fussing about with her gloves and the fur tippet around her shoulders. "I thought we were to travel straight to Pemberley," she said as the carriage started to enter the village.

"I have a small commission to fulfil first; we shall not be long," answered Mr Darcy.

As they turned the corner into the main street, the sight that met her eyes was enough to make Elizabeth cry out in surprise; for lining both sides of the road, three people deep, was the entire population of Lambton. At the sight of the carriage up went a roar and a cheer, caps and hats were thrown into the air, and everyone burst into applause. Faces, young and old, peered into the carriage as it trundled past. Voices sang out from every side with wishes of joy.

"God bless you, sir, and God bless you, my lady. Welcome to Lambton!"

So unexpected was the tribute being paid to them that Elizabeth was moved to the point where she could not immediately find her tongue. "Oh, Fitzwilliam," she uttered at last. "Is this wonderful reception for us?"

"For you, my love. I might inspire a certain affectionate respect in my tenants, but I have never seen them turn out like this before." He took her hand again. "Welcome to Lambton, Mrs Darcy. Come, we are expected."

The carriage stopped in front of the smithy. Mr Darcy alighted first, before helping his bride down the steps to yet more cheers and greetings. Elizabeth was quite overawed, but managed to return the smiles of the happy faces around her. A crowd was gathering about them and around by the open doors of the forge as if in anticipation. Just in front was placed a gleaming anvil, polished for the occasion, with the ruddy-faced blacksmith in attendance, his large muscular arms folded across his chest. A well-dressed gentleman in clerical black stepped forward and was introduced to Elizabeth by Mr Darcy. A handsome young man, Mr Lloyd, the rector of Lambton church, cut a dashing figure—quite unlike any other clergyman Elizabeth thought she had ever met. He welcomed her to the village with a very pretty speech before explaining what was to happen next.

"We have a custom in these parts, Mrs Darcy, that when a new bride arrives at Pemberley House we celebrate this auspicious event by firing the anvil. If you will step this way, Mr and Mrs Darcy, I hope you shall enjoy what is to follow."

The blacksmith took charge, filling the central hole in the anvil with a small amount of black gunpowder, to which he added the end of a long piece of cord. The audience, which had swelled in number, now including the newlyweds, took up position at a safe distance, and as the blacksmith produced a flaming rushlight, a hushed silence fell on them all.

"Mrs Darcy, you might wish to cover your ears," pronounced Mr Lloyd, as the blacksmith set the end of the fuse alight. All but the bravest held their hands over their ears and waited, breathless, as the flame crept along the cord. As it reached the top of the anvil there was an audible intake of breath; then the flame slowed and looked as if it might go out, before it finally gathered pace to surprise them all with the biggest bang Elizabeth had ever heard. Shrieks, laughter, and exclamations of relief resulted as a consequence and the rector announced Mr and Mrs Darcy officially married. Lizzy and her husband offered their thanks, then moved amongst the crowd shaking hands with all their well-wishers who, without exception, greeted them with great affability.

"'Tis not only Pemberley weddings that are celebrated in this way, Mrs Darcy," said an elderly lady with a soft Derbyshire burr, who curtsied deferentially before Elizabeth, "but birthdays and christenings too. The heirs of Pemberley receive not only a wetting in the font, but a firing from the forge, and every birthday is remembered. God bless you, my dear. I hope we will not have to wait long before we have reason to celebrate at the smithy once more."

As she moved along Elizabeth blushed as she thought about the old lady's sentiments. The thought of a child, an heir to Pemberley, was not one she had ever considered before. Yet she knew that to provide children and an heir was one of the duties that would be expected of the new mistress of Pemberley. Still, she had been quite taken aback by such forthrightness. However, though Lizzy felt the impertinence of the woman's words, she realised that they had been spoken in true kindness. Touched by the welcome from the people, Elizabeth thought how lucky she was to have met and fallen in love with the man who inspired such affection. She turned to seek him out, realising that she had momentarily lost him in the crowd that gathered around them. However, she soon had him in her sights. Mr Darcy's unmistakable profile was highly visible, his head clearly seen above the multitude. His handsome face looked its best, his eyes crinkling with good humour, and his dark hair waving back over his forehead to fall in curls against his collar. What a striking figure he cut, all ease, though still retaining an air of stateliness. Lizzy could see him listening carefully to his tenants' words of advice and congratulations on the married state, receiving all their good wishes with grace and forbearance. His noble stature and his build, so evidently strong under the perfect cut of his black coat, were enough to overset her feelings. Not for the first time did she feel almost overwhelmed by the thought of all that would be expected of her by this powerful man, but she was determined to show him that in choosing her to be his bride, he had made the right decision. Despite the trepidation that she felt, she was confident that she would take it all in her stride.

Eventually, after thanking everyone again, with an extra show of gratitude to the rector and the blacksmith for their special ceremony, they took their leave, climbing back into the carriage for the last leg of the journey. Lizzy felt in high spirits; it had been so pleasurable to be addressed as Mrs Darcy, even if once or twice she had forgotten to respond, being quite unused to being called anything other than Miss Elizabeth Bennet.

As they bowled along, Elizabeth watched for the first appearance of Pemberley Woods with excitement, and when, at length, they turned in at the lodge she could hardly contain the mixture of fear and elation that she felt inside. It was one matter to be greeted so kindly by the villagers, but what would the inhabitants of Pemberley House think of her arrival? And how was she to undertake the job she had to do now, as mistress of the house?

Chapter 2

THE PARK SEEMED LARGER than she remembered and the ascent through beautiful woodland just as memorable as it had been in August, even if the leaves now lay on the ground in drifts of russet and copper. Elizabeth's mind was too full for conversation, and when they found themselves arriving at the top of a considerable eminence where the wood ceased, she remembered with great anticipation the remarkable sight which next came into view. Pemberley House, situated on the opposite side of the valley, was even bigger than she recalled. A large, handsome stone building, standing well on rising ground, it was backed by a ridge of high wooded hills and fronted by a stream of natural beauty creating a perfect harmonious whole to Elizabeth's way of thinking.

"Welcome to Pemberley, my dearest Elizabeth; welcome to your new home," said Mr Darcy with an extra squeeze of her hand.

The smile Mrs Darcy bestowed on her husband expressed her feelings as well as any words, her face lighting up with pure joy. They descended the hill, crossed the bridge and drove to the door, and whilst contemplating the nearer aspect of the house, which she remembered so well, all her apprehensions returned as Lizzy observed the army of awaiting staff.

Georgiana Darcy was also waiting, standing solemnly in front of the house with her governess Mrs Annesley. Elizabeth was pleased to see that her new sister was as unassuming and gentle in her manners as she remembered. Miss Darcy was tall, her figure womanly and graceful, and though not as handsome as her brother, when she smiled there was good humour in her countenance. And yet, Elizabeth felt she could discern some want of spirit. Georgiana's eyes betrayed some traces of feeling, perhaps melancholy, her new sister decided. But once engaged in conversation, she seemed to brighten and Lizzy decided that the flicker of unhappiness she had witnessed had most likely been a symptom of apprehension. Georgiana was a shy girl at the best of times. Lizzy hoped above all things that they would continue to get along together as they had on their first meetings in the summer.

"I am so pleased to welcome you and my dear brother, and to see you both together is the pleasure I have most been looking forward to in the whole world," Georgiana said, curtseying before Elizabeth. She presented Mrs Annesley, who congratulated Mr and Mrs Darcy on their marriage before taking her leave to give her charge time to be with the Darcys by themselves.

"Mrs Darcy," Georgiana said, as if making an announcement, "the name sounds so lovely. I kept thinking all the while that there was to be a new Mrs Darcy at Pemberley and how thrilled everyone hereabout will be at the news."

"Everybody has been very kind," Elizabeth answered, "but I am relying on your help, Miss Darcy. My wish is for us to spend as much time as possible together. I hope you will consider taking me around Pemberley and teaching me all about your home."

"It will be my delight, Mrs Darcy."

"Oh, please, let us not be so formal—do call me Elizabeth, or Lizzy. After all, we are sisters."

"Then you must call me Georgiana also."

Elizabeth proffered her arm and so the sisters linked arms to sally forth, Georgiana performing the introductions to the butler and the steward. Mr Darcy stared after them with the realisation that he had been entirely forgotten, but thought how glad he was to see the two women he loved best in the world getting to know each other so amicably and under such congenial circumstances.

Mrs Reynolds, the housekeeper, next came forward, her expression clearly showing that she remembered Elizabeth from her former visit. With the same deferential goodwill she had been shown in the village, the old lady bade her much fortune and happiness in her new home.

"Mrs Darcy, I hope you will find everything to your satisfaction. If there is anything I can do for you to increase your comfort, you have only to ask; I am here to serve you, ma'am."

Elizabeth was on the point of replying, offering her thanks and assuring her housekeeper of her willingness to help in any household matters where Mrs Reynolds might require her assistance, when somewhere in the distance a loud boom echoed across the hills followed by several smaller blasts.

Lizzy looked with some alarm toward her husband. "Good heavens, what on earth was that? It sounded louder than the blacksmith's firing."

"I daresay Jack Rudge had a spot of gunpowder left over and thought he'd frighten them all again," said Mrs Reynolds, gesturing the way forward. "Please come along in, Mrs Darcy, it's far too cold to be standing outside."

· Elizabeth looked up at her husband who had made no comment. He was looking toward the hills in the direction of Lambton with quite a scowl on his countenance.

"What does Rudge think he is doing?" demanded Mr Darcy, whose question was clearly rhetorical.

Mrs Darcy entered the hall with half a mind on Mrs Reynolds's unceasing conversation and half on that of Mr Darcy. She was more than a little surprised to see how quickly her husband's mood appeared to have altered and was, for an instant, reminded of the proud and disagreeable man she had first met in Hertfordshire.

However, Mr Darcy's spirits were soon restored when he saw Elizabeth's reaction to her new surroundings. They followed Mrs Reynolds into the dining-parlour, a large, well-proportioned room, handsomely fitted up. Elizabeth, remembering the view from her last visit, went to a window to enjoy its prospect. Crowned with wood, the hill from which they had descended was a beautiful object. Every disposition of the ground was good, and she looked on the whole scene, at the river, the trees scattered on its banks, and the winding of the valley with undisguised delight. Mrs Reynolds quickly excused herself, saying she would send their nuncheon along in a moment, for she was sure they must be famished from their journey. Georgiana followed her out of the room, keen to make herself useful and make sure that everything was in order for Elizabeth's first meal at Pemberley.

Elizabeth stood looking at the scene with every appearance of rapture. "I think I must be dreaming," she said, looking up at Mr Darcy, who joined her to stand at her side. "To think that I shall be able to enjoy this vista whenever I choose. Oh, Fitzwilliam, I have rarely seen such beauties of landscape. I know I shall be so happy here; indeed, how could anyone ever be unhappy faced with this outlook every day? You won't ever take me away, will you?"

Mr Darcy smiled at her with the particular smile that he seemed only to reserve for her, especially in their private moments. "I will keep you here forever, Mrs Darcy, I promise, though I expect after a month or two, when the winter becomes severe and you tell me that you cannot keep warm, and that the gossips hereabout have dried up all their tales, you'll be begging me for more varied society."

"I do not think I could ever tire of Pemberley, Fitzwilliam, and I'm certain the society here will be exactly what I wish. To be holed up here in winter by a cosy fire with you is exactly the sort of society I crave."

"Do you not wish to go to London for the season?" asked Mr Darcy, clearly astonished. "I thought all young women love to go to London, if not for society, at least for the shopping! And it may be selfish, but I wish to show off my wife at all the assemblies in town."

"I should like to go one day, but now we are here, I would much prefer to stay put, at least for a while. Indeed, I cannot think of anywhere I should be tempted to go. I know I have a lot to learn about the running of a grand house and I want to do it well. I wish you to be proud of your wife, Mr Darcy."

"I rather thought my being proud was one of the traits you despised in me," he answered, looking her straight in the eye but with a twinkle in his own.

"Indeed, Mr Darcy, to be proud of your wife, I believe, shows you have no improper pride. To have pride in a spouse displays a certain satisfaction and contentment, respect even, for your life partner. I do not think you guilty of vanity or conceit for having pride in me."

Mr Darcy laughed. "I thought you might see it that way, my dearest, Elizabeth." His voice softened as he added, "I am very proud of you, Mrs Darcy."

Mrs Reynolds returned at that moment, followed by Georgiana, with two housemaids bringing plates of cold meat, warm bread rolls, slabs of fruitcake, and a dish of rosy apples.

"I think we had best make the most of our solitude today," said Mr Darcy, inviting his wife and sister to join him at the table with a gesture of his hand. "No doubt we shall be inundated with visitors over the next few days or so. My neighbours will be anxious to call on the new bride. Will you mind very much being scrutinised by the entire district, do you think?"

"I suppose I had better get used to the idea of being an object of interest. You are an important man, and the families in the vicinity are bound to be curious about the woman who has shackled herself to a man who requires so much in the way of accomplishments. I hope I do not disappoint them."

Elizabeth grinned at Georgiana, who looked so shocked that anyone could speak to her brother in such a fashion and not be scolded for it that Lizzy started to laugh.

"Your teasing is too severe, Elizabeth," replied Mr Darcy. "I suppose you are referring to that conversation so long ago in which I claimed I knew only a half dozen accomplished ladies."

Elizabeth's expression was serious, as she gave full attention to her apple. With movements deft and precise, Mr Darcy watched the ribbon of peel grow longer as Lizzy pared the fruit with her knife. She looked up for a moment, her large dark eyes sparkling at him from under fine, arched brows. "I am sure I shall be a great curiosity," she said at last. "People will be bound to quiz me as to the extent of my knowledge of music, singing, drawing, dancing, the modern languages, and whatever else an accomplished woman should possess." She paused to look up with a bemused expression in Georgiana's direction and rested a single finger on her rosy cheek. "Now, what else must she have? Ah, yes, I remember, she must be endowed with a certain something in her air and manner of walking, the tone of her voice, her address and expressions, to but half deserve the word."

"Oh dear, do not remind me. I know I was a party to this conversation," declared Darcy with a groan. "I really was unbearably disparaging. Tell me, Mrs Darcy, how could you have tied yourself to such an abominably impossible man?"

"Truly, I cannot say, except to add that I fell in love with him despite all his faults, which are lately much improved. And I think the people who know you best will understand why I married you. Indeed, I have no regrets and I have no intention of disappointing your neighbours. They will see distinction and accomplishment, I promise."

"And what is more, they will see the most beautiful woman in all of Derbyshire. Do you not agree, Georgiana?" said Mr Darcy.

Georgiana spoke up at once. "Yes, I do. I think Elizabeth the most beautiful lady of my acquaintance."

A knock at the door interrupted the conversation and a maidservant appeared with a salver. "Please sir, this letter's just come by express."

Fitzwilliam Darcy picked up the letter and Elizabeth

witnessed a frown instantly change his congenial expression as he examined the handwriting. He nodded at the servant, muttered his thanks and waited until the latter departed before tearing open the seal. Elizabeth watched as he instantly fell silent, his mouth setting in a hard line. She began to feel quite fearful. Darcy's colour was rising in his cheeks, his dark eyes flashing beneath his black brows. His agitation increased with every word read, until finally, in a spontaneous act of temper, he tore the offending missive into shreds, managing simultaneously to send a glass flying across the room to shatter onto the stone hearth in a thousand brittle shards.

"And this is her letter of congratulation and felicitation on the event of my marriage, is it? Does she imagine that I crave her approbation; that I even care for her opinion? This is insufferable, an unspeakable affront of the vilest kind!"

"Fitzwilliam, what on earth is the matter?" Elizabeth put out her hand to cover her husband's as a gesture of concern.

Darcy instantly withdrew his hand before Elizabeth had a chance to touch him, and immediately rising, he marched over to the fire to scatter the offending scraps of paper into the flames. He stood for a moment before the fender, his head bowed and shoulders hunched in an attitude of defeat. But in the next second Elizabeth saw his change in posture; he seemed taller than ever as he turned in an attitude of defiance. Now in total command of his emotions, his voice cut through the air like a steel knife after sharpening on a wet stone. "Never will she return to Pemberley whilst I am living," he declared darkly. "I have been insulted by every method and I will have no more of it."

Elizabeth ran to his side. She was very concerned, not only by his alarming behaviour, but also because Georgiana was becoming increasingly distressed. "Please, my love," she whispered, "Georgiana is very upset. May I ask what has disturbed you so?"

"Forgive me, Elizabeth, Georgiana, but I was overcome by my feelings for a moment. I did not mean to worry you. I have received a communication of the direst sort, so despicable that I would rather not have you know its contents. My aunt, Lady Catherine de Bourgh, a lady you know who does not hold back when divulging her true opinions, has chosen to insult me in such a way as can never be excused. She has made her thoughts quite clear and I feel I have no choice but to act on them. I am only sorry that the last link with my dear mother's family must finally be severed."

"Dearest, come now, think what you are saying," said Elizabeth, who was stricken by her husband's appearance. "I daresay she was not in her right mind when she wrote the letter. We both know that Lady Catherine was far from happy about the news of our engagement, and we would be fooling ourselves if we thought that the event of our marriage was going to make her sanguine. She is angry, but her displeasure need not affect our happiness. Dearest, please do not be upset."

Although calmer, Mr Darcy's anger did not subside, his complexion paled and the disturbance of his mind became visible in every feature. "That woman has slighted you in an abuse of words that I would not use against my worst enemy and she has irrevocably offended me for the last time, Mrs Darcy. No one speaks of my wife and my family in such despicable terms and gets away with it. That is my last word on the matter."

Darcy walked back to the table to his sister's side and putting out his hand took up Georgiana's small one to pat it reassuringly.

"I am sorry if I frightened you, Georgiana, but I was rather cross. I am quite composed now, do not worry."

Miss Darcy looked up and smiled, her affection for her brother clearly etched on every feature. "I am not worried, you know; however rude Lady Catherine might be, her bark is always worse than her bite. I am so sorry, Fitzwilliam, that such a lovely day has been spoiled."

"Oh, do not worry about that, my dear little sister. Nothing could spoil this day for me, which has to be the happiest I have ever known."

Looking over at his wife, Elizabeth caught his eye and the look of love that passed between them made Georgiana smile again. She placed her napkin on the table and rose to leave. "I must go and see Mrs Annesley now, if you will excuse me. There is a drawing I have to finish." She paused at the door and turned toward the happy couple. "I am so delighted that you are both here, especially you, Lizzy."

After she had gone, Elizabeth was concerned that Georgiana might still feel upset about the letter. She felt perhaps her own behaviour had not helped matters and was fearful that she might have embarrassed Georgiana by her forthrightness. "I do not think your sister is used to people teasing you or being rude to you. I do hope she was not affronted."

"Not at all. I should think if anyone's behaviour induced embarrassment it must have been my own. Not just that I was outspoken and impulsive with regard to my aunt's letter. I confess I am forgetting my manners of late when I am with you. Being in the company of lovers is somewhat tedious for anyone else, especially when they must listen to the protestations of love from a newly wedded husband."

"Oh, Mr Darcy, I can find no fault in your manners," said Elizabeth, returning to the table to stand before her beloved husband. "Indeed, they have improved so much that I declare I am quite delighted by your protestations."

"How delighted are you, Mrs Darcy?" he cried, pulling her towards him. "I need proof of such a declaration."

"Oh, my love, I cannot imagine how to accomplish such an avowal to your satisfaction."

"Can you not, Mrs Darcy?" he whispered, enfolding his wife in his arms and planting a tender kiss on her cheek. "Then please let me be the one to enlighten you."

The afternoon disappeared in blissful companionship. Relaxing on a sofa in their private sitting room before a log fire dozing in each other's arms was as close as Elizabeth imagined earthly paradise could be. The day was drawing to a close, shadows creeping stealthily inside and out. Through the floor-length windows, Elizabeth could see the wintry sun low on the horizon, like a scarlet ball sending ribbons of flame and crimson across the sky, making silhouettes of the trees and gilding the water below to a burnished copper. The soft candlelight within mirrored the scene to perfection, so where the interior finished and the garden began seemed indistinct. Happiness filled her soul at everything she observed, but most especially at the sight of her handsome husband slumbering at her side. She kissed him on the cheek but had no wish to wake him; he looked so very peaceful. Lizzy stretched and, getting up, looked about, wondering if she could remember which of the doors was the one to her dressing room. She could not resist another peep into her bed-chamber, even if she thought she had better start getting ready for dinner. The heavy door opened onto a scene of delight to

Elizabeth's eyes. Decorated in hues of her favourite yellow, her bedchamber looked a sunny room even in dim candlelight. Little had she realised in all their conversations at Longbourn that all the while Mr Darcy had been making mental notes of her preferences in all matters of style. Fitzwilliam had executed every single wish that she could possibly have had. Fresh lavender-scented linen on the bed and plumped pillows embroidered with the Darcy crest looked so inviting that she wished she could dispense with dinner entirely. At the foot of the huge oak tester bed, complete with floral drapes to keep in the warmth, a bowl of potpourri filled with dried roses on a chest assailed her senses with the fragrance of a summer's day. Elizabeth sat down at her dressing table and, glancing at her image in the glass, she was astonished by her reflection, at the sophisticated young woman who looked back at her. How much she seemed to have changed, she thought, in the short time she had become Mrs Darcy, although she readily acknowledged that the appearance of a well-dressed young woman did not altogether reflect the true state of her inner feelings. No matter how much she had convinced herself that being Mrs Darcy would be a matter she could easily take in her stride, wanting to prove her worth as a fitting consort for her husband delighted and unsettled her in equal measures.

Her thoughts turned to the events of the day. Recalling the old woman who had talked of Pemberley heirs, Lizzy could hardly contemplate the subject that filled her with not only a sense of fear, but also of excitement. How soon would there be another firing at the anvil, she wondered. That was a prospect to delight in, even if the very thought was disturbing. A picture of the man she adored smiling at her with that expression she loved most came uppermost to her mind, but whilst she contemplated, she also recollected that today had brought its troubles as well as its joys. Fitzwilliam had seemed very upset when the anvil had been accidentally fired as they arrived at Pemberley; his reaction had startled her, she had to admit. That incident coupled with the letter he had received from Lady Catherine had really ruffled Darcy's feathers. But it had been an eventful and emotional day for them both. Elizabeth thought how much she had to learn about her husband and about being a new wife. One of her first duties must surely involve helping Fitzwilliam be united with his aunt. Proud and disagreeable as Lady Catherine had proved, Elizabeth did not want to be the reason for ending their intimacy. How she was to accomplish such a feat would bring all her powers of cunning, tact, and persuasion to bear. No matter, it would be done somehow and she hoped sooner rather than later. But for now she must look forward to a pleasant evening and the prospect of their first night at Pemberley House. Elizabeth fixed a silk flower in her hair, blew out the candles, and went in search of her darling husband.

Chapter 3

MR DARCY WAS PROVED right. A constant flow of visitors eager to see the new bride arrived every morning during the following week. Elizabeth met all the notable families in the area—the Calladines, the Eatons, the Vernons, and the Bradshaws—whose invitations to dine soon mounted on the mantelpiece. Lizzy was happy to meet her neighbours if slightly overwhelmed and exhausted by the experience. As pleasant as the local gentry appeared to be, she soon gained the impression that here, as in any other locality, gossip was rife amongst its inhabitants, and she had to admit she felt most disconcerted by much of what she heard. All she could do was to put such tittle-tattle out of her mind, although one particular tale left her feeling most perplexed. That it involved the Darcy family, albeit indirectly, Elizabeth knew must be at the heart of her uneasiness.

The evening before last had promised to be a trial before it even began. Their hostess, Lady Rackham, was an old acquaintance of Darcy's aunt, Lady Catherine de Bourgh, and Elizabeth had no doubt that she would be under particular scrutiny. Before dinner there had been the usual polite but pointed conversation aimed at discovering as much about Lizzy's past and social connections as possible. That this examination had amused her there could be no question, but when the conversation turned to the connection with Darcy's aunt, Elizabeth knew she must be on her guard for her husband's sake. She had the feeling that Lady Rackham had been influenced in her disapproval of Mr Darcy's marriage and that Lady Catherine's opinions of Elizabeth had swiftly become Lady Rackham's own before she had even made the acquaintance.

"Mrs Darcy, I expect you will be staying with Lady Catherine in town for the coming season," said Lady Rackham. "I know Mr Darcy always looks forward to being in London with his aunt, and that she too depends very much upon his company."

Before Elizabeth had a chance to answer, however, Mr Darcy spoke out. He had overheard the conversation and gave his reply, which was abrupt and to the point.

"We have no plans at the present time to go to London, Lady Rackham."

"Oh dear, Mr Darcy, I know your aunt quite depends on your attendance for her comfort."

"I am sure my aunt will find she has enough diversion in London. Besides, it is my wish to stay in Derbyshire."

"I do hope your aunt will not suffer too much under her disappointment at your absence in town. But, I daresay you and Mrs Darcy have your reasons for staying away. And in any case, I expect Lady Catherine will be making her usual visit to Pemberley after Christmas," she said. "She has many friends who welcome her visits; I look forward with great anticipation to her coming to Derbyshire. We have so much to discuss."

Mr Darcy turned away at that moment to address Lord Rackham as if he had not heard her speak. Elizabeth felt mortified by his rude manners and, deciding that she must answer in the affirmative, declared that they were looking forward to a visit whenever Lady Catherine wished to call.

"I know how much she and her daughter look forward to coming to Derbyshire," continued Lady Rackham. "It is a pity that Miss de Bourgh suffers so much with poor health, but I am sure the Derbyshire air does her good. Of course, in the old days when Mrs Darcy was alive we had such splendid gatherings at Pemberley. She and Lady Catherine were the celebrated sisters of their day, such noble blood, with all the elevation of rank— the epitome of fine, aristocratic connections. But with Lady Anne Darcy's untimely death it all came to an end."

"It must have had a devastating effect upon the family," ventured Elizabeth.

"The consequences of that poor lady's death cannot be underestimated—the cost to Pemberley, I do not think we have ever fully appreciated until now. That her influence in all matters is no longer felt is a true detriment. As Lady Catherine said, its history is taking a turn I am certain she would not have endorsed."

Lady Rackham scrutinised Elizabeth with such an expression of hauteur that she felt as if she had personally been accused of causing the lady's demise. Her none too subtle hints seemed to be suggesting that if Mr Darcy's mother had still been alive Elizabeth would certainly not have taken her place. Too shocked to immediately respond, it was with some relief Elizabeth heard that they were all being asked to take their seats for dinner. Holding on to her husband's arm and feeling his reassuring presence as they entered the room, Elizabeth reminded herself that she knew there were always going to be those people connected with Lady Catherine whom she was never going to please. By agreeing to marry Mr Darcy, she had known that there were going to be many trials ahead. Rising above them was a matter she had to overcome.

The dinner passed in the usual way with much consumption by the gentlemen and little from their partners, who were all engaged in the pursuit of talking too much to be eating. At the correct time the ladies withdrew from the table leaving the gentlemen to their drinks and speculation on the sport that was to follow the next day. How Elizabeth wished she could stay with them, even though shooting was not a subject that held much interest. The thought of more searching questions and sneering remarks filled her with dread. She knew it was a matter of time before she would be singled out for the usual probing inspection and it was not long before Mrs Eaton sought Elizabeth's company. They had only met once before but that lady had established herself as a gossip and inquisitive to the point of offensiveness. Elizabeth was on her mettle.

After making enquiries about how Mrs Darcy had been enjoying the hospitality of the people in the surrounding district, the subject of Pemberley, Georgiana, and of Mr Darcy's mother arose again.

"Miss Georgiana is growing into a fine young lady," said Mrs Eaton. "I expect she'll have her coming out soon and we shall see her being courted. I cannot believe she is of an age for dancing with all that that entails." Shaking her head, she sighed. "To think all that time has passed, and that poor girl never knowing her mother. I cannot bear to think of her never experiencing the warmth of maternal love."

"It is true, a mother's care is of a special kind," Elizabeth commented thoughtfully, "but surely it does not follow that there is necessarily any neglect if a child receives love from a devoted parent or sibling—a father or a brother may also bestow much affection, and in my opinion, show quite as much attachment."

"Mrs Darcy, I did not mean to imply that there was ever any absence of care for Miss Georgiana. Indeed, I would say that generally speaking there was more than enough attention lavished on Miss Darcy. No, I believe love has never been wanting in her case. And to speak plainly, she certainly didn't suffer for want of love from one particular quarter."

Elizabeth met Mrs Eaton's eyes and bore all the study of her careful observation. With great alarm, she suddenly felt on her guard; surely this lady had no knowledge of Georgiana's unfortunate past affair with the scandalous Mr Wickham. If she had prior knowledge of the sad business Lizzy was unsure, but she felt relieved that Mrs Eaton did not allude to the comment again as she continued without a pause for breath.

"I daresay you've heard tell of old Mrs Darcy's lady's maid. She was like a second mother to Miss Georgiana until she went away."

The turn in the conversation took her aback, but Elizabeth assured her that she knew of no such lady. "Indeed, I know very little about Mr Darcy's mother, I must confess."

"The poor lady was very fond of Rachel Tissington, I can tell you. When Mrs Darcy died giving birth to Miss Georgiana, her maid lavished as much love on the babe as if she were her own. I daresay if things had not turned out quite as they did, she'd have seen her grow up into the young woman she is today."

Elizabeth instinctively knew that Mrs Eaton was referring

to some unpleasantness and desperately sought to change the subject. But her companion was undeterred.

"Between you and me, that's what started it—tending for the babe and longing for a child—as it often does with the lower orders. I am not one to gossip, I can assure you, Mrs Darcy, but when a penniless servant girl is set up for life in a cottage of her own and finds a husband and a baby within a few short months, it is bound to be commented on. Well, it is a blessing Mrs Darcy knew nothing of it, that's all I can say. I am sure it would have broken her heart."

Elizabeth could scarcely hide her astonishment. Unperturbed, Mrs Eaton continued, "Master Tissington was celebrating his birthday on the day you arrived, I believe." Mrs Eaton smiled at Elizabeth. "Well, it was all some years ago now. He's growing into a tall, handsome young man, not a bit of the farm boy about him, they say."

Lizzy had long since formed a very poor opinion of Mrs Eaton on the last occasion of their meeting, but this outburst confirmed her very worst suspicions. How she could have attracted the affable Mr Eaton, Lizzy could not think. On reflection, she decided that it was highly likely that Mrs Eaton's fortune might have prompted Cupid for she was certain it could not have been her charms.

"Well, it's happened before and it will happen again, I daresay, and I don't suppose the boy will ever learn anything of his true heritage. 'Tis a terrible place for gossip, but some very spiteful people say that Master Tissington's father is of noble descent. You might think so, for his mother certainly puts on airs in her little cottage at Birchlow."

Elizabeth felt her heart beating so fast she was sure it might burst. Every feeling of indignation and protest at this woman's horrid, unfeeling intimations filled her with a sense of disgust. It was fortunate that Lady Rackham chose that moment to call upon one of the ladies to play upon the pianoforte or the temptation to tell her what she thought of her uncivil and distasteful discourse might have been effected.

Not long after that the gentlemen joined them, Mr Darcy seeking her out and immediately putting her at ease merely by being there. But despite the reassurance of her husband's company, Elizabeth felt out of sorts. On the journey home in the carriage she could not help recalling Mrs Eaton's words. There had been something so underhand in her manner of communication, an attempt to unsettle her, Elizabeth felt. It was hardly a subject for discussion, and yet the hints Mrs Eaton had made left her feeling that there was more to this tale than one of the servant girl and the child it involved. If only Jane were here to discuss and have it over. A picture of her sister came to mind, and the thought that Jane would have dismissed Mrs Eaton's nastiness as not worth worrying about eased her mind for the present. Neither did she consider that she would mention the episode to Fitzwilliam. Thinking that it was not a matter to be brought to her husband's attention and determined to put the incident out of her mind, she refused to contemplate the matter any further.

Elizabeth longed for a moment of peace and solitude with a chance to explore her new home. There had not been much opportunity to walk about the grounds as much as she would like, but she supposed it was inevitable that there would be constraints on her leisure time, at least until things settled down. When a letter from Netherfield arrived from Jane, she immediately felt the delight of such a communication with her sister as it became clear that she too was suffering under the same engagements, even if she seemed able to bear it all with far more presence of mind.

On the following Tuesday afternoon, finding the time to take a stroll together at last, Fitzwilliam suggested they walk high into the woods, taking the path past the water cascade. The day was fine, the November sun melting the crystals of ice frosting the grass and the remaining leaves on the trees. The sound of the rushing water falling down the hillside, bubbling along, was a joyful noise to Elizabeth's ears, and as they walked she admired all the views around.

The subject of their conversation soon turned from nature to nurture and subsequently to that of Miss Darcy.

"It is so good to have Georgiana with us," said Elizabeth, taking his arm as they progressed up the steeper part of the hill. "If only we can make Pemberley into a cheerful home for her once more, I will be happy. I am conscious that she has spent considerable time in London and must have missed her childhood home greatly. I am most anxious that she may come to feel the happiness she formerly knew in this house when your parents were alive."

"It is a relief to have her with me again, with us, Elizabeth. I am so fortunate to have you help me with Georgiana, as I know you will."

"I only hope there are not too many memories to haunt her, ones that might give rise to the unhappiness and melancholy that she suffered in the past."

"Never will I forgive that blackguard George Wickham for

his treatment of my sister. To think how I might have prevented it if I had spent more time with her."

He stopped and Elizabeth observed how altered his mood became when the displeasing subject of their brother-in-law was touched upon. His black eyes seemed darker than ever and his smile, which usually softened his features into gentleness, was replaced by a scowl. It was evident that he struggled with his composure.

Elizabeth could not bear to see him so upset. "Fortunately for your sister, there was no great harm done, which cannot be said for my own."

"There is always great harm done where that gentleman is concerned," he answered. "At least in Newcastle he has a chance to redeem himself. We can only hope that their marriage will succeed, even if I feel my hopes for such an accomplishment are quite in vain."

"I cannot help but feel for my heedless sister. Lydia will have to live with him for the rest of her life. However silly and imprudent her behaviour, in my heart I do not think she deserved such a fate, even if I know there was nothing more that could be done."

They gained the top of the hill and, looking down, saw the valley and the rising prominence on the other side of the vale. "I do not mean to sound so ungrateful, Fitzwilliam. Without your intervention, who knows what would have become of Lydia. No doubt, when Wickham had become tired of her... Oh, I cannot even contemplate such a thing!"

"Let us not worry our heads over people who do not deserve such attention," Mr Darcy continued. "Let us look forward to our future, to being all together again. I have longed for this time to come to pass, a chance to be settled at Pemberley once more and amongst my fellow Derbyshire neighbours. This county, this land of high peaks and lush valleys, all you survey before you is in my blood; it forms part of what it is to be a Darcy. Oh, Elizabeth, I hope some day you will feel as I do about our home. Georgiana, I know, was unhappy in town and longed to come back. I see the change in her already. Soon she will have to make her own establishment, but I see no reason for her to go very far from us. A neighbouring estate will do very nicely. We shall have to look about for a husband for her in the not too distant future."

"Surely there is no need to do that just yet," Elizabeth implored. "Besides, I cannot think of anyone suitable in the vicinity."

"Hugh Calladine would make a good match."

"But he is at least ten years older than Georgiana, and besides, I thought it was common knowledge that he is in love with Eleanor Bradshaw. Mrs Bradshaw entertains high hopes of there being an alliance between the families."

"Hugh Calladine is a good gentleman of suitable standing, with a fine property, a sizeable inheritance, and what is more, a title to come. He has ambition, despite his friendship with the Bradshaws. They are a respectable family, but there is no fortune. Hugh Calladine will not make an imprudent match; he is very sensible. He is a young man and like all young men he has had his share of falling in love and breaking one or two hearts. That is the way of life; there is no harm done. Besides, I like the fellow. It is true, he is older than Georgiana, but I think he would be a settling influence on her."

"Do you mean to tell me that you would encourage him? And what does Georgiana think of him? I'm sure she would have no interest in a man who loved another. Darcy, you cannot be serious. Please tell me that you are joking, that you are teasing me for some cruel amusement. You do not really mean to marry Georgiana off for money and position alone, do you?"

Darcy let go of her arm, and turning away from her continued to speak. "Georgiana is a wealthy young lady and, as such, will be the prey of fortune hunters. It is imperative that a suitable marriage be made for her. There is no reason to delay."

"But surely you will let her find her own love," said Elizabeth, lightly running to catch him up slipping her arm inside his again. "Georgiana has not yet attended her first ball or had the pleasure of meeting any suitable young men who are nearer to her in age. She is just at the beginning and learning how to overcome her shyness. Even talking to young gentlemen will be a sore trial at first, let alone to someone of more mature years who might require a certain sophistication. Besides, you surely cannot deny her what you have allowed for yourself, can you?"

"I can think of no other gentleman more suitable; my parents would have been delighted if they had thought my sister would make such a match. It is all they dreamed of for their only daughter. You do not understand these matters, Elizabeth. Romance and sentimentality have no place here. Georgiana is a dutiful girl; she knows what is expected of her."

At this point Elizabeth lost her temper. "So, you are determined on this course for Georgiana. Oh, Fitzwilliam, I do not understand you. The poor girl has hardly set foot in Derbyshire and you have her married off to a man we know little about except for the fact that he is rich and enjoying the charms of another, less fitting candidate. Well, I cannot be a party to such folly and I will not discuss this matter further until you have come to your senses."

Elizabeth turned on her heel and, before her husband could stop her, she left. He stood, half amazed and half angry at the sight of his new bride running down the hill as fast as she could to get away from him.

Almost as soon as she got to the bottom of the hill Elizabeth began to doubt the wisdom of speaking out in such a manner, but she was convinced she had been right to do so.

"Impossible man!" she said to herself. "He claims to love his sister and have her best interests at heart and yet he would enslave her in marriage before she is ready, and to a man she does not love. To think that I thought he had changed for the better, that his disagreeable prejudices and notions of superiority were changed. Oh, Georgiana, how you will wish you had stayed in London."

Elizabeth hastened to her room. She felt so cross she could not trust herself to do anything else, but once there, she paced up and down, all the while trying to reason with herself. However hard she tried, she could not forgive Darcy for his belief that Georgiana must do her duty in marriage to a partner he would select. An hour passed during which every torment of feeling, every contrast of emotion from indignation to remorse unsettled her. But she was most sorry that she had stormed off, surely leaving him feeling quite the superior by his attitude. "I must learn to curb my tongue," she thought, "for I am sure that shouting at my husband will only antago-nise him. It is my temper I must control. I was too quick to show my exasperation and this will not endear me to him or change his views, I fear. In any case, I don't doubt he wishes to see Georgiana safely married. I know so little about her, truly, but from what I have gleaned from others, she has something of the Darcy spirit. I daresay I am being unfair, but a girl who was so easily persuaded to run away with George Wickham must have her own faults."

More important and uppermost in her mind was the problem she now faced of how to apologise to her husband for her rash behaviour. Though not wishing him to think that he had been right, she knew her impulsive actions had done nothing to further her argument. With this in mind, she hurried downstairs to search for him.

On poking her head around the saloon door she discovered Mr Darcy within standing by the blazing fire, which considerably cheered the aspect of this north facing room in winter. He turned as he heard her enter and they both began talking at once, declaring together their heartfelt sorrow at their misunderstanding. Within moments all was forgiven and forgotten, the lovers united by a tender embrace.

"I wish we did not have to go out to dine this evening," said Elizabeth.

"Oh, Mrs Darcy, I think you can read my mind," her husband answered with a smile. "How I wish we could stay here alone, away from the inquisitive eyes of our neighbours."

"I must admit I have had quite enough of being stared at to last me a lifetime," Elizabeth replied. "Well, I daresay I can endure it for another evening if I must."

"Perhaps I was not entirely honest when I described how our life at Pemberley might be, omitting to tell you how often you would be called upon to perform duties which are bound not only to be tedious but also irritating. Dining at the Eatons' tonight is, I fear, the last straw."

"I do not consider such evenings to be so very tiresome, and

I have enjoyed meeting the majority of your neighbours. I must confess, however, that I do have a particular dislike for Mrs Eaton who has on the two occasions of our meeting displayed an unsurpassed aptitude for conversation of a particular variety. She can relate an amusement in detail, tell a ludicrous story, and laugh at her friends with much vigour. At least it is not a requirement to join in. She is happy enough to supply her own replies."

Mr Darcy laughed. "I am fortunate that her long-suffering husband is a good deal more pleasant."

"Well, at least I shall be able to talk to him during dinner. It is after dinner, the ladies withdrawing from the dining table that I dread."

"They will no doubt quiz you and question you as to the kind of man you have married, Mrs Darcy. I hope you will not disappoint them or they will have nothing to gossip about."

"Gossip: the fuel of village life. It doesn't seem to matter where one lives, there is certainly no escape from hearsay and scandal. For my own part, I thwart it whenever I can, though it is impossible to avoid when talking with Mrs Eaton." Elizabeth paused to consider whether she ought to discuss the story related by this lady, yet she was curious to discover if Fitzwilliam had any notion of the gossip surrounding his mother's former employee. "I have been quite unable to put some of her tittle-tattle out of my head. She told me about a lady's maid who was formerly in the employ of the Darcy family. There is a rather unpleasant tale going about that her child's father is a gentleman of some distinction. It was in many respects a disconcerting story. Do you know anything of the matter or circumstances?"

Fitzwilliam Darcy turned once more to the fire. He picked up the poker and stabbed at the glowing logs before picking up a size-able chunk of wood to add to the flames roaring up the chimney.

"I know nothing of these tales," he answered in a voice that immediately discouraged further discussion on the subject. "You should not concern yourself or listen to these gossips. My mother's maid was of exemplary character—that is all you need to know."

Chapter 4

THE SECOND WEEK IN December heralded much excitement for Elizabeth. Her aunt and uncle Gardiner with all the young Gardiners arrived from London in preparation for Christmas. Lizzy had the pleasure of fulfilling her aunt's dearest wish on her arrival, by taking her round the park in a low phaeton with two ponies as had been that lady's suggestion several months before.

"I needn't ask if you are happy," said her Aunt Gardiner, turning for a moment from the view to take Lizzy's hand and squeeze it hard. "Your face is a picture, my dear niece, glowing with health and vitality, but also with something more—dare I say it, with pure unadulterated joy."

"Oh yes, Aunt, I never was so happy in my life. My husband is so generous, so kind, so loving. I can truly say I was never so loved in all my life."

"And are you enjoying your new role as mistress of Pemberley? I hope your neighbours have been kind."

"I am very busy and fortunate for the most part with our neighbours. It was very daunting at first, but I am feeling more confident than I admit I felt when I was first faced with the county families. So confident, in fact, dear Aunt Gardiner, that I have decided that we will have a grand Christmas ball."

"Oh, Lizzy, I am so proud of you. To think that I too will be a part of such a lavish entertainment; I've no doubt that such a diversion will be on a grand scale. I suppose you will be inviting everyone in the district."

"Yes, indeed, but I also have some other guests arriving, those to whom we are both related. Papa writes to me constantly and though his letters are full of news and as amusing as ever, I have detected a little unhappiness within the well-scripted pages. I happened to mention this to my husband and he insisted that my parents be reminded of their Christmas invitation with my sisters. Of course Lydia would not come without Wickham, but the invitations have been sent to Longbourn and Netherfield. Indeed, Mr Darcy first made the invitation to my father on our wedding day, leaving him to understand that he was most welcome to come to Pemberley to see me whenever he wished. Fitzwilliam had not told me and I think Papa thought he should wait for an official invitation."

"Oh, Lizzy, your mother will be so pleased."

"Yes, I am sure she will," said Lizzy softly, looking away. They both were silent for a moment, lost in their thoughts. "I know I am probably being very unkind, but Aunt, the prospect of my family coming here does fill me with some trepidation. My mother will not keep her tongue and has the habit of saying such unfortunate remarks before she considers what she is saying. I am worried that she may not behave with all due decorum and expose my husband and myself to the ridicule of our neighbours, some of whom are difficult to please at the best of times. There, now I expect you will consider that I am a most unfeeling and undutiful daughter."

"You must not worry; I do understand, you know, and I feel honoured that you are able to speak to me in such a confidential manner. But I am sure that your mother and father will do you proud. Concentrate on the things that matter. Organising such an event will be quite enough for you to think about, without worrying your head over anything else. If I can be of any assistance, it will be a great delight to help."

"Thank you, Aunt, I knew I should feel instantly better about everything with you here. But tell me, what would you like to do whilst you are in the area? There must be acquaintances you long to see from the old days or perhaps you would like to call on the friends you met in the summer. I can have a carriage put at your disposal at any time if you would like to go visiting in Lambton."

"Elizabeth Darcy, I should love that very much. You are a very kind girl, no matter what you say to the contrary. Perhaps you would like to come with me when I go visiting. I would like to see how my old friend Martha Butler is faring. We have corresponded for many years but I missed her in the summer as she was visiting her son in London. It would be so very good to see her again. What do you think, Lizzy? Should you like to come with me?"

"I would love to, if you do not think I would be in the way. There are bound to be many topics on which you will wish to converse and I should not wish to disturb you."

"Certainly not. Mrs Butler will consider your coming a great compliment and will, no doubt, have her status within the village highly elevated as a result."

"Then let us make a visit tomorrow."

"Splendid! Perhaps we could ask Georgiana to come along too. She seems to be blossoming under your care, Lizzy. I remember she was so shy and could hardly speak a sentence in company when first we met."

"Yes, though I doubt whether I have made any significant difference to her behaviour in the few weeks we have lived under the same roof. And Mrs Annesley is to leave us tomorrow for a little holiday, so I am sure Georgiana will miss her company. But are you quite sure Mrs Butler will want to be so overwhelmed by visitors?"

"When you meet her, Lizzy, I know you will see I was right. She is a very genteel but very affable lady, and I am sure you will become friends. I would trust Martha Butler with my life and all my most prized possessions. It would be a comfort for me to know that you will have an acquaintance you can call on who is someone to be relied upon at any time."

"Then let us call on her tomorrow and we shall all have an outing to which we may look forward with pleasure."

Georgiana was delighted to join the party that set out next morning after breakfast, driving along in the carriage away from Pemberley taking the road to Lambton. The three women travelled alone with the coachman and his boy, leaving Mr Darcy and Mr Gardiner to their shooting and all the little Gardiners to their lessons with their governess.

"Thank you so very much for inviting me, Mrs Gardiner," said Georgiana. "I'm rather embarrassed to admit that I am not really acquainted with anyone in the village, though I've always longed to have more friends in the area. But having been in

London for such a long time meant I did not have the opportunity to meet with many people round about, apart from the families that called when I was here in the summer."

"There is no reason why you should be acquainted with anyone in Lambton, Miss Darcy," replied Mrs Gardiner. "I know the circles you have moved in all your life are very different to those of my own and I am sure there was never the chance to enjoy a very wide society."

Georgiana looked thoughtful. "I do remember my brother telling me that my mother was very conscientious in her duties and often called in the village, especially on the needy and sick. It is a practice I would like to rejuvenate; I know my mother was very well regarded in Lambton. What do you think, Elizabeth? Would you like to revive the habit?"

"We shall go together if you should like it," agreed Elizabeth warmly. "I know Mr Darcy has always tried to help the poorer families where he can, and I think we could certainly find other worthwhile occupations and enterprises to which we may give a helping hand, especially if it can be done without giving offence. The people here are very proud, hard-working, and for the most part self-sufficient, but we can do much to improve their general happiness and condition, I am certain."

"If any two people can undertake such work with sensibility and discernment, I am sure you both can," said Mrs Gardiner. "There is always someone or something that needs attention in a place like this, where those who do fall on hard times often find it difficult to ask for largesse."

The carriage turned into the High Street and Elizabeth could not help noticing the excitement their arrival was causing amongst the inhabitants going about their business. Being Mrs

Darcy was going to take some getting used to, she decided, as she witnessed passers by nudging one another, curtseying or bowing and doffing caps, as they travelled the length of the thoroughfare to a good-sized stone house with gables set back from the road.

"Here we are. I am so looking forward to seeing my friend, though I have to tell you, it shall be a visit tinged with sadness," declared Mrs Gardiner. "Dear Mrs Butler's lovely husband passed away last year. He was a naval captain until his health took a turn for the worse and an upstanding member of the community, always willing to help those less fortunate than himself. He succumbed to consumption after a long illness and poor Martha is left quite alone. Her only surviving son has gone to seek his fortune in London and is doing well, I believe, and although he has tried to persuade his mother to join him there, she would never consider leaving Derbyshire or the home she shared with John."

"I can easily understand that," said Lizzy peering out at the house before them. "To leave a house full of memories shared with the one you love would not be easy, even if you were going to make a new home with those you adore. Her son must be a generous, affectionate young man to take such care of his mother."

"I have not seen him for some time, but I do remember that he was the very image of his father and with the same gentle ways. I know he would have tried very hard to persuade his mother to join him."

The coachman was at the door in a moment and the ladies stepped down to make their way along the flagged path leading up to the house with its central door set between mullioned windows. They were soon shown into a comfortable yet old-fashioned parlour furnished in country style. On one side of the gleaming mahogany fireplace was an oak dresser displaying a wealth of pewter, illuminated by the bright flames of the fire in the grate, and in the opposite corner, a grandfather clock with a painted face of flowers and cupids stood ticking the hours away. Placed before the hearth an ancient settee draped in chintz and a sturdy settle adorned with blue check cushions were arranged to make the best use of the heat of the coals.

Georgiana looked around her with wonder. Such a cosy room and stuffed with objects of varying interest, though not necessarily of great worth. It had the feeling of what she imagined it would be like to enter a ship, with its low beamed ceiling and dark panelled walls. Every surface displayed some treasure, from exotic shells, oyster pink and glossy with a finish of pearl, to spiky sea urchins and stiff, bony sea horses. A mahogany box brimming with bright fishing flies lay open on the shelf before the window, in between a Chinese bowl decorated with peonies in vivid blue and the skeletal remains of what appeared to be a large and rather sinister looking fish.

Martha Butler bade them sit down after the introductions and immediately addressed the Darcy women, telling them what an honour it was to receive them. "And to see you again, Mrs Gardiner, after all these years and under such splendid circumstances. I cannot think of anything that would have pleased you better than to see your niece as mistress of Pemberley. Lambton was always so dear to your heart and now you have an excellent excuse to visit us both very often, I hope."

"I am very lucky to have been invited to stay so soon and I hope to visit you often, my dear friend," Mrs Gardiner replied.

Mrs Butler glanced at Georgiana who despite herself could not help look with fascination at everything around the room. "It's a very queer room, is it not, Miss Darcy?"

"Oh, Mrs Butler, on the contrary, it is a lovely room, but you must think me so rude for staring."

"Not at all, my dear, and if there is anything that takes your fancy for a closer scrutiny, I hope you will have a look. See these old panels on the walls? My late husband rescued them from a ship he served in that was broken up for scrap. I never felt so far away from him when he was at sea, so long as I could see these lovely pieces of timber worked on and polished by his own hand to fit into my parlour."

"Mr Butler was a skilled carpenter as well as being an admirable sea captain," joined in Mrs Gardiner. "I remember he made you a sewing box on your marriage, a most beautiful object to my mind."

"I have it still, though it is locked in the cupboard this morning. I'll fetch it out in a minute, Miss Darcy, and you can see what my husband had to keep himself occupied during those long days on board ship when he was a mere midshipman."

At that moment the party heard the sound of the front door shutting and a man's voice booming with cheerful resonance to the maid in the hall.

"Oh, my goodness me, I quite forgot to tell you in all my excitement in seeing you again," Mrs Butler declared, her face lighting up with pleasure. "Master Thomas is home for a holiday. He has just finished on a scheme of work at Lord Featherstone's house in Richmond, but I expect he will tell you all about it himself."

Just as she spoke, the door of the parlour opened to admit a tall young man with an air of affable good nature and with such pleasing looks that Georgiana, who had started to become quite at ease, felt quite unequal to meet the eyes of those that alighted so eagerly upon her countenance.

Chapter 5

THOMAS BUTLER, THE APPLE of his mother's eye, was twenty-one years old and generally convinced those on first acquaintance to the impression of dashing good looks by his lively disposition, rather than by the evidence of a handsome countenance, though most would agree that he was a very good-looking young man. He was possessed of a fine figure and gentlemanly appearance which, combined with his happy manners, resulted in the appearance of wholesome affability. After the inevitable introductions and Mrs Gardiner's enquiries as to his health and well-being, he disappeared momentarily before returning with a dining room chair, which he placed in careful proximity next to Miss Darcy and sat down. Georgiana felt disquieted by this rather bold behaviour but was relieved when he neither spoke nor looked in her direction.

Mrs Gardiner spoke again. "Your mother has told me that you have been in London and Richmond of late, Mr Butler."

"That is correct, Mrs Gardiner. I have been trying to make my way in the world by seeking my fortunes abroad. I suspect my mother has not told you of all my ventures, but after having been a drawing master and artist, I decided to try my hand at landscape gardening, for which I have discovered there is a great demand by those who are blessed with lots of land. I am fortunate that amongst my father's friends were those who were eager to help me make suitable introductions, and Lord Featherstone decided to take me on. He seems delighted with the improvements I have made to his estate and I too am much pleased with the whole experience, which has been profitable in more than one direction."

"And what sort of improvements did you offer to Lord Featherstone for his estate, Mr Butler?" asked Elizabeth. "Are they all picturesque?"

"I would like to think, Mrs Darcy," Tom answered carefully, "that although I take into consideration many of the ideas that influence my clients as to their wishes, that the practicality and usefulness of a design are my first considerations. I am sure you are aware, ma'am, that not all design based on the 'picturesque' is either entirely functional or sensible. I do not think the landscape at Pemberley was created on such principles."

Elizabeth laughed. "No, indeed. I think the designer of Pemberley's grounds did an excellent job; the whole effect is natural without pretension. I believe the majority of the work done was executed many years ago. Did you ever look over the estate?"

"No, Mrs Darcy, I have not had that pleasure, though I would dearly love to see a landscape I have heard much talked about," answered Mr Butler.

Elizabeth turned to Mrs Butler. "You must come, you must both come and visit us. I do not know enough about the gardens myself, but I know Georgiana would be only too happy to show you around. Georgiana is something of an artist herself and has executed many sketches of Pemberley grounds."

Georgiana cast her eyes down to her lap and immediately answered, but in a timid voice scarcely audible to her audience, "Oh, but Lizzy, you praise me too highly, they are just the drawings of an amateur."

Tom turned to Georgiana. "I am sure if Mrs Darcy commends them to us all they must be good. Do you paint as well, Miss Darcy?"

"I love to draw and paint, though I think I find pastels most satisfying," Georgiana managed to answer, blushing as she regarded young Mr Butler, who leaned forward so as not to miss any of her quiet speech.

"I would be very interested to see your vision of Pemberley," Mr Butler added. "You are very fortunate to have had such wonderful inspiration for subject matter on your doorstep."

"I am indeed. I never was so happy to draw or paint if I was outside in the countryside I love so well. I have not had the opportunity lately as I have been in London for some considerable time, but now I am home I hope to start work on my portfolio once more."

"Ah, yes, London has its amusements but it is not so conducive to the creative spirit, I agree. And in London there are so many diversions and other distractions that one runs out of time for leisurely pursuits. I only associate London with work, Miss Darcy, I confess."

"Do you have much chance to pursue your own painting, Mr Butler, if you are busy designing gardens?" asked Elizabeth.

"I paint whenever I can, Mrs Darcy, and especially when I am at home here in Lambton, for it not only gives me immense pleasure, but it is essential that I keep my hand in it for my work. I use my paintings as a way of presenting my work to my employers."

"I see, how very interesting," Lizzy replied. "I'm sure we would all like very much to see how your designs are executed."

"I have one of my books here, but forgive me, I feel rather as if I have taken over the conversation. Mama, I am sorry to be commandeering your guests."

Martha Butler smiled indulgently at her son. "No, indeed, it is a pleasure to see you young people talking about the things you enjoy. And I have missed having a house full of people with such lively conversation. Tell me, Mrs Darcy, do you share this love of painting?"

"I enjoy looking at paintings very much," said Elizabeth, "but I have to tell you that I am only tolerably capable with a pencil and nothing I ever produced was good enough to put in a frame." She looked toward the young couple who were still engaged in conversation on their favourite pursuit. "Two artists with a love of drawing," said Elizabeth. "How I envy them. Now what I should like to see is how they each perceive the same scene. Wouldn't that be interesting?"

Elizabeth was so pleased to see Georgiana emerging from her usual shy state of being. Still quiet, but with more animation than she usually displayed, she looked to be entirely engrossed with Mr Butler's conversation.

"I'm sure we would all love to see your designs, Mr Butler," interrupted Mrs Gardiner.

Tom looked up and grinned amiably before begging his leave for a moment. He returned minutes later with a large book bound in green cloth which he placed on the dresser where they all gathered to inspect it.

"I like to present my clients with a view of their grounds as they are at this moment in time and with one as they might be once altered by my design," he began, turning the pages of the book to show how he achieved this through overlays on the original paintings.

"How very clever," enthused Elizabeth, "and your work is exquisite. I would love Mr Darcy to see what you have done. There are many fine works of art at Pemberley, some of which have been collected by my husband. I know he would appreciate your fine talent."

"Mrs Darcy, you do me a great honour by your praise," Tom said quietly, as if taken aback and unprepared for such an admiring speech.

"Well, it is not often that one meets with such passion or dedication and application, Mr Butler. I wish you every success in your endeavours."

The conversation turned back shortly after this exchange to reminiscences of old times between Mrs Gardiner and her friend. The workbox was fetched out for Miss Darcy's inspection, and they all admired the skill and handiwork of the lovelorn sailor who had carved such affection into an object his wife still treasured. After another half hour passed, it was time to go home. The party rose to say good-bye, everyone agreeing that they hoped it would be possible to meet again very soon.

Elizabeth repeated her wish of seeing Mrs Gardiner's friends at Pemberley. "I do hope you will make a visit soon, Mrs Butler, and do come too, Mr Butler, if you are free to do so."

As the Pemberley ladies gathered their belongings together, Tom observed that the weather outside had taken a turn for the worse. The skies were grey and it had started to rain.

"Do not worry," said Elizabeth, "I have my umbrella which we can share. We have only to walk to the end of the path."

"I'll fetch another," cried Tom, reappearing in a second with a large green silk umbrella. Mrs Darcy and her aunt followed the maid to the front door. "Please allow me, Miss Darcy, to escort you to the carriage," Tom insisted, stepping out and putting up the umbrella before Georgiana had a chance to pass through the doorway into the rain. It was coming down very fast now, dripping off the eaves and gurgling in the gutters.

"How kind he is, even if he strikes me as a little bold," thought Georgiana, as Tom held the umbrella over her head down the length of the path, insisting that she take especial care on the wet flagstones. The other ladies could be seen being settled in the carriage by the coachman and as Georgiana stepped up to take her place, Tom held out a small package, which he pressed into her hand.

"I thought you might like to make a study of this," he said, smiling down at her. There was no time to look at the contents of the rumpled paper which she hastily pushed into her pocket and besides, Miss Darcy's confusion made it impossible to look, let alone speak any words of gratitude. Once inside, she steeled herself to look out of the window to make the effort of returning his smile and managed to wave as the carriage moved off. The small package felt hard and knobbly, but though Georgiana was most curious to know what lay within the wrappers, she did not want to draw attention to it. She had a feeling that her sister Elizabeth might take the opportunity to tease her about Mr Butler and she did not think such raillery could be borne at present. Besides, Tom Butler, though kind and gentleman-like was rather too sure of himself for her liking. And that was part of the trouble. Georgiana did like him, but his charm and manners reminded her too well of someone else she had at one time preferred to any other and too much for her own good. Men were not to be trusted, she decided, as they trotted along away from Lambton village, and was thankful that it was unlikely that she should see much of him in the foreseeable future.

Chapter 6

ONCE HOME, ELIZABETH COULD not wait to tell Mr Darcy all about their new acquaintances and rushed along to the room where he spent a portion of his day working on estate matters with his steward. Lizzy was glad to find him alone and ran to his side, stealing a kiss before there was any chance of them being disturbed. She had soon told him all about their visit to the Butlers' house in Lambton and about how impressed she had been by young Thomas. "I'm sure you would like him, my love, and it would be something to help the family. I do not know how Mrs Butler fares financially and whether her husband left her well provided. I am sure she has a comfortable home, but that she is not wealthy is plain to see. The fact is that her son Thomas provides for her and he is only just starting off in his chosen profession. What do you think, would you be prepared to meet him? I'm sure we could think of something that needs doing on the estate."

"By all means, my dear. If they are friends of Mrs Gardiner's I am sure they must be decent people. A widow's lot is very hard and it would seem her husband was a commendable gentleman. Let it be your scheme, my love. You decide what should be done; I'm sure we could do with another prospect and a temple or two up on the higher reaches of our grounds. Perhaps we should give your proposal a name. What do you think? Mrs Darcy's Dell has a good ring to it, don't you think?"

"Fitzwilliam Darcy, I believe you are teasing me. Well, I shall take on the challenge and you shall see. Mr Butler and I will make something quite new for posterity that will combine elegant improvement with sense and economy."

Mr Darcy turned back to his desk and picked up a pile of papers waiting to be dealt with.

"I know what that shuffling of papers means," cried Elizabeth. "You have a lot to do and are trying to get rid of me. Very well, I shall go, but on one condition only," she said, standing next to him and giving him the benefit of a long look from her fine dark eyes.

"I have conditions of my own, you know," Mr Darcy said, taking her with a swift movement into his arms and holding her so tightly she thought she might stop breathing altogether. "If you will kiss me, Mrs Darcy, I promise never to shuffle another piece of paper as long as I live."

Elizabeth willingly submitted, allowing Mr Darcy to kiss her as many times as he wished. She did not consider herself to be artful, but she did wonder as she gazed up at him if now might be a good time to try and talk to him about his aunt and how he might write to her with an invitation to Pemberley. A further fifteen minutes of temperate persuasion, gentle reasoning, and considered rationale punctuated with the caresses of a loving wife did the trick.

"You must show your aunt that you are undaunted by her behaviour and forgive her folly, for you are the greater person for not allowing such a resentment to take hold. Please invite her to Pemberley, Fitzwilliam. I do not want to cause a permanent rift between you and your family. After all, Lady Catherine is your dear mother's sister. I am sure Mrs Darcy would have expected you to do what is right. Ignore her pettiness: Georgiana is quite correct. You'll see, Lady Catherine's bark is worse than her bite; she will not be able to resist coming to see us, if only to observe what she perceives as the downfall of Pemberley under my influence."

"It is one of my greatest faults, I know: implacable resentment. I cannot forget the follies and vices of others so soon as I ought, nor their offences against myself."

"I know you can and will, my darling. Please promise me that you will write to Lady Catherine this very afternoon and attempt a reconciliation."

"At one time I used to say that once lost, my good opinion was lost forever, but you have taught me not to be so rash, so decided in my pronouncements, my outbursts of temper. I promise, Elizabeth, I shall do what I can."

Mrs Darcy's arguments were so tactfully debated and so charmingly delivered that as she left him, Mr Darcy could be seen by anyone who chose to pass by the study door sitting in deep and docile contemplation with pen in hand engaged in the very task Elizabeth had anticipated.

By the afternoon, Elizabeth was full of ideas and suggestions, which she had great enjoyment talking over with her aunt and uncle, her cousins, and Georgiana. It was proposed that a walkabout be had on the upper slopes just before thick woodland made it too difficult to achieve very much and with a view to finding a suitable spot for Lizzy's plans. Georgiana was invited to accompany them all but declined, saying she had some drawing to do, an exercise she was inclined to start, which could be accomplished most comfortably at her desk in her sitting room by the warmth of a fire.

Elizabeth set out with the Gardiners and their children, who were soon running up the slopes and watching their breaths on the cold air turn into puffs of smoke. The scene was noisy and playful, Elizabeth happy to help pull along the little ones who held out their hands eagerly for her assistance.

"It is very kind of you to try and help Tom and Martha in this way, Lizzy. The Butlers are the most deserving people I know," said Edward Gardiner. "Her husband left her reasonably well off, but any assistance that can be made for young Thomas to help him make his way can only be of benefit to both of them."

"It is my pleasure, Uncle. I am determined to help anyone deserving if I can. Between you and me, I also think it will be good for Miss Darcy to have the company of a young friend with similar interests. Did you notice, Aunt, how well she and Mr Butler got on? I have never heard her speak so well to another soul."

"I did notice. Forgive me for saying so, but do you think it altogether wise to be encouraging this sort of friendship? Mr Butler is a very pleasant, if rather forward, young man, but to speak plainly, Elizabeth, he does not belong to Miss Darcy's class. He has no money and has yet to make his fortune, and besides, I am sure Mr Darcy must have plans for Georgiana's future that do not involve penniless gentlemen."

"Aunt Gardiner, I am very surprised at you. He may not have money, but she has; in fact, Georgiana has enough money to take on any prospective husband that she wishes. Besides, they have only just met and I am not suggesting that she marry him, merely that she spend some pleasurable time in his company."

"She seems to me to be a girl that might be easily persuaded," Aunt Gardiner commented, "and though I am reasonably certain of Mr Butler's character, I would not like to see such a vulnerable girl easily influenced. And I must say, Elizabeth, I did not like the familiar way he sat next to Miss Darcy on so slight an acquaintance. His manner was perhaps a little too forthright."

"Oh, Aunt Gardiner, he is just young and suffering from over enthusiasm, I am sure. I thought Tom Butler quite delightful. I cannot put my finger on it, but I kept thinking I knew him, almost as if we had been previously introduced, though I know that cannot be. His manner of talking, so utterly charming and artless, somehow…"

Elizabeth hesitated as the realisation of the person to whom she had been comparing him came to her mind. Mrs Gardiner arrived at the same conclusion at the precise moment. "Oh, no, Aunt, I do not believe it. His manners may be similar and he has that same goodness of expression, but I refuse to believe that in essentials he is the same."

"Of whom are you talking?" butted in Mr Gardiner, who had paused to catch his breath as they gained the top of the hill. "I have to confess I am quite baffled by this turn in the conversation."

"It's probably just as well, for Mr Butler is not advantaged by this comparison," Elizabeth replied. "Poor Tom has the unhappy fate to resemble someone we once thought was of good character, a man we were completely deceived in as to the worthiness of his nature, though I live in hope that he is improved sufficiently for my sister's sake."

"Oh dear, you mean Mr Wickham, I suppose," uttered Mr Gardiner rather breathlessly. "No, I cannot believe it. Tom's father was an excellent man and I'm sure his son is the same."

"I'm sure you are right, Uncle," said Lizzy, taking his arm, "it is just that I have become prejudiced against good-looking young men, which surely cannot be fair in Mr Butler's case."

"And we do know of one very handsome gentleman who is not only of excellent character but who also married a splendid girl, do we not?" Mr Gardiner went on.

"And despite what she says, she hasn't a prejudice she ought not to possess," agreed Mrs Gardiner, looking directly at Lizzy.

Elizabeth turned to regard her uncle and aunt who were smiling at her. She laughed and shook her head before gesturing toward a clump of trees in the distance. "Now, what do you think of that vista over there? Is it a handsome enough spot for Mrs Darcy's Dell?"

On their return from what Elizabeth decided was a very successful mission, she went in search of Georgiana to tell her about the place she'd found for Mr Butler to create a new design. Lizzy wanted Georgiana's opinion and approval, hoping to persuade her to take a look on the morrow. She found her as expected, still at the desk before the window surrounded by drawing paper and pastels.

"We'll take a walk up there on the morrow just the two of us, what do you say, Georgiana? We haven't had a chance for a tête-à-tête for so long and I do so want your approval of the idea. Let it be our secret; I do not want to tell Fitzwilliam about the place I've discovered just yet, if at all. Do you not think that it will be a wonderful surprise?"

"Oh, Lizzy, that is exciting and I am sure I will love the spot you have found. Tomorrow I shall wrap up and we will go walking."

Elizabeth sat down to observe the drawing that had occupied Georgiana all morning. Several discarded, crumpled sheets of paper were lying on the carpet. Her eyes alighted upon the object that Georgiana was studying. "What an unusual shell," she remarked. "May I look?"

She glanced at Georgiana who instantly blushed a deeper pink than the pretty shell itself. Elizabeth immediately guessed from whence it had come and smiled. "Did Mr Butler present you with the shell? That was very kind of him to notice how much you admired them. He must have thought that you might like to draw one."

Georgiana bit her lip and nodded, not once taking her eyes from her sketch or the paper on which she worked so fine a drawing that Elizabeth thought she had never seen such delicate workmanship.

"You'll have to show him when he comes. I am sure he will be interested to see your work," said Lizzy, patting Georgiana's back in a reassuring fashion.

Georgiana immediately looked up, her expression a mixture of astonishment and fright. "Is he to come here?"

"Why, yes, I thought that we had already mentioned that possibility when we were visiting the Butlers."

Elizabeth looked directly into the eyes of her sister. "Poor girl," she thought, "the prospect of seeing him again appears to give her some distress."

"Would you not like to see Mr Butler again?" she continued.

"I thought you two seemed to enjoy one another's company. Indeed, I have rarely seen you so at ease with someone you know so little."

"It is not that I did not like Mr Butler…"

"But? What is it, Georgiana? Are you afraid of seeing him again?"

"Oh, Lizzy, I do not know… that is, I do not feel at ease with any young man; there is the truth of it and, I confess, there was a boldness about Mr Butler which puts me on my guard."

"It is as well to be careful where gentlemen are concerned, but my advice would be to give him a chance. It will be good for you to have the company of a young fellow who is closer to you in age than your brother and myself. You have so much in common and I am sure you will have lots to converse about and share. I expect he will want to see the drawing you have made when he comes. Indeed, I rather suspect that his motive for giving the shell to you was a belief that he may in future have a reason to legitimately strike up a conversation with you on the subject."

Georgiana blushed deeper than ever as Lizzy kissed the top of her head before departing, saying, "Don't forget our walk tomorrow, Georgiana. I shall want to know what else Mr Butler had to say to you."

In the quiet of her room, Miss Darcy picked up the shell and turned it over in her hands. Despite her misgivings, she had to admit she was almost looking forward to seeing Mr Butler again.

On the day that Martha and Thomas Butler returned the visit to Pemberley, they were at last very pleased to meet the man they had often observed in Lambton but never met before.

Mrs Butler was almost overcome by the sense of occasion, but Tom, who instantly realised the opportunity that Mr Darcy was conferring on him, rose to the challenge of presenting his work with confidence and aplomb.

Mr Darcy was clearly impressed with Tom's green book, and after they had talked about the possibility of working on some designs for the estate, they were all able to relax a little. "You must come as often as you choose, Mr Butler. I am sure there will always be someone willing to show you round the grounds. I know Mrs Darcy has already fixed upon some places which she thinks might be of interest to you."

"I have taken the liberty of finding a site, but I must confess I have no idea as to its suitability for such a scheme," said Elizabeth. "I hope you will advise me, Mr Butler."

"I will do the best I can, Mrs Darcy," Tom promptly answered. "May I say how very grateful I am to you for giving me this chance to prove myself. If I may come tomorrow with all my equipment, I can start work immediately."

"That is splendid," said Mr Darcy, shaking hands heartily with Mr Butler. "We shall look forward to seeing you on the morrow."

The Butlers' visit was brief. Georgiana, who had been present during the short half hour they were there, could not help but feel a little disappointed. Mr Butler had barely glanced in her direction, nor made any communication with her apart from what could only be described as a hint of a smile on admittance to the saloon. But she guessed that might, in part, be due to the presence of her brother, who had an alarming effect on most people when they first met him. Mr Darcy's stature, his mien and bearing were such that she had seen other men almost diminish into nonexistence when meeting him face to face. On the other hand, she had not witnessed any such timidity on Tom's part. Far from it, he had been composed, very civil, and self-assured. More likely, he was not really interested in her at all, she thought. When she had seen him at the Butlers' he had been merely polite, and what she had mistaken for a curious attention in her favour had been simply courteous behaviour after all. Perhaps she should have entered into the conversation a little more, she wondered, but no sooner had the thought popped into her head than she knew she had not been equal to opening her mouth at all, let alone joining in any discussion. Georgiana had felt at her shyest, compounded by the fact that Mr Butler had seemed not even to notice she was in the room. Well, Lizzy was wrong after all, she decided. Mr Butler must have enough friends of his own without wishing to add her to the list.

Chapter 7

Georgiana knew that Tom Butler had arrived, for she had been watching for him after breakfast from the safety of her sitting room, which afforded a splendid view of the drive and the little bridge crossing the stream, over which all visitors must come. She was thinking about how she might start another drawing on a completely new subject and considering how unnecessary it was to go and introduce herself to Mr Butler again. After all, he was here to do some work for her brother and he would be completely taken up with that. Georgiana positioned two vases of varying heights with a Chinese bowl into a suitable arrangement and was just sharpening her pencil with the knife she used specially for the purpose when there came a rapid knock upon her door.

It was Lizzy looking most harried. "Oh, Georgiana, I am in a panic. Will you help me? I had completely forgotten that I promised Mrs Gardiner that I would take her to see the market and shops in Matlock whilst she is here. It is market day today and there will not be an opportunity to go again before the

Christmas festivities begin. She was so looking forward to going with the idea of looking for small gifts for the children."

"Oh, Lizzy, I know what you are about to say. Please do not ask me!"

"Please, Georgiana, you have only to take Mr Butler to the upper slopes where we walked and then you may leave him. I beg you; no one else will do. I feel it looks bad enough that I am not going to be here to do the honours, but at least with you, the other mistress of the house, I shall not feel quite as if I have neglected my duties so much. Please say you will help me."

Mrs Darcy's expression was such that it was quite beyond Georgiana's power to refuse her; indeed, she felt she could never refuse anything Elizabeth asked of her. Lizzy was so kind, always behaving like the sister she had never had. How could she decline such an appeal to be of assistance?

"Very well, Lizzy, I do it because I love you, my dearest sister, but I have to tell you that every inclination in my body is against it."

"Thank you, my dearest girl," said Lizzy, not stopping to assuage Georgiana's feelings further with any more platitudes. "Come, make haste, there is not a moment to lose. I've left the poor man in the library looking at a stack of your sketches. I told him I would be back in seconds."

"Oh, Lizzy, how could you show him my poor sketches?" cried Georgiana.

"Listen, not only are they remarkable drawings, but also you will have something to talk about, so you need not feel so shy," added Lizzy, taking her sister's hand and almost pulling her out of the room.

Mrs Darcy left Georgiana at the library door, running away

before the latter had a chance to change her mind. With her heart hammering, Georgiana observed Mr Butler through the open door. He was sitting at a table by the window and so engrossed with the drawings before him that he was unconscious of her presence. Dressed very smartly in a dark blue coat, and with his hair falling in fair tendrils against his collar, he made a pleasing picture. His long fingers seemed almost to caress the paper, so gently did he turn the pages. Georgiana watched his hands and noted not only his movements, but also his quiet strength. "He does have an expression of kindness," she thought, "but I am so afraid to go in. It is such a curious feeling, so alarming that I do not know what to feel; though if I must describe it to myself, it is somewhere between fright and excitement. If only I could run back to my room at this moment, I would!"

At last she found the courage to step forward, remembering that she did not want to let Elizabeth down. "Good morning, Mr Butler," she said, trying to meet his eyes which stared into her own with a clarity she found unsettling. "I am so sorry that Mrs Darcy has a previous engagement, but I hope you will allow me to show you around."

Mr Butler rose from his seat, at once reminding Georgiana of his stature. Her own height often made her feel too significant. She quite liked the fact that he made her feel almost dainty by comparison. "That is very considerate of you, Miss Darcy," he said, as he bowed in her direction. "I am most sorry to put you out, for I am sure I must be disturbing you. I could come back tomorrow if you have other plans."

For a second, Georgiana was tempted to say that sounded an excellent idea, but realised in time how rude that would appear and was able to reply with an assurance she did not feel that it was her pleasure to escort him.

"I have been looking over your work, Miss Darcy," he announced before she had time to think of what she should say next. "I have rarely seen such draughtsmanship. You have a great talent."

"You flatter me too well, sir," Georgiana replied with difficulty. She was most overcome that he had praised her work so highly, but immediately thought that he must be teasing her. There was certainly something in his expression, a hint of mischief about the twinkle in his eye. Perhaps he was laughing at her?

"No, Miss Darcy, I see what you are thinking. I am most sincere. You draw exceedingly well. I was a drawing master for some time and I assure you, I have never seen such aptitude for the subject amongst any of my former pupils."

"I expect that was because your pupils had no natural inclination for the subject. I do not mean to say that you would not have been an excellent teacher or that you could not have inspired them with enthusiasm," she added, watching his expression change, "but I have often observed that when masters of any subject have been engaged by well meaning parents, unless the pupil has an earnest desire to learn or a real interest in the subject, it is not only a wasteful but also expensive exercise."

Tom laughed. "Miss Darcy, you are quite correct, but I assure you, in this case, I see great aptitude and application. Your style reminds me very much of the French artist, Madame Vigée Le Brun. About ten years ago I was lucky enough to see her paintings in Rome whilst on a tour with my uncle."

"Oh, how wonderful, and how lucky you were to see her

work, which I have long admired, though I admit only to having seen her paintings in a pamphlet."

"Without a doubt, Rome was wonderful, but I understand you have spent a great deal of time in London, where you must have attended many fine exhibitions."

"Oh, yes, Mr Butler, I have been to Somerset House and studied the masterpieces of the day. There is nothing like seeing great painting for one's own inspiration."

"Yes, that is very true, and talking of inspiration, I'd best be getting on with my work," Tom said, promptly shutting up the folder of work, as if suddenly conscious that he was talking too much. "Mrs Darcy told me you knew of the area in the grounds that she would like me to redesign."

"Yes, of course," answered Georgiana, relieved that employment and action would now take the place of conversation. "We will go directly I have found my cloak and bonnet."

As soon as they were ready, the couple made their way out to the rear of Pemberley House taking a shortcut through the formal gardens and making their way towards the upper slopes of the wild garden. They strolled across the open landscape, following an ancient stone wall which ran along the slope like a pointing finger, silvered with lichen and frost-covered mosses. The larch wood at the top of the hill was their destination, and as the incline increased so did the effort to keep moving. The higher they climbed, the shorter was their breath, which came out in bursts, and Georgiana felt her heart race with the effort of keeping up with Mr Butler. It was wonderful to be outside in the crisp air, and although she had imagined that it might be easier to converse outdoors in such a beautiful setting, nevertheless Georgiana and Tom did not exchange one word.

Tom had become most business-like in his manner and carried his bag containing his books and pencils with some importance. Georgiana glanced sideways at him once or twice, but his expression was so solemn and he looked so thoughtful that she thought better of disturbing his reverie. She kept her eyes to the ground, challenging herself to differentiate between the footprints of rabbits and foxes, pheasants and partridges imprinted on the frosted grass.

At last, the ancient stone dwelling place where they were headed on the edge of the wood came into view. But having observed the old ruin, it suddenly disappeared from view as the high hedge looming before them obstructed their vision and their way. Further along, a gap produced a stile. Mr Butler jumped over in a moment and without further ado, held out his hand on the other side to Miss Darcy. She hesitated, and it was only when he smiled encouragingly that she allowed him to take her hand.

"Be careful, Miss Darcy, there is a muddy puddle on this side. Please, will you allow me the liberty of helping you over it?" She grasped his hand tightly and climbed over the stile, slipping a little on the greasy, wet plank. As he witnessed her unsteadiness, instead of waiting for her answer, he immediately took her up in his arms and carried her over the puddle. Georgiana was so shocked that she could not speak besides muttering her thanks, which sounded to her own ears like a strangled squeak. She could not think about anything except how he had picked her up as if she were no weight at all. In his strong arms she had felt quite small and, for all the shock it had given her, felt relieved now it was all over. Tom strode on ahead as if nothing of any consequence had occurred. Georgiana hurried behind him, running to catch up, feeling her face burning with what she hoped would look like exertion but which, she knew, was as a result of her consciousness of what had just happened.

Mr Butler stood in front of the old stone hut. One of its walls was missing, it had only a couple of struts left for a roof, and most of its old stones were lying tumbled before the open doorway whose solid door had disappeared long since. Sheltered by a beech tree and smothered at its foot in brown bracken and ferns, it looked a sorry sight.

Georgiana found her tongue at last. "This is the spot Mrs Darcy thought might be improved. I hope it is to your liking."

Tom nodded and turned toward her at last, saying, "Mrs Darcy has a good eye. I think there are great possibilities here. Well, Miss Darcy, I am sorry that you had to be so troubled this morning when I am sure you have plenty to occupy you. Thank you very much for bringing me up here, I will get on immediately whilst the light is good."

Georgiana stood for a moment, not quite knowing how to answer. Eventually she uttered, "It was my pleasure, Mr Butler." There did not seem anything else to say. Mr Butler had fetched out his things and taken up his stance, his back to her in a most dismissive gesture. Georgiana immediately felt in the way and her companion seemed entirely involved in his work. He was sketching, making rapid movements with his pencil in a small notebook. It was clear, she thought, that he had forgotten that she was even there. Without saying good-bye, she turned quickly on her heel and made her way back down the hill, taking care to avoid a hedge and stile the sight of which would give rise to much mortification.

Mrs Darcy and Mrs Gardiner had spent a profitable day in Matlock. Laden with packages and parcels, most bought with Christmas in mind, they set off for home before darkness fell. The weather was closing in again and the temperature was dropping. Elizabeth carefully tucked a rug, kept for the purpose of swaddling cold and weary travellers, around their knees as they travelled through the villages of the Peak towards Pemberley.

"There is a feel of snow in the air," said Mrs Gardiner. "I am pleased we have managed to accomplish so much today. I know when winter sets in here it is very difficult to get about."

"Yes, I have heard from Fitzwilliam that the winters are very hard, but I daresay if it snows it will be nothing but a delight to the children."

Mrs Gardiner smiled. "You are quite right, Lizzy. But I hope there will not be too much snow to prevent your family from arriving or stop your plans for a ball."

"No, that would be most inconvenient. Well, if we should have snow soon perhaps it will have melted by the time I give my ball. I have sent out many invitations and I have not yet received one refusal. I still have a lot to do, but I know with your help and that of Mrs Reynolds, we will soon be able to forget about what has to be done and enjoy the coming festivities."

The ladies became quiet, lost in their own thoughts as they travelled. They were entering Birchlow, a village still seven miles from Pemberley and typical of the area with its stone cottages. There were not many of its inhabitants about and those that walked along the side of the road walked quickly, with collars turned up against the icy wind, hats and bonnets firmly in place, and cloaks held tightly about them. Elizabeth rested her head against the cushioned interior and stared out of the window. It did feel quite cosy and she was feeling very tired after the exertions of the day. Just as her eyes were closing, lulled into sleep by the gentle rhythm of the rumbling coach as it rolled over cobblestones, her attention was caught by the sight of someone in the dim light, a gentleman who looked most familiar. Suddenly awake, she craned her head round as the carriage rolled past. "How strange," she said to herself, but as she observed the gentleman's appearance she chided herself for being silly and dismissed the notion. Her husband did not dress like a country farmer. Besides, she reasoned, it could not possibly have been him because she recalled that he had gone to Buxton for the day on a business matter and would be travelling home in completely the opposite direction.

"Is anything the matter, Elizabeth?" enquired her aunt.

"No, nothing," replied Lizzy, "I think I was dreaming, that's all."

Chapter 8

THOMAS BUTLER WAS TO continue working on his plans at Pemberley over the next day, spending most of his time outdoors in spite of the cold weather. Georgiana watched him striding across the gardens and up to the higher slopes from a window in the saloon as far as she was able, for he quickly became a small dot in the distance. She had begun to wish she could join him up there, but reminded herself that he had not seemed to want any company the day before. He had discouraged her, she felt, and yet she was puzzled. His behaviour toward her in the library had seemed friendly enough and he had shown kindness and gallantry when faced with a muddy puddle. The recollection caused her to blush. Strong arms, warm breath on her cheek like a caress, and a smell, a heady mixture of lemon-scented cologne perfumed with the sharpness of frosted earth, filled her mind and awakened her memory. He had walked further than he need with her in his arms if she recalled, though the moment had swiftly passed and there had been not even a comment nor a look exchanged between them. Was there something in her manner that he had disliked? Had she not thanked him enough, or perhaps she had given him the impression that she was ungrateful for his intervention?

Georgiana did not know what to do with herself and could not seem to settle to anything. Drawn by any activity through the window, she had the satisfaction of seeing Mr Butler eventually reappear three hours later, head down and briskly walking. Rushing to the door, she paused, waiting to see if she could hear any sign of him come in or catch his voice talking to one of the servants. But no such sound came. "Perhaps he will not come in after all, but will go straight back to Lambton," she thought with more than a little regret. Georgiana ran downstairs as soon as she dared and, trying her utmost to appear casual when enquiring after Mr Butler, she could not help feeling disappointed when she heard Mrs Reynolds say that he would return the following day.

By the very next morning, Georgiana had convinced herself that she had offended Tom Butler in some way and was sure that he must think her proud and haughty by her manner. She blushed with shame as she recalled that she had not managed any conversation as she accompanied him on that first day, nor thanked him properly for his gallant help over the stile, and she was determined to do something about it. As soon as she caught sight of him heading off in the direction of the stone dwelling place, she set off with her sketchbook and pencil in hand. She had to run to catch him up and got within a few yards when her courage started to fail. What would he think if he turned round and saw her chasing him? The sight of his tall, imposing figure dressed for warmth in a greatcoat, the capes of which flapped on either side of him, made Georgiana think he resembled some heavenly creature, a dark angel with outspread wings. Her courage started to fail. The day was cold and the sky looked very grey with low clouds massing on the horizon. To finish it all, it looked as if it might rain at any second. What was she doing here out in the cold? she scolded herself. Georgiana had just decided to stop and turn tail when she had the misfortune to step onto an icy puddle, which cracked with a loud retort. Mr Butler immediately turned round and saw her looking not elegant and graceful, as she hoped she might always appear to him, but dishevelled and unkempt, with an expression of horror on her countenance, as she ended up tumbling backwards onto the ground with one of her ankles twisted and sunk at least six inches into a hole in the ground. Her cloak was muddied, she had a soggy boot that would not move, and her gloves were ruined.

"Miss Darcy," shouted Mr Butler coming down the hill as fast as he was able, "are you hurt? Please allow me to be of assistance. Stay where you are, do not attempt to move. Oh dear, I see you are quite stuck fast. I hope your injuries are not serious."

With sudden realisation, Georgiana appreciated the comedy of her situation and laughed. "Oh, no, Mr Butler, only my pride and my crushed bonnet are hurt. Oh dear, I was doing so very well and now I'm stuck. I cannot move my leg."

Tom caught up with her holding out his hand to assist her to her feet. She took one look at her dirt-encrusted glove and shook her head. "You'll soil your glove, Mr Butler."

"Take yours off," he directed. "You may have mine, though your slender fingers will be lost in my giant-sized ones." Georgiana watched him swiftly remove his gloves and proffer them. Such was his command and so impossible her situation that Georgiana felt quite unequal to argue with him and struggled with her wet gloves, peeling them from her fingers and discarding them on the ground. She looked up to take Mr Butler's gloves but before she could grasp them Tom's hand enclosed one of hers. He pulled her up towards him, steadying her with his other arm until she was upright.

"Let's have you on your feet, Miss Darcy." His large hand felt very warm against her cold fingers, and there was something so protective about the way that he held her that she forgot at first that her foot was still jammed in the hole. "Hang on to me, Miss Darcy," he instructed, "and pull your boot out."

Georgiana pulled, but instead of her boot coming out, only her foot appeared. On one leg, regardless of Tom's assistance, she started to wobble and hop around until he was forced into action. Up into his arms she went, very much as she had done on that other day, but this time she tried her hardest to smile and make her thanks audible, though she was unable to speak a word.

The sky was looking thunderous, it had turned slate grey and a few feathers of snow were settling on the brim of Mr Butler's hat as she regarded him. His arms held her tightly, their strength all too apparent through the thick cloth of his greatcoat. He felt so close she could feel his breath warm against her cheek stirring the curls which poked from under her bonnet.

"We'll make for the stone hut," he said. "I'll leave you comfortable, then return for your boot. It's only stuck in the mud."

He carried her up the hill, entering the ancient dwelling place when he got to the top and placing her on a large, smooth rock jutting from the ground, which did very well for a seat. "I'll be back presently, Miss Darcy, do not fear."

As Georgiana watched him run down the hill, her hands encased in the huge gloves that he had insisted on her wearing and with a stockinged foot, feeling very wet and dirty, she saw with alarm that the snow which had started so lightly was beginning to fall thick and fast. Tom returned with her damp boot in one hand, her sketchbook and pencils in the other, and with an apologetic expression on his face.

"Miss Darcy, I am afraid it is in a sorry state, it is not going to be of much use to you."

"Thank you, Mr Butler, I am indebted to you for your kindness. The boot is of no consequence; so long as I can hobble back down the hill with it on, it shall have served its purpose." She eased her foot back into it, tying what was left of the broken lace.

Tom looked up at the skies. "I think it is only a flurry; it might be as well to remain here for a little while until it is over. That is, if you are not too soggy and uncomfortable. I shall light a fire between these stones; it won't take long."

Georgiana watched him as he quickly gathered kindling and enough wood to start a small fire, which he soon accomplished with the aid of a tinderbox from his bag; the flames provided a cheerful glow and warmth. "Surprisingly, I feel quite snug," Georgiana replied, holding her hands toward the heat, "and I am sure you are right. There is some blue sky yonder, so it will be all over in a quarter of an hour. At least we are sheltered here, if not entirely by the roof then by the large arms of the beech tree."

"In that case," said Tom, "I declare it is time for a picnic." Reaching for his bag once more, from within its depths he produced a cloth-covered bundle fragrant with the smell of freshly baked bread. A hunk of cheese, a knife, and a bottle of sweet cider completed the repast. The snowy cloth was undone and the bread sliced. All at once, Tom's face fell. "Miss Darcy, do excuse me, I got quite carried away for a moment. What must you be thinking of my peasant's meal?"

"Oh, no, Mr Butler," Georgiana was able to say sincerely, "it truly looks delicious and I am honoured that you wish to share it. You are so generous and I am sure I do not deserve all this attention."

Tom became the jovial young man she remembered on their first acquaintance, assuring her that he could think of nothing nicer than to share his nuncheon, even if he was sitting with the most accident-prone young lady of his acquaintance.

"I think you mean clumsy," Georgiana remarked shyly. "I am always getting into scrapes."

"Well, I hope if you get into any more that I shall be here to help you get out of them," Tom answered with a laugh.

Georgiana forgot her shyness for a moment and laughed too, only stopping when she realised that Tom was staring at her. She did not know where to look and studied the chunk of cheese she was holding as if it were the most interesting object in the world.

"It's not true what some say in the village," he said, "that the Darcys are proud and reserved."

Georgiana looked up and, as much as it pained her to speak out, she retaliated in her brother's favour. "People only say my brother is full of pride because they do not know him. I am certain if you asked those villagers with whom he is acquainted, then you would hear a fairer report. As for myself, if I have ever given cause for offence by my manner, I am sorry for it. It was not done with intent."

"Forgive me, Miss Darcy, I have been rude and outspoken. I meant only that on closer acquaintance I now realise that what could be perceived as an appearance of cool reserve masks other traits in your personality."

"And now you are to accuse me of being haughty and disdainful, I suppose, Mr Butler, and I do not think I can refute it. On your first day at Pemberley I was not very welcoming, I think."

"No, Miss Darcy, you are quite wrong. I see before me a very cordial and friendly young woman in her close circle, but one who is rather diffident and shy amongst strangers, perhaps even uncomfortable in the company of men other than those with whom she is intimate."

Mr Butler's words startled her; it was as if he knew her mind, her most personal thoughts, and she did not like it. How dare he presume to know so much about her, she thought, as she considered his impudent remarks. Georgiana blushed and after brushing the crumbs from her pelisse, she stood up and in a defiant gesture proffered the borrowed gloves toward her companion. "I thank you for the food and for your assistance, Mr Butler, but I think I will be missed from home and must be going now. Good-bye."

"Miss Darcy, please wait. I beg your forgiveness," he implored, jumping to his feet. "I have overstepped the mark, I know. Please accept my apology. I did not mean to be impertinent. Please let me escort you back down the hill."

Her first instinct had been to put up her defences, the armour-like shield of stiff impenetrable pride she always wore when anyone threatened to become too close. She wanted to deny him the privilege of walking with her, yet knew she did not want to quarrel with him. Georgiana hesitated, not knowing quite what to do, but deciding to wait for him to gather his things said rather stiffly, "Yes, I will accept your apology."

Despite the falling snow they started to walk. Georgiana wanted to speak but could not find the nerve. "I must learn to be bolder," she said to herself before biting her lip and deciding in a rush that she would speak her mind.

"You are impertinent, Mr Butler, but that does not mean that you did not speak the truth. I do feel at ease with people I know very well, but I do not consider that there is anything unusual in that. Are you always unconstrained in the company of those who are strangers to you?"

"I am fortunate, Miss Darcy, that there are few situations where I do not feel equal to my company. Shyness is something I have never been troubled with, and I must admit I am surprised that a Darcy, a person richly born, significant amongst their society, and with every advantage of esteem by others, can suffer in such a way."

Georgiana remained silent. There was too much to say that she could not possibly relate. Let him think what he wanted. Besides, she thought him quite arrogant. How dare he speak to her in that way.

"I did not mean to sound unsympathetic. Miss Darcy, you must think me cold and unfeeling, as well as rude. Perhaps a little shyness might be a better trait for me to cultivate than those attributes of arrogance you have witnessed in me today."

All at once Georgiana found the courage she did not think she possessed. "You talk of my shyness and reserve and of your own confidence, but I saw none of that self-possession when you first walked up here with me the other day. You were as reserved as I have ever been."

"The truth is, Miss Darcy, that I did wish to converse with you, but I started to wonder if I should. I am an employee of your brother and I admit, although I wanted to talk to you, I believed that your accompanying me was done out of duty and that you little wanted to be there, let alone have me constantly rattle at you. Some people would say that I should not talk to you at all."

"What on earth do you mean?"

"I am certain that Mrs Gardiner would not approve. She would think I am getting above my station to freely converse with a Darcy, and in such intimate circumstances."

Georgiana felt herself blush red again at his outspokenness. She put her head down, hoping he would not notice, but did not know how to answer him.

"I would like very much to see the shell drawing you made," he said.

"Could anyone be more brazen?" Georgiana wondered. And the fact that he was so certain that she had actually produced such a drawing and voiced the fact certainly sounded bordering on arrogance. But, entitled as she felt to be cross with him, she could not help liking him. He was direct and said what he thought, which made such a change to the young men she knew. Hugh Calladine, for instance, was an exceedingly tricky gentleman who had blindly flattered her with words on the last two occasions of his calling, but had not an ounce of the sincerity that Tom Butler possessed. Besides, she knew that Mr Calladine was in love with someone else.

They entered the house at last, brushing off the snowflakes from their clothes and Georgiana explaining all to Mrs Reynolds about the accident with her boot. All, that is, except those parts she felt the old housekeeper did not need to know. Mr Butler

CHRISTMAS EVE AND THE arrival of the Bennets and Bingleys to Pemberley marked the official start to the festive season. Elizabeth was pleased and surprised at her own feelings on firstly welcoming her parents and two of her sisters, Mary and Kitty, to her new home. For all her newfound happiness and exultation in the success of her marriage, she had not realised until coming face to face with them again how much she had missed them. It was especially heartening to see her papa again and, as he hugged her until she thought she might have no breath left, her feelings took her by surprise. The resulting misting of her eyes she quickly brushed away before his notice provoked a comment.

"I am very glad to see you, Elizabeth, and for this invitation from you and your husband, we are very grateful," he said, standing back at arm's length to admire the daughter he loved best. "I have missed you and it does my heart good to see you looking so well."

Mrs Bennet was, for once, struck quite dumb on their entrance into the hall and did not utter a syllable for the first ten minutes. Her eyes darted everywhere, alighting on the marble floors, staring at the grand curving staircases, the statues in the niches, and the paintings adorning the walls and the ceiling. She looked almost frightened and had such an appearance of stupefied shock upon her countenance that Lizzy felt quite concerned.

"Are you quite well, Mama?" asked Elizabeth, taking her mother's hand and rubbing it between her own. "Indeed, you do look very tired. But the journey is such a long one, I know. Come inside and get warm by the fire."

Mrs Bennet shook her head and spoke at last. "I am astonished, Lizzy. I knew Pemberley must be a great house, but I never expected this; not in all my born days did I expect to see such opulence, such finery! The floor alone must be worth a king's ransom, not to mention the gilded balustrades, the paintings and statues, the drapes, the chairs and settees, and I know not what. And this is only the hall! Lord bless me! I shall have to sit down. And as for the grounds, I thought Christmas would be over before we arrived, so long did it take to get from the road to the house. What a prospect! The finest house, the grandest park, the most magnificent hall that I ever did see. What a pity that Lydia cannot be with us to see it. I know she would have loved to see Pemberley, and dear Wickham too. I'm sure he would have enjoyed seeing his former home."

"But, Mama, though I admire your feelings of benevolence in consideration of Mr and Mrs Wickham's lack of invitation," observed Mary, who loved to reflect and sermonize on the folly of others, "in my opinion, such deliberation is ill conceived. If you dwell for just one moment on the real likelihood of such a summons to our misguided sister and her husband from Mr

Darcy, who we know to be a rational man, you must also know it to be highly improbable."

"Oh, Mary, hold your tongue. Mrs Wickham can come to Pemberley whenever she likes, whatever you might think on the matter," rejoined Mrs Bennet loudly, with an expression of exasperation.

Mrs Gardiner advanced quickly to reach Mrs Bennet's side, to greet her and divert the course of conversation, just as Mr Darcy entered the hall to welcome his guests. He had thought it prudent to allow Elizabeth a little time with her parents and sisters before he came on the scene. His manners were as impeccable as ever and Mrs Bennet became quite girlish in her manner at his attentions, patting her curls and looking at him under her lashes. When Lizzy was able, she could not resist catching her husband's eye, raising her own heavenwards. She felt such a mixture of pride and love for all that he represented to her, the man who in disposition and talents suited her to perfection.

No sooner was the Bennet family installed—dispatched to become acquainted with their rooms over which Mrs Bennet was soon exclaiming, not only at the size, but also at the number assigned to them—than Elizabeth's sister, Jane Bingley, her husband, and his sister arrived. Never was a reunion more joyful between two sisters who adored one another and who had never before in their lives been separated for so long. Jane still had the glow of a new bride about her and Lizzy was overjoyed to see Bingley again. Elizabeth was not so pleased to see Mr Bingley's sister Caroline, who had in the past been the cause of a temporary rift between Jane and her husband during their courting days, not only separating them but informing Jane of her wish that her brother be married to Miss Darcy. But she received her with much civility, which in the circumstances was highly gratifying, as she recalled with a certain glee that Caroline had at one time fancied that she might take on the role of the mistress of Pemberley herself. How very satisfying it was to be addressed by Caroline Bingley as Mrs Darcy.

"My dear Mrs Darcy, how splendid it is to see you again. It is exceedingly kind of you to invite me to Pemberley for Christmas, which, as I am sure you have heard, is always unsurpassed in both hospitality and by its splendour." She turned to Mr Darcy, who was regarding her with what Elizabeth had come to recognise as the expression he reserved for those he could not tolerate—a look of polite indifference, but happily undetected by the person on whom it was bestowed. "Oh, Mr Darcy, we have enjoyed one or two merry Christmases together, have we not? Such parties and balls that I have been quite spoiled forever. I do not think I shall ever enjoy such entertainments again. But, forgive me, Mrs Darcy, you are hosting a grand ball on the morrow, are you not? What felicities we shall enjoy, I cannot wonder. Do you remember, Mr Darcy, when Reynolds fetched out the old fancy costumes from the attic and we dressed up? I thought I should die laughing when I saw you as Robin Hood and I was Little Bo Peep, as I hark back. What fun we had. Do you recall, Georgiana? You were the sweetest lamb, all in white with a pink ribbon on your tail."

Miss Bingley, having found a willing listener in Georgiana, immediately led her away talking at the top of her voice about the wondrous parties of the past.

Elizabeth was starting to feel quite sick with nerves at the prospect of the coming ball. She did so want it to be a success and, whispering into Mr Darcy's ear when the others were busily engaged in directing the servants with their luggage, said, "Oh dear, do you suppose we should have had a fancy costume ball?"

To which came the rapid answer, "Absolutely not. The whole idea was of Miss Bingley's engineering and I loathed every minute of it. I absolutely forbid fancy costume balls to be held at Pemberley ever again!"

Mr Darcy and Mr Bingley soon repaired to the library and Elizabeth and Jane were at last left to themselves. Lizzy took her sister's arm with much affection and led her upstairs to her small private sitting room, which on her marriage had been one of the many surprises her husband had presented. She had always preferred the style of the past to what was currently in fashion, and everything within the cosy room had been chosen with that in mind. A richly coloured tapestry, glowing with hues of yellow and rose, green and sand, hung on one of the oak-lined walls. Crewel-worked drapes framed the Venetian window, whose glass panes reflected cheerful flames from the fire in the chimneypiece, to glimmer on blue delftware bowls of dried lavender scenting the air with a fragrant potpourri. Much of the furniture consisted of pieces that had been in the Darcy family from Tudor times. A gilt-wood settee upholstered in ivory Genoa velvet and embossed with green pineapples was placed on one side of the fire opposite a Queen Anne love seat beautifully worked in needlepoint. Elizabeth's writing desk sat before the window next to her books from Longbourn, housed in a handsome bookcase in the corner, the one exception to antiquity. With the addition of a scattering of useful tables and several exquisitely painted Dutch floral pictures in gilt frames, the whole scene suggested comfortable and easy elegance, a refuge from the demands of a busy life as mistress of Pemberley.

"Oh, Elizabeth, what a perfect room," declared Jane as soon as they entered. "I've tried to imagine you sitting at your desk so many times, but I really did not do justice to this heavenly place in my mind. And now, when I am home once more, I can picture you sitting there before the window filling a page with your news."

"Oh, do not talk of going home yet, Jane, when you have been here but five minutes; I cannot bear it. Come, sit down, I wish to hear everything you could not put in a letter."

Jane laughed. "I do not know where to begin."

"Oh, my dear sister, that does sound promising."

"On which particular subject are you most curious, Lizzy?"

"There are so many. First, are you happy, Jane? No, do not answer such a stupid question. Happiness is radiating like sunshine on a summer's day from every part of you. But tell me, is Charles everything you hoped he'd be?"

"I could not ask for a kinder husband."

"And are you in love with him still?"

"I love him more than ever."

"And as a lover, is he all that you ever dreamed?"

"Lizzy, you are truly shocking! Whatever would Mr Darcy say if he knew quite how brazen the woman he married can be?"

"'Tis too late, I fear, Jane, he knows already. And I will confess to you, dearest sister, that I am quite delighted with my husband in every respect. And please forgive me, but my knowing such joy has only made me wish to discover if you too have found such happiness with Charles."

Jane nodded and blushed, turning her head towards her sister with a smile. "Sometimes I feel so consumed by his affection that it almost frightens me. I do not know what I ever did to deserve such happiness, but I am so relieved to know you feel it too. But enough of such talk, you are making me blush. One thing I must ask you. In your last letter you said you had persuaded Fitzwilliam to write to Lady Catherine. Has there been any response?"

"Oh, yes! Lady Catherine has replied in her inimitable way; she is still refusing to visit, but I am sure she will come in time. Curiosity will get the better of her resentment, you'll see."

"Oh, Lizzy, you are of a stronger constitution than I am; I do not think I could handle a woman like that."

"But you do and on a daily basis. Tell me, how does Caroline Bingley behave? Your letters paint such a generous description of that lady that unless she has undergone a complete character transformation, I am not entirely sure I can have any faith in what you have written."

"Caroline is much improved, Elizabeth. But it does not mean to say that I have completely reformed our friendship in the old way. I do not bear grudges easily, but I believe it will take me a long time to allow her into my confidence again. However, she is very civil, and I will say is improving daily. I think she was quite surprised to find how reserved with her I became after Charles and I were married. And my dear husband has made it very clear from the start, without any unpleasantness, that I am the sole mistress of Netherfield Park. I daresay that is why we have been so fortunate to enjoy her absence from home this last week. She has been visiting her sister in London. No doubt, Louisa and Caroline had plenty to discuss on the subject of my marriage and my housekeeping."

"If they have, and I think we may assume not a doubt of it, I hope the venom produced from their malicious tongues poisons them once and for all. Well, Jane, we do not have to be resentful, for we have the whip hand over those two embittered sisters."

"We do, indeed, Lizzy! Now, we shall not waste any more time on them. I've been thinking about dear Georgiana, how does she settle? It must be strange for her to be returned to Pemberley after such a long time living in London."

"Oh, Jane, what can I say? She is a delight, a true sister, but I have a little tale to relate, which you must promise not to divulge to anyone. She has settled back to Pemberley very well and made a new friend. I think she is in love, but I do not quite know what to do about it and I feel partly responsible."

"Oh, Lizzy, how could it be a bad thing for her to be in love? She is young, but I know if I had met Charles sooner, it would not have made a jot of difference to my feelings for him."

Elizabeth related the connection between Mrs Gardiner, her friend Martha, and Tom Butler and explained how the latter had been employed in producing some designs for the grounds. "Mrs Annesley has been away, and I had not appreciated quite how much time Mr Butler and Georgiana have been in company with one another since then. Last night she told me of her high regard for him. She did not say she was in love with him exactly, but I could tell there was more than an innocent interest in his talent for drawing. Apparently, they have been out every day for part of the time sketching together. I dare not tell Fitzwilliam for he is sure to be angry with me. He will think that I have not been supervising her properly. To be sure, she always told me she was working on a drawing, but I had no idea. This house and park are so enormous that it is not difficult to lose people. I feel so responsible, notwithstanding the fact that I did encourage their friendship from the start."

"I still do not know why you are so concerned, Lizzy. I thought you said he is a gentleman and that his family are respectable, even if their fortunes are not what they have been in the past."

"That is precisely the problem. Fitzwilliam means to find Georgiana a suitable match, in other words, an alliance where money and fortune will be a priority. He is hardly going to be thrilled to hear that Georgiana has fallen for a penniless landscape gardener."

"Oh, dear. But I should have thought his old prejudices were quite changed. Are you so sure that he would make Georgiana marry against her wishes? In any case, perhaps there is no reason to panic. Now that Christmas is upon us, Mr Butler will not have any occasion to visit Pemberley. Perhaps this is just a fleeting infatuation that will soon pass with a bit of figgy pudding and some other young men to dance with tomorrow evening."

Elizabeth sighed. "If only Fitzwilliam's prejudices were completely vanquished and if only Mr Butler did not have an invitation to the ball."

"He has an invitation?"

"Mr Darcy invited both Tom and his mother himself only yesterday, and they have both accepted," said Elizabeth ruefully. "Still, I daresay at her first ball, Georgiana will find she has so many suitors to divert and entertain her that she will hardly notice Mr Butler's presence at all. She will have no need to pay particular attention to one person. I am certain she will be sensible."

Chapter 10

CHRISTMAS EVE PASSED WITH all the usual ceremony that such occasions bring, but to Elizabeth, her first Christmas celebrations at Pemberley combined the elements of anticipation, excitement, fulfilment, and trepidation, in that order. Christmas morning started well with prayers in the family chapel, which looked a picture wreathed in greenery and glowing with candlelight. Lizzy prayed more fervently than usual that everything would go according to plan and that by tomorrow morning her husband would have more reason to feel proud and love her (if that was possible) even more than it seemed he did now. She did have some trouble keeping her attention fixed on the voice of Mr Lloyd, the rector, who arrived to take the short service before giving his own in Lambton church. Elizabeth's mind would keep wandering back to the recollection of her early rising. On waking, Mr Darcy had presented her with a gift, an enormous box wrapped in marbled Florentine papers, bound with ribbon.

"Happy Christmas, my darling girl," he had said, planting

a kiss on the top of her head. "This is just a small token of my esteem and love to mark the occasion of our first Christmas spent together."

"Well, it doesn't look very small," she answered, pausing to smile at him. The look he returned was enough to overset her feelings. "Do not look at me like that, Fitzwilliam," she said softly, "I cannot concentrate and these ribbons must be undone."

His answer was not spoken, but his fingers assisted where they could, his feelings displaying, only as an ardent lover can do, what was very much uppermost in his thoughts; so it was not until very much more time had passed that Lizzy actually accomplished the task of opening her gift. Able at last to give her fullest attention to her present, she carefully undid the gold ribbon around the large box. With each layer of wrapping, some of fine paper, some of ribbon and silk, came a different package. New boxes were discovered within each, until finally she was left with just three. By their very appearance Elizabeth knew they would contain something special. On opening the first, she gasped. Laid on a silk and velvet interior was the most beautiful diamond necklace she had ever seen.

"Open the others," he urged.

Long, pear-shaped diamonds for her ears were revealed, followed by a stunning diamond ring to match.

"Oh, Fitzwilliam, what a heavenly present. It is too much!"

"Nothing is too much for my wife, Mrs Darcy. Besides, I thought you should have something to wear for the ball tonight."

"I cannot wait to wear them," she cried, unable to resist picking up the heavy necklace, turning it in the light to watch the myriad of sparkles from the glittering stones catch the light. "Indeed, it is such a long time until seven o'clock." She sighed.

"It is no good, Mr Darcy. Do not protest, I beg you, but I have no patience and must wear them now. What do you think? Is it too shocking, or should you like to see Mrs Darcy in diamonds before breakfast, sir?

With her dark curls tumbling over her shoulders through which diamonds twinkled like stars in a velvet sky emphasising the brilliance of her dark eyes, Mr Darcy sat back to admire the wondrous vision before him. He did not speak a word, but merely watched her with the same forbidding expression she had often witnessed but now knew was a façade of restrained emotion, hiding much that he did not wish to reveal.

"I think by your expression that you might prefer this attire to any other," Lizzy laughed, as she revelled in her husband's captivated and studied observance as he gave his fullest attention to Mrs Darcy's diamonds and a whole lot more besides. If any man could have loved his wife more at that moment, he did not think it was possible. Could any woman have looked more beautiful, he thought, than the girl sitting before him amongst the bedclothes, her skin lustrous as the diamonds that flashed and dazzled as she moved to lean over him, expressing her love, gratitude, and the desire he had awakened in her once more.

A breakfast of cold meats, bread rolls and cake, chocolate, wine, and ale was a jolly affair after early morning prayers, sitting in the dining room with all the various factions of family attending, before they all set off for church to hear the sermon and greet friends and neighbours.

The Darcys and their relatives took their seats in the family pews; Mr and Mrs Darcy sat in front with Mr and Mrs Bennet and Mr and Mrs Gardiner. Mrs Bennet was making the most of the situation, but Lizzy was finding that her behaviour, far from being worrisome, was most amusing to observe. For Mrs Bennet, since appearing at dinner the night before, had taken on the regal airs of a personage no less than a queen. Her spiteful tongue, which often lashed out at home, was not heard once during the whole course of the dinner, and her smiles and nods, compliments and greetings were not only freely given to everyone, including Miss Bingley, but were also quietly effusive meted out at appropriate times and calculated to induce the utmost respect and admiration in the listener. Elizabeth could only hope that her mother would not buckle under the strain, but was hopeful that her great character shift might last as long as the ball's duration at least. It was clear that Mr Bennet was most amused by his wife's transformation. He sat on the other side of Elizabeth and when no one was taking much notice caught hold of her hand, squeezing it hard.

"Well, Lizzy, this is a turn-up for the books! I could get quite used to this, and I think in future I must send your mother to Pemberley more frequently. She tells me she has never felt better, that her nerves are entirely done away with, and that she has never noticed before this morning that Miss Bingley is an attractive woman. I declare there must be something in the very air of Pemberley, not to mention the waters, to warrant such a change. She has even kissed me on the cheek. What do you say to that?"

"My mother certainly seems swept away by a sense of the occasion and also of her new importance, I think, as mother-in-law to the 'Great Mr Darcy' as she calls him. For my part, I cannot say which I prefer, the old Mrs Bennet or the new. At least with the old version you felt you knew what was coming. I do not know that I feel quite so comfortable with so many compliments that have been heaped upon my husband, myself, and all of our guests this day, and I cannot rid myself of this dreadful feeling of foreboding that it cannot possibly be sustained."

"Do not worry, my dear. If I should witness any reversal to her old habits I shall swiftly remove her from the vicinity. But I daresay she will do you right in the end. She may not always show her feelings, but in her heart she is very proud of you, Lizzy, that I do know."

Elizabeth turned to her father and squeezed his hand back. "Oh, Papa," she said quietly, "I have missed you."

Two young ladies in the congregation had their thoughts on entirely different objects but were trained along similar lines. Elizabeth's sister Kitty was, against her usual inclination, very much enjoying this morning's sermon. Adam Lloyd, the handsome rector, was a lively orator and delivered his sermon with dash and flair. Even the verger at Longbourn, whom both she and Lydia had formerly considered handsome before the militia arrived, was nothing to the good-looking gentleman who stood at the pulpit to deliver his address. Once or twice she thought she caught his eye, but he looked so serious she could not be sure of anything.

Georgiana Darcy had spotted Thomas Butler as soon as she walked in and was so overcome with shyness at the sight of him that she could not bring herself to look in his direction immediately. At length, however, curiosity got the better of her and she glanced sideways at him under the cover of her bonnet as soon as she dared. Her heart turned over. Mr Butler dressed in his Sunday best was more handsome than she had ever seen him. Clothed in a dark coat, which showed up the fairness of his curls to perfection, his blue eyes dazzled in contrast. When it was obvious that he was looking at her with the same intent and that he was also smiling, she coloured and turned her eyes instantly to her Bible.

There was no opportunity for Georgiana to talk to Tom, but she was able to acknowledge him with a smile out in the cold churchyard as Mr and Mrs Darcy exchanged greetings with other parishioners. Kitty was introduced to Mr Lloyd to her delight and determined on writing to her sister Lydia in Newcastle at the earliest opportunity to tell her all about him.

Lizzy was soon waylaid by Mrs Eaton, who made it clear that she was not to be fobbed off by a mere polite "good morning." Mr Darcy rapidly made his escape, becoming quickly lost among the throng, for which Elizabeth could not blame him. She forced herself to look as interested as she could, though it was difficult to concentrate when faced with a barrage of dull information and scurrilous gossip, but she did the best she could. When the subject arose of old Mrs Darcy's maid being in attendance and Mrs Eaton's questioning her about whether or not she had been introduced to the lady, Elizabeth could bear her company no longer. On suddenly remembering that she had left her Bible in the church, a perfect excuse was instantly formed and executed in order to make her release possible. Elizabeth made her way back into the deserted building, hurrying along before she was missed. As she entered the church through the porch door the sound of hushed voices caught her attention. In the vestry opposite, the door was slightly ajar. She could just see Mr Lloyd returned from his duties to his parishioners outside and hear him engaged in conversation.

Trying not to disturb him she found her seat and the forgotten Bible and was just returning to the door when her attention was caught by the sound of her husband's voice. A glance through the vestry door revealed that it was indeed Mr Darcy in conversation with the rector, a well-dressed lady, and a young boy. The boy she noticed for his striking and handsome features with wavy, dark hair, curling back from his forehead. He had a distinctive mien for a boy of his age and Elizabeth was quite fascinated by him, not only by his manner but also by his countenance, which seemed familiar. Yet she knew she had never set eyes on him before. The lady was now curtseying before Mr Darcy and it was evident that their conversation was at an end. Elizabeth did not know what to do. She felt caught, almost as if she had been spying. It was too late to rush outside. Elizabeth observed Fitzwilliam turn to leave and then he saw her. His face was grave, but he smiled as he approached and taking her arm reached for her hand, bringing it to his lips before tenderly planting a kiss.

"Shall we go home, Mrs Darcy?" he asked.

Elizabeth looked up at him and nodded her assent. "Who were you talking to, Fitzwilliam? I neither recognised the lady nor the child."

"No, they do not live in Lambton," he replied, squeezing her arm affectionately. "The lady was my mother's maid, a very long time ago. I had to pay my respects as she always attends the service on Christmas morning. Mama was very fond of her and would be pleased, I think, that I still bestow a token in memory of her affection. Her son is growing into a fine boy; my mother would have been most delighted." Mr Darcy paused on the step outside to take a lungful of air, his breath exhaling in puffs of cloudy vapour on the freezing air. "What's next, Mrs Darcy? Present giving, revels, and Christmas dinner; I can hardly wait!"

Elizabeth was sure that the lady must be the Rachel Tissington that Mrs Eaton had told her about, but there was no more time to ask any questions, surrounded as they were by well-wishers as they emerged.

The Darcys and their guests left the church first, hastening back to Pemberley in their carriages to prepare for the arrival of their tenants who would be gathering in the hall waiting for their Christmas tokens: a pouch of money and a Christmas pheasant. Elizabeth met and greeted every farmer and worker with a handshake and a gift. Her audience instantly warmed to her, so unaffected was she in her manner and so obviously interested was she in their lives, listening to their tales about the Pemberley Estate from their childhood days of yore. Mrs Reynolds and her maids plied them all with porter, ale, and mulled wine, so it was a happy band that soon left to make merry with their own families.

Fortunately, Elizabeth was kept so busy that she did not have time to think about the imminent ball. One of the tasks set for their guests on Christmas Eve had been to invent a charade for an after dinner amusement the next day, a game which was traditionally played sitting around the table, according to Georgiana. Miss Bingley too had been in raptures about the game and spoke constantly on the past wit and intelligence displayed by former guests who had graced the Pemberley dining room. Elizabeth knew that Miss Bingley was probably trying to discompose her, but she must admit she was rather concerned that one or two members of her family might not be capable of rising to the challenge. When her mother confessed that she was where a sheaf of paper and ink were set out ready to accomplish such a task. Making up her own charade had been fun, but trying to think of one suitable for Mrs Bennet was a little more difficult and the constraint on time was having the very worst effect. Her mind seemed blank and she was increasingly unable to concentrate. Lizzy got up to peruse the books on the shelves. Hundreds of leather bound titles lined the room, each one proclaiming its title in gilt letters. She would have loved to spend the time with a selection of books indulging her passion for reading, but she quickly selected an old Shakespearean volume, thinking that here she might be rewarded with the stimulation that was immediately required. However, she was disappointed; no matter how hard she tried, nothing would come despite a promising array of characters, situations, and plots. The book went back on the shelf, but realising straight away that it would not fit back comfortably into the space and that something behind was preventing its return, she took it out again to investigate. Whatever was proving to be an obstruction was out of her line of vision on the high shelf and it was necessary to stand on tiptoe so that she could explore the space with her fingers. What felt like another book had fallen down and wedged itself at the back of the shelf. Elizabeth could only just grasp the volume with her thumb and forefinger, and she pulled hard knowing that if this attempt failed she would have to fetch out the library steps. Her efforts were only partly successful, for after refusing to budge for what seemed like an age, the book came out all of a sudden with such a force that she dropped it, scattering pages from the loosely bound book.

On bending to pick it up, however, she could see that the papers lying on the floor were not in fact part of the book, but letters, one of which had come undone. The book itself was a very dry tome, a Treatise on the History and Chemistry of Mineral Waters and other Aqueous mixtures, that at first held little interest for Lizzy until flicking through the pages to determine where the letters might have been inserted, she came across a flower pressed and dried within its pages. Such an unexpected article raised her curiosity, and though she determined on instantly putting back the letters to their original placing, she found herself turning the opened one over in her hand. There was no date, the hand was clearly feminine, and the words seemed to leap from the page, willing her to take note of them. It was read before she knew what she had done.

> *Darling Orsini,*
>
> *I know we promised that there would be no communication between us, but I am compelled to write after seeing you this afternoon. When you declared your love in that place which has become the dearest spot in the whole world to me, I can only tell you that a cherished dream came true. I adore you and to know that finally you feel as I do fills me with such pleasure as is impossible to describe. I love you more than you can ever know and you have made me the happiest girl alive.*
>
> *We may be young but we know our hearts to be true. What does it matter that we have only known one another for a short while—how are love and constancy to be measured by time alone? I need no approval from those who would not understand. It is our secret, indeed, I have not yet told the person we best love, who is dearest to both our hearts for fear of something dire happening to prevent us from being together. I know you may not*

always talk to me in company, but a sign, anything, will suffice to remind me of your love. Till I see you again (please let it be this evening),

I am yours,
Viola

Elizabeth wished straight away that she had not read it. The letter was so heartfelt, so personal. A love letter, without a doubt, and one that was clearly shrouded in secrets written by a lady whose name and that of her lover were clearly assumed. Orsini and Viola, Shakespeare's lovers from *Twelfth Night*, Elizabeth recalled. It was all rather mysterious, but no doubt guests of the Darcys staying at Pemberley some time ago had penned it. Well, whatever the letter was doing hidden away in the book, Lizzy thought she should replace it, folding the worn paper along the lines so that it looked much as it had done before it was disturbed. She picked up the other letter and placed it over the top of the first, closing the book with the intent of putting it back on the shelf. The temptation to open the second letter was great, but she reminded herself that neither letter was addressed to her nor were they on public display. Whoever had hidden them had intended them to remain that way, though she felt that something so private as a love letter should have been better concealed or burned if the lovers were worried about their missive falling into the wrong hands. On reflection, she thought she might ask Mr Darcy about it to see if he could shed any light on its composer but then thought better of it. It might seem to him as if she had been snooping around and ferreting amongst what, after all, were his belongings. It was a pity, she thought, for she was sure he would be extremely diverted.

Chapter 11

To say that Elizabeth was relieved when Christmas dinner was over is something of an understatement. But she was satisfied that the meal had been an excellent one and, when washed down by the majority with several glasses of wine, found everyone in congenial spirits for the game of charades. Mr and Mrs Darcy started, followed by other willing volunteers, and soon the assembled guests relaxed and started to have fun. There were some excellent puzzles and even Mrs Bennet began to enjoy herself when it came to her time, delivering hers with what she imagined was an erudite air.

Miss Bingley's turn came next. She waited until everyone was silent for the greatest dramatic effect before she recited her charade by heart.

"My first has the making of honey to charm,
My second brings breakfast to bed on your arm,
My third bores a hole in leather so fine,
While united the whole breaks the heart most kind."

She looked around the table with a smirk upon her face and played with her bracelets as if she must find another amusement to keep her occupied from waiting for answers which surely would never come. Charades were her speciality, she knew, and surely this dull company did not have a clue.

Mrs Bennet piped up immediately. "Bees and honey go together rather well to my mind, Miss Bingley. I wonder if 'my first' is a bee."

"Well done, Mrs Bennet," cried Mr Darcy, hardly able to keep the astonishment from his voice. "I am sure you are right, an excellent thought."

Mrs Bennet instantly flushed as scarlet as the berries on the holly leaves adorning the portraits. She directed her best smile at her son-in-law and glanced at him in a coquettish manner when she thought he looked at her.

Kitty was next to surprise everyone as she proclaimed that the second was a tray, and before they could even worry over the third, Mr Bennet declared he knew the complete answer to the riddle.

"Miss Bingley, I have found you out," he said, raising his glass to her across the table. "Duplicity, falseness, and treachery are your game, are they not?"

Miss Bingley held his studied gaze over the table and did not flinch.

Mr Bennet smiled before delivering the solution with triumph. "The word 'betrayal' is the answer to your charade, I think."

For the first time Elizabeth felt some discomfort. She knew her father too well to imagine that his remarks were not given without his intentions being satirical. She knew exactly what he thought of Miss Bingley and of her mistreatment of Jane.

But she need not have worried; Miss Bingley seemed not to notice, graciously accepting her defeat, and when Mrs Bennet declared how clever Miss Bingley was to devise such a riddle, the latter fairly glowed with pride and almost, but not quite, returned the compliment.

"I am so pleased you enjoy charades as well as we do here at Pemberley, Mrs Bennet," she said. "It is an old tradition that I believe our host started in his youth. But, in my recollection, I do not think I ever heard of a charade based on betrayal, although the very word has such connotations that I will forever associate with Pemberley. Mr Darcy, what do you think?"

Mr Darcy looked rather discomposed for a moment. "I cannot think to what you refer, madam," came his answer, and his expression, which formerly had been congenial, immediately altered to one of haughty disdain.

"You remember, Mr Darcy, I am sure," said Miss Bingley, who to all intents and purposes was smiling at him. "I can never think of that word without summoning up a picture in my mind of Christmas theatricals. Shakespeare: love and betrayal, his universal themes. You must remember *Twelfth Night*. You were Duke Orsini and I was Olivia. How you pined for me!"

Elizabeth was all attention. Her heart began hammering as she recollected the letter she had found in the library. So, Fitzwilliam had played Orsini, but it did not follow, she reasoned, that the Orsini implicated in the letter was her husband. There had probably been dozens of theatricals over the years, and in any case, the letter's recipient might have nothing to do with any of it. She waited to see his response.

"My dear Caroline, I can barely recall such an event, and I

must admit, although I can remember being dressed up for many a part, the particulars escape me. Tell me, was I any good?"

This brought a laugh to echo round the room. Mr Darcy stood up and with a mock bow announced that, as there were scarcely two hours left before the dancing was due to begin, they might all wish to repair to their rooms for restoration and preparation.

In her dressing room Elizabeth prepared for the ball, and though the looking glass told her that she had never felt more pleased by her appearance, her feelings were in turmoil. Caroline Bingley, it had to be said, always had the power to make her think irrationally and tonight was no exception. That lady's allusions to the past, to a time before Elizabeth had known her husband, made her feel not only uncomfortable but also quite envious. It was silly, she knew, but she must admit a certain jealousy when she thought about the Christmases he must have spent in the company of Caroline Bingley and every other young woman in the vicinity.

"I know very little about my husband," she thought. "I know he was never in love with Caroline Bingley, but does that mean that he was never in love with anyone before he met me? I have not considered such a thing before today, but I am certain that a man does not reach the age of twenty-nine without experiencing an affection or infatuation or maybe something more."

Could the letter she found implicate her husband in some way? she considered for the first time. Lizzy did not want to think about it, but she felt sure that her mind would be put at rest with just one more enquiry. For now, she would forget about it and concentrate on the matter in hand. She scrutinised her reflection with a critical eye and was satisfied enough to smile at the young woman who stared back at her. Elizabeth's gown of white sarcenet fitted beautifully, accentuating her slight and graceful form. With her headdress of lace and feathers further emphasising her colouring, her skin glowed, setting off her sparkling eyes as they glittered with vitality.

There came a soft knock upon the door and when she called out, expecting to see her maid, she was delighted to find her husband instead. He carried her jewel boxes and before long he had assisted Elizabeth with their fastenings, performing this simple task in such a way as made her feel that she must be very precious, as he lingered over adjusting the diamonds in her ears, placing her necklace just so, and holding her hand in the gentlest manner to slide her ring onto her finger. When he had finished he stood back to look at her with such an expression of love in his eyes that Elizabeth could hardly meet them with her own.

"I love you, Mrs Darcy," he said, leaning forward to kiss her lips. "Come, let us go, it is time to open the best Christmas ball Pemberley has ever seen."

Georgiana Darcy entered the ballroom on her brother's arm, conscious that the whole room of people were staring at her but knowing, to her relief, that the majority were engaged more particularly in observing her sister-in-law on the other side. It was quite mortifying to be looked at with such close study, and she hoped Elizabeth was more equal than she to the examination. There had always been times at Pemberley when she had to suffer such agonies, but this was by far the greatest challenge she had met, for this was her first ball, her coming out. She could hardly meet the eyes of those who watched her every move and was grateful for any familiar countenance she spied. There was only one face she wanted to see and when she did catch sight of him on the other side of the room standing with his mother engaged in conversation with Mr and Mrs Gardiner, she felt her heart involuntarily leap. As if he were aware of her glance, Mr Butler immediately looked up at precisely the same moment, smiling and bowing in her direction. Even though her heart was beating wildly, she managed to return his smile before Mr Darcy moved on, leading her away in quite another direction.

"Ah, Mr Calladine," pronounced Mr Darcy as a young man stepped out before them. Though not tall, Mr Calladine had a gentlemanly air and appearance, a well-cut coat, and breeches of the best silk and style.

"It is my pleasure to meet you all again. May I offer my compliments of the season, Mrs Darcy, Miss Georgiana," Mr Calladine said, bowing as he spoke and immediately turning towards Georgiana. "I do hope you will allow me the honour of the first dance, Miss Darcy, if I have not been pre-empted by another suitor."

Georgiana did not immediately know how to answer him. She must admit, if only to herself, that she was rather hoping Mr Butler might be first to ask her to dance. But even as the thought occurred to her, she knew her brother would heartily approve of Mr Calladine's offer.

"I am sure Miss Darcy would be delighted, would you not?" Mr Darcy was heard to say before Georgiana uttered a word.

She looked up at her brother's expressive countenance, which seemed to urge her to accept. Georgiana knew she could not possibly refuse and found herself nodding in agreement, her curtsey not only acknowledging but gratifying both her brother's and Mr Calladine's requests.

"I shall look forward to leading you out onto the floor, Miss Darcy," said Mr Calladine, who bowed once more and moved off, not stopping for further conversation.

"He is an excellent fellow, Georgiana," said Mr Darcy. "I like him very much."

Georgiana could not answer. She felt quite miserable at the prospect, and besides, her pulse had started to quicken once more as they headed toward the very gentleman whose presence thoroughly discomposed her. But before they had got much further their neighbours Mr and Mrs Eaton stopped to salute them. Mr Darcy immediately fell into conversation with Mr Eaton but Elizabeth could only reflect on the last discourse she had had with Mrs Eaton and the memory of observing Mrs Darcy's former maid in the church. Such misgivings and recollections must be dismissed from her mind and their conversation, Elizabeth decided, trying hard to steer the topic of conversation onto an agreeable subject.

"Mrs Eaton, how do you do? I do hope you are ready to enjoy some dancing."

"I am ready to dance, Mrs Darcy, but whether I shall enjoy it is another matter. It has always been my belief that such physical activity ignites certain passions amongst those in whom such demonstration would be better suppressed. There is a tendency, I think, amongst the lower orders and the intellectually challenged to prefer dancing to everything else. It is an amusement that encourages profligate behaviour amongst the young and adultery amongst the happily married. I cannot approve of such exertion, but a ball calls for certain sacrifices on one's part. If I must dance, I will, however my inclination against such practices informs me."

"It is very kind of you to put yourself out quite so much," answered Elizabeth, hardly able to suppress a smile. "I find dancing exhilarating and, I confess, Mrs Eaton, to experience a certain pleasure in the activity. I met Mr Darcy for the first time at a ball in Hertfordshire, though we did not dance a step. However, it is not to say that we disliked dancing; we later found we were both prodigiously keen on the diversion so long as we were engaged with the other. It is my belief that to be fond of dancing is a certain step towards falling in love."

"Precisely, Mrs Darcy, my point exactly." She turned to Georgiana. "And how do you like dancing, Miss Darcy? I saw Mr Calladine press his request to open the ball. I daresay we'll have you married by Easter, will we not, Mrs Darcy?"

Georgiana coloured instantly and looked to Elizabeth for assistance.

"I do not think one dance ever decided anyone's future, Mrs Eaton," said Elizabeth, "and Georgiana is full young, I think, to be contemplating matrimony just yet. I hope to see her dancing with several of the young men here tonight."

"I suppose it is all very well if properly supervised, though, mark my words, Miss Georgiana, Mr Calladine will not be satisfied with one dance."

Mrs Bennet surveyed the scene in wonder. She felt she had done her daughter proud by the efforts she had made with her appearance and was much gratified by the attention she received from the Darcys' acquaintances and neighbours. She simpered and smirked, saluted and smiled at them all with the dignity she felt fitting for such an auspicious occasion. Kitty stood between her parents with her sister Mary feeling equally happy, her exhilaration caused by having had Mr Lloyd ask for the first dance.

"He is handsome, I suppose," said Mrs Bennet, "but if Mr Calladine should ask you to dance, be sure to smile at him. You may not have your sisters' looks, but a man could go a long way to see good teeth like yours, my love. You have a pretty mouth when you are not sulking, so make the most of it. And if Mr Lloyd asks for another, as it is certain sure he will, tell him you are already engaged."

"I will do no such thing, Mama," Kitty declared. "In any case, why should I not dance with him more than once? Lydia and I always used to dance with whomever we liked."

"But Lydia is married and you are not and we know, do we not, just how grasping clergymen can be? Mr Lloyd wants to get his feet under Mr Darcy's table, that's for certain. He'll be after what pickings he can get. They're all the same and I daresay he's a distant relative of that other odious clergyman, your cousin Collins. I'm surprised he isn't here making the most of his connection with Mr Darcy's aunt."

"But you know Charlotte is indisposed, Mama. She is nearing her time."

"The addition of a miniature Collins would not stop him. And his hint to your father about the rectory being too small to raise a family will not bring his entailment any quicker. No doubt he spends his days praying for your father's demise. My only comfort is that at least I now have three daughters married and will be spared a life in the hedgerows. If you and Mary could just secure one of these nice, rich young men that

GEORGIANA AND MR CALLADINE opened the ball with Mr and Mrs Darcy, to great applause from their guests. Mr Calladine was pleasant and attentive, but talked too much to Miss Darcy's mind, and was rather too familiar holding her hand for longer than she liked, pressing her fingers with too much insistence. His lack of height made her feel too significant and ungainly; she felt as if she were towering over him. Relieved when the dance came to a close, she was looking around the room before it had finished to see if she could catch sight of Mr Butler. But Mr Calladine had other ideas when Georgiana tried to affect her escape.

"You cannot leave me now, Miss Darcy, you will break my heart. The entire ballroom is watching you and they will all be disappointed if you do not dance a second with me."

Georgiana could see Mr Butler in the distance making his way toward her. She tried to release her hand without any success and, on looking up, saw her brother standing a little apart smiling encouragingly, clearly delighted by Mr Calladine's repeated request to dance. She did not feel she had any choice but to accept, and was made more forlorn when she witnessed Tom's expression when he saw her being led onto the dance floor again.

"He will never ask me to dance now," she thought as he turned away, their eyes having met across the room. "Mr Butler will think that I prefer Hugh Calladine's company and there could be nothing further from the truth."

At the same time, Charles Bingley had taken Elizabeth's hand and Jane was to dance with Mr Darcy. Such friends rejoiced in their partners; Mr Darcy and Jane looked very elegant, each complimenting the other by their grace. Lizzy and Mr Bingley appeared most relaxed and happy in one another's company, as close a brother and sister as they could be.

"May I compliment you, Mrs Darcy, on a most excellent ball?" began Mr Bingley.

"You may, indeed, Mr Bingley," answered Elizabeth brightly. "I am having such a lovely time and have to keep pinching myself that I am not dreaming. But I admit I am very nervous about the whole affair and can only hope that this Christmas ball will live up to the expectations of all our guests."

"I do not think Pemberley has ever seen such a magnificent or happy day," entreated Bingley. "You must not worry. Look around for yourself; everyone is enjoying themselves immensely."

"But the talk of Christmases past and the fond memories you all share have made me realise that I could not hope to supply such an entertainment to equal those festivities."

"All exaggerated, I assure you, Mrs Darcy. I think this by far the best ball I have ever attended in my life."

"I always knew you'd be my favourite brother-in-law,"

Elizabeth said with a laugh. Their conversation paused as they moved down the set and Elizabeth wondered if she could pluck up the courage to ask him the question which plagued her most. "Perhaps we should put on a play next year," she began when they met up again.

"And you would have us all acting again, I suppose, Mrs Darcy. Well, I don't know. Not that I wouldn't mind resurrecting the old theatricals, but Darcy always said he would never do another after the last one."

"Was that *Twelfth Night?*"

Bingley looked puzzled for a moment, trying to remember. "Yes, I believe it was, but why he was against another, I cannot recall now."

"I should have loved to have seen Darcy as Orsini. Whom did you play?"

"The fool, of course, I played the fool," Bingley repeated, laughing at the memory and at his own joke. "That was one part Darcy would not consider."

It was Elizabeth's turn to be amused. "I daresay Darcy was far too proud at the time to play anything but a nobleman, but, between you and me, I've always considered that Feste the fool was the wisest character of them all." She took a deep breath. "So Caroline played Olivia, did she not? Tell me, who played Viola?"

Bingley scratched his head in a thoughtful manner. "For the life of me," he said at last, "I can't remember."

Elizabeth watched him, trying to decide whether he simply could not recollect or whether there was another reason, some design involved by hiding the truth. After all, there must have been a reason why Fitzwilliam did not want to continue with the plays. The moment the thought was in her head, she realised she was being ridiculous and she also knew as she observed him that Charles was far too open and honest a creature to be capable of concealing such a thing.

"No, it's completely gone," he said, as the dance came to a close. "You'll have to ask Caroline."

Kitty had enjoyed dancing with Mr Lloyd and was rather hoping that he would ask her for another, but no such request came, to her great sorrow. He was very polite, thanking her profusely, but he moved away quickly as soon as he returned her to Mrs Bennet's charge. Her eyes followed his progress across the room and she saw him stop to talk in a kindly way to a young woman who had a most melancholy air about her.

Mrs Bennet, who had also been watching, sniffed with contempt. "That young lady with a face like a sour lemon is Eleanor Bradshaw, who is no better than she should be according to Mrs Vernon, whom I had the pleasure of conversing with just now. Apparently, she is in love with Mr Calladine and though he's shown a certain interest in her at the last few assemblies, I don't doubt he'd like to further his interests elsewhere and align his fortunes with Miss Darcy."

"Oh dear, poor girl," said Kitty, "has Miss Bradshaw no fortune?"

"Don't be so silly, girl. Whether she has a fortune or not is beside the point. How on earth can she compete with Miss Darcy's wealth and position in society? I saw Mr Darcy grinning from ear to ear when they danced twice, and I would not put it past him to encourage another, you'll see. Perhaps you'd be better off sticking to your clergyman or some other young man, Kitty. I'm not at all sure you'd get anywhere with Mr Calladine now, however good your teeth."

Kitty fumed. Her mother really was the most exasperating

woman that ever lived, she felt. She opened her mouth to retort but decided against relieving her feelings, knowing it would be of little use. It was time to seek refreshment before she said something she knew she might later regret.

Georgiana had also gone in search of refreshment. At least that was what she told herself. She longed to bump into Mr Butler. Perhaps if she did, he might ask her to dance, she thought. Entering the room where tables had been set up for the purpose of serving food and drink, she looked around the vast crowd, a sea of people waving and gesticulating, chattering and laughing, and all making so much noise with a constant frenzied movement about the place that she could not see anything clearly. Tom was nowhere to be seen and it was impossible to progress further into the room, so tightly packed were the bodies. Someone stood on her train and she felt the back of her gown pulled, making her stagger backwards and almost falling over in the process.

"Miss Darcy, please forgive me," said a voice in her ear that she instantly recognised, making her cheeks blush. Before she turned round Tom Butler, grave but apologetic, took steps to further arrest her progress into the room and bowed before her.

Georgiana was delighted to see him but could tell immediately that his manner toward her had changed. There was no warmth in his eyes and certainly no hint of a smile to his lips, just a flush about his face as if he were as embarrassed as she. She plucked up the courage to speak. "Please do not worry, Mr Butler, there is no room to move in here. It was an accident; there is no harm done."

His eyes looked everywhere about him and he shifted his feet, as if looking for an excuse to walk away, but there was such a crush that it was impossible for him to go anywhere. Georgiana's mind had gone blank. All their easy friendliness had disappeared and she felt so shy before him.

"How are the plans coming along?" she said eventually, wishing she could have thought of something clever or witty to say.

His returning glance was quite cold, she felt, and the answer he gave made her feel no better. "The plans are finished. I shall send them to Mr Darcy presently, as soon as Christmas is over."

"But could you not bring them yourself?" Georgiana dared to say, speaking up for once and immediately regretting her outburst.

Mr Butler looked at Miss Darcy's face, whose expression, sweet and imploring, could not help but move him. It was evident that she was not asking out of civility. His answer was just as daring. "I will bring them myself if you promise to indulge me in one small matter."

Georgiana hardly heard his next speech. She was too busy drinking in his smile and the soft expression in his eyes, which seemed to tell her more than his words alone.

"Dance with me, Miss Darcy. Please, will you take a turn in the ballroom with me? It is Christmas, after all."

Georgiana felt a glow of happiness, immediately taking Tom's arm and allowing him to lead her away. Being pushed and jostled by the throng who clamoured in the other direction seemed almost pleasurable, especially when Mr Butler was forced to place a guiding hand in the small of her back whilst shielding her from the mob. She delighted in the touch of his fingers and thought she would never be miserable again.

Elizabeth watched Georgiana and Mr Butler from the side of the room and bit her lip involuntarily. Her sister-in-law's performance was of such a marked contrast to the one she had endured with Mr Calladine that she couldn't wonder if she was the only person that observed it. Such wholehearted joy in the application of the dance Elizabeth felt she had rarely seen, but there was more than that. Sparks, unseen sparks of desire flew between them; their attachment for one another was as visible as a candle flame before the touch paper is lit.

Looking around, she was relieved to see her husband deep in conversation with Mr Gardiner. Somehow, she had a feeling he would not be very amused to see Miss Darcy enjoying herself quite so much with another partner and one that she felt he would hardly approve. She had no more time to reflect on either, however, for Mr Bingley suddenly appeared at her elbow.

"I've just remembered who played Viola," he said with a certain sense of triumph. "I cannot think how I could have forgotten because she was rather good, a very talented actress. Can you guess, Mrs Darcy, from all of Pemberley's friends and neighbours, who such a creature could possibly be?"

Chapter 13

Miss Darcy and Mr Butler were inseparable. When they were not dancing, they were sitting down talking or walking about the room together. Their behaviour began to draw the attention of some of the elders at the ball, particularly those spiteful ladies from the county families. Mrs Eaton's enquiries as to whom Miss Darcy's inclinations seemed particularly favoured did not immediately bring her satisfaction. No one seemed to know anything about him. In desperation she asked Miss Bingley. Mrs Eaton always liked to see Miss Bingley at the Pemberley parties and knew she could be relied upon for any spicy gossip to be had. But she was disappointed. Miss Bingley had no idea who the charming Adonis could be but was sufficiently motivated to find out, especially when Mrs Eaton informed her that Miss Darcy had danced with him no less than three times.

Seeing Mr Darcy on the other side of the room completely engaged in conversation with a fellow neighbour, Miss Bingley made her way around the edge of the ballroom, all the while observing Miss Darcy and her partner. There was something rather too familiar about the behaviour of the young man, she thought, and had quite decided against him before she even reached Mr Darcy's side.

On seeing her approach, the gentleman discussing the Christmas sport due to take place on the following day bowed and took his leave, assuring Mr Darcy of his attendance on the morrow. Mr Darcy, who was feeling rather pleased and proud with himself and delighted by the way that the evening was progressing, smiled warmly at Miss Bingley. "A ball to surpass any ever held at Pemberley, I think, Miss Bingley," he said. "However, I am sorry to see you are not dancing."

"Oh, do not worry about me, Mr Darcy, I've had my share of partners this evening. I find I am happy enough to observe the splendid company before me, and to meet with so many old friends is a delight."

"It is indeed. There is nothing like a ball for cementing intimacy amongst neighbours. Everyone talks at once, information and compliments flow, and when each is satisfied that they are the envy of their peers, they go home rejoicing in the pleasure of an evening well spent at no expense to themselves, convinced of their own unrivalled good fortune and superiority."

Miss Bingley laughed in a coquettish manner. "Mr Darcy, if I did not know you better I might accuse you of being satirical."

Mr Darcy smiled again. "Come, Miss Bingley, do you mean to contradict me?"

"Oh no, not in the slightest, I never did see anything differently from you. Our neighbours give us much diversion in many ways, I agree, and the observation of their behaviour bests any sport one might get out in the fresh air, in my opinion. And whilst we are on the subject of your guests, Mr Darcy, there is one here to whom I have not been introduced and a young man who is quite a figure of curiosity amongst your friends, I might add."

"Really? There is someone here that you have a particular wish to be introduced to, Miss Bingley? Can you point the gentleman out to me? I will present him at once."

"Yes, of course. But you must know why we are all anxious to meet the young man. He has been most particular in his company this evening and has not left Miss Darcy's side for the last three dances. Is there something you have been hiding from us, Mr Darcy? Is an engagement about to be announced?"

Darcy's face fell at this intelligence and when he followed Miss Bingley's gaze across the dance floor to alight his eyes upon his sister dancing in a very animated fashion with Mr Butler, his whole expression changed. His dark eyes glittered with anger and his whole countenance could not have displayed more discomposure.

"Excuse me, Miss Bingley," he said immediately, giving a short bow before he strode off, circumnavigating the room in pursuit of his wife.

Just at that moment the supper bell rang and the confusion that ensued as the hungry revellers quickly abandoned the ballroom for the dining room had Mr Darcy caught up in the crowd. He was forced to abandon his search for the present. He knew Elizabeth would already be engaged with Mrs Reynolds and her staff, supervising the proceedings and ensuring that everyone was happy. There was nothing he could do for the moment.

Elizabeth was happily employed in the dining room, moving amongst her guests and hoping that her feelings would not betray her. The intelligence that Elizabeth had earlier received from Mr Bingley had been a great shock, but although she had been almost stupefied by the information at the outset, she was now convinced that something about the whole matter was not quite as she had at first thought. The more she contemplated, the more she was completely amused by the idea, for no matter how the situation looked, in her heart she could no more put two such dissimilar personalities together than jump in a basket and fly over the moon. Louisa Hurst! Charles and Caroline Bingley's elder sister, who was as equally disagreeable as her sibling, was the person who had played Viola. Louisa was in London for the season with her husband at present and no ball at Pemberley would have induced her to miss one in the metropolis. Elizabeth felt enormous relief. Whoever the correspondents of the letter had been, she was certain they were not Fitzwilliam and Louisa. She laughed inside at the very idea. And now she had had time to think over the whole thing, she was able to come to the conclusion that even if her husband had ever been in love before, as was highly likely, it had not stopped him from marrying her. Elizabeth bore his name, they loved one another, and she would not think or dwell on whatever may or may not have happened in the past. She was, therefore, delighted to see her husband coming with all speed into the room, though as she regarded his countenance at some distance, she could immediately see that something was wrong. He looked most displeased.

As soon as she was able she asked him the reason for his obvious discontent. "Are you feeling unwell, Fitzwillliam? You do not look yourself."

His face was scarlet and Elizabeth became most concerned as

she was led away to a quiet corner of the room. "I want Mr Butler removed from my sister's side immediately," he began. "He has been making an exhibition of her, I have been told, behaving in a disreputable manner, and exposing her to the curiosity and insults of the entire neighbourhood."

Elizabeth tried to soothe him straight away. "I daresay you are mistaken, my love. From whom did you receive this information?"

"I've seen it with my own eyes, thanks to Miss Bingley and the knowledge she gleaned from others. There is talk of an engagement, would you believe? The boy needs whipping for his impertinence."

So Miss Bingley was bent on revenge and had found the perfect weapon with which to accomplish her acts of retribution. Elizabeth immediately sprang to the defence of Mr Butler. "There is no harm done. Young people love to dance and Georgiana is no exception. Mr Butler is very gentleman-like, and I am sure if they have been a little carried away by their enthusiasm for the spirit of the occasion, a gentle word will set everything to rights."

"I think if you will observe the Gardiners' table, Mrs Darcy, you will see that it is far too late. Not only is the young upstart sitting next to her, but he is rattling away, talking nineteen to the dozen in such a way to make the entire room cognisant of their conversation. What are your relations thinking about to allow such a thing to carry on? The damage is done. Hugh Calladine will not ask her to dance again this evening."

Elizabeth, though determined to remain calm, initially found herself unable to listen any longer without feeling extreme indignation. Not only was he being completely unreasonable, but also he had insulted her aunt and uncle and, by so doing, had offended her in such a way that she knew she could not easily forgive. But she had no wish to cause a scene. There was quite enough going on for their guests to enjoy as it was, and Lizzy was determined that nothing was going to spoil this long planned evening.

"I will request that Georgiana join us at an appropriate moment. Do not worry, all will be accomplished without any fuss and you will see that your fears are unfounded. Georgiana is too sensible to place herself in such a predicament and I am sure Mr Butler is only being a gallant guest. Excuse me, Fitzwilliam."

Elizabeth walked away, determined not to be angry, though all the while feeling her emotions rising with every step. She could see Georgiana looking so happy and chatting away with confidence in a way she had never seen her before. It seemed cruel to separate them, but she felt there was nothing else she could do without making difficulties for everyone concerned. Fitzwilliam had been unforgivably rude, but she knew that his fierce protection for his sister was at its core, though forgiveness seemed quite impossible for his behaviour.

Unhappily, Miss Bingley chose the same moment to move across the room towards the Gardiners' table and arrested Elizabeth on her way.

"May I congratulate you, Mrs Darcy," she said, "on an eventful evening and for expanding the society of dear Miss Darcy. I hear her gallant suitor is a gardener, no less. Indeed, it quite puts me in mind. The Darcys always did have a penchant for keeping low company, as I recall hearing, and it appears as if Miss Darcy is making the same mistakes as her brother once did. But I do not wish to talk out of turn. I daresay the old days are best forgotten."

Elizabeth knew that Miss Bingley was making a reference to the friendship Fitzwilliam had at one time shared with her sister Lydia's husband Mr Wickham. The son of Mr Darcy's father's old steward, George Wickham had grown up alongside Fitzwilliam, playing together like brothers and sharing their lessons. He had turned out to be a disreputable character and the enforced marriage after Wickham had eloped with her sister Lydia still left Elizabeth feeling shamed. "If you have nothing else to add, Miss Bingley, I must take my leave of you," Elizabeth managed to say, though her voice could hardly be heard over the noisy accompaniment of the diners all around.

"Well, I do not think it lasted long, his infatuation with George Wickham's step-sister. But she was a beauty, I've been told, quite dark, a similar colouring to your own, I imagine. Now then, what was her name? Ah yes, Viola. Viola Wickham; I wonder where she is now?"

Chapter 14

THE SHOCK ON ELIZABETH'S face prompted another response from Miss Bingley. "My dear Mrs Darcy, I do beg your pardon. You appear quite unwell. I did not mean to upset you, but I see the astonishment upon your countenance betrays your feelings wholeheartedly. Come; allow me to find you a seat. I should never have said a word if I thought you would be so overset. I assumed, as you and your husband appear so very confidential, that you must have some knowledge of his past."

Before Elizabeth had a chance to utter a syllable Miss Bingley took her arm and attempted to steer her in the direction of the door. Lizzy, however, halted their progress immediately. She was determined to recover her composure and though her thoughts raced around her head with more questions than she could ever hope to have answered, she rallied in time.

"Please do not concern yourself, Miss Bingley," she managed to say. "I was a little shocked, I confess. I had no idea that George Wickham had any siblings at all."

"Or that husbands are capable of keeping such secrets, I

daresay," interrupted Miss Bingley. "I suppose a young gentle-man must enjoy a little youthful dissipation, and Viola Wickham was very willing to supply that diversion, I have heard. I've no doubt of Mrs Eaton's authority on the subject; she is a lady who knows everything. I will tell what history I can recollect. George Wickham's father was married twice. When the first Mrs Wickham died his father married again, I believe. She already had two daughters, but their mother wanted a fresh start and they were sent to live with her sister. A short while later, George Wickham was born. The forgotten girls never were returned to live with them and so Wickham grew up not knowing he had any step-sisters. He was separated from them for many years until after his mother died, and he was reunited with one of them. Wickham's father invited Viola to Pemberley with old Mr Darcy's permission, thinking that she might have a settling influence on the boy, who was becoming a most troublesome young man. Little did he realise what havoc she would create. I believe Darcy and the Wickhams were inseparable for several months from what Mrs Eaton told me."

"I do not wish to know any more, thank you," said Elizabeth. "It was not necessary to inform me of any of this tittle-tattle and I would be very obliged to you if you would leave me now, Miss Bingley."

"Of course, Mrs Darcy, but I do reiterate: it was not my wish to upset you but merely to inform you. However, in light of my further considered opinion, I do think, dear friend, that perhaps it might be prudent not to mention this conversation to Mr Darcy himself. I would hate to be the cause of any distress to his good person. As I say, I am most regretful if I have caused you any suffering."

Elizabeth was not going to give Miss Bingley the satisfaction of knowing just how dreadful she felt at her report. She chose to stare steadily back at her foe with an expression of contempt, so it was Miss Bingley who chose to depart swiftly without another word. No, Lizzy was sure that Darcy would be mortified, not only that Miss Bingley had told her, but also that she knew about any of the circumstances. When Elizabeth recollected the letters in the library, she now almost certainly knew who had written them. It had all happened some years ago, she was certain, if Mrs Eaton had some knowledge about the affair. Perhaps Fitzwilliam and Viola had not been as discreet as they should; youthful love was inclined to be rash. Perhaps the theatricals had brought them together and maybe that was the reason Darcy could not face performing again, especially if subsequent performances had brought back painful memories of Viola. That the whole episode must be put out of her head was paramount, Lizzy decided. It had all taken place before she had met any of them and to dwell on such things might drive her mad. Caroline Bingley clearly had been unable to control her desire to provoke a rift in Elizabeth's relationship with her husband, but she had realised in divulging such information that she had taken a step too far. Of course Lizzy would say nothing to Fitzwilliam; what was in the past must stay there. And for now she had more pressing matters. Georgiana must be spoken to with tact and reason.

When Elizabeth explained to Georgiana how she was concerned that her behaviour might appear to be too particular, she was pleased to see that her young sister-in-law understood her worries.

"Oh, Lizzy, what have I done? I did not mean to confine myself to dancing with Mr Butler only, but he has been so kind to me and I did not want to disappoint him. I do love to dance with him and he makes me laugh."

"I do not think there is any real harm done, but perhaps it would be wise not to dance with him again this evening. People do love to gossip and I would hate to see you at the mercy of some of the less agreeable people here."

"Do you think I have distressed my brother by my behaviour? I would not upset Fitzwilliam for the world," Georgiana said, looking most anxious. "Oh, thank you, Lizzy, for advising me in such a lovely way. I will not dance with Mr Butler again. I am quite mortified to think that my behaviour might have caused you both pain. I hope Fitzwilliam is not cross with my friend."

"Of course not," lied Lizzy, thinking how overcome Georgiana would be if she really knew the truth. "Now, we will go back to the ballroom and you may dance the night away with all the other young men who are waiting to have their chance to dance with the most beautiful young lady at the ball tonight. This is your very first ball, and I'm sure you will not be found wanting a dancing companion."

Georgiana knew that the one thing that would please her brother would be to dance with Hugh Calladine. She kept her distance from Mr Butler, avoiding that part of the room where she knew he stood, and when Mr Calladine presented himself again with an offer to dance, she accepted willingly, making sure that Fitzwilliam was witness to some very enthusiastic dancing. Mr Calladine begged that she join his family party afterwards, and so despite her feelings of trepidation she submitted herself willingly into their circle. Nervous and shy amongst company she did not know well, her thoughts turned to Tom as they talked over the top of her. She hoped he would forgive her for ignoring him. Lost in reverie, Miss Darcy was brought back to the present by the shrill tones of Mr Calladine's mother asking her a question. Once Lady Calladine had finished interrogating her she almost sighed with relief. On looking about the room again searching for a glimpse of Tom, his cold expression told her all she needed to know as their eyes met. He turned away at the soonest opportunity and Georgiana felt grieved. Torn by duty to her family and her feelings for Tom, she nevertheless wished that she could rush over to him and attempt to bring back the smile to his lips.

Elizabeth and Darcy stood side by side at the edge of the ballroom watching the dancers. To the rest of the room Lizzy fancied that they looked as happy as everyone else. The ball was a success, she knew, but whilst she was most grateful for this fact, Mrs Darcy was desperately upset. She felt most disquieted, for all her efforts to set aside those thoughts that Caroline Bingley had inspired. Recognising the wisdom of speaking to Georgiana, she was pleased with the outcome, yet still she had witnessed a certain disappointment in the girl's eyes. Worst of all, there was a distance, a silent uneasiness between Elizabeth and Darcy which seemed to hang in the air above them. She could not think how to talk to him. That he was gravely disappointed in her she was absolutely convinced. All she could do for the present was watch the company, who in contrast were excited and happy. The country dances were starting next, beginning with an Irish reel.

"Do not you feel a great inclination, Mrs Darcy, to seize such an opportunity of dancing a reel?"

Elizabeth smiled but made no answer. Fitzwilliam repeated the question wondering if she would remember a conversation they had had long ago that he was sure would provoke a laugh on recollection. He wanted to make her smile, but his pride inhibited him still. He knew he was wrong to have been cross with Lizzy over Georgiana, but saying sorry was not easy.

"Oh!" said she, instantly remembering, "I heard you before, but I could not immediately determine what to say in reply. You wanted me, I know, to say 'Yes,' that you might have the pleasure of despising my taste; but I always delight in overthrowing those kind of schemes, and cheating a person of their premeditated contempt. I have, therefore, made up my mind to tell you that I do not want to dance a reel at all—and now despise me if you dare."

"Indeed, I do not dare. Mrs Darcy, I can only beg you to reconsider." He held out his hand and she took it gladly. "Please, will you dance a reel with me?"

"Nothing would give me greater pleasure," Elizabeth said with a smile and a toss of her curls as she allowed her dashing husband to lead her onto the floor.

There was a very late breakfast on the following day. Everyone was in good spirits and all arrived downstairs at once with the exception of Caroline Bingley, who was late and appeared to be in ill humour when she did make an appearance. Elizabeth made a point of saying good morning, giving her also the benefit of her widest smile and asking if she had slept well. Miss Bingley muttered something back that was hardly audible. She looked most shamefaced and took her seat, remaining unusually quiet.

"I think last night's ball was quite the best I have ever attended," said Jane generously. "Oh, Lizzy, you have so many affable neighbours, and everyone adores you and says how lovely it is to have a new mistress at Pemberley."

"To be sure, Lizzy is admired wherever she goes now she has such a handsome husband as Mr Darcy," observed Mrs Bennet. "Of course, looks are not his only endowment; no one has more friends than the rich, and how many friends you have, Mr Darcy. But if we are talking of looks, as I recollect I was at the start, in my opinion Miss Georgiana was the belle of the ball. You were never without a beau, were you, my dear? You were Mr Calladine's first choice and Mr Butler's first choice and I daresay every other young man's first choice if they could only have got near you. I thought it very amusing to see Mr Calladine and Mr Butler fighting for your affection. It quite put me in mind of dear Colonel Millar and Mr Bennet sparring for my attention in the old days. Well, you enjoy it, my dear. When you are no longer in the first flush of youth, you'll look back on these times with fondness."

Georgiana, who was sitting on the other side of the table, blushed scarlet at this outburst. Lizzy felt mortified and glancing over at her husband could see his dark eyes clouding under the black brows, his expression changing gradually from amused indifference through indignant contempt to a composed and steady gravity. Elizabeth noted that Caroline put her hand to her mouth and coughed loudly, her expression displaying a half-hearted attempt to disguise a snigger.

"I sincerely hope that you all enjoyed yourselves. I must say that everyone was so warm and friendly," Lizzy spoke up, determined to change the subject and wishing her mother would be silent. "All the old families who have always lived in these parts were particularly kind, saying that they were reminded of the good old days at Pemberley and all of them remarking how like his great father is Mr Darcy."

Mr Darcy's features softened a little and a smile played about his lips. "It was a splendid ball," he began, "to rival the greatest events of the past. I must thank my wife for the success of the evening; she has endeared herself to the people of the neighbouring villages, town, and county in a very short time and I am insufferably proud of her."

"Hear, hear," came the cheers from Mr Gardiner and Mr Bennet, jovially thumping on the table, with all the little Gardiners joining in and clapping loudly too.

Mrs Darcy glowed with pride. She looked across at Fitzwilliam with adoration. He had continued to make further amends after the ball and a night of such sweetness had followed that made Elizabeth wonder if vexing one another might be a pleasurable occupation that she would not mind repeating regularly if the outcome was always to be as blissful. Out of the corner of her eye she was aware that Miss Bingley was regarding her with a mixture of envy and dislike, however well her countenance was arranged in an expression of good humour. And there was a certain satisfaction in knowing that Miss Bingley had been a witness to Mr Darcy's praise.

A servant bringing in a large parcel with a note for Mrs Darcy was a welcome interruption, though as soon as Lizzy guessed what the package might hold she felt most grieved. It could only contain the book of plans that Mr Butler had produced. That he had not brought it himself would, she knew, be devastating to Georgiana. However biddable Miss Darcy had been in regards to partnering other suitors, Elizabeth knew how fond she was of Mr Butler. She glanced over at her sister-in-law and saw the disappointment in her eyes. It was not necessary for Elizabeth to say anything; Georgiana had already guessed what was held within the mysterious parcel. Lizzy's only hope was that the note accompanying it might contain a crumb of comfort for her sister.

"Oh, Lizzy, whatever is it?" cried Mrs Bennet. "Open it at once, girl, do not hesitate. How exciting, I wonder what it can be."

But Elizabeth was not to be drawn. "I am afraid that I cannot oblige you, madam," she said with a knowing smile at the gathered assembly. "It is a great secret which cannot yet be exposed. If you will excuse me, I promise that all will be revealed in time. Georgiana is the only person privy to the mystery, and so, my dear family, we will leave you for the present. Come, Georgiana, we have much to do."

"You quite delight in vexing me as much as your father, Mrs High and Mighty," professed Mrs Bennet as she watched Elizabeth and Georgiana heading for the door. "As if I should breathe a word. Everyone knows I am the very soul of discretion! And, I'd like to know, why does it have to be such a secret? To my mind, there's something very underhand about such clandestine operations."

"Lizzy, it is the book of Mr Butler's designs, is it not?" asked Georgiana as she watched Elizabeth undo the letter in the privacy of her comfortable sitting room. "What does he say? Why did he not bring it himself?"

"He was not able to come because he has had to go back to

London early this morning, to see about some new work," said Elizabeth, handing her the note. She was not looking forward to seeing Georgiana's reaction. Even though the letter was written for Lizzy, she knew Georgiana would be searching for any reference to herself and there was not one.

"He did not even come to say good-bye," said Georgiana in a small voice.

"Perhaps he did not have time to come. He is still making his way in the world, Georgiana, and he cannot afford to delay if he is needed, nor is he in a position to turn work away. I expect we'll see him again soon when he visits his mama."

"But he gave no hint yesterday that he was about to leave."

"I do not expect he knew himself; perhaps his patron summoned him urgently. I'm sure we will have the pleasure of his company soon enough. In any case, Georgiana, I know you are fond of him, but you are very young to be forming such a serious attachment. Time apart never did any harm where true hearts are concerned. Love and affection will be sustained if it is really lasting, and besides, one cannot live on love alone. If Tom is serious in his intentions he will want to secure his prospects and finances first before he considers taking a wife."

"But Elizabeth, I have money enough for both of us; there is no financial impediment to a match between us. I could marry any man I wish with my fortune."

"Tom is a proud young man, Georgiana. I am not sure he would wish to take such a step. I think he would want to provide for a wife and family himself."

Georgiana nodded. "Yes, you are right." She paused in contemplation of the matter. "There would be no other obstacles to a marriage between us, do you think, Elizabeth? Except that I know precisely why I am asking you that question. I do not think Fitzwilliam would really approve of such a match."

Elizabeth could not respond. Georgiana, she felt, already knew the answer to that question.

"No, it is quite hopeless," Georgiana said at last. "And I think Mr Butler realises the futility of our situation. That is why he has taken himself off to London. We cannot all expect to marry for love. Well, I daresay he will forget all about me in a day or two. Indeed, I wonder if I have not been mistaken about him in any case. How could he go away like that without saying good-bye if there were much affection in the case? I am fooling myself to think differently."

At a loss to know what to say for the best, Elizabeth could see that Georgiana was becoming most distressed. Instead of saying anything at all she joined her sister on the opposite sofa and put her arm round her in a comforting gesture. Georgiana's tears flowed as she sank against Lizzy, giving in to her emotions. "Georgiana, please do not be upset. Everything has a way of working out in the end. Life has a way of turning out in the most unexpected ways and sometimes even for the better."

"Oh, do not worry about me, Elizabeth, I am more trouble than I am worth. I shall get over Tom Butler; indeed, I have already put him out of my mind."

"Dear Georgiana, I do not believe a word of it, but I admire your spirit. That's the way. Now, let us think of something pleasurable we can look forward to doing together. Employment and diversion are what we need and something to get us through these gloomy winter days."

Georgiana dried her eyes. "I always find comfort in drawing, Lizzy. Perhaps we could do some sketches of one another."

Lizzy laughed. "Now, that is a novel idea! I'm prepared to try my hand, though I warn you, drawing was never considered to be a talent of mine. Sketching it shall be then. And talking of which, are you feeling strong enough to have a look at the designs yet?"

"I think I would prefer to delay that for the moment, Lizzy, if you do not mind. Not that I should be distressed to see them, but I do not care for them at present. I do not think I am very interested in Tom Butler's designs now. He could not be bothered to show me them himself and I do not care to see his efforts."

And rising swiftly to her feet, Georgiana immediately excused herself after planting an affectionate kiss upon Lizzy's cheek.

Before she had reached the door, however, she was checked by the appearance of one of the housemaids.

"Begging your pardon, ma'am," she said with a curtsey, "but the master asked if you and Miss Georgiana could come downstairs. Mr Calladine has called and he is most anxious to pay his respects to you."

Chapter 15

Mr Darcy and his guest were waiting for them in the drawing room. Mr Calladine did indeed pay his respects to the ladies and was gentleman-like and courteous. Georgiana sat on the sofa next to Lizzy in her usual state of nervous fear at the prospect of being spoken to by a comparative stranger and kept her eyes diverted. Elizabeth was happily engaged in the small talk she knew was necessary for such occasions and hoped that the call would not be of too long a duration. For all her brave words, she knew that Georgiana was most upset and she wished to spare her any unnecessary misery.

After an interval of five minutes, Mr Darcy stood up and, addressing his wife, requested that she accompany him. There was a small matter he wished to discuss with her if Mr Calladine would excuse them for a few moments.

Elizabeth was horrified. To leave Georgiana on her own was highly imprudent, she thought, and gave Mr Darcy the benefit of an expression of disapproval from those fine eyes he loved so much. But her husband appeared either not to notice or had decided to ignore the frown wrinkling between Lizzy's brows. He took Mrs Darcy's arm without further delay and escorted her from the room.

As soon as they were out of earshot Elizabeth protested. "Fitzwilliam, what do you think you are doing? Georgiana will be terrified. How could you leave her on her own like that with a gentleman she hardly knows?"

"She'll know him soon enough, Mrs Darcy," he said, leading her down the corridor and into the library. He closed the door firmly before adding, "Everything has been arranged most satisfactorily."

Something in his tone of voice made Lizzy most apprehensive. She could not for a moment find her tongue to speak.

"I had expected Mr Calladine to call this morning after he requested to see me last night," he continued. "We have been discussing Georgiana's future and also that of his own. He made an offer that anyone would be a fool to turn down. Hugh Calladine will be bringing a fortune of considerable size to add to that of my sister's, an alliance which shall make her the richest woman in the county, if not all England."

Elizabeth was stunned into silence.

"He has come to make his intentions clear to Georgiana. I am sure they will both be happy in time. He is a gentleman, Elizabeth, a very respectable, straightforward sort, who on first addressing me was most keen to advise me that all past relations with a certain young woman he has been associated with are at an end and have been for some time. He is very taken with Georgiana and believes himself in love."

As this speech came to its shattering conclusion Lizzy felt unable to control her emotions any longer. "And did you once consider Georgiana's feelings in all this talk of finance and matrimony?" she asked, trying to remain calm. "He may fancy himself in love, though I doubt for one moment he is in love with Georgiana. He is exactly the sort of man who is only interested in increasing his own fortune and though he might profess his heartfelt affection now, I am certain it will diminish as rapidly as it has grown once they are married. She is young, Fitzwilliam. Nothing need be settled now. Let her find her own way with a gentleman who can really love her. Hugh Calladine is not the only young man with an inheritance. Why the hurry?"

"With respect, Elizabeth, I think I know my sister's needs better than you do. Remember, she is a vulnerable girl, easily persuaded into fancying herself in love, and I will not let her ruin her life. George Wickham was a lesson for us all. The quicker she is wed, the better it will be. For her own protection against the likes of fortune hunters like Thomas Butler, my sister and her legacy must be safeguarded. Georgiana will marry Hugh Calladine and that is the end of the matter."

Elizabeth stared at Mr Darcy in disbelief. Not for the first time in the last few days did she stare at the man she had married to consider how little she really knew him. She had been so sure of his character in Hertfordshire and now, for the moment, she could not reconcile any of her former beliefs. Looking at him, his countenance flushed from his passionate speech, his face solemn and sober, she realised it was useless to debate the matter. Without further ado, she excused herself, determining not to leave Georgiana longer than was necessary. The poor girl would be overwrought, she was sure.

As she hurried along the corridor Elizabeth could see that the drawing room door was shut tight which gave her such feelings of unease that she did not dare dwell on the thoughts that immediately sprang to her mind. Lizzy's heart was hammering as she approached and all she could think was how she had let Georgiana down. Taking a deep breath, she gave a warning knock before turning the handle. On opening the door she perceived her sister and Mr Calladine standing closely together over the hearth, as if engaged in earnest conversation. As soon as she saw them, she knew it was too late.

"Oh, Lizzy," cried Georgiana, who could not hide her expression of startled confusion. "Mr Calladine has proposed. He has asked me to marry him."

The shock of hearing such a statement took Elizabeth by surprise. She needed all her wits to think how she must react. Turning to Mr Calladine she ignored the outstretched hand proffered in her direction saying, "Mr Darcy would like to speak to you in the library this instant, Mr Calladine."

"Yes, of course, Mrs Darcy, I am certain he is most anxious to discover the outcome of my declaration to Miss Darcy in light of the interview we had this morning." He bowed toward Georgiana. "You have made me a very happy man, Miss Darcy. Do excuse me, ladies."

As soon as he had left the room Elizabeth questioned Georgiana in earnest. She observed her nervousness, the agitation in her manner. "What did you answer, Georgiana? Please tell me that you refused him."

Georgiana's eyes were very bright with tears. She bit her lip and did not immediately answer. Elizabeth watched her swallow hard before she spoke in agitation. "I accepted him, Lizzy. I could not refuse him; he had already spoken to Fitzwilliam and everything was decided between them. We are engaged."

"Engaged! No, that is impossible."

Georgiana nodded her head and repeated that it was indeed true.

"Oh, my dear," cried Elizabeth, falling into a chair, "you did not have to say yes, whatever he implied."

Georgiana took the seat next to hers, talking non-stop. "But he was so persuasive, and everything he said seemed to make perfect sense. I made him very happy when I said yes, and I know that my brother has wished for this engagement for some time."

"Georgiana, think before you say any more. You do not wish for this engagement yourself. Listen, it is not too late. Come, we will go to Fitzwilliam and tell him that you have changed your mind, that you cannot go through with it. We'll tell him that you were rushed into making a decision too soon and that you need more time before making a commitment. When he sees how upset you are he will realise his mistake. I know he desires you to be happy above all things; he could not bear to see you in tears like this."

"No, Lizzy, it is no use," whispered Georgiana, brushing away her tears with the back of her hand. "Not only did I disgrace him at the ball last night by my behaviour, but I have disappointed my brother too many times in the past. At last I have a chance to please him and to do the duty expected of me. I know it is what my parents would have wished also, and I must reconcile myself to the fact that I will be married to Hugh Calladine. It is time I grew up and recognised that real life is not a fairy tale. It is useless to dwell on what I know will never come to fruition. Mr Butler will marry elsewhere; I will learn to forget him and marry the man that has been chosen for me. I trust my brother's judgement implicitly; he has always had my best interests at heart. My parents learned to love one another; in my turn, I will learn to love Mr Calladine."

"I think you may regret your resolution, Georgiana. Your life will be changed forever because of a decision hastily and rashly made. You know this cannot be a sound basis for such an important commitment."

Georgiana rose to her feet, and Lizzy witnessed a look of determination in her countenance, a look that Elizabeth could only describe as displaying the Darcy spirit.

"Thank you, Elizabeth, I know you are trying to help me, but the truth is you cannot. My mind is made up, I shall marry, and as far as I am concerned, the sooner, the better. I will not be the first young woman to enter into such a contract and I am certain that my chance of happiness with Mr Calladine will be as good as most people can expect."

Between Elizabeth and Georgiana there followed a restraint which kept them mutually silent on the subject of the engagement over the next few days; the former confidence they had shared seemed to have entirely evaporated. Elizabeth's disappointment in both her husband's attitude and that of Miss Darcy, neither of whom were prepared to listen to her point of view, made her turn to her father who did his best to listen to her concerns. Mr Bennet did not dare oppose his daughter, but he did suggest on more than one occasion that he felt ill-qualified to sit in judgement on the methods and modes of the Darcy alliances. What was good for the gander was not necessarily good for the goose, but he was convinced that Mr Darcy had his sister's best interests at heart. It was a long time before

Elizabeth became at all reconciled to the idea of so unsuitable a match. The strangeness of accepting an offer of marriage in such extreme haste with little reflection on the outcome was in total antipathy to Lizzy's own thinking. Coupled with the insistence of her husband to such a marriage, it called into question everything she thought she had formerly believed about his whole philosophy. She had always felt that Fitzwilliam's opinion of matrimony was not exactly like her own, but she could not have supposed it possible that, when called into acting for his sister, he would have sacrificed every better feeling to her worldly advantage. Elizabeth was distressed by the conviction that it was impossible for Georgiana to be tolerably happy in the lot she had chosen and confounded by the fact that her husband was so little known to her. That everyone else appeared to be overjoyed by Georgiana's news was clear and made Lizzy feel more frustrated than ever. She could not help but wonder what Mr Butler himself might think when he received word, which he undoubtedly would before much more time passed.

A fortnight elapsed during which Elizabeth fought by every process to quell her feelings and find a peaceful equilibrium, but to no avail. However, one letter giving information of expected joy arrived from Charlotte Collins to give Elizabeth some feelings of delight for her friend. Mrs Collins had given birth to a baby girl to be called Catherine named in honour of Mr Darcy's aunt, the Collins's esteemed patroness. Both mother and baby were doing well, which raised a smile to Elizabeth's lips and gladdened her spirits. But when more surprising news arrived later that morning from a most unexpected quarter, her initial feelings were of abject disconsolation.

"I have received a letter from my aunt, Lady Catherine,"

said Mr Darcy, as he donned his riding jacket and turned to glance at his reflection through the long cheval mirror in the bedchamber. "I think you should read it. I would like to know your opinion and thoughts, Elizabeth," he said, with a gesture towards the parchment missive which was lying unfolded upon the washstand shelf.

Mrs Darcy looked over at her husband. He looked very fine in his dark green coat, cut to show off his manly figure to perfection. With his dark curls falling over his collar above broad shoulders, he looked the very epitome of a handsome hero. As he caught her staring, he swung round and his brooding eyes met hers. She could not look at him without her heart leaping, but Elizabeth averted her eyes as quickly as his engaged hers. He had that expression again, that look of disappointment that she had witnessed ever since they had quarrelled over Georgiana. She had finally accepted the engagement and the inevitable wedding but still showed him her disapproval from time to time and made her feelings clear. They were still conversing on a superficial level, and while anyone else would not have known that anything was amiss, Elizabeth was quite aware that things were not quite right between them. There was reserve and detachment like the cold wind blowing across the hills out on the peaks, which she felt not only during the day, in their solitary moments together, but also at night. For the first time since they were married Fitzwilliam was choosing to stay up until the small hours and did not retire to the bedchamber when she did. Elizabeth lay down in a cold bed; she lay in the dark waiting for the sound of the door handle and the familiar, warm and spicy fragrance of Fitzwilliam's cologne. Roused from sleep when he did make an appearance, he made little attempt to be close to her and on waking, he arose immediately, washing and shaving in his dressing room attended by his valet. Lizzy was uncertain what she should do to change the situation. Although she longed for the world to feel right again, she knew that they were both as stubborn as the other and that each in their turn felt they were right about Georgiana. Dismissing these thoughts and glad that at least Fitzwilliam wanted to share his letter with her, she walked over to the washstand with a heavy heart and picked up the sheet of hot-pressed paper. Sitting down and making herself comfortable on the edge of the bed, she started to read, ever aware that Fitzwilliam was watching her. His eyes felt like glowing torches burning into her mind, and she knew that she blushed under his scrutiny.

Harrogate, January 17, 1803
Dear Fitzwilliam,

I am writing to congratulate you on the news received this last week of the engagement of dear Georgiana to Mr Calladine of Bridestones Hall. That such a propitious union has been contracted on your sister's behalf shows a measure of sense and wisdom I had begun to think you had lost forever. At least one Darcy is to make a prudent marriage, and I know if your mother and father were alive they would join me in considering the alliance to be a very worthy connection. The Calladines are blessed with Darcy blood in their ancestry and are in many respects descended from the same noble lines, those of respectable, honourable, and ancient families. Their combined fortune will be splendid—Georgiana will one day achieve her title and become the lady her mother wished she should be. What a pity my dear sister will not be here to witness it, but then if she were, she would have had to bear the disappointments of other, less desirable associations.

But I will say no more on that matter except to say that reports received pertaining to recent seasonal celebrations at Pemberley House are less alarming than I would ever have warranted and I find I am much relieved to hear that your wife, at least, conducts herself in a manner befitting her new station.

Send my affectionate love to Georgiana,
I remain most faithfully,
Your aunt, Lady Catherine de Bourgh

Elizabeth sighed. "Praise, indeed," she said with a grimace. "At least I have not been completely vilified in this letter."

"Did you see the postscript, on the other side?" asked Fitzwilliam, standing before her.

Elizabeth turned over the letter.

I am at present staying with our cousins the Granvilles in Harrogate and on my return to Rosings shall break my journey at Pemberley on Tuesday, February 8th, for one night only. I trust you will be able to accommodate me.

Elizabeth raised her head to see Fitzwilliam towering above her. His eyes were still regarding her closely; he was studying her form with such intimate intent that her heart quickened.

"I know I ask too much, but I hope you will help me receive

my aunt at Pemberley," he said, sitting down on the bed beside her. "I cannot do it without you, Elizabeth." He faltered. Lizzy knew he was trying to find the right words and she patiently waited to hear him out. "I know you do not understand or approve of my actions concerning Georgiana's engagement. It is settled, however, and I hope in time that you will see everything come right in the end, and understand that I did the correct thing by my sister. I would like your blessing even if we do not agree on everything. I so dislike being at odds with you. I'm sorry, Elizabeth, I know I should have discussed the matter with you. But I think my reticence to do so was because I knew we might disagree. I do not think you have changed your views, yet I hope you can see that I only have my sister's future happiness and comfort in mind."

Elizabeth had thought long and hard on the subject of Georgiana's engagement. She did not agree with alliances based on fortune alone, and the idea of a marriage without affection was one she knew she could not have borne herself. Yet she also knew that an engagement of this kind for Georgiana was expected in the society she now moved in. Fitzwilliam truly believed that he was doing the best for his sister; she saw that his motives and his heart were pure. "I know that you wish for the best for Georgiana, Fitzwilliam, even if I do not completely agree with your methods of attainment."

"Will you forgive me?"

"I forgive you, of course I do. And do not worry; I will be the perfect hostess to Lady Catherine. Everything will be fine," she heard herself say, as she entwined her fingers with his, simultaneously admiring their clasped hands held together so tightly. "I am not alarmed by the thought of a visit from a cross old woman who is only coming to satisfy her curiosity. Do not worry, Fitzwilliam," she said, as he took her hand and kissed it before enfolding her in his arms. "You know very well that there is a stubbornness about me that never can bear to be frightened at the will of others. My courage always rises with every attempt to intimidate me."

Mr Darcy's lips sought hers; sweet and passionate were the kisses he'd denied himself for too long. Elizabeth no longer had any command over those feelings which had kept them apart as she gave herself up willingly to his caresses.

"Then I hope to witness that boldness for myself," he whispered into her ear, "as I have every intention of intimidating you, right here and now, with a little coercion of my own."

"Oh, Mr Darcy," Lizzy replied, returning a kiss on his cheek, "indeed, sir, you do not alarm me, but I confess, in the circumstances, I would be most obliged to you for your intended duress."

Chapter 16

THE BEGINNING OF FEBRUARY heralded not only the imminent arrival of Lady Catherine de Bourgh but also the departure of Elizabeth's relations. She was sorry to see the Gardiners leave, particularly her aunt whose wise counsel had given Lizzy much food for thought. Mrs Bennet talked of postponing their leave-taking and extending their visit, but to Lizzy's relief they left all the same. She was not sorry when the day came to say good-bye; it had been a busy, eventful, and pleasant few weeks, but Elizabeth craved some quiet days, exempt from the thoughts and contrivances which any sort of company gives. To be alone with her husband, or at least, as far as they might be permitted to be alone in a house filled with people, was her greatest desire. There was one person she was very sorry to see dressed in her travelling clothes, but for the moment she still had the delight of her sister Jane's company for another hour or two. It had not been easy to confide in her whilst the house had been so occupied and now the others were gone, Elizabeth took the opportunity of discussing Georgiana's engagement.

They sat in Elizabeth's sitting room, cosy from the winter day outside, partaking of a last cup of tea together. The scene through the window upon which her eyes rested showed a landscape glittering with frost in the sunlight, the hills reflecting shades as blue as the duck egg sky. Elizabeth did not know quite how to broach the thoughts innermost in her mind, but that she needed to confide in Jane for her own peace of mind was paramount.

"Tell me, Jane, what did you honestly think when Georgiana's engagement was announced?"

Jane put down her teabowl and ventured, "I have never been so shocked in my life before, except perhaps when you divulged that you were going to marry Mr Darcy."

Elizabeth could not help but smile. "No, seriously, you were surprised, I am sure, as I was myself, especially knowing Georgiana's feelings for Mr Butler."

"What I meant to say was not that I was surprised about the engagement itself, rather in the unexpected way it came about. I suppose she will go through with it?"

"Not a doubt of it, she will not upset Fitzwilliam. Yet it cannot be the right course, can it? I do not think she can conceive of the years she will spend in unhappiness. Surely nothing can be compared to the misery of being bound without love, bound to one and preferring another. Georgiana does not deserve such a sentence, and all the money in the world will not change her situation. But equally dreadful, Jane, and I hardly know how to tell you, is the realisation that Fitzwilliam can allow, even insist, that she be married to such a man. I would not say this to another soul except you, but I feel this event proves that his pride is as great as it ever was and though I have tried to bury my feelings and attempted to understand his point of view, I find I cannot. Tom Butler is not considered to be good enough for Miss Georgiana, in exactly the same way as Mr Darcy first considered me to be inferior. Do you remember? He told me once that he could not bear the thought of my lowly connections, relations whose condition in life was so decidedly beneath his own. I have tried to reconcile my feelings for the sake of my marriage, I have told Fitzwilliam that the alliance has my blessing, but I still feel so at odds. Georgiana does not fool me; she is not happy. Oh, Jane, I love Darcy, or at least I thought I loved the man I married, but this is causing a rift between us, which I do not think will easily be healed. We go on as if nothing has happened, whilst underneath the tensions are still the same. Why will he not allow Georgiana what he has done himself? I'll tell you why, because he regrets his marriage to me. I don't doubt that he loves me in some ways, but he will always consider that he married beneath him."

"Lizzy, you know that is not true. It is clear for all to see how much your husband adores and reveres you. Whatever he might have said in the past he has wholly refuted in his actions. His behaviour to us all, to the whole family has been exemplary; you cannot accuse him of prejudice against us now. In any case, Georgiana has been brought up differently, with an expectation of marriage to unite alliance and fortune; you know that. We did not have a similar prospect; indeed, we had few prospects. I am sure you are more upset by this engagement than she appears to be."

"I sincerely hope you are right, my dearest sister. You always were the voice of sweet reason."

"I think you must trust Mr Darcy in this case," added Jane, "or else risk the happiness of your own marriage. Pride and prejudice may be faults indeed but are not confined to your husband alone. Perhaps you should give Mr Calladine a chance to prove himself; he may win Georgiana over in the end. He is a gentleman, after all, and Georgiana might find lasting happiness with a man who is not only wealthy but also completely accepted in her circle. If Charlotte Collins has managed it, I'm sure Georgiana can."

"But her case was entirely different, Jane. There was no prior attachment."

"No, you are right, Lizzy. I know I could never have considered such a marriage for myself especially after meeting Charles." Jane paused to regard her sister, her head on one side as she searched the beloved countenance she knew so well. "But I think more than Georgiana's predicament upsets you. Perhaps the idea of Lady Catherine's coming here is making you more anxious than you realise."

"I daresay the thought of Darcy's aunt is at the root of some of my troubles, and not least, I shall be so sorry to say good-bye to you. How can you think of leaving me to a tongue lashing from Lady Catherine de Bourgh?"

Jane got up from her seat to hug her sister for the last time. "I could not if I had the least worry that you would be incapable of holding your own. I recall your retort as you reported it to me on the occasion of your last interview with that lady: 'I do not pretend to possess equal frankness with your ladyship. You may ask questions which I shall not choose to answer.' Lady Catherine knows when she has met her match, I am certain. I don't doubt you will manage very well!"

Elizabeth was more worried about the impending visit from Mr Darcy's aunt than she was prepared to let on, but was determined not to dwell on any misgivings she might have. There was quite enough to deal with simply organizing such details as food and menus, and which bedchamber Lady Catherine was to occupy, without being anxious about any conversation they might share. At least Miss de Bourgh, Lady Catherine's daughter, would not be accompanying her. Apparently, Anne was staying behind with her companion Mrs Jenkinson in the hope that the change of air and spa water would do her some good. Sickly, pale, and cross, the spoiled cousin of Mr Darcy had never enjoyed good health, and Elizabeth knew that no expense would be spared in the efforts to revive the spirits of this despondent creature, though she considered it unlikely that any amount of money or treatments would make a jot of difference. Privately, Elizabeth felt quite sorry for the girl who had never been allowed to live a normal life. In her opinion Anne had not only been spoiled, but had also been fussed over and mollycoddled to the point of suffocation. No wonder the girl was awkward in company and socially inept—she was never allowed to speak and would not dare oppose her mother's beliefs or statements on any topic. Besides all this, Lady Catherine's hopes for an alliance between her daughter and Mr Darcy had been thwarted, and as such, Lizzy was sure that Anne would avoid coming to Pemberley altogether if she possibly could. At least Lady Catherine was not due for another week; Lizzy would have time to prepare fully.

Elizabeth's own spirits were subdued. The Christmas celebrations and Georgiana's engagement, not to mention the awkwardness that subsisted between Lizzy and Darcy as a result, had all taken its toll. Mrs Darcy was feeling tired and lacking in carriage or dressed in her best pelisse it might have been a different matter. It was lovely to be anonymous for a change and the sense of freedom that she felt such as she had enjoyed in the old days almost overwhelmed her. Chiding herself for being silly and sentimental, she continued over the bridge and turned into the lane leading to the High Street. It had been her intention to turn round and walk straight back to Pemberley, but now she was here she was struck by the idea of calling on Mrs Butler. That she could send news to her Aunt Gardiner about her friend seemed a wonderful idea.

Mrs Butler was surprised but exceedingly welcoming at the sight of her visitor. Lizzy was made to sit next to the fire, where Mrs Butler soon had the kettle on a trivet over the burning logs until it sang, hissing with steam. Her best china was produced and a cup of fragrant tea placed before Elizabeth on the small Pembroke table at the side of the sofa.

"My dear, you must be perished with the cold coming such a long way on foot," said Mrs Butler.

"I love to go walking and as the sun did keep peering out from under the rain clouds I thought I would make the best of it. I do not feel the cold and walking always warms me up." Elizabeth sipped her tea. She was very curious to ask after Tom, but she was reluctant to start up any conversation regarding that gentleman. Whether Mrs Butler knew about Georgiana's engagement or not she had little idea. There was a possibility that her aunt had informed Mrs Butler of it and news travelled fast in the countryside, but she could not be sure, nor of how much the lady knew of what had formerly happened between Tom and Georgiana.

Mrs Butler was the first to speak. "I must offer my

congratulations on Miss Darcy's engagement, Mrs Darcy. You must be very pleased."

"Thank you, Mrs Butler. I shall pass on your good wishes to Miss Georgiana." Elizabeth made no further comment. Even with a desire to make polite conversation she could not profess to be pleased. She picked up her teacup, once more contemplating how she might ask after Mr Butler to find out why he had left so quickly after the ball.

"Have you any news of young Thomas?" asked Elizabeth tentatively, unable to resist asking for information. "We were disappointed not to see him before he left for London."

She need not have worried. There was no awkwardness in discussing Tom's activities. Mrs Butler declared that his patron, Lord Featherstone, had use of him again and he would be in Richmond and London for the foreseeable future. Indeed, he was so busy that she was not sure of seeing him for some time. Still, his mother was pleased that he was needed and being introduced to many important people who had expressed great interest in his methods of landscape gardening with a view to having their own gardens improved upon.

"I am not in the least surprised," said Lizzy. "Tom is a very talented young man. I am so pleased with the designs he did for me. As soon as the weather improves, work will start on the upper slopes. It is a surprise for Mr Darcy and I can't wait for him to see it."

"Tom will be so pleased to hear you are happy with everything. He left in such a hurry, only arranging at the last minute to send the book over. I did think he would come and present it to you himself at Pemberley, but I'm afraid he insisted that there was not a moment to lose. I do hope you understood, Mrs Darcy.

Tom does not mean to be rude, but he has a habit of flying about the country and setting off in a moment."

"Of course. It is a habit of many young men, I think. Mr Darcy's particular friend Mr Bingley is rather like that in his practices."

"That reminds me, Mrs Darcy. Please do apologise to your husband for not stopping to speak to him the other day in Birchlow. I had been visiting a friend when I saw him and it was only when he had passed by me on the opposite side that I realised who he was, and by then he had disappeared. I cannot think why I did not recognise him straight away, but you know what it is like on these dark winter afternoons when gentlemen are swathed in greatcoats and hats. I'm sure he didn't see me, in any case, but if you would mention it, all the same. I would not like him to think I was discourteous."

"I'm sure he would think nothing of the sort, Mrs Butler. When was this, did you say?"

"Hmm, let me think. It must have been last Friday, market day. Yes, that's it. I remember now, and perhaps the reason for not recognising Mr Darcy straight away was because he was dressed in country fashion, as if he had been to market himself. I didn't recognise the young gentleman he was accompanying, a fine tall boy. They seemed to be in a hurry, so it's just as well he didn't see me; he didn't look as if he had a moment to lose."

"He didn't mention going to Birchlow, but I'll certainly pass on your felicitations. I know he does attend market occasionally with his steward, especially if there are horses to be bought."

Elizabeth was puzzled. Fitzwilliam told her most of his activities, but she couldn't remember this outing or that he had mentioned calling on the Tissingtons. Lizzy was certain it must have been George Tissington that Mrs Butler had described. She put down her teacup. All of a sudden she felt very weary. Sitting by the warm fire was making her feel very drowsy. Despite her efforts, her eyelids flickered shut momentarily.

"Forgive me, Mrs Darcy, I think you are feeling tired. I hope you will not mind my saying this, but you are very pale. Are you feeling quite well?"

All of a sudden Lizzy felt as if she had become a leaden weight; her limbs felt heavy and aching and the tiredness was so consuming that she felt sleep steal over her like a dose of laudanum. She was feeling rather strange again, and a wave of nausea washed over her so strongly that she thought she might faint.

"Oh, Mrs Butler, I am so sorry, you must think me so rude coming here unannounced and then falling asleep the moment I sit down. I do not know what the matter is with me, but I admit I have not really been feeling quite myself these past few days. I thought air and exercise would do me good, but I admit I do not feel very strong. What would you advise, Mrs Butler, for the sickness I seem to be suffering of late? I can hardly eat and it is so unlike me to lose my appetite."

Elizabeth looked up to see Mrs Butler smiling at her. "Oh, my dear, I do not think you should worry unduly about your sickness; it is an excellent sign in cases such as these. Forgive my impertinence, but I think you must take good care of yourself in your situation."

Elizabeth met Mrs Butler's eyes, which twinkled with merriment.

"Oh, my dear Mrs Darcy, do forgive me, but with your welfare in mind, your aunt asked me if I would keep an eye on you just before she left. As your aunt and your mother are so far away, I hope I may be of some use to you. That is, of course, if you should wish it."

With a dawning realisation at her insinuation Lizzy blushed as she caught the sense of Mrs Butler's speech. Could it possibly be true? She looked over at the kind lady beaming on the opposite side and remembered what her aunt had said about Martha, her oldest and most trusted friend. To have someone to confide in, someone who knew exactly how she was feeling would be wonderful, if what Mrs Butler was implying was really a possibility.

Elizabeth tried to find the words. "Do you mean? Are you suggesting…? Oh, my goodness!" cried Lizzy, in amazement as the reality of her situation started to sink in. "Mrs Butler, I can think of no one else I would rather turn to for advice than your good self. If what you say is true I know your advice will be invaluable, thank you."

"You must arrange to see a physician as soon as possible. And rest assured, Mrs Darcy, this conversation is private and strictly confidential. Do not worry; I should never repeat anything you have to tell me. Now, whilst the idea of this splendid news is sinking in, I shall leave you for a moment. I have a seed cake in the pantry, which I will fetch just now. A slice and a fresh cup of tea will do you good and help you get your strength back. And when I return we will consider how best to get you home."

Elizabeth fairly hugged herself with excitement, but until she had more proof or seen the physician, she was not quite sure she could believe it. Besides, it was early days and she knew that she would have to wait a little longer before confiding in anyone else, even Fitzwilliam. To have his hopes raised before everything was certain would be disastrous if it turned out she was mistaken, or worse, if something went wrong. "A baby, perhaps an heir to Pemberley," she thought. "Am I really having Mr Darcy's baby? Is it possible that I am going to be a mother?" The very idea was enough to make her want to burst with pride, and how she would keep her secret she could not contemplate.

Mrs Butler returned bearing the promised cake, which was cut into slices and elegantly arranged on a colourful Newhall plate. Surprisingly, Elizabeth thought that, considering how nauseous she had felt earlier, she now felt absolutely ravenous and devoured the cake with ease. Mrs Butler urged her to take another piece, adding that it would help her to regain her strength for the journey home. "Not that I shall be allowing you to walk home, Mrs Darcy. If you have no objection you can have a ride in my donkey carriage."

"I do not want to put you to any trouble, Mrs Butler, but the idea of your donkey carriage is a lovely one. Thank you so much, I do not think I could manage the walk home at present."

So it was settled. Mrs Butler's manservant Nicholls would drive her home.

"Well now, Mrs Darcy, if it's not too impertinent of me, I'd like to suggest that we get you home before it gets dark and they send out a search party for you. Remember, if you need me for anything at all, just ask; I am always here. And when you next write to your aunt, if you can include amongst all your exciting news that you have seen me, I would be most grateful. She will understand. Take care of yourself, my dear, and keep your walking to a gentle stroll around the garden for the present."

"I will, Mrs Butler. Thank you so much for a lovely after-noon and for all your kindly advice."

The little carriage soon stopped outside the gate, and after

Mrs Butler had shown Lizzy in and wrapped her up in blankets and shawls, they set off at a gentle pace. It was rather lovely to be out clopping along at a donkey's pace in an open carriage, the air fresh in her face. As Lizzy contemplated the excitement of all that had passed during the afternoon's conversation, she could not help but dwell on what Mrs Butler had said about seeing Mr Darcy in Birchlow. That he had been seen accompanied by a young man was rather strange; his steward could hardly be considered to be fitting the description, and that he had not mentioned the trip made it all the more puzzling. Birchlow, she knew, was home to the Tissington family. Master Tissington was a fine, tall boy. But what was Mr Darcy doing with the boy? She supposed he must have called on the family; after all, the boy's mother had been a servant of the Darcy family. She would ask him about it when she got home. For now, she could think of little but the reasons for her tiredness and of how thrilled she was at the idea. The little cart picked up pace as they turned over the bridge, and Elizabeth delighted in all she saw of Lambton village around her. Lamps were being lit and she could see into the windows of some of the cottages, into cosy kitchens where mothers with babies on their shoulders nursed them to sleep. Elizabeth fell into a delightful reverie imagining how it might be to nurse her own babe, when just as they were approaching the crossroads, another carriage coming along in the opposite direction was travelling with such fearsome speed that it seemed a collision was inevitable. Nicholls pulled on the reins, ensuring that his docile donkey halted, but nothing was going to stop the other carriage, which appeared not even to notice the little donkey cart until it was almost too late. Watching with increasing alarm Elizabeth saw the other carriage swerve within a hair's

Chapter 17

LADY CATHERINE DE BOURGH looked Mrs Darcy up and down with such an expression of horror and contempt it was all Lizzy could do to keep her nerve. "Does your husband know that you are running around the countryside dressed as a gypsy riding in a donkey cart, Miss Bennet?" she asked in scolding tones. "What on earth can you mean by disgracing Mr Darcy in such a fashion? Have you no idea of decorum, are you insensible to the honours bestowed on you by him, that fool of a nephew of mine who has singled you out above all other women to bear his name?"

"A name, ma'am, which you clearly have trouble in remembering," thought Elizabeth, feeling indignant not only at the rude manner in which she had been spoken to, but also at the fact that she had not been addressed by her new title: Mrs Darcy. In any case, what was Lady Catherine doing here? She was not expected for another week. And now the worst possible beginning that she could imagine for any new understanding between them had just taken place, in the mere twinkling of an eye. It was not her fault, but she had been rather outspoken, goaded by Lady Catherine's offensive and discourteous behaviour. Conscious that she might undo any reconciliation and the chance of true appeasement between this offensive woman and Mr Darcy, Elizabeth swiftly came to the conclusion that it might be best to take a superior position and try her utmost to smooth over the situation.

"Lady Catherine, I must admit that I was not expecting you until next week, but I do hope you are on your way to Pemberley. Mr Darcy is so looking forward to your visit."

"Is he indeed, Mrs Darcy?" came the reply, short and succinct.

"You must be very tired after your journey, Lady Catherine, and after the shock of the accident I think you need the comfort of a good fire and plenty of sweet tea. I will not keep you talking any longer. Let me assist you to your carriage."

"I thank you, Mrs Darcy, but I only take my own particular blend of tea, and I could not bear to have its delicate balance of flavours corrupted by cloying sugar. I am tired of travelling and unable to tell you if I shall put up at Pemberley at all, though if you insist, I might sit by a fire in the hall for a half hour. Harrogate has no charms left; I am entirely fatigued by the North Country and its odious people, and I am in no humour to waste any more of my time in the company of those who pretend to court me. I suppose you would like to take the rest of your journey in my carriage? Well, what are you waiting for? Only remove those hideous shawls before stepping up; I cannot be seen conversing with someone dressed as a washerwoman."

Through gritted teeth Elizabeth did as she was bid, taking care to make sure that the garrulous woman was settled before she took her seat. For one who professed to be tired Lady Catherine did not cease talking all the way to Pemberley, and Elizabeth had quite a headache by the time she was home. With so many impertinent questions to answer she had to be on her mettle. All her tiredness disappeared for the moment; she was determined not to say or do anything that might reflect badly against her husband and for that she had to be wide-awake.

What a commotion ensued on their arrival. Elizabeth could tell that poor Mrs Reynolds, though as accommodating as ever, was quite upset that she was not prepared for Lady Catherine's arrival. Maids and servants flew about them removing luggage and bandboxes. As they entered the hall Mrs Reynolds took Elizabeth to one side. "Begging your pardon, ma'am, but I think you should know that the master has been in a bit of a lather since you left this afternoon. He's had all the footmen out looking for you on the peaks. I did tell him that you like to go off on your own sometimes, but he wouldn't listen. Don't judge him too badly if he seems a little fractious, but he's been that worried, I can't tell you."

Elizabeth fumed inwardly. She had not been gone for long. Why must she tell the entire household if she wanted to go for a walk? Mr Darcy's reaction seemed entirely ridiculous if what Mrs Reynolds said was true.

Lady Catherine was refusing to leave the hall. She had set up by the fire insisting that she would be gone again in a quarter of an hour. "I am not stopping," she said. "I shall rest for a moment before heading home to Rosings. At my time of life, too many demands placed upon one's time are positively injurious to the health; though I must add that there is not another traveller in the whole of England as stalwart as myself, and those half my age would agree there is no one they know with more stamina. And that is precisely the problem with Lady Cathcart's circle in Harrogate; they could do with taking a leaf or two out of my book. It seems to me a very stupid sort of person who does not appreciate good advice when it is being offered to them. It's small wonder that she suffers so dreadfully with every ache and pain known to man when she refuses to try my frugal diet of vegetables and poached fish, highly recommended to me by the Earl of Southampton. If she followed my strict regime, all her digestion troubles would be entirely eliminated. And as for the perils of crow's foot she has entrenched upon her countenance, I truly despair. If she had taken the recommendation I offered her last winter of a daily application of Gowland's lotion, she would look half her age. Well, if people don't know what's good for them, I don't know what I am to do about it."

Mr Darcy could not come soon enough, thought Elizabeth, though as she took in his stern expression as she met him by the door, she could see that he was not best pleased. "I cannot begin to tell you of the upset you have caused this afternoon, Mrs Darcy," he began. "Why on earth did you not inform someone of where you were going?"

Elizabeth opened her mouth to speak, but Mr Darcy interrupted, saying, "I have no time to discuss this now, I must see to my aunt."

He swept past without another glance at Lizzy, rushing over to the cantankerous lady who was eyeing them both with great suspicion. Lady Catherine extended her bejewelled hand as Fitzwilliam approached, greeting her warmly and bending his head to place a kiss.

"I would like to say what a pleasure it is to be at Pemberley again, Fitzwilliam, but I have endured such a day that nothing could afford me any pleasure. The singular activities enjoyed by your wife have very nearly brought me to grief this afternoon. I cannot think why a donkey cart would be a preferable convey- ance to that of a Darcy coach ornamented with the family crest, but I daresay it has something to do with her old habits."

Elizabeth wished the ground to open up. Mr Darcy was looking at her with an expression so severe she thought for an instant that she might burst into tears. The day had been so exacting on many counts; she felt so weary, and how she was going to explain everything she could not think. Her brain and her body would not work properly together.

"I called on Mrs Butler, and she offered her cart to take me home. We met Lady Catherine on the road…" Elizabeth faltered.

Mr Darcy looked away and toward his aunt. "I hope you are going to stay, Aunt. We have both looked forward to your visit with great pleasure and would be sorry if you were to leave so soon."

Lady Catherine pursed her lips. "I have no motive to disap- point my dear nephew. Perhaps I will stay. Despite my great shock at being almost overturned in my own carriage today, I find my appetite returning, and, as I always say, the de Bourghs and the Darcys know more than any families in the kingdom how to keep a good table. I hope, Mrs Darcy, that you see to all the menus yourself?"

Mr Darcy spoke up. "Mrs Darcy does an excellent job in all domestic matters, I think you will find, Aunt Catherine."

"I enjoy my household duties very much, Lady Catherine," Lizzy spoke up as soon as he had finished. "The discovery of the late Mrs Darcy's receipt books has been a very useful source for inspiration in the kitchen. Written in such a beautiful hand and with such tried and tested methods, I have been able to draw on her expertise with the help of Mrs Reynolds."

"My sister did have a superior hand and a talent for the culinary arts. It is a trait with which I too am most fortunate to be so blessed. When you next come to Rosings Park, Mrs Darcy, you may have my receipt for herb dumplings. You will find no better authority nor softer dumplings than mine, let me assure you."

Elizabeth could hardly suppress a smile. To flatter Lady Catherine must surely be quite the best way to win her over. "I am certain I would find such advice invaluable, Lady Catherine. I know Mr Darcy prefers soft dumplings to any other kind."

Mr Darcy glanced over at his wife, a flicker of a smile and a quizzical expression on his countenance, but his wife returned his perusal just as steadily and with as solemn an expression as she could muster. How dare he be cross with her, she thought; she would not give in to his smiles so easily.

"Please allow me to show you to your room, Lady Catherine," Elizabeth addressed her. "Mrs Reynolds will lead the way. We thought you'd like to have your sister's room. There is such a charming portrait of you both as young girls on the wall, set between the windows. She was so very beautiful, and you are so alike in looks. You must miss her very much, and an elder sister is always of such comfort."

"Mrs Darcy was my younger sister by five years, but we were often taken for twins in our youth. You are not the first to remark on the similarity of our features. Noble blood and aristocratic noses are those features which mark out the truly genteel. One can only pray that they will continue to grace the Darcy lineage." They had mounted the stairs and were almost at the top. Mrs Reynolds, several steps in front, disappeared quickly into the room to make sure everything was as perfect as it could be. As they reached the door Lady Catherine turned. "Have you told your husband yet, Mrs Darcy?"

"Forgive me, I'm not certain to what you refer, Lady Catherine," answered Elizabeth, blushing furiously, unsure as to her meaning and feeling quite conscious of all that had passed during the afternoon.

"Come now, Mrs Darcy, do not insult me. I knew as soon as I saw you. A little ginger in your tea will cure the worst of the symptoms. Ask your friend Mrs Collins; she will tell you how she was still able to see to the pigs after my intervention. I don't doubt you will produce a healthy offspring. Of course, those persons not so highly born are often generally better suited for breeding, and this may be where you have the advantage over a refined, aristocratic gel of a delicate frame and constitution. For the purposes of crude procreation, I daresay my nephew has chosen wisely in plumping for a girl of well-built proportions; I pray the excesses of childbirth are not injurious to your health. Many a young woman has been snuffed out in her prime, if not after the first, then after half a dozen or more confinements." Lady Catherine looked Elizabeth up and down as if she were examining a prize cow. "Now, I shall leave you. I suppose dinner is at six, as it always has been at Pemberley. I am feeling raven-ous—a hearty dinner tonight, I think. The Earl of Southampton recommends frugal diets only in the summer months."

Lady Catherine turned and entered her bedchamber without a backward glance. Elizabeth stood for a moment on the thresh-old, desirous of following her and telling her exactly what she thought, but she knew that to do so would be a fruitless exercise.

Besides, there was someone else who needed a talking to, and she must find him straight away.

Elizabeth went in search of Mr Darcy as soon as she could. It was imperative that she speak to him before Lady Catherine divulged her suppositions whether outright or by none too subtle hints. He was getting ready for dinner and looked so striking in his black coat that she almost felt shy as she entered his dressing room. How to begin on such a subject she could not think. Before she had a chance to speak, however, Mr Darcy gestured to her to sit down. She sat upon a chair before the window and looked up to see him scrutinising her most severely.

He spoke in measured tones. "I am very disappointed, Elizabeth. What on earth were you thinking? I have had every man looking for you over the entire estate; nobody knew where you were. Did you not consider for a moment how worried I might be? To go off without informing me or anyone else of your whereabouts is utterly irresponsible. Not only have you had me almost out of my mind with anxiety, but then I also find that you are dressing like a peasant to go off donkey riding in the countryside. To wholly disregard your position here at Pemberley and that of myself shows such little consideration that I find myself unable to credit. You have submitted yourself to the derision and ridicule of our neighbours. What they must think of me for allowing you to conduct yourself thus is anyone's guess. And then to be seen in such a state by Lady Catherine herself is quite unforgivable. Are you trying to make a fool of me? Please explain your actions, Elizabeth, for at this moment, I do not comprehend you."

"No, sir, you do not comprehend me, that is very certain. I was not aware when we married that I was from that day restricted, unable to move, speak, or voice an opinion without your approbation or permission, but it is becoming increasingly clear that I am no longer able to enjoy a free will of my own. I am sorry if you think my conduct has been unbecoming or if I gave you cause to worry, but it was not done with any intention of shaming you or belittling your noble standing in the community. As for your aunt, Lady Catherine de Bourgh, whose unannounced arrival has thrown everyone into disarray, I hope you will recall that if it were not for myself, the reconciliation you hope to accomplish would never have been a remote possibility."

Elizabeth was becoming increasingly angry and indignant. And the reason for her sole purpose in seeking him out was no longer a subject she felt she wished to reveal, a confidence she could not discuss with him now. She waited for him to answer, and when none was forthcoming Elizabeth decided to leave. His countenance was suffused with colour and the obvious suppression of yet more bitter proclamations seemed to emanate from every pore.

"I will see you at dinner, Mr Darcy. And if you have no further instruction as to how I must conduct myself at the dinner table under the eagle eyes of your aunt and those of your good self, I will take my leave."

For all her outspoken words Elizabeth showed a united front with her husband at the dinner table, though it was difficult to be the light, bright, and sparkling conversationalist that Mrs Darcy had become renowned for amongst her neighbours. Thankfully, Lady Catherine made no further reference to their earlier conversation and Elizabeth resolved to keep the matter to herself for the time being. Lady Catherine had not had her questions confirmed and Lizzy decided that if she was so impertinent to hint at such a thing again that she would deny all possibility. Mr Darcy's aunt held court, much as she had done at Rosings when Elizabeth had been invited there with Charlotte Collins the previous summer. Poor Georgiana was bombarded with questions and with so many recommendations as to the correct conduct of an engaged young woman that Elizabeth wished she could have intervened more than she did. At length the evening was broken up. Mrs Darcy retired to her bedchamber feeling as weary as she ever had. The fact that her husband did not instantly follow her had only a momentary regret; the instant her head touched the pillow she fell fast asleep.

When she awoke, however, he was not there. Whether he had risen early or whether he had not slept in their bed she could not decide at first, but the neatness and lack of depression upon his pillow finally persuaded her that he had not in fact slept there during the night. Elizabeth sighed. He was the most stubborn man she had ever known, she decided. Fitzwilliam was behaving like a child who could not get his own way. "I am not going to report to him for everything I do or say," she said to herself, "and if I give in to him now I shall never be my own person again." Yet despite her brave thoughts and her self-assurance, she was very upset that he was not lying there beside her. In their short married life together they had never before spent a night apart. Disagreements were unpalatable; she had never felt at such variance with any other person in her life; and to dispute in such a manner with the man she loved most in the world was so dreadful and alarming. Quite what she was to do about it, she did not know.

A knock on the door had her alert and sitting up in bed in expectation. Her disappointment she felt deeply when her maid entered, though the sight of a cup of tea with the post was most cheering.

There was a letter from Jane which she eagerly read first, a letter from her sister Lydia in Newcastle asking for money, and the third, scribed in a hand she did not recognise, not only gave her cause for great upset but was also anonymously written.

> *Dear Mrs Darcy,*
>
> *Your husband's heart belongs to someone else. If you need proof ask Mrs Tissington of Birchlow about Master George's true parentage. If not for certain conditions imposed upon his real mother and father, he would be the next rightful heir to the Pemberley fortunes.*
>
> *A well-wisher.*

The postmark was a London one, a district she did not know. This hastily penned, cruel missive written in a scribbled hand with the sole design to cause mischief left Lizzy feeling greatly disturbed. Despite telling herself that it was all nonsense, an invention created to wreak havoc in her marriage, she could not help but dwell on the message it contained. That Fitzwilliam had lately been seen in the vicinity of Birchlow village and talking to a boy matching George Tissington's description gave rise to great feelings of apprehension and trepidation, but what should she do about it? In any case, Darcy had never disguised the fact that he knew the boy and his mother. Questioning her husband or showing him the letter would suggest that she considered him under suspicion. The more she thought about it, the more Elizabeth rejected the ideas and the contents of the cruel note. The implication that George Tissington's father was Mr Darcy was the worst possible insinuation. To do nothing seemed the favoured option; to contemplate anything else was too awful. Besides, Elizabeth refused to believe such a lie, such a degradation of truth, and getting out of bed she threw the vile paper on the fire, watching it smoulder and burn until it vanished into smoke.

Chapter 18

Mr Darcy, Georgiana, and Lady Catherine were already seated at breakfast in the parlour set aside for its special use. Lady Catherine looked up as Elizabeth entered the room.

"I have given instructions to Reynolds for the special tisane I was telling you about, Mrs Darcy," she began. "It will help to alleviate the symptoms with which you suffer."

Aware that she had blushed to the roots of her hair, Lizzy muttered her thanks and sat down, averting her eyes from Mr Darcy who stared at her in that uncompromising way he had. "I hope you slept well, Lady Catherine," she said, helping herself to a bread roll. Unable to face anything else, her symptoms felt stronger than ever this morning.

"Quite well, thank you," the lady replied, keeping her eyes firmly fixed upon Elizabeth's countenance. "Perhaps you would fare better if you slept late in the mornings, Mrs Darcy. Take my advice, you cannot be too careful in your situation."

Mr Darcy looked from his aunt to his wife with a quizzical expression unable to comprehend the subject of their discourse.

"What a pity it is that you are unable to stay longer, Lady Catherine," Elizabeth persisted, determined to change the subject.

"Yes, my hosts are always grieved when I must leave, but I must hasten to Rosings to prepare for the London season. I hope to see you there, Fitzwilliam and Georgiana. You have never yet missed my first soirée of the season, Darcy, and my friends will expect you."

"Oh, but I am not sure if we plan to go to London this time," said Elizabeth, knowing that they had already discussed the fact that they wished to be at Pemberley for the foreseeable future.

"But Georgiana will want to enjoy everything London has to offer in the company of her fiancé, I am sure," barked Lady Catherine. "Surely you do not wish to deny her that great pleasure. You long to go to London, do you not, Georgiana?"

Georgiana looked down into her hands. Elizabeth thought she had never seen anyone look less willing to go anywhere.

"We have not yet made any firm decision," announced Mr Darcy, contradicting his wife and glancing at her over the breakfast table.

"Good, that is settled then. I shall expect to see you shortly in town, Darcy," said Lady Catherine, an expression of triumph on her countenance. "The first Friday in March is the date, as you well know, and I will expect to see you all, your health permitting, Mrs Darcy. Well, I cannot sit here in idle chatter any longer; I must be away. Have you a letter for Mrs Collins, Mrs Darcy? I expect you are in constant communication at present and on a most particular subject."

"I wrote only yesterday to Charlotte, thank you, Lady Catherine," Elizabeth replied, wishing she would hurry up and go. Her comments were bound to instigate some queries from

Mr Darcy and she did not want to talk to him about anything at present. She would fulfil her role as dutiful wife whilst Lady Catherine was present, but she was not sure that she was ready to forgive Fitzwilliam for yesterday's tirade. Besides, there were other matters on her mind that had to be resolved before she made her peace with him.

Lady Catherine left for Rosings eventually, without making many more insinuating remarks, to Elizabeth's great relief. She was ashamed to admit it to herself, but she was glad that Darcy's aunt had gone. The old lady had wavered at the last moment before flouncing off to her carriage as if mortally wounded by all she witnessed about her. At least the steps towards a reconciliation had taken place and Fitzwilliam had resumed a relationship with his aunt, a fact which Lizzy considered her doing. It would take more than one visit, she knew; Darcy would still have to be the person to engineer the rift, but he had made the first move to accomplishing this very thing.

Mrs Reynolds appeared the moment Lady Catherine departed with a request for Elizabeth to advise her on what was required for dinners during the forthcoming week, so Lizzy was glad of the excuse to leave her husband's side. He had estate matters to attend and so she knew he would be occupied for the morning, at least. The discussion with Mrs Reynolds did not take long, leaving Mrs Darcy with time on her hands. Needing to think, she took herself off to her sitting room, but on passing the library door en route she had another idea—one which, however much she told herself might not be a good one, nevertheless took hold, taking her footsteps in that direction.

Recalling the shelf where she had found the book on Christmas day was not difficult and by using the library steps she managed to find what she was looking for with ease. Her heart was hammering as she took out the slim volume, her fingers shaking as she removed the letters from their hiding place.

The first was the one she recalled reading. The second she did not hesitate to open.

November 20, 1792
Darling Orsini,

I am writing to you in good spirits under the circum-stances. I am well; indeed, we are both in good health. Everything has turned out much as could be expected, but I miss you more than words can express. It was not your doing to send me away, I know, yet the cruelty of my situation is one that nobody should ever have to endure. Not that I blame you, my love; I know left to you I would not have been treated so shabbily.

I expect you are curious to hear about little G. whom you have not yet seen but that, I trust, will be a pleasure soon afforded. The babe is fat and healthy—with dark, curly locks, not unlike those I've seen in countless family portraits at P. I wish you could see him; when he opens his eyes he has such an earnest way of looking; he is quite the little gentleman already. Your wish to provide, to look after us is exactly the gesture I hoped you would make, and I know that your word is as good as your heartfelt actions. Fate has cruelly separated us for the time being, but I know you too well to expect anything less than unerring devotion for myself and little G. They cannot and will not separate us forever. I love you more than words will ever express and, if he too could show his adoration, I know he would. When the time is right I am certain that you will redress the situation and accomplish what is right for us all. Believe me when I say that you have never been from my thoughts; if it had been in my power we would never have parted.

> *Come soon,*
> *My love always,*
> *Viola and little G.*

Elizabeth knew she had made a terrible mistake as soon as the letter was read. To her mind there was only one interpretation. The date, the information, everything confirmed what Elizabeth suspected. Eleven years—the lapse of time seemed too exact a science to be a mere twist of fate. George, little G. must be Viola Wickham's son, George Tissington, and his father... could there be any other explanation? Elizabeth could not bring herself to voice his name even in her mind. It would appear that the discovery of the union between Viola and Darcy had ended with them being parted by the family. Miss Wickham must have been sent away in disgrace, but quite what had happened when the baby was born still seemed unclear. That he had been taken away from his mother, perhaps unwillingly, seemed a great possibility. Placed in the custody of Mrs Tissington, at least the Darcys had scruples enough to see to the boy's welfare, but it all appeared to be a very wicked business. Had Darcy been in love with Viola? Was he bound by duty alone to look after the boy? Two questions plagued her more than any other. Had he broken off all ties with Viola, and was there any fragment of that former regard Mr Darcy had had for her? Did he perhaps still secretly love Viola with the passion of a love thwarted? She struggled with all these notions, but there didn't seem to be any straightforward answer. And there was another thing: Miss Wickham and Mr Darcy may have been in love, but how much better could he be said to have behaved than Mr Wickham in his seductions of Georgiana and Lydia? This was such an awful thought that Elizabeth buried it as soon as it surfaced.

Just touching the letters was distasteful; she wished she had not read them, and replaced them as soon as she could. Satisfied that the bookshelf looked as it had before she entered the library, no one would be any the wiser, she thought. She must go and find solace in her sitting room where she could think about it all rationally and look for any other explanation that could ease her present mind.

Balanced as she was on the library steps, the next step down was lower than she realised and in her haste to get away she completely missed her footing, which caught her off balance. Too late did her senses combine to inform her of the mistake. With an almost silent cry for help, which she knew she could not command, she fell in a heap, landing painfully on her back, banging her head hard on the floor. An overwhelming sensation of nausea engulfed her before she submitted wholly to the darkness, instantly blanking out every other sensation in mind and body.

Chapter 19

WHEN SHE CAME TO, she could not at first think where she was or what had happened to her. The room slowly came into focus as she opened her eyes, and the anxious face of Mr Darcy, who was holding one of her small hands between two of his large ones, loomed into view. Dressed in her nightgown and cap with the covers tucked neatly around her, she was lying in her bed. The memory of the fall and what had happened prior to it came back in a sudden rush. Elizabeth pulled her hand away as she struggled to sit up.

"Rest, Elizabeth," urged her husband. "You have had a nasty fall. I have sent for the physician. Please don't try to sit up. I shall not be easy until you have been examined."

Looking up at his face, Mr Darcy's concern was etched on his features. Such a kind and handsome countenance, thought Elizabeth, as she watched him take her hand once more and raise her fingers to his lips, his dazzling dark eyes never leaving hers for a moment.

"I am worried about you," he said tenderly. "I do not know what I should do if you were to be taken from me, Elizabeth."

Apart from a blinding headache and the feelings of nausea that had dogged her for the past week, Elizabeth felt fine and able to assure him, "I just took a tumble, that is all. There is no need to worry."

"I am sorry we quarrelled," he continued, his eyes averted before he found the courage to look into hers again. "Will you forgive me, Elizabeth? I was wrong to speak to you like that, but you must understand that you are no longer Miss Bennet of Longbourn. Mrs Darcy of Pemberley House must take care of herself, if not for her own sake then for that of the man who loves her beyond all measure."

Leaning toward her, he dropped the softest kiss upon her lips. "I love you, Mrs Darcy. Please tell me that you forgive me."

The physician chose that exact moment to arrive, accompanied by Mrs Reynolds and a flurry of housemaids fussing about with bowls of water and tea for the invalid. Mr Darcy was shooed out of the room, followed by all the attendants, until finally Elizabeth was left alone with the doctor. Their discussion and the ensuing examination included the topic of Lizzy's state of well-being and her queries were finally satisfied. What she had hardly been able to imagine these last few days was confirmed as the truth, and she was given strict instructions to stay in bed for a day or two in case the shock of falling had done any damage.

Now that the truth was substantiated, her feelings were so mixed and her emotions so intertwined that she seemed to rapidly course between the highs of elation to the depths of despair in a moment. Unadulterated joy merged with fear; a new worry that she might lose this precious baby was coupled with the dreadful knowledge that she had about the possible existence of another child who most likely belonged to her husband. With difficulty she tried to put these thoughts into a more considered perspective. What had happened eleven years ago, before she met Mr Darcy, belonged to a different time. She had no control over those past events, and nothing could change what had happened. Until her husband could tell her himself, she would have to be patient. And if he did not, then she would have to accept that there would always be an enforced lack of trust between them. But the failure to divulge his secret and, no doubt, his shame would illustrate a lack of real devotion in their relationship, Elizabeth decided. To take her into his confidence, to confess all would define a new intimacy between them. It would be the greatest example of his trust and faith if he were able to share his past. It was not likely, she considered, but perhaps when she told him her news, he might divulge something of the history and tell her about George. It might all be impossible, but she would have to bury the knowledge she had gained for the present, and of course, there was always the hope and the slightest possibility that none of it were true. Love would find a way, Lizzy told herself, and no matter what had happened before, she would continue to love and adore the man she had married. Besides, there was a new life to consider.

When the doctor had gone, Mr Darcy soon reappeared looking as anxious as ever. He sat down on the bed, stroking her hair with one hand whilst reaching for her fingers with the other. "The doctor has given me strict instructions to make sure you do not get up," he said gravely. "You are not to go waltzing along to Lambton for any reason, whatever you may think on the freedoms of the individual. I am sorry, Elizabeth, but in this case I must be firm."

"Yes, Mr Darcy, I quite agree."

He looked back at her, the shock on his face plain to see. "You agree with me?"

"Yes, on this occasion I do agree with you, wholeheartedly. At least for the present." A smile played about her lips.

"Did you hear me properly? I said you must stay in bed."

Elizabeth nodded and began to laugh. "I will do as you say."

"And may I ask exactly what has brought about this complete transformation in your character that you are inclined not only to agree with me, but are also willing to obey my every word?"

"I am having a baby, Mr Darcy, and as such, I must take care of myself."

Fitzwilliam Darcy was stunned into silence. His expression gradually changed from serious reflection to joyous exultation. He whooped and hollered, throwing back the bedcovers to snatch his wife up into his arms to twirl her round, squeezing her so hard that she could only laugh all the more. The worries and fretful anxieties of the afternoon disappeared as he embraced her, celebrating her beauty in laughter and words of praise. It was only when he speculated on the sex of the child that her thoughts turned briefly to George Tissington, but nothing could spoil this moment nor remove the pride she felt at having achieved her husband's greatest wish for a child so soon.

There followed such a period of happiness between the young married couple that Elizabeth was able to bury any misgivings she had learned of her husband's past. Now she had had time to reflect and consider the matter, she even began to wonder if she might not have been fanciful in her estimation of his role in the Tissington affair. Despite all indications to the contrary, there was no proof that the letter from Viola was written for him, and the anonymous letter could have been penned by anybody who wished to be malicious. She felt rather ashamed that she could have jumped to such a conclusion, yet was prepared to forgive herself, realising that her suppositions had first arisen when she had been feeling under great strain. She was determined to put the past behind her and this was made even more possible by Mr Darcy's own very attentive and loving manner towards her welfare.

With every passing day Elizabeth bloomed and her husband never failed to tell her how much she was blossoming, admiring her soft and burgeoning womanly contours, which to the rest of the world were not yet apparent. Lizzy was feeling strong and delighting in the changes, transformations that gave her husband even more pleasure than herself. Only one thing marred her happiness. Georgiana was becoming increasingly subdued as time went on. To Lizzy the girl had never looked as a blushing bride-to-be should appear and Georgiana's spirits seemed very low. Hugh Calladine called dutifully twice a week, but to Elizabeth, who had been courted with greater insistence and zeal, she watched them in dismay. A polite civility subsisted between the young couple, no more, and as February came to a close Georgiana's health took a turn for the worse. When Mr Darcy repeated his aunt's request to take a trip to London, assuring her that it would be of only a month's duration, Elizabeth agreed. Something had to be done for Georgiana, and perhaps London with all its diversions would cheer her up. Elizabeth was rather curious to see her London home though dreaded the society of Lady Catherine and her friends. However, to be with her husband, to be loved by him and spend time with him was all that mattered at present. If he had asked her to go to the end of the world with him she would have gladly gone.

Georgiana did not much care where she went, but so long as she could enjoy the society of her brother and his wife she was as happy as she could be. But she also took pleasure in solitude, whenever she could escape from Mrs Annesley and Elizabeth's well-meaning instruction and employment. She knew they were worried about her, yet she needed time to be alone and think. "I will never love Hugh as Elizabeth loves Fitzwilliam," she thought as she sat at her pianoforte playing melancholy songs. "But then, I do not know of any other couple so much in love, except perhaps Mr and Mrs Bingley. I cannot help but wonder about Tom and what he is doing, even if I know that he has most likely forgotten all about me." Looking out of the window across the hills she could just make out the line of trees to where she knew the stone hut stood. Her heart lurched at the thought of Mr Butler, with his laughing eyes and generous smile. She could feel the warmth of his fingers, his large hand enfolding hers as if he were in the room beside her. But it was no good to dwell on such things. Conjuring up a vision of Hugh, she tried to convince herself that he was the man she loved. She tried to placate herself with thoughts of Hugh's grand house, richly decorated, with every modern convenience and comfort, filled with the finest furniture and art that money could buy, but knew in her heart that if only she could be with Tom, she would have been happy to dwell with him in the stone hut with no roof. Remembering the picnic they'd shared brought back an image of Mr Butler, his tousled hair curling against his brow, which wrinkled in concentration as he tried to make a presentation out of the simple meal. It was no good; however hard she tried, she could not replace his countenance with a picture of Mr Calladine. "I wish I could have told Mr Butler how much I enjoyed his company," she thought as tears pricked her eyelids. "But it is too late now, and he will never know how much happiness he brought me during those few weeks when he was here at Pemberley." Wiping her eyes, she resolved once more to attend to the present and not dwell on the past. Picking a song sheet with a lively melody she resumed her practice, declaring to herself that she would dedicate and sing this song to her fiancé when he next called. Time was on her side, she considered, as Mr Calladine had called the day before and did not usually make a habit of calling again until at least the better part of the week had passed.

Downstairs in the drawing room, a favourite place other than her sitting room to sit and read her letters, Elizabeth settled down on an elegant settee. Mr Darcy fussed about her with cushions, which he piled high against the scrolled arms insisting that she put her feet up upon the plump velvet seat. A fire roared in the grate, the reflections of which burnished the little table beside her with flickers of gold illuminating white snowdrops in a glass vase, the delicate petals reminding her that spring and all that the season promised was not far away. She had a letter from Jane, which she eagerly opened, reading its contents with feelings of surprise and hope, followed swiftly by bleak despair. Her sister had written to say that she and Charles had formed a plan to make a trip to the north, that they intended travelling as far as the Lakes at the beginning of March with a view to taking a house. Charles's Uncle Bellingham, a single man with poor health, had offered them his house for a few months whilst he went in search of the healing air of a spa in Switzerland. Would Elizabeth and Darcy join them, as they could think of no one with whom they would rather share such an adventure?

The letter went on:

> I know you have wished to see the Lakes for yourself and were disappointed when you could not make the trip as promised by our Aunt Gardiner, even if you were not dissatisfied with the eventual outcome! Just think, Lizzy—did it ever occur to you that if you had gone further north you might still be unmarried and living at Longbourn? My aunt and uncle have been invited also, so we will be a merry party.
>
> My dearest sister, if you have no other plans, please write soonest to assure me that my wish will come true—even if I think you might now prefer men to rocks and mountains in contradiction to what you once professed!
>
> Yours ever,
> Jane Bingley
>
> P.S. I do delight in so writing my name, do not you?—I do not think I ever wrote so many letters in my life before, simply to have the pleasure of signing it.

Elizabeth put the letter down upon the table and sighed audibly. It was done before she was cognisant of its volume. As she railed inwardly, trying not to think about how much she would prefer to go to the Lakes in her sister's company than be in London with Lady Catherine, Mr Darcy looked across at his wife, dismayed to see the despondent expression on her face.

"What is it, my love? Are you ill? Let me ring for some tea. What can I do for you? Perhaps you are too close to the fire. Let me adjust the sofa—don't move, stay where you are!"

Elizabeth smiled. Fitzwilliam had always been a very attentive husband, but since she had made her news of the baby known to him Darcy was a man possessed. Nothing was too much trouble; indeed, she wondered if she might be allowed to take a step unaided ever again. But she could not mind. To be so loved was like discovering hidden treasure, and she could only love him the more for his concern.

She explained, trying to disguise the disappointment that she felt, yet knew he would detect it—if not in her words, then in her voice.

"And if you could choose, where would you most like to go?" he asked with a solemn expression.

"Oh, Fitzwilliam, that is not fair. You are teasing me, I think."

"No, truly, would you prefer to see your townhouse in London or enjoy a trip to the Lakes?"

"I am very curious to see the house and to spend time with you in London, seeing all the sights together, but I would not be truthful if I said the prospect of the season and all it entails does not fill me with a certain apprehension. If I really had a choice, I would prefer the Lakes."

Darcy paused. He was lounging in a fireside chair, but he sat upright to regard his wife with a huge smile on his countenance. "Then we shall go to the Lakes."

"I beg your pardon, Fitzwilliam?"

"If that is your wish, dearest, loveliest Elizabeth, we will go to the Lakes."

Elizabeth stared at her husband. For a moment she thought he had gone quite mad. "You cannot mean it! And risk the displeasure and possible ostracism of Lady Catherine? No, Darcy, I cannot believe it. Please do not tease me so."

"My aunt will get over it. In any case a journey to the Lakes will be far less fatiguing and even she will be aware that is the case. Your health is of paramount importance. Indeed, if the physician advises it, we will not be going anywhere. Besides, I think my sister would enjoy the trip. I admit, Elizabeth, to feelings of great concern for her." He continued, staring into the fire, unable to meet Elizabeth's astonished gaze, "I think I am guilty of huge misconduct. I spent too long persuading myself that I was following the correct course and doing my duty to my family, instead of acting on what I knew to be in my sister's best interests. Georgiana is not ready for matrimony, whatever she professes to me. That she would do anything I ask of her is a power I have abused. I have never seen her in such low spirits and it is entirely my fault. My pride, the Darcy pride as some have called it, has been exhibited in all its worst excesses. Too proud to admit that you were right, I am ready to admit that I was wrong, yet I do not know what can be done at present. It is a situation that requires careful handling. At least we have time on our side to consider the best course. Well, there is no hurry for her to be wed, and being away from Pemberley and Hugh Calladine will do her good. In the meantime, perhaps Georgiana may come to know her own mind on the matter. She needs to consider what will be best for her peace of mind and her happiness."

Elizabeth did not know whether to feel relieved or angry. Yet there was little point in going over old ground. Georgiana had willingly made her choice, despite Elizabeth's entreaties to consider what an engagement really meant. How anything could be done to alter the situation seemed impossible unless the couple came to a mutual decision and that was hardly likely to happen. Hugh Calladine had probably been waiting for years to press his suit, and Georgiana's reputation would suffer irrevocably if she broke off her engagement. It was a mess, Elizabeth knew, brought about by stubborn pride and folly. Still, if the wedding could be delayed then that was all to the good. Elizabeth felt she was quite wicked in her thoughts, but the idea that Mr Calladine might be tempted to fall into old habits whilst Georgiana was away was one idea that gave her comfort. Perhaps Georgiana could be saved after all.

Everything was settled for a tour of the Lakes. No scheme could have been more agreeable to Elizabeth, and her acceptance of the invitation was most ready and grateful. "My dear Mr Darcy," she rapturously cried, "what delight and felicity! Oh! What hours of transport we shall spend! And when we return, it shall not be like other travellers, who cannot give one precise idea of anything. Lakes, mountains, and rivers shall not be jumbled together in our imaginations; nor, when we attempt to describe any particular scene, will we begin quarrelling about its relative situation. Let our first effusions be less unbearable than those of the majority of travellers."

Mr Darcy laughed. He loved more than anything to see his wife happy and, coupled with the secret of the new life that they shared, she was his first priority. If she was contented, then so was he. Lady Catherine would be placated with the promise of a return trip to Rosings at a later date. Even Georgiana seemed pleased at the prospect of a trip, collecting together armfuls of paper, paint, and paintbrushes to capture the entire landscape in watercolours.

About a week before travelling, Elizabeth received a letter from her aunt. Mr Gardiner was unable to make the trip as business required him to stay in town, but she was delighted to say that Mrs Butler, her dear friend, was to be invited to join them in their party. Lizzy received this news with mixed feelings, being on the one hand delighted that Mrs Butler and Aunt Gardiner would enjoy such an expedition together, but on the other rather anxious about what her husband might have to say on the matter. She thought it best to tell him out of Georgiana's earshot, but far from seeming displeased, he was perfectly amiable and even said he should be delighted to see Mrs Gardiner's friend.

On the following morning, Elizabeth persuaded Georgiana to accompany her to call on Mrs Butler after they had visited several homes in Lambton where Lizzy made her regular calls. To be greeted so warmly and to see the delighted countenances of those on whom she called was a pleasure in which she revelled. There was hardly a family in the village that had not benefited in some way from Mrs Darcy's assistance. Georgiana's increasing confidence with strangers resulted from the kindness of the villagers. They seemed to love her and were instinctively protective toward her, only engaging her in conversation when she seemed ready.

Georgiana felt very nervous about visiting the house where she had memories of Tom's first acquaintance, but she was determined that she should speak comfortably with his mother.

They were going to be constantly in one another's company shortly and she wanted to make sure there was no awkwardness. Whether his mother had guessed how Miss Darcy secretly felt about Tom she had no idea, but Georgiana liked Mrs Butler very much and she wanted to get to know her better.

Elizabeth rang the bell whilst Georgiana did her best to hide behind her sister-in-law. At least, she thought, even if the recollections might be all consuming, he would not be there. Safe in London, and at the opposite end of the country to where they were headed, she knew however much she dreamed of seeing Tom she could not have borne coming face to face with him.

However, when the door opened, to Georgiana's enormous shock and surprise the very person she dreaded seeing most was standing before them with his hand upon the doorknob, as if used to performing a manservant's duties daily. Her start was clearly audible to them all, and she instantly felt that she was the greatest simpleton for allowing her feelings to overwhelm her at such a moment!

Chapter 20

For a few seconds she was unable to gather her wits; she was lost to confusion; but when she had scolded back her unforgivable senses, she observed Mr Butler greeting Elizabeth as warmly as he ever had. Some moments later, she found herself seated upon the settle in front of the fire, not quite knowing how she had got there, and did not at first realise that Tom was speaking to her, offering his cold congratulations on her engagement. Muttering her thanks she felt such mortification that to endure anything, even being snubbed by him, would have been infinitely preferable.

"I am sorry my mother is not here to greet you herself, but she has gone shopping with our maidservant this morning. I would have thought she would be back by now—she is only in the High Street—but I know how ladies love shopping and I expect she has been detained."

Georgiana wanted nothing more than to go home. Keeping her head down, she saw nothing of Tom or the room; her heart was beating so loudly she feared they must all hear it.

Just as Elizabeth started to say that they must go, that they should not delay Mr Butler any longer, he interrupted, declaring that he could observe his mother coming down the path. As he left the room to open the front door, Georgiana appealed to Elizabeth with a look that spoke volumes. But it was impossible to leave; Mrs Butler entered the room with her usual cheerful bustle with enquiries after them both, giving Lizzy's hands an extra squeeze when the latter remarked that she was very well and in stronger health than when last she had been there.

Listening to their conversation, Georgiana was aware of Tom's eyes upon her. She avoided any glance toward him, keeping her eyes firmly fixed on Elizabeth's face. The talk centred on the exciting prospect of the Lakeland excursion and the logistics of planning such an operation; Georgiana was quite happy to sit back and listen.

After a while, Mrs Butler turned toward her and said, "Oh, Miss Darcy, just listen to us rattle on. Hearing all these plans must be very irksome for you; I am sure you do not want to hear how many gowns I can fit in my largest trunk or whether two hat-boxes will be sufficient." She directed her next words to her son. "Thomas, take Miss Darcy to see the new kittens out in the stable yard. Five kittens, Miss Darcy, and I do not know what to do with them. They will have to be found homes before I go away."

For the first time Georgiana looked over at Mr Butler. His countenance was quite grave until he regarded her, and seeing the look of apprehension in her eyes he adjusted his expression accordingly. "Come, Miss Darcy, come and see them. I know you will not be able to resist them."

Everyone turned to see how she would answer. There was nothing else to be done except to follow him out of the room along the panelled corridor to the outside door. He did not speak, but merely held it open for her. She stepped through the space into the passage leading to the outbuildings aware of his close proximity, breathing in his cologne as she passed by, all too conscious of the intimacy of such a moment.

They were soon in the stable yard. Two adorable kittens were leaping through the straw as the others slept in an oblivious state, snuggled up asleep near their mother. Tom bent down to pick up the smallest—a tortoiseshell kitten with round, grey-green eyes. He could hold the tiny creature in one hand. Cradling it in the crook of his arm, he tickled the kitten under its chin. "Would you like to hold him?" he asked, staring straight into her eyes.

"I..." Georgiana faltered, astonished at the effect that his piercing eyes had upon her ability to speak, but with a step, Tom was beside her, the kitten squirming between his fingers.

"Quickly, before he escapes," whispered Tom. "Put your hands together." He transferred the little ball of fluff, and in doing so, caught hold of Georgiana's fingers partly in an effort to keep the kitten from falling and partly because he could not resist the temptation to touch her or the opportunity to witness her reaction.

Georgiana did not know how she kept her nerve, especially when she realised that Tom had no inclination to remove his hands. They felt warm and strong and his touch provoked such emotions that she had thought buried forever. She hardly wanted to move in case he withdrew them, yet she desired her release at the same time. The kitten wriggled and writhed until at last Tom released his hands and she was able to take a firm hold of the animal, gathering it into her arms, stroking him until he was settled enough to sleep. Feeling completely tongue-tied, Georgiana could not utter a word; and though Tom's silence matched her own, she wished she were capable of speech. No, more than that, she wished she could be clever, witty, and amusing, show him that she was a happily engaged young woman confident of a splendid future with the husband who had been chosen for her. Yet in her heart she desired to tell him the truth about what his friendship had meant to her and how she would think of it all her life. If she could have told him how sorry she was that they had parted without really saying good-bye, Georgiana would have been partly appeased. But she could not; it was useless to try and mend what had been irrevocably broken.

It was Tom who spoke first. "It is good to see you again, Miss Darcy."

Georgiana scolded herself into conversation. "I am very surprised to see you, Mr Butler. I thought you were working in London."

"I was, and still am, but my mother wrote to tell me of her trip and I wanted to say good-bye, so Lord Featherstone very kindly gave me leave. Mama is very excited to be joining your aunt and to be included in the Darcy party. I confess I was concerned. Forgive me, but I am astonished that she has been invited. After our last encounter with the Darcys, I had the distinct impression that our company was distasteful."

"Oh, Mr Butler," Georgiana cried, "I am so sorry about what happened on the night of the ball. My brother was angry with me, but with good reason, I fear. I was behaving without true propriety; I know that now. My family advised me to stop being so particular, to dance with other partners, and I fear his disapprobation extended to you. We had danced together too many times… Well, my sister was right to tell me that I should not confine myself to one partner."

"It did not seem to matter how many times you danced with Hugh Calladine."

Georgiana blushed and bit her lip. In an attempt to hide her face she put the kitten down on the straw and watched it gambol with its brothers and sisters. She must find the courage to speak.

"I do hope your dear mama enjoyed the evening, that she did not feel uneasy or uncomfortable, I trust. No slight was intended, I assure you."

"Mr Darcy is well-bred and civil, but your brother's manners are not inviting. He does not make one feel readily at ease. However, I do not think Mama felt the snub nor indeed did she notice. But I felt it, I assure you. Heavens, what else could I expect? I am only a gardener in his eyes and certainly not worthy of dancing with his sister."

"Mr Butler, my brother was very wrong if you felt he treated you badly, but I am afraid his behaviour toward me was quite justified. I am a very troublesome creature, and I am under his guardianship. My brother has looked after me since my father died, a thankless task at times, I declare. Mr Darcy is zealous, but I fear with good reason," Miss Darcy replied, knowing that she could not fully explain just why her brother behaved in so protective a way towards her. His challenge of being snubbed because he was a gardener was a question she did not wish to answer, suspecting that there may be an element of truth in what he said.

"Are you in love with Hugh Calladine?" Tom cried in a sudden outburst.

Georgiana gasped at the question. Tom was looking at her carefully, scrutinising her expression. He had taken up his stance in front of her, and when her first words were uttered so quietly as to be inaudible, he stepped closer.

"We are to be married, Mr Butler," she replied in a whisper, looking down at the floor and studying the antics of a gambolling kitten.

"Yes, I am aware of that fact. Why are you marrying him, Miss Darcy? Oh, he has a fine house, and it is an alliance that will make your brother very happy, but what of you, Georgiana? You cannot be in love with him. I refuse to believe it."

"I am very grateful that my brother has chosen someone who will give me a comfortable life. To do my duty by my family is the correct course, I believe."

"Do you love him?" he persisted.

"I love him," Georgiana spoke at last, though her words, she knew, were spoken in defiance. What good would it do to tell him of her heart's desire? She must not let Tom think anything else. "I beg you will stop this questioning, Mr Butler; I do not feel quite myself."

"And will he love you in return, Miss Darcy? Have you thought about that? Are you content to live a life without love… without passion or true feeling?"

"I am happy enough, Mr Butler, and if you do not mind my saying so, I think you are rather impudent to be discussing my fiancé with me in such a manner. I do not think you should be speaking to me about such personal matters which have nothing whatsoever to do with you." Georgiana was aware that she was lying to him, that she was rebuffing him in the rudest possible way, but she could not bear to think about any other alternative. It was one thing to daydream about Tom, but to have him here, to acknowledge all she really felt about him to herself was unbearable.

"But it has everything to do with me," insisted Tom, "and I cannot let this moment pass without telling you how much your happiness has to do with me."

Georgiana felt tears spill over her hot cheeks before she was aware of Tom's cool fingers under her chin raising her head until her eyes were in line with his own. He held her face in his hands, his fingers caressing her soft skin as he brushed away her tears. His blue eyes stared into the pools of the grey eyes that looked up at him, the connection broken for a moment as he lowered his gaze to rest upon her lips. He was going to kiss her, she felt sure. More than anything, she wanted him to kiss her, to show him how much she loved him. Georgiana stared back at his mouth and closed her eyes in anticipation. Tom looked down at her skin, warm and glowing like a soft peach in the sunlight, her wet lashes curling against her cheek, her lips pink and inviting. He thought how beautiful Georgiana looked, but Tom knew he would be very wrong to take advantage of such willing submission. The temptation to kiss her was very strong and he had to fight every inclination to touch the lips that looked so bewitching. Georgiana opened her eyes to see a look of defeat in his eyes. How she longed to tell him that he could steal a kiss, that she wished he could take her in his arms, however wrong she knew that would be.

From outside Georgiana thought she heard her name being called. The sound of footsteps approaching brought them both back to an overwhelming sense of reality.

"Georgiana!" a voice called from just outside the door. "Come, it is time to go home."

Politely, Miss Darcy held out her hand to him. "Good-bye, Mr Butler," she said.

Chapter 21

GEORGIANA WAS LYING IN bed on the following morning quite unable to rouse herself, partly because of the recollections of the previous day, which kept her dreaming, and partly because she knew as soon as she stirred out of bed she would have to face the fact that what had happened must never happen again. Resolving that she must never be alone with Mr Thomas Butler again, the acceptance of this idea threatened to completely banish the feelings of great happiness stirring within her; so Georgiana stretched before curling up again, pulling the covers over her head once more. A knock at the door alerted her to the arrival of her maid, who entered with a tray of tea things. The tray was set down whilst she drew back the curtains to let in the sunshine. Spring was in the air, the sky was blue, and the birds were singing as if glad to feel the warmth of the sun.

"Oh, Miss Darcy, look what we have here," Mary said, as she returned to the bedside fussing about her charge, pummelling pillows and straightening the bedclothes. Georgiana sat up, rubbing her eyes but smiling at the sight of Mary, who looked most excited. "There's no note with them, Miss," she began, "but I expect these beauties are from Mr Calladine."

A bunch of blue violets, their delicate heads nodding against the glossy green leaves that bound them, were wrapped in waxed paper and tied with a purple ribbon. "That's so romantic, Miss," Mary continued. "My dear old mum says there's hardly such a romantic flower for lovers. Faithfulness, I'll always be true is what a violet says, and a bunch as big as this—he must have been up for hours picking them. Ooh, Miss Darcy, smell them! Just a moment, I'll fetch a vase of water."

Georgiana held the posy to her nose and breathed in the sweetest perfume redolent of the scents of woodland in early spring. Hugh Calladine could not be responsible for such a delightful gift, she thought. The only flowers she had received from him were a bunch of hothouse blooms forced from one of his greenhouses on the day after the announcement of their engagement. The only person who really understood flowers and would be aware of their symbolism and meaning was the only man who truly empathised with Georgiana, she knew, and as she buried her nose deep into the tussie mussie, her happiness at the idea knew no bounds. To think of Tom wandering through the woods collecting the tiny flowers, to know that she must have been in his thoughts at such an early hour was to render her almost delirious with elation. But whilst the sense of euphoria was almost intoxicating, the antithesis of feelings in desolation and despondency soon took hold. Knowing that their love, however sweet, was forbidden and could never be gave rise to feelings of despair.

However, Georgiana had more to worry about than just trying to come to terms with accepting her situation. A further ordeal was yet to be faced. There was to be a reception in the evening given by Elizabeth in order that the family could say good-bye to Pemberley and all their friends and neighbours. Martha Butler and her son had been invited—and so too had Hugh Calladine.

It was Elizabeth who had come upon Georgiana and Tom in the stable, but to Miss Darcy's relief nothing on the matter had been said. Not that she thought Elizabeth had witnessed any-thing that had gone on, simply that to be seen with him talking together in such intimate circumstances would normally have prompted questions. There had been none, though Georgiana blushed all afternoon at every mention of Mr Butler's name and finally when all reference to him ceased, she breathed with sweet respite. Yet how she was to get through an evening having to face Tom whilst standing at the side of her fiancé she did not know. Every effort to keep them apart must be made, she felt, and no acknowledgement of what had passed between her and Tom must be allowed. It must be forgotten, she told herself. In any case, such was the experience she almost wondered if she had dreamed it. But to think about that, to deny the truth was impossible. If she could but skip through time and be at the Lakes! What feelings of mortification would she escape? With a sinking heart and a sense of desperation, she finally roused herself, placing the violets in the vase that Mary produced on her return. Just looking at them made her smile. If only she could look at them as a lover might and not feel guilty at the sight of them. "I should not have behaved as I did," she scolded herself. "I almost let Tom kiss me, and if he had I know I should have kissed him back. I am engaged to Hugh Calladine; I am betrothed. What could I have been thinking?"

The sun shining through the window warmed the petals of the nodding flower heads, turning the scent of violets into a heady fragrance. One moment the posy brought her joy and in the next such feelings of shame that she hid them behind the curtain where she could not see them. Struggle and conflict each took their turn within Georgiana; the battle for her heart, the fight between true love and false commenced. But she recognised that duty or honour to her family and to herself had little to do with her disconsolation. Lying to herself about her feelings for Tom gave way to the lies about her devotion to Hugh. Before the evening party commenced, Georgiana had convinced herself that she felt nothing for Tom and everything for Hugh. Her commitment was paramount; she was engaged to Mr Calladine, Georgiana reminded herself, and in an effort to counteract all thoughts to the contrary, she convinced herself that Tom had not only taken advantage of the situation in the stable yard but also had behaved outrageously.

Georgiana believed that she was impervious to Mr Thomas Butler's charms as she entered the drawing room dressed in her finest white muslin. What harm was there in wearing just one or two of the violets in her sash at her waist or woven amongst her tresses, she thought. And the more she considered it, the more she was persuaded by Mary's insistence of their having been a present from Mr Calladine.

When she entered the drawing room, she found her fiancé standing alone by the fireplace. Well dressed and with a slim figure, he had an air of distinction about him which made up for his height. With her hair dressed on top of her head, Georgiana knew he looked at a disadvantage when they stood next to one another, but she hoped that the fact that she had no heels on her slippers would make up for it. She curtsied before joining him by the fire, facing him not unlike the way she had stood before Tom on the previous day.

"Georgiana," he said, by way of a salute, and then looked her up and down in the critical way he had of observing people. "Those wild things you have in your hair are wilting, you know. Did your mother never tell you not to wear such woodland weeds about your person?"

"They're violets, don't they smell heavenly?" she asked, tilting her head toward him. This gesture was ignored and Hugh turned to stare into the fire once more. For the first time Georgiana realised how little they had conversed with one another during their short engagement. She didn't think they'd had a proper conversation about anything at all. Miss Darcy looked at the man she was to marry and discovered that she did not know him. "Don't you love the woodland at this time of year?" she asked, aiming to learn if he loved nature as she did.

"Now the shooting's coming to a close, I can't say it holds much fascination," he answered.

"I meant how lovely the woods become with all the spring flora," Georgiana went on. "I love to take some paper and paint out with me so that I can make a study. There'll be primroses and cowslips soon, butter yellow and quite beautiful."

"I daresay you ladies like that sort of thing, but all the turn of the season means to me is a halt to my beloved sport."

"I wish you were coming to the Lakes," said Georgiana, trying to convince herself that she was bereft at the thought of him staying behind.

"Do you, my dear?" he asked, looking at her in surprise. "Yes, I rather think you do!" Georgiana was looking up at him with an expression he had seen on his best pointer waiting for his master to give his command. "Don't you worry about me, old gel. I am going to London for a few weeks."

Georgiana did not know what to say next. There was an awkward silence.

"Miss Darcy, I think we shall rub along very nicely together, all things considered. We should set the wedding date rather sooner than later, don't you think? I intend to speak to Darcy this evening. When you get back from the Lakes, it must be sorted out immediately. Perhaps tomorrow afternoon we might enjoy a walk out on our own. What do you say? Would you like that, to be alone with me, my dear? A parting kiss before you leave me: might not that be the very thing to gladden your heart before we are separated?"

As he leaned in toward her she flinched at his advances. Georgiana was repulsed, utterly and completely. She was quite ready to burst into tears, but as she despaired at the prospect of his touch, never mind his caress, they were joined by Mr and Mrs Darcy who entered upon the scene as Miss Darcy was trying to conceal the shock she felt at her fiancé's request and think of a suitable answer. Mr Darcy was soon taken up with Mr Calladine to Georgiana's relief, so that when Elizabeth stepped up to take her arm saying that she looked a little flushed, she allowed herself to be led away. The room was filling with guests and it was impossible to speak to Elizabeth confidentially. Before many minutes more had passed Mr Calladine claimed her again, taking her arm and whispering what he imagined to be the sort of phrases to set a young lady's heart aflame.

Martha Butler and her son soon made their appearance with several other villagers and neighbours. It had been

Elizabeth's idea to ask some of the farmer's families along with the local gentry, and though Mr Darcy had raised one or two objections at first saying that the two would never mix, he had listened to Elizabeth's arguments in favour and finally acquiesced. Elizabeth seemed to be able to make her brother do anything she liked, thought Georgiana, and it struck her that she was sure she would never have the same power over her spouse. She watched her brother greet Mrs Butler with great affability and his behaviour toward Tom was equally good, she noted. Whatever Tom had accused her brother of in the past could surely not be held true now. Georgiana watched them conversing as she stood at Hugh's side, completely ignored as he rattled away to a fellow sportsman. He had her arm trapped within his own. How she wished she could let it go, especially since she knew Tom had caught her eye and was staring at her in that unnerving way he had.

Taking her chance, she excused herself, moving through the throng and stopping to greet those neighbours and friends that hailed her. Conspicuous by their absence were the Bradshaws. Not for the first time did Georgiana think about poor Eleanor, whose heart must be broken even if she had found herself a man willing to marry her. She knew Eleanor and Hugh had formerly been sweethearts, a fact that had made her feel wretched about accepting Hugh in the first place. The whole business was a disaster. Georgiana felt as if she were on the edge of a precipice that was crumbling rapidly, about to send her hurtling into an abyss of misery. Why had she accepted him? she asked herself for the hundredth time. Why had she not listened to Elizabeth instead of trying to please Fitzwilliam? All at once the room confined her, and her feelings threatened to overwhelm her. In need of fresh air, Georgiana slipped out of the drawing room and along the corridor undetected, or so she thought.

Finding her way outside, she paced the terrace, breathing in the sharp, frosty air in an effort to steady her nerves. Spring might be on its way but the night air of early March was very cool. Stars studded the black velvet sky with a million diamonds; beams of moonlight caressing every surface with a finger of mellow light, gilding the balustrades and glimmering on stone urns. It was quiet; she needed the silence in order to collect herself and think. But a noise from behind startled her and she suddenly realised that she was no longer alone.

"Georgiana," a voice called out in a hoarse whisper.

Spinning round she saw the outline of a figure she recognised standing in the shadow of the door recess.

"What are you doing out here, Mr Butler?" she whispered, hurrying toward him.

"I wanted to say good-bye; that is, I need to talk to you alone," he answered.

"I do not think you should be here with me alone," Georgiana protested. "Go back. There is nothing we have to say to one another. Please leave me be."

As Georgiana made an effort to sweep past him he caught her arm.

"You cannot marry that man, Georgiana. You know you cannot."

"I am marrying Mr Calladine as soon as I return from the Lakes."

"Think of what you are doing, Georgiana. You are throwing your life away. He can never love you as I love you, as you need to be loved. If you marry him, you will be his chattel, his possession; he will consume everything you own, all that you are. Georgiana, I refuse to believe that you can submit your life to him in this way. Do you wish to lose everything? You must know that he will expect you to forget everything you have ever learned for yourself to become just like him. I doubt you will even be allowed your own thoughts... everything, your ideas, your independence will be gone forever. He will steal your very soul and leave you with nothing. It's not too late; tell him you cannot marry him. For your own sake, tell him."

"It's no use, Tom," said Georgiana facing him, her head bowed. "I made a promise to him and my brother; it cannot be broken. You do not understand; there is nothing that can alter the fact that I am to be Hugh Calladine's wife. I must go back now, excuse me."

"Promise me something, Georgiana," said Tom urgently, catching her hand. "I know I may ask too much, but will you write to me from the Lakes, tell me all that you are doing? I have long wished to visit the area, and to see it through your eyes would be the next best thing. Of course, I realise that to ask such a thing is most improper, but if you could just send one note to tell me that all is well in your world, I would be most grateful." He paused, watching her face as the blush rose in her cheeks. "I know what happened yesterday was very wrong of me, and I beg your forgiveness. I would not have taken you in my arms if I had not thought that I might never have the chance again. Please forgive me, Georgiana, it was the hardest task I ever faced not to kiss you. And this last request is just that, I promise. Just one letter before you are lost to me forever."

"I must go, Tom," Georgiana muttered, aware that the feelings of the day before had not dissipated between them and were feeling ever stronger. "I will write to you if I can, I promise, as a sister might write to her brother. Good-bye."

Georgiana opened the door and ran down the corridor back the way she had come, her mind racing with everything Tom had said. Despite everything she had said to him and even though she had rebuffed him, he had shown that his interest in her was undiminished. On entering the drawing room she saw nothing, thought nothing about the gaiety of the scene. Her happiness came from inside. With glowing cheeks and bright eyes she recollected her last moments with Tom and everything he had said. His expression, his manner, and especially his looks had been such as she could only interpret one way. Perhaps she was wrong to be so happy, but she could not help herself. Tom, she decided, must truly be in love with her!

Chapter 22

THE APPROACH TO KENDAL over moorland and heath-clad
hills was slower than expected. Besides their own carriage
and that of the Bingleys and their guests, Elizabeth did not
see any other travellers on the road apart from a long train
of coal carts. The district was remote, the landscape wild
and beautiful, with mountains and peaks topped with snow
seeming to soar into the heavens or disappear under veils of
thunderous cloud. Elizabeth was longing for another stop in
order to stretch her legs and was just wondering if undertaking
such an arduous journey had been a sensible decision when at
last she observed Kendal, white and smoking in the dark vale
before them. As they travelled nearer, the outline of a ruinous
castle was just distinguishable through the gloom on the top
of a hill, and at the entrance to the town the river Kent
gushed and foamed down a weir. Beyond the fortress remains,
Elizabeth could just see a half-hidden church obscured by
trees, grey fells gloaming in the distance. It was a scene to
cheer them all.

Crossing the bridge brought the existence and bustle of habitation into view. Here were the townspeople going about their everyday lives in the same way that Elizabeth had observed as they passed through hamlets and villages by the score on their journey. Signs of society were here, men going about their business, women and children out shopping, and the sight of a stagecoach, tourists alighting laden with bandboxes and trunks. The orders were soon given to stop the carriage on Highgate at an inn. The weary party clambered down, each glad to get out and savour the welcome smell of hot food wafting under their noses.

Mr Darcy ushered them all inside. The landlord was expecting them and showed the party into an upstairs room that looked out from ancient windows half hanging over the street. Everyone spoke at once; they were full of the journey and of the spectacular views that no artist, engraver, or poet had ever before done true justice. They were all famished and before long a meal of roast beef with all the trimmings was set before them.

Having soon satisfied her appetite, Elizabeth felt in need of some exercise and a chance to alleviate her headache, so she rose to make her way back downstairs. Mr Darcy was just insisting that he should accompany her when the landlord suddenly halted him on a matter of some importance concerning the horses. Lizzy was pleased to gain her independence, slipping out before he or anyone else could stop her. It was good to be able to walk about after sitting for so long in the carriage, and she strolled along the street, finding much interest in the old timbered buildings of the town. She decided to walk as far as the market cross and stopped to look in the draper's window at the selection of ribbon and lace displayed in the window. After walking on in perusal of the milliner's, where she found a bonnet or two worth a second look, she turned to make her way back again and was just passing the doorway of another inn when some people all talking and laughing in a very animated fashion walked straight into her without even looking where they were going. When she had recovered herself enough to speak, for she had almost been knocked over, she could have keeled over again in shock.

"Lizzy, good Lord, Lizzy! What are you doing here?" asked a voice belonging to a very smartly dressed young woman whom she instantly recognised. "Look, Wickie, look who it is... isn't this a good joke?"

Elizabeth's youngest sister, Lydia, lately married, after first scandalously eloping with George Wickham, was standing before her laughing out loud as if she had just heard some hysterical jape.

Elizabeth nodded towards Mr Wickham, who bowed obsequiously. "Mrs Darcy, what a great pleasure it is to see you, my dear sister. I trust you are well?"

"I am, thank you. I must admit, I am very surprised to see you," she said, also glancing at the couple standing next to them. There was something very familiar looking about the woman, but Elizabeth was certain she did not know her.

Lydia suddenly stopped laughing and put on her most serious if rather silly expression. "Mrs Darcy, may I present Mrs Younge and her friend and ours, Captain Farthing. Mrs Darcy is my elder sister and is married to Mr Darcy of Pemberley. He's the richest man in Derbyshire, isn't he, Lizzy?"

"How do you do?" said Elizabeth, ignoring Lydia's embarrassing comments. She was trying to remember why she instantly knew that the name of Mrs Younge was one she had heard before, but she could not for the life of her think where and under which circumstances.

Mrs Younge, a handsome looking woman with dark curls that peeped out around the sides of her bonnet, was well dressed if a little showy for Elizabeth's taste. She proffered her slim hand sheathed in York tan to Elizabeth, who took it. Mrs Younge immediately encased Elizabeth's with both of hers in a gesture that felt oddly inappropriate. "My dear Mrs Darcy, I have heard so much about you from your sister. I have longed to meet you!"

"I am pleased to make your acquaintance, ma'am," Elizabeth returned before extracting her hand and turning toward her sister. "Are you here to tour the Lakes, Lydia? I must confess, I would not have thought walking over mountains was quite in your line of amusement."

"Lord, no… what an idea! We are on our way to stay with the colonel of the regiment. He has a country house at Hawkside and we shall be there for a month complete. Well, it will certainly save on our expenses, and darling Willie Arbuthnot has promised me balls and parties every night. My sweet Colonel says that a party is not a party without Mrs Wickham, and so you see, I am quite indispensable. Half the regiment is here… at least, the half that are not needed to protect our shores. Between you and me, it's the dull lot that is left behind: the ones that can't dance! La! The Lakes are full of off-duty officers, Lizzy, can you think of anything more diverting?"

Elizabeth did not think she should give her answer, as her sister would certainly not welcome her views if she knew them, so she smiled and said she must really be getting along.

"You are not staying at Hawkside, are you, Lizzy?" asked Lydia.

Elizabeth imagined her sister would be most distressed to have Mr Darcy in the vicinity and was glad to give her reassurance.

"Oh, no, we will be near Winandermere, which I am sure you know is at least ten miles in the opposite direction. We are staying with Jane and Mr Bingley. Our aunt Gardiner is also of the party."

"Well, Lizzy," said Lydia with a theatrical sigh, "I am most put out, I assure you. What a pity we could not all enjoy a family reunion, but as you say, we will be so far apart. Kiss me, dearest sister, for I do not know when I shall ever see you again."

Elizabeth suffered her sister's exuberant embraces and protestations on parting with friends, but at last was made free to hurry back to the inn. Her experience had left her feeling quite flustered. If Mr Darcy found out that her sister and Wickham were in the vicinity, he would probably make a scene, she thought, ordering them out of Westmorland within a moment's notice. It would surely be better not to mention the fact that she had seen them, saying that she had taken a turn down the street and now felt fully recovered. This last sentiment was far from the truth; if anything, her headache was rather worse, but in the interests of peace and harmony, a small deviation from the complete truth was absolutely necessary.

Entering the passage at the foot of the stairs leading up to the dining room, she was most relieved to see Jane, who had come in search of her and, before long, had told her the tale of her encounter, unburdening her worries and swearing her to secrecy.

"Oh, Lizzy, do not worry, I am sure we will not see them again. I feel sure you have done quite the right thing. Mr Darcy would be upset; you are merely thinking of him in all of this and being considerate of his feelings. It is a pity that we cannot know our sister and her husband better, but in any case, I daresay they should not have any time for us."

"No, indeed, I should say not. Lydia will be completely occupied in Hawkside by all accounts. I am relieved that we shall be on quite the other side of the district."

Mr Darcy appeared on the stairs at that moment, rejoicing and scolding his wife simultaneously for her safe return. She gave her excuses, soothing his irascible mood by diverting the conversation to that of a discussion of the scenes to be witnessed on the next leg of the journey, a favourite topic with her husband.

They were soon off again, relieved to know that their destination was not far off. Little over an hour passed before they found themselves winding through an undulating road over low promontories and spacious bays, which gradually rose over the hills. From here Elizabeth grasped Fitzwilliam's arm in excitement as, like a majestic river, Winandermere swept along in gentle beauty, the shores and hills as richly wooded as a pleasure ground. Here and there the land opened up through the landscape to the sight of some distant villa, a sign that society had even found its way to this remote corner of England. The weather was showery with sudden bursts of sunshine, the tops of distant mountains concealed in vapour ascending in grey columns. Hues of blue and purple enveloped the tops of hills, whilst lower down shades of olive and brown ranged over craggy heathland and wooded slopes, which appeared to fall into the water like soft green velvet cushions.

Bellingham Hall came into view at last, glimpsed through trees on a gentle eminence of the shore with the silver lake spreading before in all its translucent splendour, crowned beyond by the fells, which were half obscured in clouds. An Elizabethan

just after all the scandalous business with Lydia had been tied
up and in response to one she had sent after discovering that
Mr Darcy had been at Lydia's wedding. Elizabeth had been
ignorant at the time of the part Mr Darcy had played in bringing about the marriage and paying off Wickham, not only to
induce him to marrying her foolish sister but also in paying off
his debts. Mr Darcy had gone to London when he first learned
of their elopement and Lizzy remembered her aunt's mention
of him going first to call on Mrs Younge who had at one time
been governess to Miss Darcy, and ultimately dismissed from
her charge after it had been found that she assisted Wickham
in the attempted elopement with Miss Darcy. When searching
for Wickham and Lydia, Mr Darcy went immediately to Mrs
Younge for intelligence of him as soon as he got to town. But
it was two or three days before he could get from her what he
wanted. She would not betray her trust without bribery and
corruption, for she really did know where her friend was to be
found. Did Lydia realise she was keeping company with someone
who had such little integrity? Elizabeth would have liked to
believe that her sister was completely innocent and naïve, but
she knew her sister too well to believe that she would not be
aware that Mrs Younge's character was unsound and that she
was a disreputable person, not at all to be trusted. But then,
Lydia never had been a very good judge of character and, being
seriously flawed in her own nature, was quite incapable of seeing
defects in others. She would be attracted to Mrs Younge for her
pretty face and vivacious manner; Lydia would scarcely look
beyond her companion's physical attributes before deciding to
become best friends. Thoughtless Lydia! Elizabeth did not know
what to do, but resolved to speak to her aunt at the earliest

opportunity. In the meantime, her husband was looking at her with a bemused expression.

"Am I interrupting your thoughts, Mrs Darcy?" he asked. "You seem rather pre-occupied."

"Oh, no, Fitzwilliam," she whispered, drawing closer to him, blocking all thoughts of the Wickhams and Mrs Younge from her mind. "I was just thinking how lucky I am to have a husband who brings me to witness the quiet delights of Westmorland instead of taking me to town. I am so very grateful to you, my darling; I could not have enjoyed myself half so much with all of London society, however diverting. To be here on our own and with those we love is heaven indeed. And to add to all of this, we have such beauty before us in every outlook."

The views through their windows made her catch her breath with wonder. Veils of white mist hung over the lake and on the mountains yonder where the peaks iced with snow almost disappeared into the vapour. The rain had stopped and the day was turning fine; wisps of blue sky lit up by shafts of sunlight descending through the clouds were reflected in the water like an ethereal looking glass.

"I cannot wait to explore everywhere," said Elizabeth. "Is it not a beautiful sight, Mr Darcy?"

"Indeed, I have rarely seen such beauty," answered her husband, gazing into her eyes and planting another kiss on her lips.

"I am talking of the view," she protested half-heartedly with a laugh as he pulled her yet closer.

"Oh, so am I, Mrs Darcy, so am I."

Chapter 23

A FORTNIGHT OF SWEET felicity soon passed in the company of those Elizabeth loved best. She was feeling strong, energetic, and in blooming good health. The walks around Winandermere exhilarated her, with every day bringing fresh discoveries. The problems and anxieties that she had encountered at Pemberley seemed to belong to a different world, as if none of it had happened. She had never felt so close to Fitzwilliam before and she refused to dwell on any unpleasant recollections that sometimes threatened to overwhelm her. Even Georgiana's spirits seemed lifted. To hear her laugh again was a joy to both Elizabeth and Mr Darcy.

"I wonder if I was not a little quick to decide that my plans for Georgiana were flawed," he said as they prepared to go down for breakfast one morning. "I think perhaps a little holiday was all that was required to put the spring back into her step. No doubt she has Hugh Calladine painted as a romantic hero in her mind's eye and sees his handsome face in every rock and twisted tree. There is nothing like absence to swell the pangs of love, or a romantic landscape to inspire affection, especially for a swain across the miles."

"I do not know about all that. Like you, I am pleased to see Georgiana in better spirits, but I am not convinced of it having to do with any romantic notions about her fiancé. I have to admit that you have me completely intrigued by what you say about absence swelling love's pangs. You sound quite the expert, Fitzwilliam," said Elizabeth, trying not to laugh at him but failing to do so. "Am I to believe that you have suffered such agonies of affliction yourself?"

"Mock me, Mrs Darcy, all you choose, but I will admit to having suffered love's pains when we were apart. For four months I did not see you after Bingley and I left Netherfield for town. I am not ashamed to tell you that you were never far from my thoughts."

"Ah, yes, but your pain was quite of your own making, was it not? And I am certain your suffering was more to do with the agony of acknowledging that you had feelings for me than to do with being apart. I believe you were vexed with yourself for falling in love with me; cross and quite angry that despite all your efforts to despise me, you could not help yourself."

"Mrs Darcy, you have a very cruel streak. Do not remind me of the man I was then. But you will not have it all your own way. Whatever may have been my misguided thoughts about the situation, I knew I was in love with you."

"Did you?"

"You know as much. I have told you before."

"Well, Mr Darcy, I wish to hear it again. When did you first realise that you were in love with me?"

"I cannot fix on the hour or the spot or the look or the words which laid the foundation. It is too long ago. I was in the middle before I knew that I had begun."

"Yes, you have said all that before… but there must have been a moment when you knew there was no escape from my allurements, that, as your aunt would say, I had drawn you in."

Mr Darcy laughed. "I always knew your abuse of me was by design, that you drew me in by pretending to be as unflattering and critical of me as you dared. You thought you could not win me by your form, wit, and fine eyes alone, so you resorted to pretending to dislike me in an effort to gain my attention."

"By design, how can you say so, you incorrigible, infuriating, provoking man? Indeed, Mr Darcy, no deception was necessary, I assure you." Elizabeth took his arm in hers before stating, "I hated you then as much as I love you now."

Fitzwilliam put his hand over hers. "Do you love me, Elizabeth?"

"You know I do, darling."

"Well, Mrs Darcy, I wish to hear it again."

"I love you," she whispered, pulling him toward the door and, looking up at him with a mischievous glint in her eye, added, "but only on days with a 'y' in them."

Almost everyone was seated at the breakfast table when the Darcys made an appearance. No one batted an eyelid at them; they were quite used to the couple being last to sit down, each privately assessing the reasons for their perpetual lateness. But this morning they were not the last to arrive for breakfast.

"Where is Miss Georgiana?" asked Mr Darcy as he helped himself from the platters of ham, eggs, and soft rolls upon the table.

Jane spoke. "She has gone out to the village to collect the post."

"There is no need for her to do that. One of the servants can go. I am not sure she should be wandering around on her own."

"It is but a short walk, Fitzwilliam," Elizabeth said. "She likes to go out walking by herself. I am sure she will be here in a moment."

At these words Georgiana came flying into the room clutching a handful of letters, her cheeks flushed by the exercise and with an air of animation and high spirits. "I have letters for you all!" she exclaimed. "Mrs Biddle in the village says she has never been so busy with so much correspondence. Mrs Gardiner, I think you have the most, seven letters in all."

"Oh, they will be from the children, I daresay," said Mrs Gardiner, "full of news of London."

The letters were handed out and a few minutes passed where silence reigned as the missives were read.

"Well, I never," said Mr Bingley at last. "I cannot quite believe it, but I have it in writing here that my sisters are leaving London and Mr Hurst behind, as I speak, to head north to the Lakes."

"Caroline is leaving London and all its entertainments to come up to the North?" asked Jane, who sounded as astonished at this piece of news as she looked disappointed.

"It seems Caroline has been finding society very dull of late. But listen to this… perhaps the inducement to travel lies in other directions. Not all society is so very tedious to my sister Caroline, it appears."

"Whatever do you mean, Charles?" asked Jane, whose heart was sinking at the prospect of spending any time with her sister-in-law.

Charles Bingley cleared his throat and read out loud.

*"At one of Lady Metcalfe's drawing rooms, Louisa
and I were introduced to a fellow by the name of*

Dalton. He is a painter, an advocate for the pictur-esque, of which he is a great exponent. Lord Dalton prefers not to be known by his title, and indeed, I have only just discovered that he has one, that he is not only of noble ancestry, but also that he is one of the richest men in Westmorland. This gentleman's work and his philosophy is all the rage in London, and he is fêted wherever he goes. His talks on the simple pleasures of life in the Lakes, where he was born, have moved me to the extent that I shall not rest until I have experienced it for myself: nature in all its sublimity. As Dalton says, truth and refined taste can only grow from studying nature. To be at one with nature, to define and expe-rience the picturesque can only be truly appreciated from close observance of the landscape. I am, therefore, following him to the Lakes and will reside in a cottage near Hawkside to live as simply as I can. Society holds no attraction for me anymore. Dearest Charles, I have cast off the shackles of a civilisation that no longer has any charms for me. I believe there will be several disci-ples following in his wake, but I do not think I exag-gerate when I say that Lord Dalton and I have become particular friends. I shall write to let you know when Louisa and I arrive at Robin Cot, Hawkside."

During this speech Elizabeth had found it increasingly difficult not to laugh out loud, especially when she happened to catch Jane's eye from across the table. The thought that Caroline Bingley with all her pretensions to grandeur could swap the high life for a humbler existence in a cottage was extraordinarily comic. She could not resist saying, "Do you think there may be more than an appreciation of nature at work here, Mr Bingley? Is there some love in the case?"

"My goodness," said Bingley, "I am beginning to wonder."

"Has Miss Bingley always enjoyed such an appreciation of nature?" Elizabeth continued, ignoring the nudge of her husband's foot under the table.

"I can't say I ever noticed it before," Bingley muttered, scratching his head. "It doesn't make sense. I can no more see Caro in a cottage than I can myself. What the deuce has happened to her, do you suppose?"

"Love does many strange things, and the most unlikely pairings take place in springtime," answered Mrs Darcy, gazing into her husband's eyes with a wink and a smirk.

However, Mr Darcy was not to be diverted from Charles's conversation or from the perusal of his own letter, in which he had suddenly become most engrossed. "Good God!" he exclaimed in an agitated voice.

"My love, whatever is wrong?" cried Elizabeth, feeling quite alarmed at the flush spreading over her husband's face. Everyone's eyes turned toward him in concern.

"It seems this Dalton fellow has been creating havoc wherever he goes," he said, re-examining the letter he held in his hand. "My aunt, Lady Catherine de Bourgh, informs me that she is taking a house further along the shore here at Winandermere on the recommendation of her friend Lady Metcalfe. She is bringing a party from London immediately, including not only the painter and poet, Lord Henry Dalton, but also her friends, Lord and Lady Metcalfe, Lord Featherstone, the Miss Winns, Mr and Mrs Collins, and one or two others I have never heard of before… literary types, poets, I believe. She claims that this Dalton fellow is not only a painter of the highest order, but that he is a great orator and has charmed London society as no other has done before him. Her soirée is postponed until they arrive as she is anxious for us all to meet him."

"And how many more will follow in their wake?" cried Elizabeth, quite unable to hide her disapprobation for the scheme. "I do not think I am ready for the whole of London to arrive in smart barouches clogging up the lanes and throwing balls and parties every night."

The table fell silent as each person reflected on their own misgivings.

"Well, I expect they will be far too busy running around the countryside with easels and writing books to do much entertaining," said Mr Darcy perusing the letter once more. "I confess, even my aunt seems to be given over with scribbling verses. Ah, here it is, she says… 'there are few people in England, I suppose, who have more true enjoyment of art and literature than myself, or a better natural taste. If I had ever had the benefit of Georgiana's masters or the luxury of time spent away from an ailing child, I should have been prolific. As it is, I must content myself with the fact that Lord Dalton says he has rarely witnessed such superb enjambment as he finds in my work.'"

"Forgive my ignorance," said Mrs Gardiner as both she and Mrs Butler looked on with a mixture of puzzlement and incredulity, "could you please enlighten me?"

"Enjambment comes from a French word meaning to put one's leg across or to step over," answered Elizabeth mischievously, "but, in this case, I imagine that Lady Catherine is referring to the running over of a sentence from one verse or couplet into another so that closely related words fall in different lines."

"Here we are," continued Mr Darcy, "my aunt has been kind enough to include one of her verses for illustration with the note that she has recited the very same before Lord Dalton's friends with the most flattering success.

"Not far from Ambleside's banks and bay
An humble dwelling rose;
Around its walls the woodbine twin'd,
Encircled with the rose.
The purple violet at their feet,
Perfum'd the ambient air,
And those who view'd the lovely cot,
Thought it—a shield from care!

"There is more, but I am sure you get the picture."

"Oh, I like the part about the perfumed violets," cried Georgiana. "Fancy my aunt a poetess!"

For Elizabeth, now close to exploding with mirth for the image conjured in her mind of Lady Catherine reciting her poetry before an audience all trying to outdo one another with romantic idylls, tempests, and spontaneous lines addressed to nature, it was all too much. "Oh dear," she could not resist adding, "do you suppose we shall have to communicate in verse when we meet?"

"Lord, help us all," muttered Mr Darcy under his breath, but not so quietly that the whole company could not hear him. "Bingley, I hope you know the difference between an epic and an epigram, or I fear you'll be cut and snubbed by all of new Lake society! Mrs Bingley, be most careful when you are out walking this afternoon in case you feel a sonnet coming on, and Mrs Gardiner, Mrs Butler, beware the ballad and the ode!"

The tension was broken at last and everybody laughed.

Georgiana excused herself when she could to escape to her room in order that she could read her letters. It was no accident that she volunteered daily to fetch the post, disappearing before anyone else had risen, to go down to the village further along the shore. Her personal correspondence over the last fortnight had been a source of constant delight. She had kept her promise to Mr Butler and had written to him, but far from writing only once, she had corresponded whenever she could, letters to entertain with snippets of her daily routine accompanied by notes and drawings on the landscape, which by all accounts he was enjoying very much. To her enormous excitement, Tom had written back just as much telling her of his escapades in London. His patron, Lord Featherstone, was there for the season and, besides attending to the work Tom had to do, he had been invited to stay with the old bachelor who had taken him under his wing. Having no wife or children, Lord Featherstone enjoyed the young man's companionship and was invited everywhere with him.

Georgiana tore open her letters with impatience. Firstly, one from a friend in London was read, followed by one from Mrs Annesley, who was enjoying her stay in Weymouth with her sister. The third she saved until last and with a mixture of excitement and elation opened the seal with trembling fingers.

> *Dearest Georgiana,*
>   *I hope this letter finds you as well as I am. Thank you for your last—I loved the drawing of a sunset over*

Winandermere—it was so good I could smell the air moving over the water stirring the lake into ruffles of crimson sateen. How I wish I could be there to see such a sight with you, to sit at your side, each with a pencil in hand to draw the beauty around us.

London is filling up; there are more carriages arriving every day, and there is such a ceaseless bustle and hustle about the place that I long for the solitude you have. To be able to sit at the side of a lake with ne'er another soul in sight must be wonderful. Still, to see it all through your eyes is reward enough if I cannot have the real thing.

I hope you enjoy the enclosed. We made a visit to the Tower of London and I have drawn some of the wild beasts to be found there. I am not sure who is the more curious, and the animals have such a way of looking at you that I almost began to feel that I was the caged one. Do write and tell me what you think! I must away, as Lord Featherstone is calling me—I shall endeavour to find the time to write some more before I catch the last post.

Since writing the above, I have just heard some incredible news. It seems that my patron has been invited to the Lakes, to a house party. I know none of the particulars, but it is too much to hope that I shall also be asked to come. Lucky, lucky Featherstone!

I will write again as soon as I can with any more news.

Affectly yours,
Thomas Butler.

Georgiana was all hope. She had heard her brother mention Lord Featherstone's name at breakfast, and now she was filled with anticipation, trusting that Tom's patron could no more do without him in the Lakes than he could in London. If she could just have one glimpse of Thomas Butler that would be enough to satisfy, she told herself. Ever since they had arrived, despite all attempts to blot Tom out of her mind, she had been unsuccessful. His letters were her solace and pleasure. Mr Darcy had been quite right about Georgiana's romantic sensibility, but not with any reference to Mr Calladine, who had sent no missive of any kind. No, her thoughts and visions were all centred on Tom, whose countenance she espied on every distant hilltop vista and Lakeland scene.

Chapter 24

AT THE VERY START of April, as the daffodils danced on the quiet shoreline of Lake Winandermere, an untidy procession of coaches, carriages, tilburies, and phaetons noisily wound their way along the roads from Kendal to their various destinations, some toward the lake itself whilst others travelled on to more remote hideaways.

Caroline Bingley and Louisa Hurst looked out of their carriage window in expectation as they bowled along.

"How soon do you think we shall see *him*, Louisa?" said Miss Bingley, who could not speak Lord Dalton's name out loud for fear of raising her blushes higher. Caroline, who had never felt anything remotely like love for anyone in her life before, was completely smitten. Such a change had come over her that she hardly recognised herself. So softened by her notions of amour and romance had she become that even Louisa looked quite handsome today in her eyes, which was saying a lot, because apart from the sibling rivalry that prevented her from ever admitting anything in her sister's favour, she privately thought that Mrs Hurst was very fortunate to have caught herself a husband with a countenance that she considered would make a turbot appear attractive.

"You gave him our forwarding address, did you not, Caroline? I am sure he will find us if that is his desire," answered her sister with a look of discontent spreading over her face. In her opinion, there was little chance of Lord Dalton calling often, if at all, but she kept her thoughts to herself. She started to gesticulate through the window. "It all looks rather wild out there. Are you quite sure this is such a good idea? To turn down Lady Catherine's kind invitation so you can cavort in a cottage is not my idea of fun. What did you mean by it, Caro? Have you gone mad?"

"I confess, I think I am a little mad, dearest Louisa... mad in love, if you please. And I think when you hear me out, you will see that my reasons for choosing a sweet cot are very sane."

"There's nothing sane about wanting to stay in a tiny hovel a peasant wouldn't thank you for, with no servants to light the fires and no cook to wait on us. I do not know how you talked me into staying with you."

"Oh, Lulu, you know I must have a chaperone, especially one that likes to take herself off for long walks when a certain gentleman comes calling. It is so romantic! I can see it all! Just picture it: a cosy sofa by the fire and Henry on his knees before me. Louisa, this is my chance, you must know that."

Louisa knew nothing of the sort and privately thought that her sister had as much chance of winning over Lord Dalton as she had of winning the State Lottery, which she never did. The fact that he seemed similarly smitten with one of Lady Catherine's circle, the unassuming yet beautiful Miss Theodora Winn, was a truth that Caroline refused to acknowledge or admit.

Presently, the carriage stopped, the door opened, and the steps were let down. "You'll have to get out here," said the driver of the post chaise. "I can't get down that track; I'll never get back again."

"But how far is Robin Cot from here?" snapped Mrs Hurst who was less than impressed by the coachman's attitude.

"I can't say, ma'am, it depends who's doing the walking," he answered gruffly, observing their fine kid shoes. "Though by just looking I'd say fifteen minutes if the mud's baked, twenty-five if not. That's Robin Cot yonder."

The sisters followed his pointing finger to the sight of a small dwelling, which could just be seen through a clump of trees on the brow of a hill in the distance. The narrow lane they must walk down was three inches deep in mud. Neither sister was equipped for such a jaunt nor did they relish the prospect of undertaking such a feat. They looked at one another in horror. "But you cannot leave us here," wailed Caroline, as she watched the driver climb back onto the box.

"Company rules, ma'am," he shouted, with a dismissive wave as he set off to leave them. "I'll arrange for your luggage to be brought up to the cottage, but you'll have to pay extra for a man to carry it all. Good-bye, ladies, I hope you enjoy your stay!"

As the sisters were struggling down the lane, each berating the other for anything and everything, Lady Catherine de Bourgh, accompanied by Mr and Mrs Collins, was calling at Bellingham Hall. Mr and Mrs Darcy and Miss Georgiana attended their guests in the Chinese drawing room. Elizabeth greeted her friend Charlotte with the liveliest pleasure and her husband as formally as his manners entailed. It was so good to see her old friend again, and though they had much to discuss, little could be accomplished with Lady Catherine in the room. There was nothing to be done but to listen to this formidable woman talk, which they all did without any inter-mission till the tea things came in, delivering her opinion on Winandermere, Lord Dalton's sublime painting, and her poetry writing in her usual decisive manner. If she paused for breath, Mr Collins supplied what was missing with much flattery in his usual grave tones punctuated with deferential bowing in Mr Darcy's direction.

"You and all your guests are invited to come along to my first soirée at Golgarth Park," Lady Catherine announced with a slight nod of her head, as if bestowing a gift of great worth. "It will be an occasion not to be missed. Everyone is arriving from London; in particular, Lord Dalton and Lord Featherstone are my very special guests. Featherstone was such a great comfort to me when my husband died, Mrs Darcy, I cannot tell you. He is a great man. Of course Lord Dalton has promised to speak about his work and will be reading from a selection of my poetical writ-ings. Mrs Darcy, you will be interested to know that your friend, Mrs Collins, has been most fortunate to be present at all our meetings and will, no doubt, enlighten you as to the methods and philosophies behind the arts we shall be discussing."

Elizabeth looked across to where Charlotte was sitting. Poor Charlotte had blushed pink and was looking as if she wished to be anywhere else but in the room. Mrs Darcy was quite certain that Lady Catherine had coerced her friend into attending the meetings and could not begin to imagine what agonies she must have suffered at the hands of the poetry and painting circle.

Lady Catherine spoke again to Elizabeth. "Do not be alarmed that your ignorance of fine art and poetry will leave you at a disadvantage in the first instance, Mrs Darcy. Mrs Collins will be there to advise you."

"I do not know how to thank you enough, Lady Catherine," answered Elizabeth, feeling quite mortified, not only for herself but also for poor Charlotte who bit her lip in embarrassment at Lady Catherine's rudeness.

"If I," said Mr Collins, "were so fortunate as to be able to compose poetry, I should have great pleasure, I am sure, in obliging the company with a sonnet, for I consider poetry as a very innocent diversion and perfectly compatible with the profession of a clergyman. However, the rector of a parish has much to do of a more practical nature, and so I am obliged to leave such composition to those with the leisure to pursue their literary craft. Lady Catherine is the finest exponent of the *petits vers de société*, and I must add that although I consider my dear Charlotte and I to have but one mind and one way of thinking, I bow to her superiority when it comes to the written word."

"But, Mr Collins, is it not a fact that you must write sermons for the benefit of your parishioners, and as such, a well-crafted lesson which has ramifications not only for their understanding but for their moral well-being is surely as fine as any piece of poetry committed to paper?" asked Elizabeth, with a perfectly straight face.

"Mrs Darcy, I am most sincerely complimented by your sentiments. Firstly, whilst a humble clergyman as myself dare not flatter himself to be most fortunately blessed in this capacity, according to those who judge such matters, I am assured of setting the example of excellence in sermon composition in my parish for the optimum benefit to all. Secondly, I am convinced that such a gift—which is surely disposed from above—dispenses not only spiritual balm ensuring the welfare of my flock, but also essentially assists in their general happiness; and thirdly—which perhaps I ought to have mentioned earlier—that it is the particular advice and recommendation of my very noble patroness to allow such time for the exercise that will improve and enhance my method and delivery. I think, if pressed, Lady Catherine would concur..."

"Darcy," interrupted Lady Catherine, talking over the top of William Collins, forcing him into silent apologies and yet more frantic bowing, "we shall take our leave. It only remains for me to say that I shall expect you all on Friday se'nnight. Dearest Georgiana, do not be afraid of such august company. The possession of a superior bent for artistic merit is endowed only on the minority. Learn from your betters where you can. Your cousin Anne will be present. You will be pleased to see her again, no doubt. It is such a pity that ill health has robbed my only daughter of attaining excellence at the hands of the Masters, but I welcome Lord Dalton's very particular interest in her society. He hardly leaves her side when he visits. There is something very pleasing in the sight of a young, handsome couple engaged in conversation on a subject of mutual interest. Do you not agree, Mrs Darcy?

"I do, indeed," said Elizabeth, instantly curious about the physical appearance of Lord Dalton whose looks had been compared to Anne de Bourgh's. From what Elizabeth remembered of her, she was small and thin; a pale, sickly creature; and her features, though not plain, were insignificant. During Elizabeth's stay at Hunsford, Anne had spoken very little. The thought of Miss de Bourgh engaged in animated conversation was impossible to imagine. The whole idea of spending time at Golgarth

Park was too dreadful to contemplate, but she must admit she was curious to see this nonpareil that was all the rage of London. For a nonpareil Lord Dalton must be, she decided, for half of the city and so many females to be descending on the Lakes, especially when she considered that Caroline Bingley had never expressed any former passion for painting.

"I bid you a good morning, Darcy. Georgiana, you may accompany me to my carriage, and Mrs Darcy, I will add this recommendation. You need to exercise more, for you are looking decidedly sallow and peaky. Take my advice and walk; you will look and feel much better for it," said Lady Catherine as she swept out of the door.

Mr Collins immediately rose and followed, practically running behind her, but as soon as she could, Elizabeth arrested Charlotte, making her promise to visit the next day and to bring the baby if she could manage to do so.

Chapter 25

THE NEXT MORNING FOUND Georgiana up early to go on her regular walk to collect the post. Although she was looking forward very much to seeing if there was another letter from Tom, she could not help feeling disappointed. On accompanying Lady Catherine to her carriage the day before, Georgiana had questioned her aunt on all her guests in minute detail. She had learned that Lord Featherstone had no one accompanying him, so that meant that Tom would still be in London and not in the Lakes as she had hoped. She was very disheartened, but perhaps it was for the best.

Georgiana took the route along the lakeside, not the quickest, but the most beautiful. Everyday there was something new to see in the ever changing scene, whether it was of wildlife frequenting the water or the effects caused by weather transforming the mere into one of ethereal fantasy as the light and mists descended to play upon the surface. This morning, swathes of white vapour draped like bridal veils across the water rose in filmy clouds up to the blue heavens, transforming all she could see into shades of lilac and cerulean so that the fells and the water met one another in mutual harmony. She must remember to describe the scene to Tom, she thought, and could not resist pulling out her pocket sketchbook she had made for such a purpose. The sun was breaking through the clouds, fanning sunbeam fingers restlessly, caressing the surface of the mere like a pianist scaling up and down the keys. Everywhere was silence and for a moment Georgiana felt as if she were the only person in the world, and so small did she feel against the majesty of the mountains that made such a stunning backdrop, as well as the surrounding beauty of the landscape, that she was filled with a sense of the divine. Her pencil made rapid strokes. It was no good, she decided. It was impossible to do justice without using colour and she vowed to return later with her paints and brushes. As she emitted a long sigh, resolving to continue her journey, she was disturbed by the sound of breaking twigs; someone or something was moving along in an obvious hurry, down through the clump of trees some yards behind her. Georgiana turned at the sound. For a moment she contemplated the gentleman in the distance who stood stock still at the sight of her as if she witnessed an apparition. The shock was great and her natural instinct was to withdraw into the shelter of engulfing trees, but as he ran toward her Georgiana's face lit up with joy on contemplation of his smiling countenance. Her pencil and pocketbook fell to the ground.

Miss Bingley tried again to light the fire in the tiny room that served as both kitchen and parlour. Louisa, sprawled in one of the only two chairs they possessed, looked on with impatience. "Caro, let us get some help. I do not understand why you are being so stubborn. If you'd only let me get someone to come in from the village, or better still, have us de-camp from here entirely to take refuge with Lady Catherine or one of our other friends, we would be much happier and infinitely warmer! I'm sure you're doing it all wrong."

"Well, your efforts did not produce a single spark let alone a flame, so I do not know why you are criticising me," snapped her sister. "At least there is a smoulder in the grate even if it is only smoking now." Caroline pushed back a tendril of hair that had fallen into her eyes, leaving a black smudge across her face.

Louisa howled out loud with laughter.

"What's the matter now?" shouted Caroline with indignation. "You come and light it if you think it's so hilarious."

"I wouldn't dream of usurping your place as the expert on all matters domestic," drawled Louisa lazily, deciding there and then not to inform her sister of the sooty smears which rendered Caroline's countenance quite ridiculous in her opinion.

Their ensuing argument was only broken by a knock at the door. Caroline eagerly rushed to open it in the hope that she might find Lord Dalton on the doorstep. It would not matter if her hands looked slightly careworn, she thought. Her appearance would be more authentic for having a few blisters and dirty marks. Lord Dalton's paintings themselves reflected not only the romantic vision of life in a cottage, but also that of the humble peasant dirtying their hands with good, honest work. Caroline put on her best smile and flung open the door.

Lord Dalton did not speak. His eyes twinkled with amusement and it was very clear that he was suppressing more than a smile. "Good morning, Miss Bingley. Forgive me, do I call at a difficult time?"

"Lord Dalton!" cried Caroline, instantly hiding her dirty hands behind her back. "Do come in, we are so glad to see you at last."

Lord Dalton passed into the small hall, ducking his head under the doorway into the parlour. Caroline followed, gazing at his back in admiration. She surmised that he was taller and broader than Mr Darcy; a fine figure of a man were the words that sprang to mind. Flecks of grey glinted here and there through his wavy dark hair, giving him a distinguished air. From her vantage point behind him, she gesticulated wildly at her sister, flapping her arms with the intent, Louisa was sure, of removing her from the vicinity. But Louisa was not going to be moved so speedily.

"How pleasant to see you again, Lord Dalton," Mrs Hurst said, extending her hand toward him, which he promptly took and kissed. "It is so kind of you to call upon us in our simple cot. Do sit down."

He looked about him, but such were the scarcity of chairs that he denied himself the only spare seat and turned quickly to offer it to Miss Bingley just as she was signalling in no uncertain terms that it was time for her sister to leave. There was nothing to be done but to pretend that she was waving at a fly, and with exclamations she considered fitting to fly swatting continued to swing her arms in the air.

Louisa remarked with a smirk that she was about to go out and directed Lord Dalton to her seat as she rose. Delighting in both Dalton's expression (surely of horror at the idea of being left alone to entertain a deranged woman with coal smuts on her face) and by her further delay of several more minutes as she donned a cloak and bonnet, she was pleased to see Caroline almost apoplectic with indignation as she left.

Elizabeth cradled Charlotte's baby in her arms. The friends were sitting together, quite alone, in a small sitting room overlooking the lake. Lizzy was thankful that Mrs Collins had called when everyone else was either occupied or out. Mrs Gardiner and Mrs Butler had gone down to the village, Jane and Bingley were out walking, and Georgiana was sitting sketching in her favourite spot on the lawn as Mr Darcy watched, glad not only to have an opportunity to talk to his sister, but also mindful that his wife would want to have her friend to herself and not necessarily wish him to be in their company.

"Catherine is the most delightful babe," Elizabeth enthused, kissing the top of her head. Catherine gurgled with pleasure, making Lizzy smile. The thought that she would one day soon have a baby of her own to comfort was a delightful one, but she couldn't quite imagine it just yet. There were so many questions Elizabeth had for Charlotte. She observed her friend, noting her cheerful demeanour, her features and figure rounded into softness, which she had often recognised in others who led a comfortable and satisfying existence. Despite the misgivings she had felt when Charlotte had married Mr Collins, she was pleased that her fears were unfounded in every respect. Mrs Collins looked happier and more fulfilled than Elizabeth had ever seen her.

"Oh, Lizzy, you know I had wondered not so long ago if I was to go through my life never knowing what it is to be a mother. Indeed, I think I surprised quite a few people when I became a wife."

Elizabeth did not know how to answer this without betraying the fact that she had been one of those people. She smiled encouragingly instead and Charlotte continued.

"Oh, I know, Lizzy, you did have objections to my marrying him, but I hope I've proved that ours is a very satisfactory match. We are suited in many ways, not least in our ability not to expect too much of the other nor of our situation in matrimony. That way disappointment is not easily met and any small happiness is seized upon with delight. Perhaps I did not immediately feel for my spouse what you felt for yours on marrying, but I have to tell you that with Catherine's arrival this unromantic soul has taken a turn to the contrary; I am in love with William as much as I ever hoped to be. I cannot tell you the joy my daughter brings me; every day has something new to learn."

"Oh, Charlotte," enthused Elizabeth, "I am so happy for you, and more so because you deserve such happiness more than anyone else I know."

"Well, that is enough about me running away with my feelings. I want to say how wonderful it is to see you again, Lizzy. Marriage is certainly suiting you; there is such a glow about you." Charlotte paused, her head on one side as she contemplated Mrs Darcy's form. She smiled, a knowing expression on her face. "The Derbyshire air is clearly very good for one's health and… you have filled out a little, I think."

Elizabeth looked at her friend whose countenance betrayed her every thought. Lizzy laughed. "I see what you are thinking, Charlotte, and if you promise not to tell anyone yet, I shall tell you what you have already guessed."

"Is it true, Elizabeth? Oh, I am thrilled for you! I should not say it but I only had to see the way Mr Darcy behaves toward you to suspect it."

"Oh dear, is it that obvious?" Elizabeth laughed merrily as her friend nodded.

"Well, perhaps it is not obvious to all," Charlotte admitted at last. "Mr Collins has no idea, and I have chosen not to enlighten him with my conjectures. I know him too well to suppose he could keep it a secret, and I am certain you will not want everyone to know just yet. He would not resist telling Lady Catherine or making hints to Mr Darcy, I am sure, so I have kept my thoughts to myself. I suppose Jane knows, does she?"

"Yes, of course, she was one of the first to hear of it, and Aunt Gardiner. Lady Catherine has already made many impertinent remarks, though I hope I have not given her any true reason for suspecting my condition. But, Charlotte, please promise not to mention it to your mother, for I have not told mine and I do so want to keep it secret for a little while longer."

"Not a word shall pass my lips, you know that," said Charlotte with a pat of Lizzy's hand.

"Now tell me," said Elizabeth, trying not to laugh again, "how might I improve myself enough for an evening amongst the august company of Lady Catherine's circle?"

"Dear Lizzy, I cannot tell you what I have endured, though I am sure you would have found it all extremely diverting. Follies and nonsense such as you have never witnessed before, believe me. I do not think I shall tell you all for fear of spoiling your pleasure. That is if you think you shall be coming to the event of the year!"

"I wouldn't miss it for the world," Elizabeth replied. "Do you know exactly who has been invited?"

"Well, we have many people staying at the Park who will be in attendance, like Lord Dalton, Lord Featherstone, and Lady Metcalfe. Then there is Theodora Winn and her sister Emma, two lady poetesses, the Misses Tankerville and Ponsonby respectively, three gentlemen painters, Mr Richardson, Mr Hunter, and Mr Ellis, as well as Mr Fraser and Mr Murray who write poetry and plays, I believe. Caroline Bingley and her sister have been invited also, of course. I expect they will have called to see you."

"No, I did not know they were yet arrived," said Elizabeth. "Is it true that they are staying in a cottage?"

"Apparently so," said Charlotte with a nod of her head. "Between you and me, Miss Bingley has a soft spot for Lord Dalton, and I have a feeling that her residence in a rural idyll is for the benefit of gaining his admiration. He has a passion for tumbledown dwellings which are shown to great effect in his latest series of paintings."

"Oh dear, poor Caroline," said Elizabeth, suppressing a laugh. "I cannot imagine how she is coping."

"Nor I. Lady Catherine was most put out when she heard that they had refused her invitation. She was so piqued that she set about immediately trying to find a replacement. It seems she had the fortune to bump into some old acquaintance of her husband in Kendal. Apparently the Cathcarts had been staying with a colonel of some Northern regiment in Hawkside and were on their way home when Lady Catherine persuaded them to put up at Golgarth for a few days."

Elizabeth instantly recalled the meeting with her sister and Lydia's mention of Wickham's Newcastle regiment. But there was no need to worry about that, she persuaded herself. Lydia and her friends were away on the other side of the Lakes and even if they were in the vicinity she was sure that an evening of painting and poetry criticism would not be of any interest to her sister and her friends. "Goodness, I hope the drawing room at Golgarth Park will accommodate so many," commented Elizabeth, unable to resist laughing again, though her expression rapidly changed on hearing what Charlotte had to divulge next.

"Oh, it's vast," answered Charlotte, "big enough for an entire regiment, which is just as well because I believe Lady Catherine has invited some of the Cathcarts' military friends for the evening too."

"Is it really you?" asked Georgiana as she gazed up into Tom's eyes. As he took her hand she prayed he would not let it go. "How can you be here?" She could not believe that he was standing before her, that he held her hand, however briefly. It was useless to deny all that Tom meant to her; just his very presence was enough to make her feel as if she were glowing inside. In that moment Georgiana recognised beyond a doubt that she was in love with Thomas Butler and there was no going back.

"My dear Miss Darcy, I knew I would find you here. Your letters described this spot so perfectly; it is exactly as I saw it in my mind's eye, such a heavenly place. Thank heaven for Lord Featherstone! I am here because of his kindness. My patron could not demand an invitation from Lady Catherine for myself, but he knew how much I would enjoy seeing the Lakes and he has long known of my wishes to explore the region. He suggested I might benefit from a holiday and he arranged for me to travel at my convenience. Besides, I think he is rather hoping to furnish some of his drawing room walls with scenes from the Lakes and I am only too happy to oblige."

"But where are you staying? Have you managed to find accommodation? Are you settled at an inn nearby?"

"That is the best part. I think I have the most wonderful employer for he insisted on finding me a small cottage of my own. It is about half a mile along the shore from Bellingham Hall. It is not a very romantic dwelling, but it is neat and clean, with a servant to cook and sweep up. I consider myself a most fortunate fellow, especially when I think I have avoided being a guest at Golgarth Park. I could not wish for anything more perfect."

"And to have a cottage of your own; I must admit, although I love my family, I cannot think of anything more splendid than to be in complete solitude amongst the lakes and mountains."

"Perhaps complete solitude might do for you, but I would prefer the company of someone with whom to share such vistas," he said, looking straight into her eyes.

"You will be spoilt for choice of beautiful views to do your paintings," remarked Georgiana, blushing as she spoke, unable to meet his gaze.

"I am sure I shall," Tom agreed, "but the only view I wish to capture is one of Miss Georgiana Darcy sitting with her sketchbook in studied contemplation of the view, the wind playing in her hair."

"I am finding my independence more and more," Georgiana continued, not knowing what to say in reply. "At first, I was only allowed to collect the post, but now my brother is happy for me to go on solitary rambles with my paints and sketchbook. I must say where I am bound and how long I shall be before I am allowed to go, but no one worries in such a safe and congenial place as Winandermere. Dearest Elizabeth has been so helpful in securing my freedom; she is a marvel. My brother will act on anything she commands."

"How wonderful. Perhaps we could meet sometimes, do you think?"

Georgiana was thoughtful. More than anything she wanted to meet Tom, but she did not want to be deceitful. Her brother, she knew, would not be at all happy about any arrangements she might wish to make. "Mr Butler, you know I would like nothing better. However, I do not think I should meet you, even if it is my dearest wish."

"If that is what you want," said Tom quietly, disappointment pronounced in every word. "Forgive me, Georgiana, I know you are in a difficult position. I should not really have come to find you, I know, but I could not help it, believe me. I will do anything you desire, even if it means I must stay away."

"Thank you, Tom," whispered Georgiana as he let her hand go at last. "I knew you would understand."

"I understand completely," he said, bowing formally before her. "I promise, Miss Georgiana Darcy, never to arrange any meeting with you, but I am duty bound to tell you that should we ever accidentally bump into one another, I shall not be responsible…"

Lord Dalton looked, to Caroline Bingley's eyes, the picture of manly perfection as she watched him on his hands and knees before the grate. His coat lay on the chair where he had abandoned it before rolling up his shirtsleeves and setting to the problem at hand. She could not help notice his muscular body as his shirt revealed what she had only imagined before. "His hands are so strong," she thought, watching him about his work. The coals had been taken off the smoking fire and were placed on a piece of newspaper. A basket of kindling and spills made of used paper had been put to good use so that now orange flames licked up the chimney in fiery tongues and the satisfying crackle of a fire spat and sputtered into life. As Henry Dalton placed coals gingerly on top of his careful arrangement, Caroline took her chance.

"Oh, do let me help," she cried, kneeling down beside him on the floor, taking care not to sully her muslin which she was beginning to realise was far too thin for such a damp cottage. She reached out for a piece of coal, trying not to grimace at the sooty marks it made on her fingers. Their heads were very close, each engaged in the task. "The smell of a man is quite intoxicating," she thought to herself, having never before been quite so close to one other than her brother Charles. Caroline felt quite elated at the near proximity of Henry. Her shoulder brushed his as she picked up another nugget and, squealing with girlish excitement, she threw it without aim. It missed the fire, bouncing back off the basket to land in her lap. Their heads turned toward the other in an instant. Caroline, overcome by the sensations she was feeling, was unable to conduct herself in any other way. She swooned, or at least she told herself that was what happened, and finding Henry's arms about her as a result looked up at him with an expression of adoration as soon as she considered it was time to come round and open her eyes.

"Miss Bingley, you've fainted straight into my arms," he said, with an expression Caroline found most pleasing. It was almost as if he were looking at her as if he had never seen her before.

"Oh, Henry," she simpered, "how can I ever thank you for saving me?"

When Louisa Hurst chose that exact moment to return, she was naturally shocked to find her sister in such a compromising attitude. She excused herself immediately, turning once more toward the door, but Lord Dalton instantly called her back, rising to his feet as rapidly as the occasion warranted, ungallantly choosing to leave Miss Bingley in a rather crumpled heap where she was on the hearthrug before the fire.

"Do forgive me, ladies," he cried, reaching for his coat with haste, "but I have suddenly remembered a prior engagement. I beg your pardon; I must take my leave this moment." There was no hint of embarrassment in his voice yet it was clear he was eager to go.

Miss Bingley was on her feet in a second. "Lord Dalton saved me, Louisa, from a most terrifying faint. I do not know what I would have done without his assistance. I might well have been aflame if not for his intervention!"

Louisa looked from her sister to Henry Dalton and considered how timely had been her return. She was certain Lord Dalton had meant to take full advantage of the hapless situation her silly sister had effected. Goodness only knew what might have happened had she not been sensible about the time she was absent. The rumours circulating London about Dalton's affairs with any eager and willing young woman were most likely unexaggerated, she thought, after having witnessed his smirking expression. And Caroline, innocent in her newfound feelings, was gazing at him in triumph as if she had secured his love forevermore. What was she to do, Louisa wondered with a sense of doom.

"Oh, Louisa," cried Caroline, after Lord Dalton had made his speedy exit like a shot from a pistol through the door, "I think Henry Dalton and I are in love!"

Chapter 26

THE FIRST TIME THAT Miss Georgiana Darcy accidentally bumped into Mr Thomas Butler, her reactions were quite divided: by initial fear on one side and by true elation on the other. She was frightened by the acknowledgement to herself that however much it was wrong to see Mr Butler and not to inform anyone of this fact, she also knew that no amount of reasoning with herself was going to prevent it. The very next morning as she went to collect the post, she was sure the thrilling sensations that coursed through every nerve on seeing him step out from the clump of trees where they had first met had never been experienced by another living soul. Every emotion was heightened, and far from thinking that she was defective in her judgement, her newfound confidence confirmed her belief that she was right to follow her heart.

"I am in love with Thomas Butler," she said to herself as she saw him standing under the shelter of the trees in the damp morning air. "Why should I not be in love with him? There are other forces at work here; it is not our choice... the Fates have thrown us together; I know it. And why should we not follow our hearts? Fitzwilliam, my dearest brother, I love you too, but you take no account of what I shall suffer if I have to marry elsewhere. Besides, you did not deny yourself the privilege of falling in love against your family's wishes. So then, why should I?"

Having justified the reasons for meeting, it was easy for Georgiana to act. On this first brief occasion both lovers knew their time was limited. Georgiana would be expected home with the post, but later, she promised, she would take the path again, and if he should be sketching this way, perhaps they might spend some time together again.

The day and time seemed to pass as slowly as the mountains weathered; every chance she had to make her escape was thwarted. Mrs Gardiner kept her in conversation, Elizabeth wanted to look over all her sketches, and her brother wanted her opinion on a book he was reading. But at last Georgiana was able to slip away with her sketchbook under her arm, her curls escaping from her bonnet as she ran along the path she knew so well, her heart leaping when she saw Tom waiting. For the following days they met again in secret whenever they could. They rambled about the countryside with their sketchbooks and paints, sitting companionably together, sometimes quietly revelling in the silence or conversing on any subject that might take their fancy. When they could not be together they left notes in a hollow under a special tree, the very one where they had first set eyes upon the other in the Lakes.

On Friday afternoon, the day of Lady Catherine's soirée, Georgiana hurried to their favourite spot only to be disappointed. Bending down to the roots of the great tree she removed the stone, catching her breath as a corner of paper revealed itself in the sandy hollow. Oh dear, she had been so looking forward to seeing him. Undoing the missive with agitation, she read:

> *Dearest G,*
>
> *Please wait! I may be late—I have had some business in Kendal to attend, but I promise I shall see you before long.*
>
> *Yours ever,*
>
> *T*

All was well with the world again. Georgiana made herself comfortable and waited.

Mrs Butler was feeling rather harried. She was divided by her sense of propriety, her strict moral codes, and by feelings of loyalty to her one and only child. A meeting with him in Kendal had been the reason for her discomposure and no amount of talking to him had had any effect. She had received a letter from him the day before which indicated that he knew she was to be in Kendal on the following morning. This was true; a trip had been arranged between Mrs Darcy, Mrs Gardiner, and herself to partake of some shopping. Mrs Gardiner needed a new piece of lace for a headband she was making over for Lady Catherine's evening party, and Elizabeth had suggested that they make the visit in pursuit of trifles. That Tom knew Mrs Butler's movements had been surprise enough, but to then find out that he was in the same part of the country, and that his intelligence of the proposed outing had come from a least expected source had set her spirits all aflutter. The meeting had been of the most disquieting kind, leaving Mrs Butler with such agitated and despondent thoughts as could not be erased. What she was to do about it all she could not decide and she wished more than anything that Tom had not taken her into his confidence. She could not even confide in her dear friend Mrs Gardiner for Tom had sworn her to secrecy. How she wished she were not involved! Above everything else she deplored lying of any kind and how she was to avoid answering Mrs Gardiner's questions about how she had occupied herself all morning after they had separated was an impossible thought to contemplate. Fortunately, when they did all eventually meet up, her friend and hostess were so engrossed in discussions pertaining to lace and fripperies that the questions were not asked.

Meanwhile, a young girl sat on a rock on the slopes of the mere, contemplating the scene. She could not be bothered to sketch; in any case it did not seem so much fun without a certain young man to share the experience. Just as she began to despair of him ever coming, she saw him and her spirits were instantly lifted. Tom raised his hand in salute. Georgiana rose and ran; she could not wait another second to be at his side.

"I hoped you'd wait," Tom cried, as the girl he loved eagerly joined him.

"I could not go until I had seen you," she answered, trying to catch her breath. "Where have you been?"

"I went into Kendal to meet my mother," he said, as Georgiana's eyes opened wide with astonishment.

"You didn't tell her about us, did you?" she asked fearfully. Georgiana liked Mrs Butler very much but knew beyond a doubt that she would not approve of her meeting Tom in so clandestine a way. As far as that lady was concerned, Georgiana was engaged to be married to someone else; not only would she be very shocked, but Georgiana thought that Mrs Butler would think the worst of her. Tom's silence on the matter confirmed her worst fears. He didn't look in the least bit concerned, but was grinning from ear to ear.

"Do not let us worry about that," he said, taking her hand and pulling her along. "Come, Georgiana, let us chase the sun. I've a passion for painting today."

Miss Darcy, caught by his enthusiasm, laughed as readily as he and allowed him to take charge for the moment. They followed the shoreline but kept away from the common paths where they might easily see someone they knew.

"Where are we going?" asked Georgiana as they hurried along.

"I've a surprise for you," he said, as they approached the little village of Bowness. Tom halted at a point well screened by trees at the side of the lake and so they stood for a few minutes watching the boats. It was early in the season and as yet there were few sailors out on the water.

"Stay there for a moment," he said. "I'll call you when it is safe to do so."

Before she could ask where they were going or what they were doing Tom had walked up to the man in charge at the boat station where they exchanged a few words before the former was presented with a pair of oars. Georgiana's mouth fell open in surprise, but she immediately advanced towards Tom's beckoning arm without a moment's hesitation. He was in the boat in a single step and held out his hand to assist her.

"Oh, Tom, do we dare?" Georgiana cried as she took it, feeling the boat rock under her unsteady feet. The swaying vessel took her off balance, forcing her to sit rather promptly. They both laughed again. What an adventure she was having!

"We're headed for that island, yonder," declared Tom, making fast progress as the oars twisted and dipped, pulling them away from the shore. "I have a passion to paint for myself today. See how the mist shrouds us, Georgiana? I wish to capture the atmosphere before it all disappears or rains down on us in a torrent."

Georgiana looked dreamily into the distance in recollection of a memorable quotation.

"Ye mists and exhalations, that now rise,
From hill, or steaming lake, dusky or gray,
Till the sun paint your fleecy skirts with gold
In honour of the world's great Author rise."

"Ah, Milton, I recall," Tom rejoined.

"I love the picture those words paint in my head; it matches this very outlook," said Georgiana, leaning back against the seat. She drew her cloak about her; it was cold on the lake despite the sun bursting through the clouds to send sparkles of light glimmering on every ripple of water made by the oars. "The island," she asked, "is it inhabited?"

"No, at least not by human kind." Tom looked across at his love. There was a small frown furrowing her brow. "Are you worrying, Georgiana? Do you think I do wrong to take you there?"

"Oh, Tom, I think there is nothing more natural and lovely than you taking me to the island where I know you have no other thought than for us both to enjoy some sketching." Georgiana hesitated, trying to find the words.

"But you are concerned nevertheless, I know. It was really thoughtless of me, I see that now, Georgiana. My mother tried to tell me but I would not listen. I just kept thinking what a surprise it would be; I wanted to see your face light up in that lovely way you have when you are not expecting something. I was wrong; we'll turn back."

"No, Tom, I do wish to go with you. I am a woman of independent thought, after all. I will not be dictated to by the stuffy confines of a society that brands the innocent as guilty merely because of their stupid codes of propriety. I want more than anything to see the island and to see it with you."

It was clear that this heartfelt speech meant much to Tom. He returned the fire in her eyes with a look of pure adoration.

Larkholm loomed before them, a thick belt of trees encircling the island so that it was impossible to see anything beyond. A sense of mystery pervaded the scene; the isle sitting in the lake shrouded in mist looked as if it had been forgotten in time. Georgiana watched the swans flying overhead and felt herself quite under the spell of such a magical place. It was as if she and Tom were lost in time; the sensation was most enjoyable.

Having secured the boat, they set to walking through the dense wood. All was quiet except for the scurrying noises of small animals in the undergrowth, the waterfowl calling from the lakeside, and the musical soughing of tree branches in the wind. Tall pines arched over their heads, scenting the air with their fragrance, filtering the sun to dapple the mossy earth with patches of gold. Coming out on the other side, the landscape appeared as if especially composed for an artist's eye with rocks, trees, and a glimpse of a ruined summerhouse placed with picturesque perfection.

Georgiana gasped. "Oh, Mr Butler, it's breathtaking, and now I am so thrilled that you brought me here. But this land, does it not belong to anyone? Someone must have built that temple even if it is now falling down."

"Isn't it divine? I had to show you; I knew you would like it just as much. I believe the island did belong to a gentleman once; there is a story that he built the summerhouse for his lover but she died before he could share it with her. He never recovered nor visited the island again. It's a sad tale, but somehow I think he would approve of us being here, don't you? If any two people were made to appreciate such a gem it is you and I, Georgiana."

With great excitement they explored the area, each vying with the other with regards to the best spot for a suitable composition. At last they were settled on an upturned log worn to silky smoothness as if designed for a seat. With paper and paint in hand and with a bottle of water from the lake to clean their brushes, they were all ready to start.

"What a sweet view: English landscape at its most sublime," enthused Georgiana. "If ever there was a more fitting illustration to the maxim that God made the country and Man made the town, then I do not know it! Here is Nature in all her glory. Indeed, if ever more proof were needed that Nature's attribution is female I would challenge any man to supply it. Perhaps God is a woman too."

"Miss Darcy, one might take you for a female philosopher with that point of view."

"One might, indeed. I would not express my opinions to anyone else in the world except to you, Mr Butler, but I am sure you understand me. I think you are not very shocked by my thoughts."

"I am not shocked. I've always suspected quiet young ladies

to be the most troublesome. Though perhaps you are not so timid as I once believed. Your voice is beginning to find itself. So you are an advocate of women's rights as well, I suppose?"

"If I had my way I would change the lot of women, I admit," Georgiana replied. "We are no more than the chattels of our families, at the mercy of those fathers and brothers who think they know best. Trapped by the laws men make, there is nothing we can do to change them. It is so helpless to be so powerless, and despite your sympathy, you cannot really know what it is to be in that situation. You can go wherever you like, say, do, and be whomever you please. There are no restrictions placed upon you whatsoever."

"And if you were free? What then? Would you cast aside all mores and live in a tent, unshackled and liberated?"

"You are laughing at me now, Thomas Butler. No, I would not live in a tent… but I would live as I wish and make my own choices about what I might do with my own money and whom I might marry!"

Tom put down his brush and laid aside his sketchbook. His countenance was suddenly grave. Georgiana watched him, his brow wrinkling into a frown. Standing up, he paced up and down for a moment or two in a very agitated manner. He stood looking away from her for a moment before he turned, suddenly falling on his knees at her feet.

"If you could… what I mean to say is… please put me out of my misery, Miss Darcy. Were you able to make that decision, the one about whom you might wed… May I ask: would you marry me?"

Georgiana looked down into Tom's eyes shining with love for her and knew exactly how she would answer him.

Before she could reply, however, the moment was inter-rupted by the sounds of activity not far away, the noise loud enough to suggest that not only were they about to be intruded upon, but by a large group of people. Raucous laughter, calling, and shouting punctuated by snorts of derision at something being said by one of the distant party were loudly heard as they gradually moved within sight. Glimpses of figures approaching through the trees could be seen, both gentlemen and ladies, though it was clear to both Tom and Georgiana that this was no refined outing. Georgiana felt quite frightened, not wanting to be discovered; however innocent their afternoon's activity had been, she did not think it would look that way to strangers. What were they to do?

"I think we had better leave," said Tom, assisting Georgiana to her feet, but it was too late, the gathering was upon them, and the young couple were forced to stand still as a member of the party hailed them.

"Miss Darcy, what do you do here?" asked a familiar figure in a rude manner. Dressed for fashion in country hues, the dashing figure of Mr Wickham stood at the front of the mob whilst his companions stared, nudging one another, making no attempt to hide their amusement at the young couple's plight. Mr Wickham's expression was one of mock civility and he bowed before them in an action that was both exaggerated and scornful. The entire assembly laughed out loud. They stared at Georgiana and then back at Mr Wickham.

Miss Darcy reddened. "How do you do, Mr Wickham?" she said, not knowing which way to look and blushing more furi-ously as she recognised the woman standing next to him. Her old governess, Mrs Younge, stood at his side with a smirk on her face looking pointedly at her former charge before scrutinising Mr Butler and raising her eyebrows in a look of contempt.

"I hope your brother knows where you are this afternoon, Miss Darcy," she said, fixing Georgiana with a look that the young girl recognised from former times. Mrs Younge had always had the ability to crush Georgiana with a single glance, an accomplishment she had used to great effect in the past coupled with the capacity to bend Georgiana's will to her own fancy.

Before she could even think or speak, someone else who appeared to have been dawdling along at the back suddenly rushed forward, admonishing Mr Wickham as she did so. "Lord, Wickie, do be quiet! Oh, Miss Darcy, it is such a pleasure to meet you at last. You know, you and I are practically sisters!"

It was not necessary for Lydia to say anything else. Georgiana guessed this must be Elizabeth's poor unfortunate sister she had heard much about. Dressed in white muslin with a tall, highly decorated bonnet on her head as if she were about to promenade in Kensington Gardens instead of ramble through the countryside, Lydia looked most uncomfortable out of doors. But Georgiana couldn't help feeling rather sorry for the silly girl who had married Mr Wickham. Despite being foolish enough to involve herself with him in the first place, Georgiana knew only too well how that gentleman would have eased his way into her confidence by his charm and pleasing ways. She had almost suffered the same fate. Wickham was a man not to be trusted.

"How do you do?" cried Lydia, holding out her hand to Mr Butler. "You must be Miss Darcy's fiancé. I'm very pleased to meet you.

Georgiana curtseyed. "We are just leaving; we have been sketching," she added, not quite knowing what to say.

Lydia winked and looked around at the company as if involving them in the joke and conspiracy. "Do not worry, Miss Darcy, your secret's safe with us, isn't it, gentlemen? We've all enjoyed a bit of sketching in our time, don't you worry. Young people like to have a bit of time on their own. I do not think I have such wonderful memories as the time Wickie was courting me. We could not wait to be on our own, but everyone knows about that." Lydia glanced over at Wickham with a coquettish smile which was completely ignored. "My lips are sealed, and if I should run into my dear brother Darcy, I should remember, or should that be forget... Anyway, Miss Darcy, rest assured that I and my friends will not say a word."

"Come, Miss Darcy, it's getting late," interrupted Tom, who could see the distress that Georgiana was feeling. "Excuse me, but we must take our leave." He took hold of her arm, pulling her away as quickly as he could. Miss Darcy allowed him to lead her away. Her countenance paled; she did not speak, so shocked and numbed was she by the experience of meeting her old foes. The young couple hurried through the trees, Georgiana's heart pumping with every footfall. Oh, the shame of it. Trying to erase the expressions of all those people who stared at her was impossible. Worst of all was the memory of Mr Wickham and Mrs Younge's faces, whose expressions not only mocked but showed their complete disdain and disregard.

Eventually, they came out of the woods but worse was to come. There was no sign of the boat they had carefully moored. There were several others bobbing up and down in the water that must belong to the Wickhams and their friends, but theirs was not amongst them. They looked out across the water in despair as Tom realised the unthinkable had happened.

Whether by accident or design, the boat was drifting to the other side of the lake by itself and there was no way of getting it back unless he was prepared to jump in and swim. How on earth it had come adrift Tom could not fathom. He knew he had left it most secure. At the sound of distant laughter that echoed round the water, he realised some treachery must have taken place. There was only one way to get the boat back. Removing his coat, waistcoat, and shoes, he took up his position at the side of the lake. Georgiana could only gasp in horror as she watched Mr Butler dive into the water.

When Georgiana had not returned by four o'clock, which was the usual hour at which the company retired to dress for dinner, Mrs Butler became extremely upset, especially when she thought about the conversation she had shared with Tom earlier in the day. Mr and Mrs Darcy had both expressed their concern about Georgiana, although Elizabeth was sure she was not far away and had merely forgotten the time. If she hadn't returned before another half hour passed, they would walk out and look for her. Mrs Butler knew she should say something; she could stand it no longer; she must tell Mrs Darcy what she knew. Mrs Gardiner would be first consulted, but how she was to tell her that Miss Darcy was probably sitting at this moment unaccompanied except by a young man in a boat, she could not think.

Fortunately, Georgiana made an appearance in time, but her general demeanour gave Lizzy some cause for concern. When questioned, Miss Darcy confessed that she was feeling ill; she was suffering from a headache, which she knew would only be removed with quiet and solitude. All that she wished was to be

IT WAS A QUIET party that left Bellingham Hall, though Jane and Charles Bingley, seated with Elizabeth and Darcy in the first carriage, did as much as they could to alleviate the subdued atmosphere that pervaded the interior with their usual light-hearted conversation.

"By all accounts my sister Caroline is enjoying herself here in the Lakes," Mr Bingley pronounced, as the carriage rolled out of the drive. "I received a note from her this morning saying she was sorry to have missed us when Jane and I called yesterday, but she has been very busy with her compositions which seemingly take up all her time. Apparently, she is immersed in the landscape, engaged in capturing the essence of nature at its most fearful and sublime. I hope you all have good constitutions; I imagine there'll be a vast body of verse on the transcendental significance of mountains this evening."

"Charles, you are in a very teasing mood tonight," said Jane. "Be careful what you say on the matter to your sister, for I imagine if she has been brave enough to pour out her heart on paper, any adverse remark might well put a stop to all creative output."

"Which might be a blessing for us all," said Mr Darcy, turning his head as he spoke to look out of the window.

"Yes, quite right," added Charles. "I must confess the prospect of this evening's pleasures do not quite hold the same charms as our usual diversions."

"You are talking of the billiard table, I suppose," Elizabeth responded with a laugh, "and the card table too, not to mention the wit, charm, and humour of one's companions at Bellingham Hall. I do not think we will find such gaieties at Golgarth Park. Our conversation will be limited to discussions on the pictur-esque... no doubt we shall have to arrange ourselves in groups of three or five when talking to Lord Dalton and his circle."

"Oh, Lizzy, you are too cruel," said Jane with a smile.

Mr Darcy, whose contemplative expression had been noted by his wife, suddenly turned toward them, becoming more animated in his composure and address. "Not cruel enough in my opinion. Well, I shall certainly hold my own in Dalton's company," he added with a smirk. "There is nothing I do not know on the subject of intricate foregrounds which command such painterly abilities for rendering the fine delights of tree stumps, nettles, thistles, and the like. My expertise on the subject of middle and far distances is, quite simply, outstand-ing... and I can spot the difference between a Gainsborough and a Claude Lorrain at thirty paces!"

They all laughed out loud.

"My dear Mr Darcy, I do believe you have been reading up on the subject," declared Elizabeth, tears of laughter misting her eyes.

"So what if I have? I could not bear to have my aunt, or worse your cousin Collins, correct me on some matter of painting or poetry."

"Well, I hope when Lady Catherine calls on you to supply the company with a sonnet that you will be able to oblige," Lizzy teased.

"I might have a little ditty for such an occasion," Darcy responded, with a wink at his friend. "But I need your advice; I fear my verse may be too scholarly and academic, however refined the company."

"Oh, do let us hear it," cried Jane, "I did not know you composed poetry, Mr Darcy."

"A hidden talent, I am certain," remarked Bingley, his eyes crinkling with mirth. "If I recall some of our past bachelor days, I feel sure I may have heard something of his proficiency as a poet before. But, Darcy, is it wise, do you think, to unleash such a masterly gift on the previously uninitiated?"

"I can think of no finer audience, Bingley, than my wife and my dear sister whose expertise in poetic creation will, no doubt, lend such worthy opinion upon my humble efforts."

"Oh, Darcy, do get on with it," cried Elizabeth. "I am beginning to fear that you have nothing to offer us but a lot of hot air."

Mr Darcy adopted his most serious expression. He coughed once or twice to clear his throat before pulling at his cuffs and commencing his recitation in as droll a fashion as Bingley had ever heard from him.

"To a Fly!
Giddy trifler, cease thy strife,
Turn thy wing, and save thy life;

Shouldst thou enter Elizabeth's eye,
That might suffer, thou must die.
Is a summer's day too long
For thee to live thy tribes among?
Is there not, in all the air,
Room enough and room to spare?
Wilt thou buzz about her still?
Silly creature, take thy will;
And warn all triflers as you die,
What dangers lurk in Elizabeth's eye."

Elizabeth and Jane could not help but laugh out loud. The prospect of Mr Darcy reciting such nonsense before the august company at Golgarth Park conjured up such images in their heads that it was impossible to do anything else. Lizzy, for one, was relieved to see her husband in such good humour. He had said very little about Georgiana since the day before, apart from saying that he wished to discuss the matter with her as soon as they could. He was avoiding broaching the subject, she knew, but was certain that he must be coming round to her viewpoint that Georgiana's engagement was wholly unsatisfactory. His last words on the matter had been to the effect that Georgiana's happiness and wellbeing were the subjects dearest to his heart.

All too soon the carriages rolled round the gravel sweep before the magnificent edifice of Golgarth Park. Lady Catherine de Bourgh greeted her guests with affected affability. Elizabeth was amused to see that affectation seemed to be the order of the day from the costumes of those who were decidedly artistic in appearance down to the way in which they conducted themselves.

"Oh dear, Mr Darcy," whispered Elizabeth, when she had a

chance, "if I had understood it to be fancy dress I would have exchanged my gown for Grecian robes and an urn. Don't look now, here comes Caroline Bingley, a vision in drapery."

Miss Bingley was rushing toward them. Dressed in white with embellishments of gold in the key-shaped motif around the hem of her diaphanous gown and her hair swathed in a voluminous turban of the same, she appeared unrecognisable, not only in appearance but also in her behaviour.

"Mr and Mrs Darcy, how delighted I am to see you. It must be an age since last we met," she enthused, her countenance beaming as her mouth broke into a wide smile. "You must come and meet Lord Dalton; he is so anxious to make your acquaintance. I told him there is not another couple in the whole of Westmorland who equal the Darcys in taste and refinement. Charles tells me you are to make your debut in our poetry reading circle this evening, Mr Darcy. I confess to be more than a little excited at the prospect. May I dare to ask on which topic your effusions have been inspired? No, do not tell me, for I am sure I can guess the answer. No doubt, Mrs Darcy's fine eyes are the stuff of eulogistic praise!"

Elizabeth was completely taken aback. Regarding Miss Bingley closely, her first thought was that the lady was merely being satirical, but on closer examination she could find no hint either in her voice or expression of sarcasm and ridicule. Caroline's countenance was open and she was smiling most sincerely. Elizabeth looked at her husband. She longed to know his answer.

"Miss Bingley, as much as it would give me great pleasure to confer such an exhibition on the present company, I feel obliged to decline in order to leave the way uncluttered for superior expertise in the field. Your brother tells me we are to hear from you, however. I could not hope to equal your command of articulation and bow to your superior grasp of poetic virtuosity."

Miss Bingley smiled and looked down with an expression indicative of modesty. "If I were ever considered vain about anything, it would certainly be of my eloquence, a fluency which involves imparting the spoken word succinctly, distilling the very quintessence of life itself within a sentence or two in the creation of the poetic form. At least, Lord Dalton is so kind as to have ventured the fact that he has rarely heard such command of the English language. He is my guide and confidant on such matters."

"Lord Dalton himself, indeed!" Elizabeth immediately responded, her countenance suitably arranged to give an impression of awe, whilst simultaneously wondering quite why she had formerly considered Miss Bingley's character to be so reformed. "You are very fortunate, Miss Bingley, to have attracted such a tutor; I believe Lord Dalton is very much in request."

"I am very privileged to have made his close acquaintance, indeed; lately, we are hardly ever separated. He listens to my work, I give him the benefit of my advice. It is a partnership made in heaven."

"Oh, I see," said Elizabeth with a knowing nod of her head. "That quite puts me in mind of a solution to the mystery I have been puzzling over. For we have all been wondering who is the inspiration for Lord Dalton's latest clutch of love poems. Who is the muse that inspires such declarations as, 'Her step was elastic, a vision so rare, a goddess divine, she is youthful and fair.' Tell me, Miss Bingley, do you know who is responsible for such an outpouring of emotion?"

Miss Bingley blushed and simpered. "Mrs Darcy, I cannot think what you mean by your wicked insinuations. Lord Dalton and I are just very good friends bound by our shared passion. The fact that he has expressed a wish to capture me in oil on canvas is neither here nor there. Oh, do come and meet him. He is about to start his talk and there is such a fine exhibition of his work."

Fortunately, Charlotte Collins presented herself at that moment and so Elizabeth had the perfect excuse to delay the meeting with the gentleman everyone else seemed eager to meet. Miss Bingley rushed away with the excuse of having to guide visitors to their seats. There was a large party gathering, Elizabeth supposing they consisted mostly of the people from London who had followed in the wake of their mentor. Mrs Collins and Mrs Darcy exchanged their news, and Georgiana's absence was explained. Mr Collins professed his disappointment whilst concurrently urging his wife and his cousin to pay heed to Lady Catherine, who was announcing in a loud voice that the exhibition was open. There was nothing else to be done but follow the swarming crowd into the drawing room. Mrs Gardiner and Mrs Butler linked arms as if in defence against those that might want to part them and perused the vast wall of Lord Dalton's paintings, which had been specially mounted for the occasion. There were so many people all crushed together that it was quite impossible to study the paintings very well. Most people paid little heed to what was on the wall, Lizzy observed; they were too busy eyeing one another and discussing their peers. Looking about, Elizabeth noticed that there were several military officers in attendance, which gave her some cause for concern, but thankfully there was no sign of her sister or her husband. Lizzy could not imagine Lydia wishing to come to any evening where poetry and art might be discussed and felt satisfied that she would not be of any party to arrive.

At one side of the room standing before the fireplace was Lord Dalton, surrounded by females all speaking at once. Handsome, yet with an air of pride and undeniable vanity as was proved by the constant checking of his appearance in a pier glass opposite, the gentleman was holding court before a rapt audience. Caroline Bingley was staring up at him with pure adoration. Poor Miss Bingley, thought Lizzy, as she noted Lord Dalton making eyes at a very young and pretty girl across the room who returned his glances most appreciatively.

Lady Catherine, who had been engaged in conversation with her many guests, finally rounded on the Darcys. Her daughter Anne, still as pale and sickly looking as when they had seen her last, stood meekly at Lady Catherine's side as they exchanged pleasantries. Henry Dalton was hailed from across the room and the introductions made at last.

"Lord Dalton has been giving Anne the benefit of his mastery and skills when her health permits it," announced Lady Catherine immediately following the formalities. "He is such a very loyal companion whether she feels like dabbling or not, sitting at her side daily, entertaining her with little *bons mots* and such-like. Is not that the case, Anne? Lord Dalton is very attentive, is he not?"

Anne did not speak; she merely nodded her head. At least, Elizabeth thought it was a nod but was not quite certain if she hadn't just been going to sneeze and had been saved from doing so at the last second.

"It has been my great pleasure, Lady Catherine," Dalton simpered. "My lady Anne shows great promise and talent; I only wish I could finish paintings as quickly."

Elizabeth scrutinised Lord Dalton's expression. Neither Lady Catherine nor Anne it seemed had registered his less than sincere compliment. His smug countenance suggested he had made a private joke for his own amusement; one he was certain would not be understood by any of them present.

William Collins, solemn and awkward, joined them in time to offer his apologies for not having attended the Darcys sooner. Turning toward the rest of the party he bestowed his compliments upon Henry Dalton and made several flattering allusions to the ladies, which were kindly smiled on by the mother and daughter. Lady Catherine took Mr Darcy's arm to lead him to his seat. Elizabeth looked about her, preparing to follow on her own. Mr Collins looked about for his wife and so Lord Dalton offered an arm each to Mrs Darcy and Miss de Bourgh.

"The rumours I've heard are perfectly true," he began, smiling at Elizabeth as they progressed about the room.

Lizzy felt a certain discomposure at this comment but endeavoured to smile back at him.

"Mrs Darcy's fine eyes are the talk of the Lakes," he said, looking deeply into her dark eyes. "Could any artist do true justice to their beauty, I wonder. Perhaps the colour and the shape might be imitated, but that expression of vitality, the fire within… now that might prove impossible for any man to capture."

Elizabeth did not know where to look. She felt herself blushing at the impropriety. There was something very artful in his way of talking, and Elizabeth did not like it. Henry Dalton made her feel extremely uncomfortable.

"With Mr Darcy's permission, I should consider it an honour to paint you," he continued. "His wife's celebrated loveliness should not forgo being recorded for posterity. Ask any of my clients here; they would not have forfeited the experience for the world. The relationship between client and artist is of a peculiar kind, formed with interests to satisfy the other. A symbiotic bond both intimate and fulfilling, an experience unsurpassed." He lowered his voice. "Perhaps something for Mr Darcy's private collection."

"Thank you, Lord Dalton, I shall certainly pass on your ideas to my husband," Elizabeth answered as politely as she could. All she wished was to be released as quickly as possible from his side and to be reunited with Fitzwilliam.

"Good, good. I see it now, the finished article with you pictured as I see you in my mind... a goddess, your dark tresses flowing in the wind like Aphrodite rising from the sea."

Elizabeth was stunned into silence for a moment. "But I'm afraid that won't do at all," said Elizabeth, finding her courage. "I could not agree to such a scheme. Aphrodite was certainly a celebrated beauty, yet she was also unfaithful to her husband, not to mention rather too scantily dressed for warmth on any English coastline that might be deemed suitable for such a project."

They had reached the rest of the party. Elizabeth was pleased to see that her bold retort had completely taken him aback. He regarded her quite simply as if he could not believe his ears.

Chapter 28

LORD DALTON'S SPEECH AND recitation had been of a lengthy duration. One by one the participants had taken their places and held forth. Lady Catherine and Miss Bingley took their turn to extol the magnificence of the Lakes with many lamentations on nature's cruelty and fearsome strength alongside many descriptive and emotive inner visions and personal feelings on their reactions to the landscape around them. It was all Elizabeth could do to keep a straight face and she wondered how her lip did not bleed, so many times she did bite it to suppress the mirth that rose inside. At last it was over and as she settled with some relief to talking to Mrs Butler and Mrs Gardiner, she was suddenly arrested by a sound from the opposite corner that left her quite disconcerted.

"Lizzy! Lizzy, over here!" cried a voice that was instantly recognisable to Elizabeth—one that she was not too ashamed to say had the effect of immediately sinking her spirits.

From the other side of the room the figure of her sister Lydia could be seen calling loudly and gesticulating wildly. There was no alternative but to excuse herself from her party as soon as she could and advance quickly to her sister's side. Mrs Wickham was standing within a circle of officers arm in arm with an older gentleman that Lizzy did not recognise.

"Fancy, Lizzy, I bet you never thought you'd see me here tonight." Lydia noted that Elizabeth was perusing the group around her as if she looked for someone. "Oh, don't worry; Wickie isn't here. I declare I never saw him in such ill humour at the suggestion of accompanying me. Well, I do not care. After all, he has Mrs Younge for company, and I daresay he did not like the idea of meeting certain people here tonight. And besides, I have darling Willie for a partner. Mrs Darcy, allow me to introduce Colonel Arbuthnot, leader of the regiment, known to his friends as Willie. He persuaded me to come along at the last. I couldn't say no; I never can refuse dear Willie!"

No, thought Elizabeth, it would have been too much for her giddy sister to refuse a night of being admired by a group of officers. At least Mr Wickham and Mrs Younge had not dared to show their faces. Nevertheless, Lizzy dreaded the remarks of those others whom she knew would not resist making comments, especially when they perceived how closely her sister stood by the colonel, almost as if she were his wife.

"When is the dancing to start?" Lydia went on jumping up and down like a small child in her excitement. "Lord, I hope there isn't going to be any more of this dull poetry they keep spouting. There's a poet or an artist in every room spouting forth such nonsense about rocks and mountains that you ever did hear in your life. And as for the painting, I never saw anything so peculiar."

Colonel Arbuthnot smiled indulgently at his partner before remarking to Elizabeth, "The young never do appreciate such fine sentiments as have been expressed in poetic or artistic form this evening."

Elizabeth smiled back whilst privately thinking that her sister should learn to keep her thoughts to herself. No matter how awful the evening's entertainments were, Mrs Darcy would never voice her real feelings to anyone but her husband, and even then she would only do so when they were alone.

"You are looking very well, Lizzy," said Lydia, drawing her sister to one side. "Is there something you should tell me?"

Elizabeth ignored her question, asking her instead about what she had been doing in the Lakes, though the answer was one she knew would not surprise her.

"Oh, Lizzy, I have been to so many parties, I cannot tell you. We have had such fun; I've danced so much I've nearly worn my legs out. But Willie shares the same passion for dancing and if Wickie will not go out, I do not know what I am to do about it! He and Mrs Younge have become such dire company. They never want to do anything, so we just leave them behind. Lord knows what they get up to for they are so dull and tiresome. They are each confined to their rooms this evening. Wickie said he was going to bed… he's just so tired all the time. I have no patience with him, or her for that matter. I feel so sorry for Captain Farthing. I tell you, Lizzy, I have my work cut out entertaining both the captain and the colonel."

So Lydia carried on talking. It was a completely one-sided conversation, and when at last she paused for breath, Elizabeth made her excuses to return to Mr Darcy. Glancing over in his direction, she was relieved to see him engrossed in conversation. Fortunately, it did not appear that he had noticed the presence of her sister, but Elizabeth knew it could only be a matter of time before he would be painfully aware of her proximity. Elizabeth felt drained. She could quite understand why Mr Wickham felt tired all the time if this was how Lydia carried on, but there was something about her sister's descriptions of her husband's conduct and that of his friend, Mrs Younge, which made Lizzy very suspicious. But there was nothing she could say of her fears to her sister. Besides, Lydia seemed happy enough and, in any case, what could she do about it?

Elizabeth returned to her husband's side just in time to be introduced to Lord Featherstone. He appeared to be a gentleman of the old school; he was chivalrous, courteous, and extremely charming; an elderly man whose silver-white hair waved back from the noble brow of a still handsome face. He and Mr Darcy were discussing Dalton's paintings.

"I must admit, Mrs Darcy, though I've never picked up a paintbrush myself, I do enjoy seeing a pretty painting on my wall. These landscapes are especially fine, just the sort of thing I like to hang in my London townhouse to remind me of greener spaces. I'm the sort of fellow who hankers for the country when I'm in the town and vice versa."

"Well, that would seem to be an excellent solution," said Elizabeth. "A painting on a wall can be quite as restful as a rural scene through a window, I am sure."

"Yes, indeed. I hope I shall be indulging in this favourite passion of mine in the not too distant future. Mrs Butler's son, you know, has been working on some sketches with a view to turning them into oil paintings for me."

Elizabeth noted Fitzwilliam's bristle at the mention of Thomas Butler.

"You must know him, of course," Lord Featherstone continued.

Darcy nodded but remained silent, leaving Elizabeth to speak once more. "Yes, we do. He is a very talented landscape designer, is he not? He produced a most delightful scheme at Pemberley."

"He should have been here this evening, but I received a message before I left to say he was a little under the weather. I expect he's been sitting out too long by the lake and caught a chill. Master Thomas Butler will go far; mark my words, Mrs Darcy. He is a young man quite out of the common way, and without his father to see him established in the world, he has proved himself both diligent and industrious. Why, I think of him like a son. As you may or may not know, Mrs Darcy, I never got around to all that business of taking a wife and having children of my own. Well, he's a splendid young man and excellent company, too. And Mrs Butler, his mother, is a wonderful lady. I've never met her before this evening, but my goodness, I can see where young Thomas gets his handsome looks from."

The news that Thomas Butler was in the Lakes was shocking indeed, especially when Lizzy considered Georgiana's behaviour of late. Elizabeth decided it was highly likely that Georgiana knew of his being in the vicinity. What would Mr Darcy be thinking about the news of this revelation? But, at least, Lord Featherstone seemed fairly smitten with the Butler family and Elizabeth could not help but feel secretly pleased that Thomas's character had been painted in such glowing colours. She could not resist a glimpse at Mr Darcy's countenance to see if she could discern any reaction to Lord Featherstone's announcement or appraisal, but his expression gave nothing away, and before Mr Darcy had a chance to enquire further on the whereabouts of Mr Butler, his wife smoothly and deftly changed the subject of their conversation.

Caroline Bingley was doing her best to claim the attention of Lord Dalton. He was always engaged in conversation—mostly female, it had to be said. Lady Catherine and her daughter Anne were ever present in his company; she could not get him on her own. At last she saw her chance to speak to him alone. Henry was starting for the door with an expression of determination. Caroline decided that a little accidental encounter would be quite the thing. He looked rather furtive as he left the room. Caroline was rather pleased. The opportunity to converse with her hero in the dim candlelit corridor outside seemed like a heaven sent opportunity. She followed him. However, once in the hallway she could perceive neither sight nor sound of him. Miss Bingley rushed along, looking into doorways for any sign. There were groups of very earnest looking young men in deep discussion in the library and two ladies leading a poetry reading in a small salon, but Lord Dalton had completely disappeared. She was just about to give up when she saw a door open to the night air leading out onto what looked like a small terrace. It was hardly likely that he was outside, but there didn't seem to be anywhere else he could be. Caroline passed through the doorway. Discerning the sound of someone speaking, she ventured forward but was stopped in her tracks by the sight of Lord Dalton standing within very close proximity to a young woman she recognised as Theodora Winn. His head was bent very low; he appeared to be whispering something in the young lady's ear which made Miss Winn laugh heartily. Her hand was held by Dalton's, and it was clear he had no intention of letting it go. Caroline knew in that moment how mistaken she had been in her estimation of Lord Dalton. All her hopes for love and marriage were dashed in a second as she observed the look in Henry's eyes for his partner. She could bear to look no longer and fearing discovery, she turned on her heel and went back the way she had come, struggling with every step and willing herself not to cry.

The evening was beginning to deteriorate in every way to Elizabeth's thinking. Her youngest sister, who had purposely avoided Mr Darcy as long as she could, finally appeared to shake his hand. Lydia was looking considerably worse for wear. No doubt she had found her courage after imbibing several drinks. It was obvious she had been making free with the punchbowl and that her companions were not only encouraging her to drink more, but were finding her general demeanour and outspoken behaviour amusing.

"Mr Darcy," Lydia cried at the top of her voice, "shake my hand, if you please. You are my brother, you know, so you are quite at liberty… or better still, kiss me!" She pressed her finger to her cheek and, closing her eyes, pursed her lips.

Mr Darcy stared, his face flushing with the all too familiar agitation that his wife speedily recognised. Elizabeth moved into action, taking her sister by the arm and steering her away. "I think it's time you left, Mrs Wickham," she said. "You are looking most ill, Lydia. Please be sensible and take my advice."

"I'm not going anywhere," Lydia declared, wrenching away her arm from Elizabeth's firm grip. "Mrs Darcy, I do declare, you are trying to spoil my fun. I want to dance! Lord, when is the dancing to start? Willie, come over here. Tell them to play some music!"

Colonel Arbuthnot, on hearing this last impassioned plea, was quite aware that Mrs Wickham had perhaps drunk more rum punch than was good for her. To Elizabeth's great relief, she saw her sister taken in hand by the colonel and Captain Farthing as they steered her toward the door, but unfortunately not before Lydia had insulted both Mr Collins and Lady Catherine as she went. Lady Catherine fixed Elizabeth with such an expression of disdain that Lizzy could only turn away with feelings of mortification.

Elizabeth wondered if it were possible to die of shame. Fitzwilliam was exceedingly cross, refusing to speak to her on any matter, and left Elizabeth's side to join his aunt, who left him in no doubt of her feelings. Removing herself from the room as swiftly as she was able, Elizabeth knew she must try to compose her feelings, but moving along the corridor only increased her sense of hopelessness. How could Lydia behave in such a manner? Elizabeth was sure that Lady Catherine and Mr Darcy were discussing the whole event. Fitzwilliam's aunt would surely be reminding him how ill conceived his alliance had been with a family of such low connections.

As she turned the corner she ran straight into the person she most dreaded seeing. However, Lizzy was immediately struck by Miss Bingley's appearance. Elizabeth felt some concern, for it was clear that Caroline had been crying and had drunk rather too much wine. With her bloodshot eyes, her blotched complexion, and a scarlet nose glowing under her slightly skewed turban, Miss Bingley looked a very sorry sight.

"I see your family are as diverting as ever; Mrs Wickham always was a crowd pleaser," she slurred, sneering as she spoke. Malice and spite positively oozed from every pore. "It must be a comfort to you, Mrs Darcy, to have such entertaining relations. Such a *bon viveur*, such a raconteur, you must be so proud of your sister Lydia. And she has such a way with the colonel of the regiment and the captain and most of the officers too. What a pity her husband could not be here to witness seeing his wife at her best. Well, I daresay he has fish to fry of his own. The Wickham family always did have zealous appetites, or so I have heard. George Wickham could never pass up on any female. And as for his step-sister, I daresay, you have heard the tales for yourself. It is not for me to say, of course, and I do not suppose we will ever know the complete truth of the matter, but I am sure I heard something on the subject concerning Viola Wickham's hasty departure from Pemberley all that time ago. Oh, yes, Mrs Darcy, I do believe her appetite for a certain dish was utterly sated, and if I tell you she left with more pudding than that with which she arrived, I think you will understand me."

Elizabeth could find no words. All she could think about was the letter she had received. The recollection of its contents came back with a clarity which left her feeling sure that she now had an answer to some of the puzzle. That Miss Bingley had written that poisonous note, she began to think must be a certainty. Suddenly overwhelmed with feelings of hopelessness and a longing to be as far away from Miss Bingley as possible, she excused herself without further delay whilst doing her best to show that she was not discomfited in the least. She moved away not knowing where she went or what she did. Only the acknowledgement that everything she had formerly refused to believe might after all be true filled her mind and left her feeling more perplexed than ever before.

Elizabeth did not want to think about what Miss Bingley had just divulged, yet she knew with certainty that there must be some element of truth in what she had said. There was too much evidence to suggest anything else. Not only must she face this fact, but she must also talk to her husband as soon as they reached Bellingham Hall. Until these ghastly rumours were either scotched or confirmed, she would know no peace. Raising the subject would be impossibly difficult. Elizabeth was sure that all discussion on any matter would be prohibited; Fitzwilliam would still be reeling from the rudeness of her sister's conduct and would most likely retreat to his own room. However, Elizabeth was determined to seek him out. He could rail as much as he liked about Lydia, she thought. Lizzy had no choice but to deal with further discussions relating to the past and the history pertaining to a certain young woman which might just as well be aired at the same time. The truth would have to be confronted.

It was gone midnight when they arrived back at the Hall. Darcy had been very quiet all the way home, sitting in silence with a frown on his countenance as Jane and Bingley chatted convivially about the evening. Elizabeth could see for certain that he was very cross with Lydia for behaving as she had and for even turning up at all. As far as Lizzy was concerned that had been dreadful, but the woman who seemed most to take delight in being malicious had spoken the unthinkable. At least it was over, and even Lydia's folly could not compare with the spite and vitriol of Caroline Bingley. Elizabeth could not begin to wonder how it was that Charles, who was always so affable and congenial, could possess the antithesis of himself in such a sibling.

On their return Mrs Darcy tried to compose herself for the trial that was to come. She bid her weary companions goodnight before making her way upstairs, passing Georgiana's door on her way. Elizabeth hoped she was feeling improved and, seeing the glow of a light still burning under her door, decided to pop her head in and say goodnight. She rapped softly on the door, but on hearing no answer she opened it as quietly as she could. Georgiana must have left her candles burning before she fell into a slumber, Elizabeth thought, on entering the room. The candles were low though still alight; one burning in a porcelain candlestick on the dressing table illuminated the detritus of ribbon, faux flowers, and combs taken from Georgiana's hair. Over by the window, ivory wax candles in tall candelabra guttered in the breeze. Dark shadows filled the corners of the room but to Elizabeth's alarm there was no sign of Georgiana: not in the bed which showed no evidence of having been slept in, nor in her dressing room just off on one side. Furthermore, a quantity of clothing was strewn over the bed in what could only be described as muddled and disordered abandon along with a variety of shoes and slippers in silk, satin, and leather. On further inspection Elizabeth found that Georgiana's painting materials, sketchbook, pocketbook, and journal were all missing too, and an upturned trunk in a dark corner of the room finally gave rise to the idea that another of these monogrammed cases had gone astray also. That Georgiana had vanished the same way there could not be a doubt. Elizabeth tried not to panic as she pushed open the casement to look down onto the garden below. With some relief she could see where Georgiana might have effected her escape.

From the window, it would have been a short leap to freedom down little more than a foot onto the terrace that ran below this old part of the house and from there down a flight of stone steps to whoever might be waiting in the shadows. Elizabeth was sure she surmised correctly. In an instant she saw how it could have happened.

Chapter 29

Such uproar ensued on Mr Darcy's intelligence of Georgiana's disappearance that Elizabeth felt quite frightened. He stormed hither and thither, calling his sister's name until he was quite hoarse. It was a pitiable sight, Elizabeth decided, to both witness her husband enraged and yet fretful for his sister's welfare. The house and gardens were searched immediately and when all returned with no sighting of either Mr Butler or Miss Darcy, Fitzwilliam ordered his horse to be saddled forthwith.

"There is nothing else to be done," he said, as Elizabeth urged him to wait. "There is no time to lose. They cannot be far, and if I can catch them I shall at least be given the chance to speak to them and make them see sense."

"Fitzwilliam, please do not be too harsh with either Georgiana or Mr Butler. I am sure they have never meant to upset anyone, but they have been driven partly by youthful folly and a sense of hopelessness."

Mr Darcy stood still for a moment and all at once looked

utterly defeated to Elizabeth's mind. It distressed her to see him so; he could hardly meet her eyes. "Oh, Mrs Darcy, do you think I have not berated myself for encouraging Georgiana to marry where she did not love? Do you not understand how much I regret my actions? You tried to tell me, but I would not listen. I have been blind and prejudiced; I know that now. I came home with the intention of speaking to Georgiana in the morning, to tell her how mistaken I have been, and with a desire to know her true feelings. All I can hope is for her forgiveness. What have I driven her to do by my own stupidity? But I must not delay, I must find them, tell them that all is not lost before it is too late."

"But where will you go? How on earth will you find them?"

"I will head south; I've a pretty good idea where they might be headed. I will make for the Peak Forest."

"I do not understand, Fitzwilliam, why should they be headed there?"

"Mrs Gardiner will supply the details, my darling. I must make haste; there is not a moment to lose!"

Charles Bingley appeared at that moment, offering to travel with his friend. However, Mr Darcy was adamant. If he had not been so proud and headstrong about his sister none of this would have happened. "Thank you, Bingley, but this is a mess of my own making and I am the only person who can set all to rights."

Mr Darcy saluted him and swept his wife off her feet with a last embrace before rushing away to his awaiting horse.

Mrs Butler was bereft. Lizzy tried to assure her as much as possible that Thomas would not be held responsible for the elopement. Elizabeth knew, however reserved Miss Darcy appeared to strangers, she could be headstrong. Georgiana had once been persuaded to run away before with a man she imagined she was in love with; how much more willing would she have been to elope with the man of her dreams? They had run away together, it was clear, yet the one hope Elizabeth entertained was that she knew in this case their feelings were mutual and that matrimony could be their only motive.

Mrs Butler was full of remorse, saying that if she had realised Tom's intentions she would have said something sooner. "He is not a bad person, please believe me, Mrs Darcy, it is just that his feelings tend to run away with him on occasion. I abhor deceit of any kind and would have told you of their meeting, but after I discussed the impropriety of his behaviour toward a young woman engaged to be married, I felt sure he would heed my words. I am certain, however, Thomas would never have any ill designs against Miss Darcy; he is his father's son through and through. Please forgive me, Mrs Darcy. I am so ashamed that I did not tell you sooner."

Elizabeth immediately went to Mrs Butler's side. "I do not blame you, dear friend. Do not distress yourself. This whole affair just proves how wrong we have been in encouraging an alliance between Hugh Calladine and Miss Darcy."

Jane felt very sorry for Mrs Butler. "People who are in love do not always behave like rational creatures," she said. "I'm sure Mr Butler could not help behaving as he did, no more could Georgiana. When any two people fall in love, prudence and discrimination often fall foul."

"But Miss Darcy is engaged," cried Mrs Butler. "And my son has caused such mischief. I will never forget the look on Mr Darcy's face!"

"You will make yourself ill, Martha," said Mrs Gardiner, who was becoming most concerned for her friend. "None of this is your doing. And besides, I am certain that it will all turn out for the best. Miss Darcy and Mr Calladine may be an alliance to secure fortune but are as ill matched as any couple could be. Mr Darcy can see how unhappy Georgiana has been made by the hasty decision to marry Mr Calladine, and I am certain that the gentleman himself will only suffer bruised pride if Miss Darcy marries elsewhere."

"But with the best will in the world, Thomas cannot offer Miss Darcy a secure future or a fortune; he is not even from the same class. It is hopeless, I am sure he knows that. Oh, that he had never ventured near."

"Where do you think they can be headed, Aunt Gardiner?" Elizabeth asked. "Mr Darcy seems to think they will have gone south, but surely if they have run away to be married without parental consent, they will be headed north, to Gretna Green. Fitzwilliam mentioned the Peak Forest before he left but that sounds such an unlikely destination."

Mrs Gardiner smiled and even Mrs Butler looked relieved for a moment. "There is a chapel in the area about three and a half miles north-west of Tideswell. The church was built in Elizabethan times on land that remains part of the Royal Forest. This means that it is still to this day without any ecclesiastical jurisdiction. Couples who are not residents in the parish can, therefore, marry without banns being read. I am sure Mrs Butler and I both know couples from our youth who went against their families' blessings and were married in the church."

Mrs Butler bit her lip and nodded, looking more worried than ever. "Mr Darcy will never forgive Thomas if they go ahead and marry. I dread to think what will happen. My son fully deserves to be punished, but I pray it will not end with a pistol."

She broke off, bursting into tears, lamenting the day Mr Butler had died leaving her with a young man she had tried her best to advise.

Jane Bingley immediately cried out, "Oh, Mrs Butler, Mr Darcy has such a kind heart. I am sure he could never consider such a dreadful act."

Mrs Darcy tried to comfort the lady as best she could. "Mrs Butler, do not fret. My husband has realised, a little late yet hopefully in time, that whatever foolishness our young couple are engaged upon, it would be greater folly to keep them apart forever. Mr Darcy loves his sister, and her happiness is his first concern. All he wishes to achieve is to find them before they do anything rash. There will be a way for this to be resolved, I feel certain, but Georgiana and Tom must learn that running away is not the best course."

"Mrs Darcy, I do hope so," cried Mrs Butler, drying her eyes. "I feel so responsible, and cannot bear to see you, Mrs Darcy, look so out of sorts. You must go and lie down, my dear."

"I'm tougher than I look. Don't worry about me, Mrs Butler," pronounced Elizabeth. "But you are right: we should all go to bed, and in the morning, I feel sure we will hear some good news."

Elizabeth had meant every word; she did feel strong. However, when she lay down her head on the pillow and the recollections of the evening's events worked their way into her thoughts, she did not feel quite so resolute. Georgiana's disappearance and Miss Bingley's words would not leave her. Elizabeth stared at the empty space beside her and at the pillow no longer moulded by that handsome head belonging to her husband. "How can it be true?" she thought. Caroline's hints were so vile she could not bear to think about it. Tossing and turning until her head ached from lack of sleep, she eventually succumbed only to spend a fitful night dreaming of an endless stream of Pemberley heirs and tolling bells in Lambton church punctuated by gunpowder blasts from the blacksmith's anvil.

Elizabeth breakfasted alone. She had woken with the dawn chorus and unable to sleep again had risen and gone downstairs to the breakfast parlour. There was already a letter waiting for her on the salver, which she instantly took up in hopes of it being from Fitzwilliam. It was immediately evident that the handwriting did not belong to her husband. Her stomach churned at the sight of the script she recognised as that of the "well-wisher" who had written to her before on the subject of George Tissington. Was it Caroline Bingley's hand? She could not tell. Reluctantly, she tore open the missive. Inside was written an untidily scrawled note alongside a scrap of paper with some writing that she recognised as belonging to Fitzwilliam. She did not examine that first but pored over the note.

> *Dear Mrs Darcy,*
>
> *If ever proof were needed, I hope the enclosed will suffice. You may find it wanting, in which case I shall be happy to supply the rest if you will meet me this noon-time by the market square in Kendal at the door of the chandler's.*
>
> *Yours sincerely,*
> *Viola Wickham*

Viola Wickham! Elizabeth had not been expecting that. So George Wickham's step-sister had been the one to send the cruel missives, or so it seemed. Elizabeth felt most disconcerted. How on earth did Miss Wickham know of the Darcys' whereabouts and what did she want? It did not take Elizabeth long to consider the most likely explanation. If she was anything like her step-brother, there was only one reason she could think of that would explain why she should be behaving in this manner: money. George Wickham had stopped at nothing to embezzle money from Mr Darcy and she was sure Viola Wickham's motives must be similar. Making mischief was never the sole aim in a case like this or her story would have been broadcast long ago. Mrs Darcy did not hesitate; of course she would go. More than anything Elizabeth wished to have this matter resolved, and she must admit that she was most curious to see the woman who had formerly bewitched her husband. The enclosed scrap of paper revealed very little. It was Fitzwilliam's handwriting, without a doubt, but apart from, "Dear Viola," and "I hope this letter finds you and the infant well," there was no more. Whatever Elizabeth wished to think about it, one thing was very clear: in order for Mr Darcy to have written such an opening meant that he was not only intimate with the child's mother, but that he also knew of the existence of Viola's offspring and cared about their welfare. Whichever way she looked at it, Elizabeth could not foresee any happy outcome from the further knowledge she was to gain in the afternoon, but there was no other course to take. Viola would be met.

Chapter 30

ELIZABETH LEFT IMMEDIATELY, BEFORE anyone else came down for breakfast but not before telling Mrs Reynolds that she had a few errands to run in Kendal, and that she would be returned by the afternoon to avoid the possibility of a search party being sent out for her. Wrapping herself in a voluminous cloak, Mrs Darcy pulled the hood over her bonnet before settling into the unmarked carriage. The last thing she wanted was to draw attention to herself by sporting the Darcy arms. The day was a dismal one. Rain fell from an indigo sky, which cast deep violet shadows over the fells, turning the mere into a sheet of tarnished silver. Alone with her thoughts, all Elizabeth could hear was the persistent drumming of water on the roof of the carriage as they bowled alongside the lake. Her emotions reflected the greyness of the day outside. She could not remember ever feeling so miserable. The man she loved, she could think of no longer in the same terms. Elizabeth could not reconcile the man she knew with this other person, a stranger secretive and guarded. She did not want to recognise the truth: that he was no longer the open, honest, and comforting presence he once had been to her. She fought hard against it, but every feeling gave way to acceptance that she must face the hurtful truth.

Relieved that she had managed to escape so easily without detection, Elizabeth urged the coachman to make haste. As the carriage jolted down the uneven lanes, she looked through the windows at the landscape flying by, thinking all the while of her beloved Darcy. Haunting images rose before her, pictures she did not want to acknowledge, of her husband as a young man in love for the first time with a girl who was prepared to do whatever she needed to ensnare him. Elizabeth remonstrated with herself for being so self-indulgent. She smoothed her gloves over her fingers, stroking and turning the thick gold wedding ring under the leather, reminding herself that whatever she was about to learn, nothing could alter the fact that she was the woman Darcy had chosen to marry. However distressed she felt, the love she bore for the man she had married was undiminished; that could never change. And then, for the first time, she felt the stirrings of the life inside her. All problems vanished for the time being as she waited with bated breath for assurance, one hand held against her gown until she felt the movement again, a flickering like the wings of butterflies, for another moment. Her child, Mr Darcy's child, was making his or her presence felt. Whatever had happened, whatever was about to happen, Elizabeth knew she would never forget this precious moment and smiled with joy.

They made good time and although Mrs Darcy was still a little early to meet Miss Wickham, she decided she would take the opportunity to sit in a coffee house situated opposite the chandler's in order to witness first sight of the woman she had wondered about for so long. A cup of warming chocolate was just the remedy on a cold and miserable day, although when it was served she knew she would not be able to drink a sip. The place was empty; she sat undisturbed watching the few wagons and carts that rumbled past the window as she waited for a first glimpse of the lady she had come to meet. There were not many people about and there was certainly no sign of anyone she imagined might resemble Miss Wickham.

The bell above the door of the coffee house jingled, breaking the quiet hum of domestic activity. A woman Elizabeth immediately recognised as Mrs Younge came into the shop. She looked steadily across at Elizabeth before walking over to her table.

"May I join you, Mrs Darcy?" Mrs Younge asked in a rather pointed and familiar way and, without waiting for an answer, pulled out a chair and sat down.

"I beg your pardon, Mrs Younge, but I am afraid I must leave in a moment," answered Elizabeth, feeling rather shocked by Mrs Younge's rude intrusion.

"I do not think you need to do that, Mrs Darcy. I believe you are here to see me."

Elizabeth was puzzled and could not help showing just how perplexed she felt.

Mrs Younge took out a folded piece of paper from her reticule and placed it on the table. The handwriting on the front Elizabeth knew to be her husband's; the letter, she could see clearly, was addressed to Viola Wickham.

"I do not understand," began Lizzy.

"I am here to represent my sister, Mrs Darcy."

Elizabeth continued to look baffled. "I am afraid I am no further enlightened, Mrs Younge. Please explain yourself."

"My sister, Miss Wickham, could not be here, unfortunately. She is an invalid and is far too weak to make the journey to meet you, however much she would wish to be here. I see you are surprised to find not only myself, but to also hear that I am related to the person you expected to meet this afternoon."

"I confess I am extremely mystified, Mrs Younge, to find that Miss Wickham is your sister, but I do not know if my being cognisant to such particulars is at all relevant. I trust that you also know that I expect to have this matter resolved discreetly and swiftly. I wish to know exactly what it is that you want, for I am certain that if you had only a desire to return this letter you could have accomplished that most easily by post. In short, Mrs Younge, let us have it out. Why did you wish to see me?"

"You will hear me out, Mrs Darcy, I will assure you of that. I shall tell you exactly what sort of man you have married and then we shall see how you defend his actions."

"Mrs Younge, I do not think I wish to stay to hear you out if you are going to address me in such a manner."

"You will stay, Mrs Darcy, because if you do not, I shall make certain that your husband's name and reputation are ruined irrevocably." Mrs Younge put out her hand to pick up the remains of the letter. "In the wrong hands, ma'am, this letter could do untold damage."

Elizabeth sat still, waiting for Mrs Younge to continue. Leaving now would not resolve anything quickly, she knew, and she must keep her wits if she were to come out on top.

"You would not know what it is to suffer, would you, Mrs Darcy?" resumed Mrs Younge. "You have no idea what it is to be abandoned by your mother and brought up in a strange family that does not want you. I hardly remember my father. When he died my mother very quickly found a new husband in the steward at Pemberley House. We took the name of Wickham, and were all set to live there, but my mother felt we would be in the way so we were sent to live in London with her sister. My aunt treated me no better than a servant. Can you imagine, having to skivvy from the age of four?"

Elizabeth hardly knew how to answer. She could not speak.

Mrs Younge's eyes flickered over Elizabeth's countenance. Her expression was contemptuous. "No, I daresay you have no idea of the horrors of my existence. Later, when my mother died, old Mr Wickham invited us to Pemberley. I was not allowed to go but my sister Viola made her fateful trip the year she also met your husband. As a consequence, George made the trip to town in order to find me and has proved to be the kindest of step-brothers ever since."

"But I do not understand, Mrs Younge. I know you were engaged as Miss Darcy's governess. Was the family unaware of the connection?"

"I had been married by then, Mrs Darcy, and I was a widow living from hand to mouth, forced to earn my money as only a woman in penury can in London. Whatever people say, George has always been a loyal step-brother to me. No one at Pemberley knew who I was or my connection to him. Mr Darcy still does not know who I am to this day. George persuaded me to come when the position of governess came up. I'd had little education in my youth, but I was smart enough to muddle through, and in my line of occupation it was easy to obtain references from willing clients. I am sure you are aware of what happened next. George and Miss Darcy were to have been married. Well, Miss Darcy was willing, but her brother soon put paid to it."

Even as she said the words Elizabeth realised the truth. George Wickham and Mrs Younge had been involved together in the conspiracy to extort money by persuading Georgiana that she was in love with Wickham.

"How dare you speak to me of such a travesty of the events that took place. It was a despicable act, to prey on a young and inexperienced woman for her fortune. You are lucky that you were not dealt with for good and for all by my husband."

"You may look at me from your position of superiority with utter contempt; you can have no idea how I was driven to act. But what would you have done, Mrs Darcy, in my position? I may be many things, but I am a survivor."

Elizabeth felt sickened. To be in company with this woman any longer might taint her in some way, she felt. She wished to leave but knew very well there was nothing to be done but see it through.

"But this is all rather irrelevant. I expect you wish to hear about the past, of the time that Viola was invited to Pemberley."

Elizabeth made no comment. She wanted to hear no more but could neither move nor speak.

"Your husband and Viola were lovers," pronounced Mrs Younge with triumph. "George Tissington is the product of their union. She was sent away immediately. Fortunately, she returned to me and so she has had me to thank for finding her a livelihood and keeping a roof over her head. But you cannot know what she suffered when they came to take her child away."

Elizabeth shuddered; her natural instinct was to cover her ears. "It's not true, I do not believe you," she cried, tears smarting in her eyes, pricking behind her lids.

"I have the evidence here," Mrs Younge whispered, leaning toward Elizabeth, in a voice low and cruel. "I want ten thousand pounds for this letter, Mrs Darcy, placed in a bank account for my use only."

"Give me the letter and I shall see that you have your money," cried Elizabeth in a last attempt to have done with it all.

"I'm afraid that will not do," snapped the harridan, pushing the letter back into her reticule. "You have by the end of the week to inform me of the new account, and when all is to my satisfaction I will release the letter."

Elizabeth felt completely trapped. There did not seem to be anything she could do. It was not possible to summon help of any kind. She felt utterly alone, defeated, and tired. "I will do as you say," Elizabeth finally managed to say. She did not know how she was going to accomplish such a feat, but there seemed nothing else to be done except agree to her terms.

"Yes, I think you will," said Mrs Younge, pushing back her chair to stand. "Good-day, Mrs Darcy."

Elizabeth could not move. Stunned like a cornered animal, she was only able to watch her adversary walk away. But with a determination to overcome her feelings, she resolved on one thing: Mrs Younge and her accomplices would never prevail, no matter what power they felt they had. There must be something she could do to protect herself and her beloved Fitzwilliam. The rain outside continued unabated. Rivulets of water ran down the panes of the bow window through which Elizabeth stared, turning everything outside into indistinct shapes and patterns, grey and sombre like the weather itself. Yet however contorted were the images she could see, none were more so than the picture she observed of Mrs Younge arm in arm with

Chapter 31

ON ELIZABETH'S RETURN SHE was relieved to find a letter
from Fitzwilliam waiting for her. She could only hope that it
contained good news, but nothing would prevent her feelings
of unease as she tore it open.

> *My Dearest Elizabeth,*
>
> *I hope this letter finds you well. I write with news
> to restore your spirits—I have found Georgiana! I am
> relieved to tell you that there is no great harm done; our
> young lovers were found by myself at five o'clock this
> morning sitting outside the very church door where I
> expected to find them, and looking most remorseful and
> penitent. Accordingly, on reaching their destination,
> the recklessness and idiocy of their plan had most fortu-
> nately struck a chord with them both. They were sitting
> within the church porch, it seems, not with any imme-
> diate plans of waking the rector to ask him to marry
> them, but with the sole intention of asking forgiveness*

and for receiving guidance of the incumbent. Georgiana broke down when she saw me, and as for her foolish suitor, I never saw such a frightened young rabbit. I did my utmost to assure them that I would listen to what they had to say, and I think I can state that you would have been proud, my dearest wife, of the way in which I conducted myself. I did not raise my voice or my hand to Mr Thomas Butler; instead, I listened patiently to their profuse lamentations on folly, forgiveness, and freedom from punishment, each of them declaring the other to be entirely innocent of any crime. I did address them in the severest manner in order that they felt the gravity of their offences, but I have given them hope that in time they might fully acquit themselves. Did I not do well? I hardly recognised myself.

I might add, whatever or however stupidly they have behaved, I could not help but feel a certain sympathy for the star-crossed lovers trembling in awe before me. The speed with which they defended the other, and in particular the way Mr Butler conducted himself throughout our interview, leads me to think that I may very well come to like my intended brother-in-law in time. Of course I have not related the fact that I shall allow such an alliance to eventually take place; we have other matters to deal with first. Fortunately, Georgiana's engagement is not generally known, and therefore I see no immediate problem with its dissolution, apart from pecuniary expenses which may naturally arise. I am to meet with Mr Calladine on the morrow in order to see what may be done. Mr Butler is to return to London in the first instance and await further instruction. I have forbidden any means of communication between them for the present; I am sure you will agree that some form of chastisement for their actions needs to be endorsed— a separation for some duration and abstinence from writing should suffice for the present.

It only remains for me to say that I have brought Georgiana home. She is sleeping now after her ordeal— I thank heaven all has turned out well enough in the end. I have written to Charles also, asking that he might bring you back to Derbyshire as soon as possible. Home—what a wonderfully comforting thought that is—Pemberley, our home, Elizabeth, and everything that pertains to our life together.

Till I can see your beloved face once more—

My love, always,
Fitzwilliam Darcy.

Elizabeth was overjoyed on first reading the letter and went in search of the others to relay its contents. She found Mrs Butler first and was able to comfort and assure her that everything would be done to help the young couple resolve the difficulties that separated them at present. Mrs Butler, though delighted to hear that Georgiana and Thomas had been found, was still overcome by feelings of sorrow and shame. As much as Lizzy persuaded her that she could not be held responsible, that lady said she did not think she could ever recover. Mrs Gardiner tried to placate her friend.

"At least they were both suitably shamefaced about their rash behaviour when Mr Darcy found them, and I'm sure regretted their decision to behave so badly almost as soon as they had departed."

"I imagine they must both have spent a miserable time of it, all in all," said Jane. "I am glad they came to see their mistake in time, and I only hope they will not be too long paying for it."

"They have caused both their families a good deal of heart-ache," interjected Elizabeth a little crossly. Although she felt immense relief that Georgiana had been recovered, she still knew she was a long way from solving the problems she still faced discussing with her husband. Elizabeth felt quite irritated that he had had to go just when she needed to speak to him most. "I think it will not do them any harm to be apart for a short while. If Georgiana had never agreed to marry Mr Calladine in the first instance we should not be enduring such a deal of trouble."

"I am sure she was only trying to please her family. Daughters are expected to do their duty by their betters; perhaps she thought she had no choice in the matter," added Jane. "Besides, it has been difficult for her not having a mother to guide her footsteps."

"You are quite right, of course," agreed Lizzy, "and poor Georgiana has not been brought up to have a single opinion of her own. Anyhow, that is all changing, thank goodness. I think we are all agreed that she is not the shy girl we knew at first, and with a little more improvement, we shall see her grow into a fine young woman."

"You have been an important influence, Lizzy," said Mrs Gardiner. "There is no doubt that Georgiana has blossomed under your care. We have seen her confidence grow as a result of your concern. This last bout of ill-considered behaviour was effected out of hopelessness and had nothing to do with lack of guardianship."

"I thank you, Aunt, for your kind words, but I seem to have failed her also. If only she had told me of her plans or given me cause to think that she might run away, I know I could have prevented it."

"But that was never likely to happen if Georgiana was intent on running away," said her aunt with a smile.

"No, indeed," remarked Elizabeth with a laugh. "It is forgivable too, now they are reconciled to their mischief. And perhaps it is not so unexpected at her age to behave quite so irrationally and without due consideration. One of the sweet taxes of youth is to act in a hurry and make bad bargains."

They were to leave Bellingham Hall first thing in the morning. Elizabeth was pleased to be leaving. Her stay in the Lakes had encompassed a whole spectrum of feelings and experiences, from her delight in the landscape and the precious moments with Fitzwilliam to the depths of mortification and horror she felt at the recollection of not only her sister Lydia's behaviour, but also that of Mrs Younge's conduct, whose despicable ways had left her reeling. Soon she would have to face the challenge of confronting her husband. Elizabeth needed to know the truth. She remembered him once saying that disguise of every sort was his abhorrence, yet she could not help believing that there must be a side to her husband's character that she knew nothing about. There was certainly a part of his life that he withheld from her when he visited with the boy. George Tissington was the proof that he had sanctioned the masquerade, and if he had nothing to hide, then why had he not informed her about the boy's true background or his frequent calls upon him?

The journey home to Pemberley was tiring and irksome. They made any stopping time as brief as possible but it seemed to Elizabeth that they would never get home. She had not been feeling well all the way; every bone in her body seemed to ache with tiredness and the only respite and pleasure she gained from the journey came from the reassuring quickening that alerted her to the knowledge of the growing life within her. Coupled with that of the delight of her sister's company and that of her aunt and Mrs Butler, Elizabeth endured it all as well as she could. At last they turned onto the road to Lambton and it was with feelings of restrained emotion that she looked out onto all the sights so dear and familiar. What did the future hold for her now? she wondered. And how would it all work out in the end? The idea of being at odds with Fitzwilliam was almost too much to bear.

Mrs Butler seemed quite overcome by the enormous hug that she received from Mrs Darcy as they parted after setting her down at her home, but she could not have known how much Lizzy derived comfort from that lady's presence. Elizabeth wished she could confide in someone, but she knew that she could not.

On her return Elizabeth was greeted warmly by Georgiana, but now was not the time to discuss the last few days. Elizabeth spoke to her sister with affection, promising when they parted that she would speak privately to her the next morning after their visitors had gone home. Fitzwilliam stood a little apart, waiting his turn. Elizabeth glanced across at him. He still had that look of concern, as if recent events had taken their toll. His greeting was tender, heartfelt, and full of anxiety for his wife's health. She was amused at the way he fussed over her, insisting that she sit by the fire and attending to some light supper by serving her himself. Elizabeth watched him as he set a tray before her on a side table with hot soup, bread, butter, and cheese, to be washed down with her favourite lemon cordial. Her heart was full of love for him. It was so wonderful to be home. Her meeting with Mrs Younge seemed like some horrible nightmare now that she thought about it. How she wanted it to fade and go away in just the same way. But she knew it would not; Fitzwilliam would have to be told, and however much she dreaded the prospect, the dilemma she faced would have to be confronted. Elizabeth would tell him everything; she would ask the questions and he would provide the answers.

Lizzy waited until she and Fitzwilliam were alone, making sure that everyone else was safely retired for the night. They were sitting in the saloon together, watching the flames dying in the grate. Elizabeth had been reading a book, to all intents and purposes, though she had not managed to read a single word. Aware that he was observing her closely, Elizabeth felt most uncomfortable. At length, Mr Darcy put down his glass of brandy and spoke.

"Are you well, Lizzy? You look very tired tonight, and you have hardly spoken a word all evening. I confess I am worried about you; you do look very pale."

"I have a little headache, that is all," she answered at last, knowing that she spoke the truth. Her head was throbbing with the anxiety of all she contemplated. Several times she started to say something, but could not bring herself to say the words.

She was about to ask him why he had not been honest, even accuse him of lying to her, for not making every facet of his past life open to her. How could she do that? she asked herself. This tremendously huge secret, which had ramifications for every aspect of their lives, could remain undisclosed. Elizabeth was at liberty to decide whether it remained buried or whether it was unearthed in all its ghastly and unspeakable detail. Certain that she did not want to have any elements satisfied, she baulked from asking the questions. But they would not go away. There was the other matter of Mrs Younge's stipulations to be considered also. Finally, knowing she had no alternative but to tell him what had happened, Elizabeth embarked on the impossible task.

"Fitzwilliam, I must talk to you," she began, trying to keep her voice even and steady. "Something has happened, something I hardly know how to begin to tell you about, and it is worrying me so much that I do not know where to start."

Mr Darcy, who was sitting in a chair on the opposite side of the room, got up as soon as he heard the distress in her voice.

"Tell me, Lizzy, I cannot bear to see you like this in such anguish. What on earth is the matter?"

"It is about George Tissington," she began. "I know the truth, Fitzwilliam." She took the portion of the torn letter from her reticule and handed it to him.

His face was very grave as he read the snippet of paper before he walked over to the grate and threw it into the fire. It caught in a second, bursting into flame. Elizabeth watched the portion of letter disappear, the blackened cinders flying up the chimney.

"What is the truth, Mrs Darcy? Please tell me," he said as he turned, coming to stand majestically before her, his face dangerously flushed with anger.

"Oh, Fitzwilliam, I know he is your son and that if only things had been different that he would be the rightful heir to Pemberley," she cried, feeling sure that this act of burning the evidence must surely confirm what she already knew. "I think you should know that there has been an attempt to blackmail me. It is the only reason I have decided to speak to you on the matter. Mrs Younge has the rest of the letter."

"Mrs Younge? What has she to do with anything?"

"I think you should sit, my love. What I am to tell you will come as a great shock. Mrs Younge is George Wickham's step-sister. She is acting on Viola's behalf and she and Wickham are up to their old tricks."

Elizabeth filled in the particulars, her knowledge of the Wickhams' history, and of her encounter with Mrs Younge in Kendal.

"Then his crimes are worse than I feared," Mr Darcy went on, sitting in the nearest seat and holding his head in his hands.

Elizabeth could only imagine that Fitzwilliam was referring to George Wickham but could not entirely comprehend his meaning.

"And did you believe Mrs Younge's testimony?" he asked, looking up, his black eyes staring at her from under his dark, finely shaped brows.

Elizabeth did not speak. More than anything she wanted to believe that there could be another explanation, yet it was impossible. She had seen written proof, not only in Mrs Younge's letter, but also in the ones she had found in the library. How could she say that she did not believe it when the voice in her head told her it was true? She looked down at the trembling hands in her lap, trying to find something to say.

Why did he not try to assure her? If it was not true, why then did he not deny it?

"And is this all the response which I am to have the honour of expecting?"

"I do not want to believe any of it, Fitzwilliam, but this is not the only letter I have seen."

"I see, and therefore, without any real explanation, you use your imagination to read what you may into any letter you happen to pick up. You would rather take the word of known scandalous, unscrupulous scoundrels who fill your head with vile and despicable nonsense than to take that of mine, your husband. For to use any other words to describe their infamy, Mrs Darcy, would be a lie." Mr Darcy paused to loosen his neckcloth. Elizabeth could see his agitation developing with every spoken word, a deeper shade of hauteur overspreading his features. "You want to know the truth. The truth you shall hear, though I always hoped I should protect you from it. I daresay my word is not deemed authority enough… it is all I have, however."

Elizabeth felt the tears prick and tried to blink them away. How foolish she had been. When she thought how he must perceive her words, nay, her accusations, she wished she could take them back. Every apology, everything she could summon up by way of saying she was sorry seemed totally inadequate. Her lips opened yet no sound came from within.

He continued, "I must confess that as a young man I did fall in love with Viola Wickham. It was a boyish love given in all innocence and never to be returned, although I did not appreciate it at the time. If you care to believe me, not even a kiss was exchanged between us. The letters you found, I thought had been lost long ago. What an unhappy circumstance that you found them. What a pity that you felt it necessary to read them."

Elizabeth winced at that remark. How could she explain that she had never meant to read them? How could she reconcile the fact that she had? She could not meet his gaze though she felt his eyes upon her.

"For a time I wanted to protect the child's mother out of loyalty and my love for her. She told me she was in trouble and I helped her with what money I had. However, in the end, it was the child's welfare that interested me. Poor soul, he could not be blamed for his condition in life. My dear mother's maid agreed to take on the child, to give him a loving home, and Viola was only too happy to give him up. I promised to help provide what I could, though I had not yet come into my money and would not do so for some time. It was all discreetly done, although in such cases as these, however careful one might be, there is bound to be talk. I kept in touch, but after arrangements were made for the child I did not hear from her again. I think as far as she was concerned I had outgrown my usefulness. It was only much later, when Viola Wickham came back into my life briefly, that I found I was duty bound to consider the child's welfare. At my father's funeral she appeared once more, demanding to see me. It was then that I learned the truth, the facts that I still find hard to contain. With my father's death her financial security withered. He did not provide for her in his will and she came to see what I would do for her."

Elizabeth hesitated. "But why should your father provide for her in his will? Was your father helping her, though you were not aware of it at the time?"

Mr Darcy nodded. "After his death, I found a letter outlining his intentions to provide for the child. Money was sent to Miss Wickham on a regular basis."

Darcy abruptly turned away for a moment and his wife heard the momentary distress in his voice.

The shock of understanding this statement gave rise to feelings of both alarm and relief of a kind. The realisation that her supposition must be correct meant that her husband was entirely innocent of the wrongs she had accorded him.

"I cannot have understood correctly," Elizabeth began, wishing she really had no comprehension at all.

Darcy nodded. "Elizabeth, I wish I could tell you differently, but there is no other explanation. George Tissington is no heir to the Pemberley fortune, but he is my brother."

Chapter 32

"I still don't quite understand how you managed to retrieve the rest of the letter from Mrs Younge," said Elizabeth a week later as they travelled into Lambton one morning to visit their tenants, "even though I know if anyone could accomplish such a task easily, it would be you."

"Our brother-in-law has his uses," Darcy explained. "When he came to comprehend that I could make his life very difficult if it was not returned to me immediately, his step-sister saw sense. I do not think we shall be hearing from Mrs Younge again, especially if Wickham wishes me to help him in the future."

"Do you think Wickham was conspiring with her?"

"Not a doubt of it, but of course I have no proof. In any case, I should not wish to make Lydia's existence any more miserable than it must be. If I'd had him bound over, it is only your sister who would have truly suffered. He is stupid enough to think that I do not know what he was about, and I daresay he thinks he has got away with it. I have my men keeping an eye on them; do not fear. At least we know that the Wickhams are back in Newcastle and Mrs Younge is returned to her usual haunts in London."

"I will never forgive myself for doubting you," said Elizabeth, reddening with shame at the recollection of all that had passed.

"No, it was not your fault. When I now consider how you must have perceived my actions alone, I cannot blame you. I should have told you, but I must admit, it is a part of my history and that of my family's past that I wished to forget and did not want to acknowledge. I still cannot believe the truth of the matter. When I consider the character of the man most dear to me, he who was the most excellent of men, honest and upright…" Darcy paused to collect himself. Elizabeth thought her heart would break as she listened to him pour out his soul. "I have never spoken of this to another living person; it is the most difficult episode of my life."

"My darling Mr Darcy, speak no more. What is done belongs to the past and cannot be changed. Only know that I am honoured that you have been able to share your thoughts with me. I love you so much, Fitzwilliam."

Mr Darcy turned to face his beloved wife. At last he could look into her eyes. "I love you too, Elizabeth."

Georgiana could hardly contain her excitement. She had never dreamed that this day would arrive when just a few weeks ago she had felt the disgrace of her foolish conduct, but today Mr Thomas Butler was being allowed to visit.

Mr Darcy had suggested to Elizabeth that she should chaperone the young couple at all times, but after sitting in the drawing room for fifteen minutes, listening to the polite conversation of those who know their every word is being heard, Elizabeth excused herself by saying she had just remembered something important she had to divulge to Mrs Reynolds about the dinner menu.

In an instant Tom crossed the room. He could not wait a moment longer. Before Georgiana could protest she was in his arms.

"Oh, do be careful, Tom," chided Georgiana playfully, "Elizabeth may return at any moment.

"I couldn't care if your brother were to walk in on us this minute," Tom cried, taking her hands in his and drawing them towards him. "How I have missed you."

"I've missed you too, Tom," cried Georgiana, gazing up at him with adoration.

Tom drew back to regard the face of the girl he loved and traced his finger down her cheek, tilting her chin to raise her lips within his view. How soft and inviting they looked; her mouth appeared more beautiful to him than in all his dreams of longing. "I have been denied this pleasure for too long, Miss Darcy," he whispered, caressing her lips with his own. "Please don't stop me now, I beg you."

Georgiana had no intention of stopping him; submitting to his sweet kisses, she felt she had never known such happiness. To have Tom at her side holding her in his arms was heavenly.

"I never thought this day would ever come," said Tom, reluctantly letting her go at last. "I have so much to tell you, and I cannot think where to begin. Oh, Georgiana, I have been bursting to tell you my news. You will not believe my good fortune."

"Thomas, tell me quickly before anyone comes. I cannot wait to hear all that you have been doing. Is it about your work?"

"It is not. Indeed, it has nothing whatsoever to do with work. I might never work again if I did not want to, but then I would become a very lazy fellow, and I am sure that Mrs Butler would not like that one bit. That is, if Mrs Butler should become my wife."

"Tom, what are you saying?" interrupted Georgiana. "You are running on the like of which I never heard before. What do you mean about not working ever again, and who is Mrs Butler? I am sure you cannot refer to your mother."

"Georgiana, I am made! Lord Featherstone is the hero of the hour. I have naturally spent a lot of time with him lately, and when I confessed to him my reasons for suddenly quitting the Lake District, he wanted to know all about it. Having never had the good luck to fall in love himself, he has taken our plight to his heart. He believes that we should be allowed our portion of happiness with no further delay. Georgiana, I am to have an estate of my own in Nottinghamshire and a settlement of six thousand pounds a year. In short, he has made it possible for us to marry as soon as we might wish. You are the Mrs Butler I hope will become my wife... that is, if you have not changed your mind. Please, Miss Darcy, perhaps I should have gone to your brother first, but I could not wait to ask. Will you marry me?"

He knelt before Georgiana, his eyes imploring her to agree to his desires.

"Thomas Butler, of course I will. I cannot wait to be your Mrs Butler," Georgiana cried, throwing her arms around his neck and kissing him once more.

The wedding of Miss Georgiana Darcy to Mr Thomas Butler took place the following month in the chapel at Pemberley. The bride looked as beautiful and as happy as a young bride should in the company of her new husband, who beamed with pride throughout the proceedings. A small family affair, apart from the presence of Lord Featherstone and Mrs Butler, the only other witnesses present were Mr and Mrs Darcy, which was just as Georgiana had wished it to be.

Despite the lack of guests, congratulations and felicitations came from all corners of England: from the Bennets, the Bingleys, the Collinses, and even Lady Catherine de Bourgh herself. Every missive contained good wishes for the young couple, who left for a little holiday to the seaside as soon as they left the church door.

Arriving too late to be read by the Butlers was a letter from Mrs Lydia Wickham. Mrs Darcy opened it one morning as she and Fitzwilliam sat at breakfast. On reading its contents, she found it most troubling and could hardly fathom its meaning. She decided to read it out loud in order to see what Fitzwilliam might think. The letter read:

> *Westcott Buildings, Newcastle*
> *Dearest Elizabeth,*
>
> *I hope this letter finds you well. We are always the last to be informed of important events within the family, it seems, or I should have sent my felicitations sooner. Wickie and I wish Mr and Mrs Butler every happiness; some people certainly appear to have all the luck! It is not as if he needed a fortune of his own, but they will be as rich as kings, I daresay.*
>
> *Lizzy, I am enclosing a letter I found when I was clearing out some of Wickie's things. I do not know what to make of it. I know you have a clever eye for a puzzle and wonder what you think it can possibly mean. Have you ever heard of Viola Wickham? I am*

sure I have not! It seems from this intelligence that she is George's sister, but I never heard of her in my life and my own enquiries have come to naught. It is something of a mystery—and I can't make head nor tail of why she should mention Pemberley if she was nothing at all to the Wickhams. There is the curious mention of duping the father and son—can she mean Mr Darcy? I wondered if your husband could throw any light on the matter—I am most anxious to learn what it is all about. George would be so cross that I have been through his things—I didn't mention the letter to him, but I would be most interested to hear what you make of it for it is a complete riddle to me. I didn't know who else to ask. It is an old letter but most intriguing. Write back soon.

Yours ever,
Lydia

P.S. I am a little short for the rent this month. Do not scold me, but I could not resist the straw bonnet on display in the milliner's!

The enclosed letter was unfolded once more. Elizabeth had read it twice through already but could not be sure she understood its contents. She read it out loud to Mr Darcy before passing it to him across the table. He read it to himself. That he was disturbed by its contents was clear.

December 20, 1792
Dear George,
Thank you for your letter, I am very well. I cannot

tell you what it meant to me to receive a letter with such heartfelt sentiments. My love for you is returned and ever constant; I trust and pray we will be united very soon.

You ask so many questions about him, I do not know what to tell you except to say that the babe has such a look of the Wickhams about him; indeed, his eyes are yours. I know you would recognise him as our own and that you would laugh to see it. I have named him for his father, of course, though our dear sister assumes that person's initials are entirely different… she has no suspicion of the truth, thank heaven, nor has anyone else. Our secret is safe, Georgie. Duping both the father and the son at Pemberley has been vastly entertaining—I have come into a little money, though how long it will last I cannot say. I am in such dire need of everything new and the rent our sister charges me is not cheap. I am assured of seeing the child from time to time if I wish it, but though he amuses me, you know he will be better off where he is going. Besides, so long as I have the comfort of your company I could not desire anything more. Georgie, will you come and see me soon? I cannot bear to be without you. Are you not a little curious to see him before he is gone forever? Such a bonny babe you never did see. I cannot write more now for fear of discovery, but I promise to write whenever I can. Come soon,

I am yours ever,
A loving sister always,
Viola.

"I have read it twice through and cannot make it out entirely. But Darcy, if what sense I can make of it were true, it would seem that what you have formerly thought about your father couldn't be the case. What do you think?"

There was a pause. There was a minute's silence during which every emotion seemed to pass across her husband's face. At last Darcy raised his head, engaging Elizabeth with his dark eyes which penetrated hers with an expression of triumph. "It is as I always hoped. My father's memory is vindicated. I have thought the worst of him and now I know he was the very generous man I always believed him to be. I knew of my father's innocence in all of this; I knew it in my heart and yet I doubted him. I do not think I shall ever forgive myself."

"You are not responsible. The duplicity of others is to blame. Fitzwilliam, you must not reproach yourself. Let us celebrate the fact that here is proof that your father is entirely guiltless in this whole affair. But I cannot help wondering about the truth of the matter, though perhaps the whole episode would be better laid to rest—I have no desire to learn anything of the Wickhams' secrets. One would presume that your father must have taken pity on the disgraced Miss Wickham. He must have been a very kind and understanding man."

Elizabeth watched her husband's countenance grow pale. Fitzwilliam sat very still in deep contemplation. His expression, though serious and grave, started to show some signs of relief after a moment or two. He raked his fingers through his hair once or twice, but his eyes were fixed on his plate as he spoke, avoiding Elizabeth's scrutiny of his countenance.

"I do not think we will ever know the complete truth, nor do I wish to dwell on it further. It does not concern us; we have all the information we need to know. My father was an excellent man until his dying day... I only hope that some day I might grow to be more like him."

Elizabeth stood up and ran to his side. "Oh, my darling, you need never worry ever again. You know your father must have been a wonderful man to show such compassion for Miss Wickham. Just like his son, who is also most excellent in every way!"

Elizabeth threw her arms about his neck, kissing the top of his head just to confirm her delight. It was most fortunate that just at that moment she could not read Mr Darcy's mind or his thoughts as he contemplated the thorough wickedness of the steward's son he had grown up with at Pemberley.

The end of May heralded the beginning of summer, sunny days perfumed with the heady scents of lilac in the syringa grove, which was a favourite haunt for the Darcys' afternoon walk. The white blooms nodding their heads in the soft breeze were a reminder that Mr Butler's design for the grove and Darcy's Hall (as the folly was re-named by Elizabeth) had been most successful. For Elizabeth it was the happiest time of her marriage to date, having found a new understanding with Fitzwilliam and a deep sense of satisfaction that life was just getting better and better. The knowledge that Fitzwilliam had chosen to share in divulging past secrets of Pemberley House had only brought them closer together, and in their newfound intimacy love flourished with a deeper profundity.

"How wonderful it is to be in Derbyshire, the most divine county in all of England. I think this will always be my preferred season at Pemberley," Elizabeth said, as they walked along arm in arm. "It is such a perfect time with everything coming into flower and blossoming into beauty."

"Just like its mistress," said Mr Darcy, laying his hand over hers in a tender gesture. "I have never seen you look more beautiful than you do today, my love. If I could paint your portrait this is how I would like to see you forever more: on this day, dressed in yellow with your dark eyes dancing with amusement."

"I am amused, I confess, at the thought of you painting my portrait. I never dreamed you had such a creative spirit when first I met you, though I have learned something of your talent for poetry. Tell me, are your artistic endeavours as exciting as your aptitude for rhyming a couplet?"

"Do not underestimate my proficiencies, madam," Darcy answered, as if perfectly affronted, stepping away from her with a mock bow.

"Oh no, Mr Darcy, I could never do that," Elizabeth cried, with a smile on her lips. "On the contrary, you have many abilities for which I declare you to be quite the genius, but I do not think the arts are necessarily your forte."

"I cannot imagine where you think my gifts tend, in that case," Darcy declared, his face as solemn as ever.

"Hmm, let me think," mused Elizabeth, her head inclined on one side as she gave him the benefit of her fine eyes. "Come closer, Mr Darcy, and if you will accompany me to Darcy's Hall, I will explain everything."

They sat high up in the stone built folly, which gave a wonderful view across the estate. Elizabeth saw the beauty of the landscape in front of them stretching as far as the eye could see. A patchwork of fields and a wood sloped away down the hillside to the river in the valley. Shadows made by the clouds swept over the long, silver grasses waving in the breeze, and in the distance on the other side, Elizabeth's eyes rested on the crest of a hill crowned by a circle of beech trees from whence the wind seemed to come, ruffling the coats of the sheep, wearing away the huge rocks which broke the surface of the earth. Nestled in the valley along the winding river, the golden stone houses of Lambton glimmered in the afternoon light.

"Penny for your thoughts, Mrs Darcy," said Fitzwilliam, watching her closely.

"Oh, my thoughts are far more expensive than that, you know," she said with a laugh, unable to resist teasing him.

"Five pounds for them then, will that suffice?" he asked, knowing she would not be at all amused by his retort.

Elizabeth would not look at him. She gazed at the horizon and maintained her expression of deep contemplation. "No money will ever pay for them. Only something precious to me might release the thoughts in my head."

"Elizabeth Darcy," he whispered, "would that be something or someone? And whilst I desire to know what goes on inside your head, there are other matters in mine which are far more pressing. I long to kiss you but I am not certain if you would think it quite precious enough a something."

Elizabeth turned her head. "One of your kisses is worth more to me than anything else in the world. Take one if you really wish to find out what I am thinking."

Mr Darcy took her in his arms. The moment was sweet and their exchange of kisses and thoughts were the happiest they had ever known.

Chapter 33

Longbourn, September, 1803

Mr Bennet leaned back in his chair with an air of self-satisfaction. He waved the letter in his hand, addressing his wife as he spoke. "I always told you she was a clever girl, did I not? And now she has surpassed all my expectations."

Mrs Bennet looked up from her cup of morning tea. "What nonsense are you talking, Mr Bennet? The only girl I ever recall you declaring to be clever is our daughter Lizzy, but not only is she now a married woman, but I also doubt she is in much of a mind to be witty and smart in her present condition. What is it all about? Who is your letter from, my dear?"

"Mr Darcy!" Mr Bennet replied, returning to his missive without another word.

"Mr Darcy! Mr Darcy! Good heavens, what does he say? Is Elizabeth near her time? Does he want me to go? Quick, Mr Bennet, we must harness the carriage. Oh, Lord! I knew it would be like this, with not a moment to prepare myself. I haven't a thing to wear! Mr Bennet! Stop sitting there opening and closing your mouth like a codfish. We must go to Pemberley."

"'Tis too late, my dear Mrs Bennet. Indeed, you are not needed."

"Too late! What can you mean? Is Elizabeth ill, or worse? Oh, I knew no good would come of it, to be confined so early in her marriage. Tell me… no, don't tell me, I do not think I can bear it."

"Then I shall keep Mr Darcy's news to myself." Mr Bennet folded the letter and placed it on one side before picking up his newspaper.

"Oh, you delight in vexing me. Well, do as you please. If it does not concern me I am not interested anyhow. I do not want to learn that he has bagged a hundred pheasants since last Tuesday; indeed, I do not. I cannot think how you can enjoy corresponding with a man who has so little to say on any matter except his sport."

"You are not interested to hear about your grandson then, I take it?" Mr Bennet asked, peering over his glasses at his wife.

"Grandson, my grandson?" repeated Mrs Bennet, whose countenance displayed the shock she felt.

"We are grandparents, Mrs Bennet. Elizabeth has been duly delivered of a fine infant boy in the early hours of this morning."

"Well, why in heaven's name did you not say so earlier? A boy, Mr Bennet. That is splendid news. But it does not alter the fact that I shall be needed instantly. Elizabeth will be fretting for her mother. Come, Mr Bennet, make haste!

"Mr Darcy has invited us to go in a fortnight's time," Mr Bennet replied. "He insists there is no need for us to go rushing up there immediately, and I daresay our young parents would wish to spend their time getting to know the little fellow without an army attending them in the first instance."

"And not have her mother for advice and counsel? How will she know the best way to hold the babe if I do not show her? And if he is colicky, as some newborns are found to be, who will recommend a little warm wine and water on a spoon?"

"I am sure they already have several nannies in place if they are needed. Mrs Bennet, let us wait until the proper time. We have been invited, after all, and I daresay we shall be as instructive as Lizzy wishes once we are there."

"Perhaps you are right," said Mrs Bennet grudgingly, helping herself to another piece of toast, "but babies soon lose that look of just having been born, and I should so like to see him."

"Have patience, my dear; we'll see him soon enough."

"Kitty will be so excited. It is all she has talked about ever since she went to Pemberley in the summer. She is sure to want to dance with him again."

"I think the little lad will be too young for dancing a while yet."

"Oh, you are ridiculous, Mr Bennet. I am talking of her dancing with Mr Lloyd, the rector."

"Well, there'll be a christening, no doubt. I expect there'll be some chance to dance then."

"I shall have to tell Kitty and Mary to come home at once. They have been with Jane quite long enough. I need them here."

"But we are not due to leave for a fortnight. Leave them where they are. I'm sure I do not want them back again just now."

"I do not want them tiring Jane out. It is early days and if she wants to have a healthy baby like Elizabeth she must learn to put her feet up and stop gadding about Netherfield."

"I'm sure Jane knows what she is about. Your fussing will do more harm than good."

"Let me remind you, Mr Bennet, that my fussing has been very productive. If I had been content to let my daughters follow their hearts willy nilly, they would not have made the matches they have. Jane and Mr Bingley, Lizzy and Mr Darcy, Lydia and Mr Wickham, Kitty and Mr Lloyd…"

"I see you have married off Kitty already. Does the rector know of your plans for his future happiness?"

"He ought to be sensible of them, but if not, I shall soon give him a push in the right direction. If only Mary could find a suitor, how happy I should be."

"Now that would be a joyous occasion for us all."

"Mr Bennet, we are grandparents, can you imagine? I wonder whom he will favour. Do you think he has Lizzy's eyes and Mr Darcy's nose?"

"They'd look a little out of place on a baby, my dear," Mr Bennet drily observed.

"And what will they call him, Mr Bennet, does it say?"

"Ah, yes, I was just coming to that. Fitzwilliam, of course, after his father, and George after his grandfather before him, and then he is to have my name."

"Oh, my dear, what an honour. The heir of Pemberley is to bear your name. Let us raise our teacups to the little cherub. Fitzwilliam George Henry Darcy, welcome to the world!"

The End

About the Author

JANE ODIWE IS AN author and artist. She is completely obsessed with all things Austen and is the author of *Lydia Bennet's Story* and *Willoughby's Return*, and author and illustrator of *Effusions of Fancy*, consisting of annotated sketches from the life of Jane Austen. She lives with her husband and three children in North London and Bath, England.

Lydia Bennet's Story

JANE ODIWE

"An absorbing read." —AUSTENBLOG

Can a girl like her really find true love?

In *Lydia Bennet's Story* we are taken back to Jane Austen's most beloved novel, *Pride and Prejudice*, to a Regency world seen through Lydia's eyes where pleasure and marriage are the only pursuits. But the road to matrimony is fraught with difficulties and even when she is convinced that she has met the man of her dreams, complications arise. When Lydia is reunited with the Bennets, Bingleys, and Darcys for a grand ball at Netherfield Park, the shocking truth about her husband may just cause the greatest scandal of all…

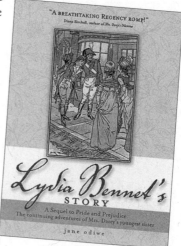

"Odiwe plays homeage to Austen's stylings and endears the reader to the formerly secondary character, spoiled and impulsive Lydia Bennet. Odiwe grants readers unfettered access to Lydia as she flirts with her many beaus…falls hard for George Wickham…and finds true happiness in the most unlikely of places."
—*Publishers Weekly*

"Elizabeth Bennet's naughty little sister takes center stage in a breathtaking Regency romp all her own, told with an authoritative period elegance by Jane Odiwe's eloquent pen"
—DIANA BIRCHALL, AUTHOR OF *Darcy's Dilemma*

978-1-4022-1475-2 • $12.95 US/ $13.99 CAN/ £6.99 UK

Mr. Darcy's Diary

AMANDA GRANGE

"A gift to a new generation of Darcy fans
and a treat for existing fans as well." —AUSTENBLOG

The only place Darcy could share his innermost feelings...

...was in the private pages of his diary. Torn between his sense of duty to his family name and his growing passion for Elizabeth Bennet, all he can do is struggle not to fall in love. A skillful and graceful imagining of the hero's point of view in one of the most beloved and enduring love stories of all time.

What readers are saying:

"A delicious treat for all Austen addicts."

"Amanda Grange knows her subject...I ended up reading the entire book in one sitting."

"Brilliant, you could almost hear Darcy's voice...I was so sad when it came to an end. I loved the visions she gave us of their married life."

"Amanda Grange has perfectly captured all of Jane Austen's clever wit and social observations to make *Mr. Darcy's Diary* a must read for any fan."

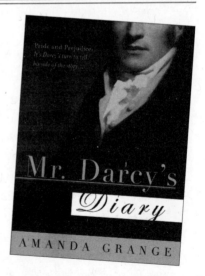

978-1-4022-0876-8 • $14.95 US/ $19.95 CAN/ £7.99 UK

WILLOUGHBY'S RETURN
Jane Austen's *Sense and Sensibility* continues

Jane Odiwe

"A tale of almost irresistible temptation."

A lost love returns, rekindling forgotten passions...

When Marianne Dashwood marries Colonel Brandon, she puts her heartbreak over dashing scoundrel John Willoughby behind her. Three years later, Willoughby's return throws Marianne into a tizzy of painful memories and exquisite feelings of uncertainty. Willoughby is as charming, as roguish, and as much in love with her as ever. And the timing couldn't be worse—with Colonel Brandon away and Willoughby determined to win her back...

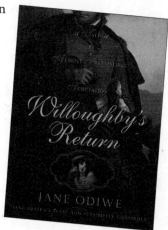

Praise for *Lydia Bennet's Story*:

"A breathtaking Regency romp!" —Diana Birchall, author of *Mrs. Darcy's Dilemma*

"An absolute delight." —Historical Novels Review

"Odiwe emulates Austen's famous wit, and manages to give Lydia a happily-ever-after ending worthy of any Regency romance heroine." —*Booklist*

978-1-4022-2267-2
$14.99 US/$18.99 CAN/£7.99 UK

"Odiwe pays nice homage to Austen's stylings and endears the reader to the formerly secondary character, spoiled and impulsive Lydia Bennet." —*Publishers Weekly*

Mr. and Mrs. Fitzwilliam Darcy: Two Shall Become One

SHARON LATHAN

"Highly entertaining... I felt fully immersed in the time period. Well done!" —Romance Reader at Heart

A fascinating portrait of a timeless, consuming love

It's Darcy and Elizabeth's wedding day, and the journey is just beginning as Jane Austen's beloved *Pride and Prejudice* characters embark on the greatest adventure of all: marriage and a life together filled with surprising passion, tender self-discovery, and the simple joys of every day.

As their love story unfolds in this most romantic of Jane Austen sequels, Darcy and Elizabeth each reveal to the other how their relationship blossomed from misunderstanding to perfect understanding and harmony, and a marriage filled with romance, sensuality, and the beauty of a deep, abiding love.

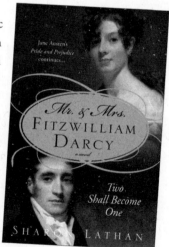

What readers are saying:

"This journey is truly amazing."

"What a wonderful beginning to this truly beautiful marriage."

"Could not stop reading."

"So beautifully written...making me feel as though I was in the room with Lizzy and Darcy...and sharing in all of the touching moments between."

978-1-4022-1523-0 • $14.99 US/ $15.99 CAN/ £7.99 UK

Mr. Fitzwilliam Darcy:
THE LAST MAN IN THE WORLD
A *Pride and Prejudice* Variation
ABIGAIL REYNOLDS

What if Elizabeth had accepted Mr. Darcy the first time he asked?

In Jane Austen's *Pride and Prejudice*, Elizabeth Bennet tells the proud Mr. Fitzwilliam Darcy that she wouldn't marry him if he were the last man in the world. But what if circumstances conspired to make her accept Darcy the first time he proposes? In this installment of Abigail Reynolds' acclaimed *Pride and Prejudice* Variations, Elizabeth agrees to marry Darcy against her better judgment, setting off a chain of events that nearly brings disaster to them both. Ultimately, Darcy and Elizabeth will have to work together on their tumultuous and passionate journey to make a success of their ill-timed marriage.

What readers are saying:

"A highly original story, immensely satisfying."

"Anyone who loves the story of Darcy and Elizabeth will love this variation."

"I was hooked from page one."

"A refreshing new look at what might have happened if..."

"Another good book to curl up with... I never wanted to put it down..."

978-1-4022-2947-3
$14.99 US/$18.99 CAN/£7.99 UK

The Pemberley Chronicles

A Companion Volume to Jane Austen's Pride and Prejudice
The Pemberley Chronicles: Book 1

REBECCA ANN COLLINS

"A lovely complementary novel to Jane Austen's *Pride and Prejudice.*
Austen would surely give her smile of approval."
—BEVERLY WONG, AUTHOR OF *Pride & Prejudice Prudence*

The weddings are over, the saga begins

The guests (including millions of readers and viewers) wish the two happy couples health and happiness. As the music swells and the credits roll, two things are certain: Jane and Bingley will want for nothing, while Elizabeth and Darcy are to be the happiest couple in the world!

Elizabeth and Darcy's personal stories of love, marriage, money, and children are woven together with the threads of social and political history of England in the nineteenth century. As changes in industry and agriculture affect the people of Pemberley and the surrounding countryside, the Darcys strive to be progressive and forward-looking while upholding beloved traditions.

"Those with a taste for the balance and humour of Austen will find a worthy companion volume."
—*Book News*

978-1-4022-1153-9 • $14.95 US/ $17.95 CAN/ £7.99 UK

THE OTHER MR. DARCY

PRIDE AND PREJUDICE CONTINUES...

MONICA FAIRVIEW

"A lovely story... a joy to read."
—*Bookishly Attentive*

Unpredictable courtships appear to run in the Darcy family...

When Caroline Bingley collapses to the floor and sobs at Mr. Darcy's wedding, imagine her humiliation when she discovers that a stranger has witnessed her emotional display. Miss Bingley, understandably, resents this gentleman very much, even if he is Mr. Darcy's American cousin. Mr. Robert Darcy is as charming as Mr. Fitzwilliam Darcy is proud, and he is stunned to find a beautiful young woman weeping broken-heartedly at his cousin's wedding. Such depth of love, he thinks, is rare and precious. For him, it's love at first sight...

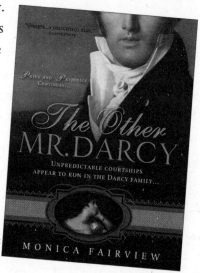

"An intriguing concept...
a delightful ride in the park."
—*Austenprose*

978-1-4022-2513-0
$14.99 US/$18.99 CAN/£7.99 UK

Mrs. Darcy's Dilemma
DIANA BIRCHALL

"Fascinating, and such wonderful use of language."
—JOAN AUSTEN-LEIGH

It seemed a harmless invitation, after all…

When Mrs. Darcy invited her sister Lydia's daughters to come for a visit, she felt it was a small kindness she could do for her poor nieces. Little did she imagine the upheaval that would ensue. But with her elder son, the Darcys' heir, in danger of losing his heart, a theatrical scandal threatening to engulf them all, and daughter Jane on the verge of her come-out, the Mistress of Pemberley must make some difficult decisions…

"Birchall's witty, elegant visit to the middle-aged Darcys is a delight." —PROFESSOR JANET TODD, UNIVERSITY OF GLASGOW

"A refreshing and entertaining look at the Darcys some years after *Pride and Prejudice* from a most accomplished author." —JENNY SCOTT, AUTHOR OF *After Jane*

978-1-4022-1156-0 • $14.95 U.S.

The Darcys Give a Ball
ELIZABETH NEWARK

"A tour de force." —**MARILYN SACHS, AUTHOR OF** *First Impressions*

Whatever will Mr. Darcy say…

…with his son falling in love, his daughter almost lured into an elopement, and his niece the new target of Miss Caroline Bingley's meddling, Mr. Darcy has his hands full keeping the next generation away from scandal.

Sons and daughters share the physical and personality traits of their parents, but of course have minds of their own—and as Mrs. Darcy says to her beloved sister Jane Bingley: "The romantic attachments of one's children are a constant distraction."

Amidst all this distraction and excitement, Jane and Elizabeth plan a lavish ball at Pemberley, where all the young people come together for a surprising and altogether satisfying ending.

What readers are saying:

"A light-hearted visit to Austen country."

"A wonderful look into what could have happened!"

"The characters ring true, the situation is perfect, the conclusion is everything you hope for."

"A wonder of character and action…an unmixed pleasure!"

978-1-4022-1131-7 • $12.95 US/ $15.50 CAN/ £6.99 UK

Darcy and Anne

Pride and Prejudice continues…

JUDITH BROCKLEHURST

"A beautiful tale." —*A Bibliophile's Bookshelf*

Without his help, she'll never be free…

Anne de Bourgh has never had a chance to figure out what she wants for herself, until a fortuitous accident on the way to Pemberley separates Anne from her formidable mother. With her stalwart cousin Fitzwilliam Darcy and his lively wife Elizabeth on her side, she begins to feel she might be able to spread her wings. But Lady Catherine's pride and determination to find Anne a suitable husband threaten to overwhelm Anne's newfound freedom and budding sense of self. And without Darcy's help, Anne will never have a chance to find true love…

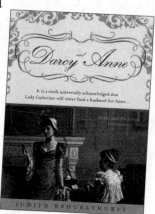

"Brocklehurst transports you to another place and time." —*A Journey of Books*

"A charming book… It is lovely to see Anne's character blossom and fall in love." —*Once Upon a Romance*

978-1-4022-2438-6
$12.99 US/$15.99 CAN/£6.99 UK

"The twists and turns, as Anne tries to weave a path of happiness for herself, are subtle and enjoyable, and the much-loved characters of Pemberley remain true to form."
—*A Bibliophile's Bookshelf*

"A fun, truly fresh take on many of Austen's beloved characters."
—*Write Meg*